This Carnival of Strange

LM Foster

This is a work of fiction. Names, characters, places and incidents are products of the author's imagination. Any resemblance to actual events, locales, organizations, or persons, either living or dead, is entirely coincidental.

Cover:
Xipe Totec, *The Codex Borgia*

9th Street Press
www.9thstreetpress.com

This book is dedicated to lefties everywhere.

ONE

It was Doomsday. The end of the world, the Apocalypse, Judgment Day, the Day of Reckoning, the destruction of mankind.

And what was I doing? Was I on my penitent knees in church, begging a merciful deity for forgiveness and redemption? Was I armed, holed up in a bunker, surrounded with canned goods, prepared to ride it all out? Was I on top of a tall building with an aluminum foil hat, waiting to welcome the aliens?

No. I was sitting on one side of a horseshoe-shaped bar in a very loud tavern with a very young girl named Maxine. Doomsday also just happened to coincide with her twenty-second birthday, and I'd promised to buy her at least one drink, come hell or high water. I'd done so, and I sat beside her while she greeted, one by one, with squeals and hugs, the many and varied friends who'd come to help her celebrate her birthday/the end of the world. The bar was filling up; apparently the young people all intended to go out with a drunken bang.

I was not one of the young people, at least not chronologically. I was thirty-seven on Doomsday, and while not a day went by anymore when I didn't wonder how I'd gotten so old – I didn't feel or think like I was a day over thirty – even thirty was still way, *way* too old for Maxine and her friends. And while it was amusing to look at all the attractive young men that came by to wish her well, I was truly just waiting until enough of them arrived so that she wouldn't notice me slinking out.

Maxine was the manager of at a vast warehouse full of overpriced junk named *Old Town Goods*, which featured itself an antique store. They had lots of cool stuff, and even some genuine antiques in there, I guess, but mostly they just had old junk. Three whole floors of it. I passed it every day on my way home from work. I stopped in now and again to see if they'd acquired anything that I might have a mind to pay too much for, and about a year and a half ago, I'd met Maxine.

Maxine was what my grandma used to call an old soul – she possessed serenity beyond her frenetic years. Sure, she had a ring in her nose and purple hair, but when you gazed into her tan-colored eyes, you sensed a strange calmness there. Though really just a child, *she had yet some smack of age in her, some relish of the saltiness of time*, as it were. She'd look right through all your barriers to your very soul, where she would then thoroughly examine it, but only with kindness. She asked intimately personal questions, but in a way that made you feel antisocial if you took offense at them. After awhile, I found myself stopping in to talk to her on my way home from work almost every day, and on Fridays we'd go to happy hour at the bar across the street, this bar. In this manner, I learned her whole life story, and she mine.

A few days after we'd met, I stopped in to visit Maxine after work, and found her crouched in the alley behind the store, attempting to feed a hamburger to a mangy, spavined tomcat with an enormous, fight-battered head. He looked at her with distrust; when he espied me, his distrust intensified.

She whispered to me, "He wants to eat this, but he's afraid. He wants to be petted, too, but he is *so* afraid. All you have to have is patience with cats. He'll come around." She cooed to the cat and held a piece of the hamburger out to him.

This promised to take a minute, so I told her that I'd meet her at the bar. They were broadcasting a police chase on the television when I walked in, and I lost track of the time watching it. When the driver finally stuffed it into a guardrail and was apprehended, forty-five minutes had passed. I looked around for Maxine. She was not there. On a hunch, I returned to the alley behind *Old Town*. She was triumphantly holding the beat-up tomcat, and he was rubbing his head under her chin and purring.

I did not approach, not wanting to spook the cat.

"See?" Maxine said, "All it takes is a little time, and a little patience." She put the cat down and he rubbed on her legs. "Now I have a friend for life." She placed the rest of the hamburger on its wrapper for him.

"What are you going to call him?"

She looked at me like I was missing the obvious. "His name is Big Head," she said and petted the aptly named stray on his big head. He stopped eating and rubbed against her hand. "Cats crave love more than food," Maxine explained. "Nothing in their world feels as wonderful to them as a human hand. That's why they always come over and bother you when you're doing something. They think you're wasting those wonderful hands if you're doing anything else besides petting them." She smiled fondly at the cat, then grinned at me. "Time for a drink." Leaving Big Head to his hamburger, we left the alley.

This incident demonstrated to me that Maxine was a little deeper than her peers. I figured that most girls her age would be too busy doing their makeup and consulting their cellphones to be concerned with a starving alley cat. I liked her blithe, kind, modern spirit, and she must've liked something about me. We became fast friends, and I wouldn't have missed buying her a drink on Doomsday, on her birthday, for anything.

2

But after about three rounds, the bar was getting louder, and the self-control I exercised in not paying inappropriate attention to any of her young male friends was waning. They were so cute, and as I knew, quite biddable. Eager to please like a puppy.

But, no, none of that would be prudent.

TWO

The year before, on her twenty-first birthday, Maxine and I had been sitting in this selfsame bar. It was considerably less crowded on that night, seeing as how the world was not slated to end for another twelve months, and four days before Christmas was not usually a big drinking night.

Maxine wasn't single then, as she was tonight. No, upon her last birthday, Maxine had been involved with a young man name Jose, who was of an age with her. He was tall and slender, possessed of all the exotic, arresting features of his race: the jet black hair, the deep brown eyes, the delicious brown skin. Maxine was very taken with him, very enthusiastic about their love story, which I knew to have been cracking on for about two months at the time.

Maxine was always very enthusiastic about her love stories, until she was not, for whatever reason. Then she'd drop the poor unfortunate like a bad habit, without so much as a polite *it's not you, it's me*. Maxine was not big on second chances with her beaux; when she was done, she was quite simply, quite irrevocably *done*. On more than one occasion, when she sighed and said to me simply, "Next!" nothing more would have to be said. I would know then that we wouldn't be seeing that boyfriend anymore.

But Jose was still Numero Uno the night of her twenty-first birthday. He came up to the booth where we sat, gingerly carrying three drinks. (He was very polite, always buying me a drink when he bought Max one). Max slid over in the booth and he slid in beside her. She planted a sloppy kiss on his mouth and said thanks for the drink.

He said, "Happy Birthday, *Corazon*." Then he whispered something in her ear. Max looked up from stirring her drink and grinned at me.

"Jose has a little surprise for you," she said. "He's invited his friend Fred to join us."

.

THREE

I'd been married once, when I was not more than a minute or two older than Maxine. And I'd loved my husband once. But things had gone south quickly, had devolved into hatred and fear and violence after only three short years, leaving me alone and shaken with two dead bolts on my door.

Then, not two years later, I'd tried again, with a guy named Mike. I was smart enough not to marry Mike, however, or perhaps he was the one that was smart enough not to marry me. I believed that I'd at last met the true great passionate love of my life. He was everything a girl could ask for: funny, smart, very, very sexy. All *that* evaporated into lies and betrayal in only eighteen too short months. I discovered that the very, very sexy aspect came in part from a completely unapologetic inability on Mike's part to keep it in his pants. I was left with a palpable, almost physical pain that I believed, for several months, would never, ever go away.

So, before I'd even turned thirty, I'd learned to be cautious with my heart. And caution doesn't lend itself to monumental love affairs. I participated in safe and boring throughout most of my thirties. Those relationships had begun, middled, and ended like time-lapse films of the sun moving across an empty room, serving as nothing more than testaments to the fact that the years had indeed passed, as boring as calendars. There were not even any commentaries, just markers. Yes, this time had passed, I'd known this one or that one; the days were X'ed off. It had all been like a movie with the sound turned off. Not one moment memorable. Yawn.

But in the six months since I'd known Maxine, my life had come alive, out of the fog. Everything was now in living color. It must be noted that the color was a trifle garish, like red light district neon reflected in rain-slicked and slimy pavement. But alive, like a salamander is alive, wet and dark.

Maxine had pushed me headfirst into the vast, untapped pool of youth that eddied around me, all unnoticed before. She introduced me to Terry, who was twenty-six. Then, through association with her crowd, I met Sonny, who was only twenty-two.

On good days, I felt like a kid in a candy store. They were all so adorable; imbued with a health and vitality that they owned strictly by virtue of being so young. It was not something that they worked at, not something that could be cultivated. They drank and smoked and fucked like rabbits, never pausing for a moment to consider how they would one day wake up and discover that all these habits had left a mark.

On bad days I felt like Henry Wotten, or even Dorian Gray himself. On those days, I admitted to myself that I had nothing but bad intentions toward these boys. They were nothing to me, nothing at all but an extremely entertaining way of passing an evening or a weekend. Or sometimes even a week or ten days, for as long as they would stick around and I could still stand them.

Madonna observed, *Satin sheets are very romantic/What happens when you're not in bed?* And this sentiment summed up my feelings for these young men, at least on the days when I was feeling guilty about my habit, this habit to which Maxine had introduced me, and to which I'd taken like the oft-mentioned fish to water. Surely, they were cute and healthy and optimistic and enthusiastic and their endurance and stamina were epic. But outside of bed they were just silly and immature and tiresome.

On days of unflinching self-examination, I felt like a roué. It was all just too easy. All you had to do was pretend to be interested in whatever drivel he was saying for a minute; after that, it was simply a matter of putting your hand on his knee and whispering a suggestion into his shell-like ear. Sometimes, with the more confident ones, all you had to do was return an appraising smile.

Seducing young men required no skill, no thought, no emotion. It was a simple game. And I took to it with gusto, except on those introspective days, when I came to believe that these practices were indeed aging me prematurely, just like that famous portrait, because I had nothing but the one use for them. And that probably was just not right.

But those days of self-examination were few and far between. On this day in December that was Maxine's twenty-first birthday, I smiled wolfishly and said, "Do tell."

Max nodded at the door, and I turned to watch the object himself as he walked across the bar. He glanced nervously about, obviously unfamiliar with his surroundings, until he spied his friends. Then he smiled and approached.

I felt my mouth drop open. I closed it abruptly, swallowed, remembered to breathe. Fred was at least six foot four, incredibly broad-shouldered and narrow hipped. He had dirty-blonde hair, cut short. He had dark brows and long, black eyelashes, framing beautiful, angelic, pale blue eyes. His cheeks were pink from the cold, in that way that only a young man's can be, and they matched his full, sensuous, boy's mouth. He was wearing faded jeans that matched his eyes, and a wife beater, covered only by an unbuttoned red flannel shirt. No wonder he was cold. He was absolutely adorable.

Jose stood, and the two of them bumped fists and slapped each other on the back, as young men do, said a few words to each other.

I whispered across the table to Maxine, "Are you sure it's not *my* birthday?"

She grinned at me, and then introduced us. I held out my hand. Fred enclosed it in both of his rough strong ones, and smiled at me. His teeth were small and even and very white. He said, "So nice to meet you," and his transparent smile revealed utterly that he had heard all about me and my proclivities and was completely down to be next in line.

I looked over at Max again, as there was no doubt who had been telling Fred about me. She said, "Happy birthday to *you*," under her breath.

I slid over to allow Fred to sit next to me in the booth, and he said, "I thought it was your birthday, Max?"

She cleared her throat and said, "Never mind, Fred."

The waitress appeared and asked Fred what he was drinking. He ordered a Grolsch, and when the waitress asked to see his ID, he patted his shirt pockets a trifle theatrically, I thought, and said, "I must've left it at home."

The waitress pursed her lips in annoyance. "I'm sorry, then. I can't serve you without seeing some ID."

"Bring him a Shirley Temple," Jose suggested, from his advanced age of just turned twenty-one last month.

"I have a better idea," Max said, her eyes never leaving mine. "Why don't we take this party to your house?"

I smirked back at her, feeling the set-up. But I wasn't too annoyed. How could I be, when I considered the fine fish she had reeled in for me? I picked up my drink, paused for effect, drained it. "Sounds like a plan. Drink up, kiddies."

I was feeling the part of the voluptuary then, but not in a bad way. One side of my mouth even curled up in an evil grin when I looked at Maxine. Hot damn, but this one was cute! *If I'm going to do these things*, I thought, *I might as well do them with zest, with relish.* It's bad enough to lie to others, but it's just sad to lie to yourself. So I admitted it. Seedy as it was, I liked it.

We drove to my house in Jose's old car. The distance was so short that Fred barely had time to put his arm around me before we'd already arrived. Work and bar and *Old Town Goods* were all so close that I always walked, but I was glad that Jose had driven us to my house, because that meant that he could all the more quickly dissolve into the mist tomorrow, and take his fine specimen of a young friend with him. The morning didn't usually show these kind of undertakings in their best light.

The four of us went into the house, and Maxine asked what everyone was drinking. Jose wanted a rum and coke, and Fred was smart enough to realize that I probably didn't have on hand whatever weird-ass foreign beer he'd tried so unsuccessfully to order at the bar. He just said politely, "I'll take a Bud if you have one," and smiled his translucently lecherous little smile at me again.

Max and I went out into the kitchen to make drinks.

She said, "I saw this guy standing in front of the bookstore today, talking to ol' Morry. Fine all day and three times on Sunday. Looked like he might be about your age."

I ignored her observational ramblings and got to the point at hand. "Jesus Christ on a crutch, Max! Young Master Fred isn't even old enough to drink?"

"I think he's old enough. Definitely grown enough." She smiled blithely. "Don't you think he's grown enough?" In addition to her serenity, Max possessed quite a bit of the libertine her own self.

But I couldn't deny what she said. Fred certainly was *grown enough*. But I insisted. "How old is he?"

"What do you care?"

I looked at her in amazement. "There are *laws*, Max." Shades of disgraced high school teachers and their incredibly poor lapses in judgment peopled my mind. Surely, I was better than them?

"Relax, Liz. He'll be twenty-one in a few weeks. What d'ya think, I hang around with children?"

I reflected that I'd been hanging around with a lot of children lately, or at least *near* children, or at least comparatively. But just then, our young men entered the kitchen to help us with the drinks, and any compunctions I might have been entertaining fled before the idea of entertaining tall, healthy, fabulous looking Fred.

Maxine turned on the television, and picked out some movie. I had a couple of chairs, a love seat, a coffee table and a large couch grouped in front of the television. Max discretely lowered the lights and joined Jose on the loveseat, leaving the couch to Fred and me.

The *what are we, in high school?* ambience stuck me immediately. It must have struck Maxine also, because not five minutes into the movie, Maxine rose, took Jose by the hand and silently led him away into the spare room in the back of the house.

Scant moments later, without further ado, Fred leaned over and kissed me. The slight whiff of sordidness that I always caught when I found myself in these situations was soon dissipated by the taste of Fred's mouth, by his eagerness.

I took him upstairs and we didn't even bother turning on the lights before falling into bed. I didn't need any lights. I ran my hands over his smooth, taut, hard-muscled body, reveling in his young perfection – I didn't need to see him, too.

He kissed my mouth, my neck. Then, when he was about to attempt an action that I was pretty sure was out of his skill set, I stopped him, made him kiss me again. Fred might learn such finesses someday, but somehow, from the way he was equipped, I thought that it would be doubtful, unnecessary. At least not any time soon. I certainly wasn't going to teach him.

I reflected on the difference between young women and older women, and young men and older men. Young women want to be cuddled and appreciated and respected and foreplayed. Young men just want to *get to it*. But as they age, young men learn that if they want to *get to it* on any kind of regular basis, they'd best learn how to cuddle and appreciate and respect and foreplay. So, by the time they get a few years on them, most men are more likely to have learned how to do these things, and to believe that they are necessary. And men being men, they think that they've learned how to do these things well.

Should a young woman be fortunate enough to encounter an older man who has indeed learned his lessons well, she finds him to be the most wonderful, considerate lover ever. Such matches are fortuitous for both parties. I'd made a few such matches myself before I got married.

But if none of these matches (or any others for that matter) stick, if one finds no happily ever after with that one perfect Mr. Right, as one slogs through the gene pool, as one ages, one can become bored. One discovers to their chagrin that men who would adjudge themselves to be thoughtful and considerate lovers are just as likely as not to in actuality be simply inept and stultifying. Counting the cracks in the ceiling or wondering if you remembered to take the garbage out are not things that should be going on during sex, and I've found myself doing just these things while I waited for some guy to be done being thoughtful and considerate.

I say that there's something to be said for just plain old animal passion, just plain old *action*, is there not? Can I get an amen?

Especially when one is not looking for happily ever after. When one is just looking for a glorious way to kill an evening, like I was.

So it only follows that, when a woman reaches a certain age, a certain state of mind, she would just as well dispense with all that thought and consideration and just *do it*. The expression *fast and dirty* comes to my mind. Here is where the young men can shine. Since they are young, *fast and dirty* can also be *over and over*. What better amusement is there than that?

In other words, Fred's youth and energy and stamina, his fine body and eager kisses, eclipsed completely a certain clumsiness and ignorance. This lack might become more glaring, might get old after a while, but for tonight he was just what the doctor ordered. He wasn't going to be around long enough for it to get old, anyway.

In that facet, young or old, all men are the same. They don't come back after you just eeney-miney-moe them out of the local bar. Not only did I know this; *I was counting on it*.

But Fred fooled me. Fred didn't disappear into the morning mists. Fred *stayed*. Within days it was perfectly clear to me that Fred believed in his tender heart and none too stable mind that I was the monumental love of *his* life. And I made the same mistake with Fred that I'd made with that cheating bastard Mike, only in reverse.

After Mike, it wasn't until months later – when the pain had finally started to subside – that I was able to go back over the whole ordeal, examine the minutia. I wanted to ascertain how I'd allowed myself to be so taken with, so taken in by, such an entirely unsuitable person. To make sure that I never let it happen again. I wasn't sure if my heart and my mind could withstand such emotional devastation again. I'd believed him to be the one, the only, the evermore, and all that couldn't have been further from reality.

What I discovered was that all the time that I was babbling on joyously about how perfect we were together, how we were going to live happily ever after, how we were going to get married and drive off into the sunset – what I'd failed to notice was that Mike hadn't been right there agreeing with me. He hadn't disabused me of my fantasies – why do that? That would only result in an argument. Tears, maybe. What he'd done was just let me roll, let me just go right on ahead and talk and plan. He'd never disagreed with me, never said me nay, but in retrospect, he'd never agreed with me, either. And at the time, I'd failed to notice that. I'd taken his silence as agreement. And that had been a grave error.

Mike knew all along that it wasn't going to last. He had just not been inclined to hep me to it.

And so it was with Fred. I have to admit that I liked the adoration. Love is a little bit of a drug even when it's a one-way street. How's that

10

for a mixed metaphor? Fred was just Fred to me, someone who was around and available at the drop of a hat. Surely, I felt no soul-lifting affirmations of love about Fred.

But it was more than a little wonderful to have someone think I was so wonderful, to have someone constantly telling me how smart and funny and beautiful I was. After a few weeks, I almost started to believe it myself.

And I liked the jealous looks the ladies at the office gave me when my big, strong, sexy, doting young boyfriend would bring me flowers or leave little gift boxes on my desk.

I enjoyed the frequent sex, even if I did always feel the slightest bit detached during it.

I'd like to think that I wasn't as conniving as Mike, that I didn't *purposely* disregard all of Fred's declarations of love and plans for our long and happy future together. I'd like to tell myself that I just overlooked them, or at worst ignored them.

But the love train crashed into the station that spring, when, on my thirty-seventh birthday, Fred got down on one knee and asked me to marry him. He'd bought a ring and everything.

I was appalled at the very idea. Oh my God, I was almost old enough to be his mother, and he thought I was going to *marry* him? What did he think we could possibly have in common enough to sustain a *marriage*? Poor, deluded Fred. It took ever so much effort to persuade him that this was all an impossible fantasy. There were many tears and recriminations.

I'd long ago stopped searching for anything that could be termed *love*, perhaps because I didn't want to risk the pain that I'd suffered because of Mike. And this congress that I'd discovered with the young men was a perfectly acceptable substitute for love. But poor Fred had *taken serious* when I'd just been *pokin' fun*, as my grandmother used to say, and I wound up hurting him as much as Mike or anyone else had ever hurt me. And I'd never wanted it to be that way.

One night, after I thought we were good and broken up, I was upstairs watching television. When I came downstairs for a glass of water, I discovered four frantic messages on the answering machine. At night, I'd been turning the phone off upstairs, because Fred had taken to calling at all hours, trying to rekindle the fires. He seemed to think that my resolve to bid him farewell forever might be at an ebb at three in the morning.

I was surprised to see the light blinking on the machine.

"Liz! Answer the phone! The cops are here!"

"Liz! The cops think I'm a burglar!"

11

"Liz! Answer the phone or they're going to arrest me!"

"Liz! Answer the goddamn phone!"

I looked outside to see two cruisers parked in front of my house.

I put on a robe and ran outside. Fred was handcuffed in the back of one of the cruisers. The cops were just about to take him in.

It turned out that Fred was drunk. He'd decided to make one more attempt at a reconciliation that would happen about the time we put an Olympic-sized swimming pool on Mars. But the gate was locked, and in his drunkenness, Fred wasn't going to take the no of an inanimate object for an answer, and had attempted, several times it would turn out, to climb over the fence.

The neighbors had seen him and had called the cops. He'd tried to explain. But since I had not answered the phone to back him up, they'd decided to err on the side of a more believable story, and were just about to run him in on suspicion of attempted burglary or something like that, when I'd finally come downstairs and then outside to rescue him.

The cops looked at the age difference dubiously, and left. We stood on the sidewalk and hashed it all out again. I knew if I let him in the house, I'd never get rid of him. When he started to raise his voice and the lights came on in the neighbor's house across the street, I finally convinced him that the cops would be coming back if he didn't leave. So he finally staggered away.

The scariest thing about it was that I hadn't heard anything that had gone on outside, hadn't heard the phone ring, hadn't heard him leaving the frantic messages. The scariest thing was that if Fred had been the type to have decided to come over to my house to break in and kill me, instead of just trying to cry me to death in the street, he might've been able to get away with it. Because I hadn't heard a thing.

This fact and the overall tedious effort that I'd had to expend to get rid of poor Fred scared me a little bit.

So, after I'd finally convinced him that I was all wrong for him, after he'd finally stopped calling me, I imposed upon myself a sort of moratorium of the flesh. No more reckless trampling of tender feelings in the pursuit of carnal pleasures, and certainly nothing as ridiculous as *love*.

After I made this declaration, Maxine would always wink at me if I seemed to be paying too much attention to the wisdom of one of her peers. Or if, heaven forbid, they seemed to be paying too much attention to mine. After the Fred debacle, she would kid me frequently about it, always doubting my vow to swear them all off.

Once, we were standing in line at the grocery. I was looking toward the windows and Maxine was facing me, about to pay the cashier. I glanced to my left, and noticed an attractive young man as he finished in the line beside us. I studied him as he walked by and out the door. When I looked back at Maxine, I was surprised to discover that she'd been watching me watch the young man.

She grinned evilly at me and asked, "How old was that one?"

I replied, "Older than you."

She said, "That still isn't very old."

FOUR

So, tonight, on Doomsday, on Maxine's twenty-second birthday, it was definitely getting to be time for me to go home. No more May-December entanglements for me, no, sirree. I communicated as much to Maxine, making my fingers walk across the table, then pointing at myself.

With that perfect grasp of the up to the minute so admirable in the young, she typed something on her cellphone and showed it to me. It said, "Give it five more minutes. I have a surprise for you." When I shook my head, she typed, "Don't worry, he's your age." And then, "You need to get a cellphone."

When I'd first met Maxine, and she'd discovered that I was modern-convenience-challenged, she'd repeated it back to me, aghast: "*You don't have a cellphone?*" in the same tone as if I'd just confessed that I didn't have indoor plumbing. I told her that I didn't need one. I didn't have anyone I needed to call so urgently that I needed to call them away from a land line.

"Besides," I told her, "you have a cellphone. You and everyone else. If I have an emergency, I can just borrow yours. Surely, if I was standing here with an emergency, you'd let me borrow your cellphone, wouldn't you?"

Since this made perfect sense to her, Maxine didn't press me too often to get with the times, except instances like this, when the bar was too loud for talking, and only texting was possible. But Maxine, always clever, had even found a way around that, typing texts that would never get sent to anyone, and then just showing them to me to communicate.

She typed on her phone, "R u sure Fred is gone 4 good?"

I took it from her and typed, "As gone as Jose."

Maxine had given Jose the boot about the same time as I'd decided to rid myself of Fred. He was not clingy like poor Fred, or even an adulterer like Mike. To Max, the old soul, he was something much worse. Jose was a gamer. He spent every moment he could spare plugged into his Xbox. And that was something Maxine could simply not abide. So he was out.

She typed, "You r 100% sure?"

"Jesus Christ, Max, don't jinx me by mentioning He Who Shall Not Be Named. It might just cause him to materialize." I said. "Seriously. He's gone. Last I heard, he moved to Long Beach. I haven't heard a peep from him since June."

Maxine shook her head. She couldn't hear me. She typed again, "R u sure he's gone? Cuz I have one for you that u must not let get away. He's even ur age."

I was skeptical, because I knew that Max's tastes ran to pretty, round-faced, big-eyed Mexican boys like Jose, who looked like they'd just stepped out of a painted-on-velvet picture. Or else mean-looking, tatted-up, pale-skinned, punk rock white boys. And everything in between. Regardless, all of them were too young for me. How would Maxine know any men my age?

She typed, "Trust, u don't wanna pass this one up. U won't wanna let this one get away. Give me five minutes."

I nodded. It was her birthday, after all.

FIVE

Less than five minutes later, Maxine nodded toward the other side of the bar. Although I couldn't hear him speak over the roar of the crowd, it was obvious that he was ordering a drink from the bartender. He was absolutely *striking* – tall, with longish, black, tousled hair, and dark blue eyes. He was wearing jeans and a white, collared shirt, and some kind of long coat.

But it was his smile that was special – he smiled and laughed at something the bartender said – his smile lit up his face. His smile was contagious. I felt myself smiling, and he wasn't even looking at me.

He was definitely no boy, as Maxine had promised, but if all men his age (my age) looked like this one, I would have no use for boys.

I glanced back at Maxine for an explanation, but she was gone. I looked across the bar again and watched her slide through the crowd and give the man a hug. He allowed himself to be hugged and bestowed an entirely fatherly kiss upon her forehead, smiled that beautiful smile at her. Then Maxine, the imp, flat out *pointed* across the bar at me.

The man turned and looked at me, smiled again, waved. Helplessly, I smiled and waved back. Now Maxine, the evil child, had taken the man's arm and was attempting to drag him back around the bar. He resisted, gesturing to her, indicating the bartender. It was obvious that he intended to wait for his drink. Maxine stopped tugging at his arm. He leaned in so she could whisper something in his ear. The man had the good grace not to look over at me again, but Maxine did not. She winked.

The bartender at last set the man's drink down. As soon as he paid for it, Maxine again grabbed him by the arm. He barely had time to snatch his drink off the bar before she began pulling him; the napkin fluttered to the floor, forgotten, like something out of a Wile E. Coyote cartoon.

I had to physically restrain myself from running my hand through my hair, straightening my blouse – all the ancient monkey tells we instinctively want to perform when we see an attractive member of the opposite sex. And this one was definitely attractive. Hot damn, Max, what have you brought for your friend this time?

The bar was packed now, and it took Maxine a minute to wind her way back through the crowd to where I was. She didn't attempt to talk to the man – it was far too loud for conversation – but she held tightly to the sleeve of his coat, like she was afraid that she might lose him in the rabble. Every chance she got, she smiled or winked at me. She paused to receive hugs and kisses on the cheek from birthday well-wishers, never letting go of the man's sleeve, and I had time to wonder what she'd said to him about me.

Funny what a narcissist I'd become in my old age; perhaps I'd always been one. But I didn't think about the man – who was he? What did he do for a living? – I only thought, *What had Maxine said to him about me?* I'm sure Maxine told him how old I was – these girls today didn't ascribe any truth to my mother's paraphrasing of Oscar Wilde: that adage that a woman who would tell her age would tell anything. They wouldn't dream of lying about such a simple fact.

Maxine might have mentioned that I was the office manager at a CPA's establishment around the corner, that I lived close enough that I could walk to and from. She'd obviously told him that I was single; had probably told him that I was long divorced.

She might've mentioned that I'd recently sworn off a penchant for young men.

Facepalm. I thought, *Oh, no, surely she hadn't told this man about all that!* That was just too mortifying to be considered, that Maxine, in her charming, youthful naiveté, would discuss something like *that* with this devastatingly attractive, *grown man*, something that might seem quite normal to her, but which was, or at least should be, an embarrassment to me. I looked through my fingers, hoping she'd left all that out.

At last she dragged him around to my side of the bar. She typed on her cellphone, "This is my friend, Tom," and showed it to me. I nodded, and she texted my name to him, actually sent it.

He looked at his phone. He didn't attempt to speak – it was absolutely fruitless in the rollicking bar – but he offered his hand and I shook it. I noticed that he had large, beautiful hands. He smiled at me, and once again I felt powerless not to smile back.

Up close, it was evident that he was at least my age, but a better preserved specimen must be rare outside of Hollywood, I thought, amused at my own humor. He had a few crow's feet, the kind you get from spending a lot of time in the sun; he had a couple grays in his black hair. These details only lent dignity to his beauty, as they always do for men. He was taller than me, sturdily built, exquisitely lean.

I imagined that he had been pretty indeed when he was Maxine's age. His full mouth would have been dewy then, maybe even a little girly. I longed to hear his voice – a lisp now, what with the enormous blue eyes and the ageless smile, might make him seem effeminate yet.

He gestured to Maxine that he was going to go outside and have a cigarette. She shook her head and turned her tan eyes to me with expectation. He looked at me too, and without a second thought, I hopped up, took my coat from the back of the chair and followed him outside to the patio.

Last year, I'd decided that it was time to make some concessions to Father Time. I wouldn't give up the occasional drink, and at that time, apparently couldn't give up the pursuit of the occasional man far too young for me, so it was smoking that had to go.

I'd never been that much or a smoker, really, more of a dabbler, a dilettante. Certainly, I was never addicted to nicotine, or at least not nearly so much as I was addicted to the formerly mentioned drinks and young men. So smoking hadn't been that difficult to give up; simply a matter of no longer accompanying the smokers outside at break time.

Once outside on the patio, the silence was nearly as deafening as the noise had been inside, at least for someone standing next to a stranger, trying to think up an ice breaker. There were a few people at the outside tables, gamely combating the Southern California cold, which comparatively, really isn't that cold at all. A few other smokers stood around, all murmuring in inside voices. Tom, still without speaking, politely offered me a cigarette. I shook my head.

I watched him take one from its tattered pack. It was a box, and the sides of the top of it were torn, the plastic missing. I wondered idly how fresh they were. He lit it and inhaled and looked at me with an appraising tilt of his head. He still didn't speak.

I smiled. Through a cloud of smoke, he featured me again with his own dazzling smile, seemingly completely at ease with not saying anything. I decided that if he wouldn't speak, then I would do so, because we couldn't just stand around all night looking at each other in silence. This man, without uttering a sound, had so far quite caught my attention, with his blue eyes and flawless smile. I would not let this unlooked for opportunity devolve into nervous laughter, when conversation was something at which I excelled.

I said, "It appears that the Mayans were mistaken."

He looked surprised for a split second but replied immediately, "Well, the Mayans never did have much of a sense of humor."

I listened to his voice more than his words: it was not a girlish voice, as I'd feared it might be, one that would've made his good looks effeminate. This man had never been effeminate, it was now obvious from his voice – even when he'd been young and pretty. His voice was wonderfully low-pitched, gruff, though infinitely well enunciated. A voice that I imagined would be stentorian, Shakespearean, if raised above conversation, but now was simply melodic in its masculinity. If his smile attracted me, his voice captivated me.

18

When I didn't immediately reply, he continued, "The Mayans always took everything so seriously." When I still didn't reply, he again held out his hand. "Hi. I'm Tom Bastion."

I again shook his hand and finally found my voice again. "I'm Liz. Liz Allen."

"So nice to meet you, Liz," he replied, without a shade of hidden meaning.

I could take no connotation other than that he was glad to make my acquaintance; there was no other unconcealed inflection revealing how much *more* he might like to get to know me. Just a generic politeness, refreshing in a way, vexing in another. I couldn't glean if he was interested in me or not.

I decided that I was just used to too many boys like Fred, incapable of hiding their obvious interest if they were indeed interested. It had been a pleasant transparency about them; but one that, unfortunately, wore thin quickly.

But this one, with his fantastic looks and his voice and his neutrality, was far more intriguing than Fred and his ilk could ever be. Surely, they were attractive and all that, but they were a veritable library of open books, with large type, and small, one syllable words. There was absolutely nothing about them to pique my curiosity, nothing about them that was going to come as any surprise to me, whatsoever.

Don't get me wrong – it didn't make them any less enjoyable, for what they were.

But this one gave me pause, made me think, made me wary in an agreeable kind of way. No encounter with a man had done any of that in a long time. I found that I had missed it, that it was actually delightful.

He gestured to a nearby table and we sat. He stopped a passing waitress, asked what I was drinking. I said gin and tonic, and he told her, "Make that two," and favored her with his killer smile.

While he talked to her, I entirely failed at fighting another monkey instinct, this one considerably more modern than the other: I glanced down at his left hand, searching for a wedding ring. I noticed a Masonic ring on his pinkie (I recognized it because my father wore one), but to my delight, I found that Tom wore no wedding ring. This sent a tiny thrill of pleasure through me, as if this absence was some kind of indisputable, beyond a shadow of a doubt declaration of his freedom, of his availability, if I should choose to avail myself of it.

I marveled at the instantaneous nature of hope, at how quickly and absolutely we will lie to ourselves when we wish something to be so. Sure, he wasn't wearing a wedding ring. So, that meant that not only was he not married, this stunning man, but it also meant that somehow he'd managed to evade the clutches of women everywhere, and didn't even have a girlfriend, either? Right.

The waitress departed, and he again turned his dark blue eyes upon me. Again it was obvious that he wasn't going to speak unless I did so first. I obliged, asking two questions at once, just to get the conversation going. "So, what is it that you do, Mr. Bastion? How do you know Maxine?"

"Ah, Maxine! What a thoughtful, intelligent child," he replied. "I met her at *Old Town*. I love that place."

"Me, too," I admitted, "but they do have an overwhelming amount of junk. You have to root through a lot of it to find anything worthwhile."

"This entire planet has an overwhelming amount of junk," he mused. "But that just makes every day an expedition, an adventure, a treasure hunt, doesn't it?" Again he smiled. "Haven't you ever found anything that completely fascinated you, that you found enchanting, that you just had to have? While surrounded by a sea of junk?"

I considered for a moment. "Yes, as a matter of fact, I did, now that you mention it. I bought a bust of a young girl from *Old Town*. I like to think that she's a genuine antique, made of actual marble, but I really can't tell."

"Yeah, the provenance of some of their stuff is doubtful at best," he said, without even placing an ironic accent on the word, as if he said *provenance* every day. "But still, if something catches your fancy, does it matter if it's truly genuine?"

"They surely had it priced like it was genuine, like it was a lost work of a Great Master. But I guess Maxine is empowered to give discounts where she sees fit, and after I went in there and looked at it five or six times, she finally knocked a couple hundred bucks off of it for me. We call her *The Maiden*."

"But if you really like something," he insisted, "if you really want it, does it truly matter where it came from?"

"No one likes to find out they got cheated. No one likes to pay a small fortune for something, and then find out that it's a fake."

"Did Maxine know anything at all about it?"

"She said the same thing she says about most of the stuff in there, that the owner bought it at some estate sale, and that she didn't know anything else about it." I paused and smiled, suddenly seeing his point. "So Maxine and I made up our own backstory about it, full of tearful, heroic romance and international intrigue."

"See? Would you love *The Maiden* any more of less if you found out that she really was sculpted by a Great Master? Or if you found out that she was mass-produced in China?"

"I guess not."

"Then why worry about it? Sometimes the stories that you can make up are so much more fun than the mundane truth. Especially if the story you make up concerns something that gives you pleasure, something that you love, like your statue. Especially if there's no way to find out what the real story is, anyway."

What a pleasant way of looking at things, I thought, as the waitress returned and set our drinks down. It was surely the credo of every charlatan, religious zealot, and snake oil salesman ever born. Believe the story that's most pleasing to you and the truth be damned.

I said, "Add the power of the State behind that attitude and you have fascism."

He looked up from signing for the drinks in surprise. "Fascism?"

"Yes, well, if I want to think that this is the truth about something, whether it's the truth or not, don't I want everyone else to agree with my version of the truth? And if I have an army or the Inquisition to back up my version of the truth . . ."

"That is indeed the definition of fascism. But I'm not talking about global ideologies." He threw out his arms to indicate the whole world. "I'm just talking about the little stories we can tell ourselves about everyday things. Haven't you ever walked around at the mall and made up stories about strangers?"

"*She said the man in the gabardine suit was a spy; I said, 'Be careful his bowtie is really a camera,'*" I said. At least I was not yet drunk enough to sing it.

Again he smiled. "And he's tracking that pale young girl over there. She's a ballerina that's just defected."

"Do ballerinas still defect?" I asked, just to be difficult.

But he wouldn't be baited by my churlishness. He just smiled again and said, "I don't know about that, but you get my point. That's why I don't mind the overwhelming amount of junk here. In fact, I take great pleasure in it. You can imagine a cool story about nearly every piece of it, and every now and again, you uncover an actual, bona-fide treasure."

If this was a come-on, some kind of round about pick-up line, it was so subtle that I couldn't be sure if that was indeed what it was. I smiled again. Oh, he was good. I liked him very much already. I'd never engaged in a single conversation with Fred or any of his peers that had been even half this interesting.

"So!" he rubbed his hands together. He pronounced it *Zo*, with a Z, like a Central Casting Freud would do. "What did you say you do?"

21

"I asked you first," I replied, saucily, I hoped.

"For lack of a more precise word, I am, you might say, an anthropologist."

"*Really!*" I exclaimed in surprise. Of all the jobs I might've guessed for him, this wouldn't have been the occupation that I would've picked. A look of pleased surprise flashed across his face, his reaction mirroring my reaction. I said, "At the university?"

"No. I don't *teach* anthropology. I am by no means qualified to *teach* anything."

"You're simply a student of mankind, then?"

The look of pleased surprise intensified. "You could indeed put it that way."

Thinking that some of the biggest, most worthless deadbeats that I'd ever known had also considered themselves to be students of mankind, I pressed, "But what do you *do*, anthropologically speaking, if you're not a teacher?"

"Whatever the experience with anthropology that I have – I couldn't earn a living with it. Not here, anyway. Or at least not without more trouble than it would be worth. And I'm way too laid back for all *that*. So I guess you could say I'm not really a practicing anthropologist so much." He paused. "But you want to know what I do, like, to earn a living? I'm the newest owner of the bookstore down the street. *Morry's*. Have you ever been in there?"

I was amazed. "You *own* *Morry's*? I go in there all the time!"

Morry's was a real bookstore, an anachronism, an establishment set down here in the up-to-the-minute by some time machine, a fugitive from an era before the digital age. It was the kind of bookstore that had all but disappeared; if *Borders* couldn't make a go of it with their bright lights and coffee and vast computerized inventory, surely a dinosaur like *Morry's* couldn't turn much of a profit either.

In a large, dim, cave of a room, stacks and stacks and *stacks* of ancient paperbacks lined cobwebby shelves above sets of ancient mismatched encyclopedias. Hardbacks with garish cover art from the 1960's and 70's stood beside obsolete textbooks from the 1940's and 50's. I could spend hours and hours just looking around in *Morry's* and had discovered far more *treasures* there than I ever had at *Old Town Goods*. *Morry's* was a wonderland.

Morry himself was a robust frog of a man, maybe sixty, perhaps ninety. He perched upon a tall stool behind an old-fashioned drafting table, drawing diagrams of I knew not what, gears and cogs, levers and switches. He was a character straight out of Dickens. He didn't suffer fools lightly; customer service was not his long suit. I was in the store, browsing, one day and overheard him tersely informing some kid that he didn't carry *Cliff's Notes*.

"We have many copies of the text itself in stock," he said imperiously. "But if you don't wish to discover its meaning for yourself, young man, then I suggest that you simply Google the title. On the internet, you'll find many excellent and learned synopses, some free and some for sale, put forth by many excellent and learned persons. You may then choose that opinion which you feel best suits you and adopt it as your own."

If you dared to approach and ask Morry what his thoughts might be on any subject, he would first study you for several seconds, through large gray eyes that never seemed to blink. If he decided that you were indeed valuable enough to receive his opinion, he would hold forth. If not, he would deliver you a curt and monosyllabic reply.

"I didn't even know Morry was selling the bookstore," I said to Tom.

He shrugged. "He didn't sell it. I'm kind of what you might call a distant relation. I sort of inherited it."

My hand involuntarily moved to cover my mouth, yet another instinctive monkey gesture we do when we see or hear something dreadful. "*Morry died?* Why, I was just in there a couple months ago!"

But Tom smiled. "Died? No. Morry's got at least a couple more decades in him, I'd say. He went back home. Retired, you might say. Returned to the *auld sod*, if you will. The place has been in my extended family for a long time, actually. Now it's my turn to run it."

"That's so cool!" I said, unable to retain my watchful aloofness, the manner I thought it was best to adopt around this striking, captivating man. "I love that place!"

Tom's smile again reflected my enthusiasm. "Stop by anytime," he said as he signaled the waitress for another drink. "I'm empowered to give you a discount."

SIX

This evening was wearing better and better. I reminded myself to thank that sweet nymph Maxine. She had indeed been looking out for me, had done me quite the solid, by introducing me to *this* guy. He was remarkably appealing while still being age appropriate, well spoken when he spoke, an anthropologist yet, that owned my favorite bookstore.

And I was getting more than a little bit drunk and having a great time, tonight, on Doomsday, with this seeming Mr. Right. I tried not to wonder what the catch was going to be.

"Maxine told me that you aren't married," he said, as if reading my mind regarding catches and all. "Why is it that someone like you isn't married?"

I blinked stupidly. The question was a simple enough one to answer: I wasn't married because I *had been* married, and I didn't want to be again. The subject of being married was quite the straightforward topic for me, but still I couldn't form words, being stymied by the *someone like you*. What the hell did that mean?

I gulped too much from my drink. "I was married once," I finally replied. "Many, many years ago. It wasn't for me." What exactly had he meant? Drink made me a little reckless. "What about you?" I said, nodding at his hand. "Why isn't *someone like you* married?"

He knew exactly what I meant when I said *someone like you*. Someone who was obviously intelligent and self-sufficient. Someone who was remarkably attractive. He smiled a trifle sheepishly. Tom was not unaware of how he looked.

"Oh, I was also married once. A lifetime ago. So long ago it was on another planet."

I had to ask the question, even though I really didn't want to know. "Does she live here in town?"

Now it was his turn to blink stupidly for a moment. Finally he pointed up and said, "Uh, no, not here in town. On that other planet." And he smiled.

His smile made me forget trying to figure out what he'd meant by *someone like you*.

Again, the conversation threatened to stall. As I watched him sign his credit card receipt for this round of drinks, I thought of something terribly clever to say. "Have you been left-handed your whole life?"

Again, he looked at me in surprise, as if it was a pleasantly ridiculous question, which I realized it was, and not clever at all. "Yes, as a matter of fact, I have. I come from a long line of the handicapped."

I laughed. "My dad used to say that being left-handed means having to constantly adapt to a world that was not set up for you."

"Definitely true. Every single thing here is designed for the convenience of the majority. But doesn't having to adapt make things more interesting?"

I nodded. Again the conversation flagged, so I noticed his Masonic ring. "My dad was a 32nd degree."

Again he smiled in pleased surprise. "It's obvious that you come from a stellar line, Liz. Your dad was a left-handed Mason? A truly stellar line." He looked at the ring on his finger. "Morry gave this to me, before he went back home."

By now the end of the world revelers had begun to spill out onto the patio. Tom shook another cigarette out of its destroyed packaging and lit it. He nodded at the crowd. "Do you really believe the world's going to end tonight?"

I took his large, lovely hand and turned it over so that I could read his watch. "Well, we only have a few more hours, at least in this time zone. Anyway, how could the Mayans be trusted to predict when the end of the world was going to happen, when they thought Hernan Cortes was Quetzalcoatl returned?"

"That was the Aztecs," he corrected gently.

"Whatever." I was beginning to feel my fifth or six or whatever it was gin and tonic. "I always thought that just because a bunch of academics tell us that the Mayan calendar says the world is going to end, that doesn't necessarily make it so. I feel that I can't really make an informed decision on the whole thing, because I can't personally read the Mayan calendar."

The look on his face said that personally deciphering the Mayan calendar was not one of his problems, what with his being an anthropologist and all.

"It just represents the end of one of their ages. It's just symbolism. Not so much an end as a beginning." I nodded. Maxine twirled by, giggling, hugged Tom, kissed me on the cheek, then twirled away again. "But what would you do if it was true?"

"I don't like it when I have to believe someone else's interpretation of something, especially if I'm not able to interpret it on my own," I insisted. "So, I'm just going with the statistical probability that it's probably not true."

"But it *could* happen, right?" He smiled deviously. "The world has to end sometime, doesn't it? Isn't that enough to make you want to find some divine stranger and go out in a blaze of debauched glory?" Maxine twirled by again, and then she disappeared into the crowd.

Wasn't *this* an interesting change of mood? Was fine Tom Bastion at last flirting with me?

I'd have to walk this line carefully. I said, "But then, if the world *doesn't* end, I'd be stuck with a potential homicidal maniac in the morning." *Like that had never happened before*, I thought. "Besides, I'm a little bit too old to be picking up divine strangers and taking them right on home, end of the world or not." At least this week.

He was looking out at the crowd, not at me, looking for Maxine, perhaps, when he said, "Indeed."

Ah, so here was the catch, I thought, with sudden drunken umbrage. Here was a flash of his true colors. Apparently Maxine *had* filled Mr. Bastion in on my former predilections and activities, and he was just as judgmental as any other man his age would be. There must be some underlying bitterness there, a bruised ego, perhaps, when he thought that *someone like me* (whatever that meant) might be generally inclined to forgo *someone like him*, someone his age, someone who might be afflicted with all the problems which came with so long a life, and choose someone fresher.

So Mr. Right thought he might judge me, did he? Didn't like my lifestyle, did he? But he didn't know me, was ignorant of my motivations, and the fact that he'd dare to think that he knew me and could judge me, after two or three drinks and a dubious introduction from a hippie-dippy child, offended my drunken sensibilities.

But I wasn't too drunk to fail to consider that perhaps I'd misconstrued his meaning. How much meaning can one really construe from only one word, after all? I was neither sloshed enough nor self-destructive enough to tell him off on such flimsy evidence. And if he did see me as some kind of aging tramp, the best way to disabuse him of this conviction was not to act like one. He'd simply agreed with me, after all, when I said that I was too old to be picking up strangers. It wasn't like he was suggesting that I consider taking *him* home, now was it?

So, my inebriated indignation evaporated as quickly as it had condensed. Still, it was time for me to make my exit, because, truth be told, the idea of taking him home had already crossed my mind more than once already, and not because I thought the world was going to end. Goddamn, but he was *fine!*

Only two things had so far stopped me from making such a suggestion to him. The first was the knowledge, gleaned after a lifetime of making the same mistake, that such a thing was simply not to be done. There was a reason it was called a one night stand. This was not some young waiter or bus boy that had grown more attractive with each successive drink. This was a very interesting grown up, and if I ever wanted to speak to him again, such a thing was simply not to be done.

Not that I thought such an act was wrong, mind you. Right and wrong didn't enter into such a discussion, as Fred and a couple of waiters and bus boys could attest. Right or wrong when it came to consenting adults was always a rather gray area to me. As long as no one was hurting anyone else, what was right or wrong?

But there was done and not done.

There was done – anything goes with the youngsters, because I couldn't possibly care less what they thought. The idea that they wouldn't come back and bother me again had always been mostly the point, until Fred had gone all off-script.

And there was not done – if I was interested in some guy beyond a mere momentary pleasure – the synapses for that idea creaked – when had been the last time that I'd been interested in some guy beyond a mere momentary pleasure?

Anyway, if I was interested in some guy beyond a mere momentary pleasure, then picking him up and taking him home five minutes after we'd met was simply not done.

The other reason that I hadn't come right out and made a drunken pass at Tom had to do with just how gorgeous he was, how intriguing I found him. I was sure that he had women throwing themselves at him all the time, and while it was obvious that he enjoyed talking to me, he hadn't indicated any further interest. So there was always the possibility that he wasn't interested at all, no matter how much I wanted it to be so. He might respectfully decline any advance I might make.

It wasn't like that had never happened to me before. I must say that it never failed to come as a surprise when it did happen, however. When they turned me down, I would think incredulously: for what other reason have you been talking to me? If a hook-up is not your aim, then why are you wasting my time? Have you been talking to me all this time because you thought I was actually *interested* in something that you had to say?

But liquor would block out both of these fail safes if I had too much more of it. A couple more drinks, and I wouldn't care what Tom thought of me if he asked and I said yes, nor would I care what he thought of me if I asked and he said no. So, if there was to be no asking and answering on this subject, as there could not be, it was time to go. As it stood, if he was interested, he could get in touch with me through Maxine. And if he was not interested, I would still be able to look him in the eye without chagrin if I ran into him again.

For my own part, I was *very* interested, and sincerely didn't want to mess everything up. It was time to go.

I said, "I was actually looking forward to sleeping through the end of the world. And since it looks like it probably isn't going to happen, it's time for me to go on home now. I'm already going to have a big enough hangover tomorrow to wish the world *had* ended." I stood.

Tom also stood. I was a little disconcerted that he didn't insist that I stay. He said, "You have my personal guarantee that the world isn't going to end tonight." He featured me with that killer smile again. "And if it would please you to stop by the store tomorrow, I'd love to buy you lunch."

Someone like me could certainly not ask for more than that, now could I?

"I'd like that very much. What time do you take lunch?" I put on my coat and started toward the exit, a wrought iron gate in the wall that emptied onto the sidewalk beside the bar.

Tom walked with me. "I take lunch anytime I want, Liz. I own the place." He took my hand in both of his and shook it, repeating, "It was so nice to meet you," again, with no discernible innuendo. "I look forward to lunch tomorrow."

"Me too," I same lamely, all traces of the poetry in my soul rendered inaccessible by too many gins. He waved to me as I started down the street, and I returned his wave, walking backwards like a school girl. Then Maxine grabbed him by the arm and dragged him back into the bar and he was gone.

SEVEN

I walked home, fighting the urge to skip along, feeling lighter and younger than I had in years. The alcohol had a lot to do with it, of course. But meeting this man, this delightful *grown* man, was the main source of my giddiness.

I considered how ridiculous I was. When I'd left work that day, I'd been the same ol' me, planning on buying young Maxine a drink, then sneaking out and going home and sleeping through the end of the world that I was pretty sure wasn't going to happen.

But that world had indeed ended, had it not? I thought, a spurt of poetry escaping. I was not that person anymore, was I? I was someone who suddenly believed that they just might possibly be starting to *fall in love*. How insane was that? After one brief conversation and entirely too much to drink? I couldn't put my finger on exactly *what it was* about Tom that was so charming. Maybe it was just his looks, which were indeed fine. But past that, there was something else there, too, something unusual. I just sensed it, even though I couldn't have defined it if asked. He just seemed to radiate some kind of overall *delight*. He projected a kinetic lust for life that seemed to sing to me from behind the blue eyes and beautiful smile.

I shook my head. Whatever it was, I liked it. I smiled to myself, then tried to think sober thoughts. It wouldn't do to be seen walking down the public street grinning to one's self.

It had been six months since Fred had finally disappeared for good. For the six months before that, I'd been wallowing up to my neck in the whole grubby business, running around with these young men, giddily using them to my heart's content. Then, in my carelessness and complete lack of either regard or respect for his feelings, I'd hurt Fred. I had not wanted to hurt anyone. The depth of his hurt had quite shocked and dismayed me.

At the time, I'd felt like a stunned junkie whose buddy had OD'd. I was sobered by the experience and had successfully not fallen back into my old habits, no matter how much Maxine had tempted me, no matter how much she made fun of me. It seemed to have slipped her mind that it was all her fault in the first place. It had been Maxine who'd shown me these dangerous habits.

But monasticism was lonely. Sure, I had a garden, and I had the women I supervised in the office, who talked pleasantly enough to me when they weren't savaging be behind my back. And I had sweet, lovely

Maxine. But still, I was lonely. I found that I missed having a man around, even if he was only a boy, and even if he was interchangeable with the next one.

And now, Maxine had introduced me to Tom Bastion, who was most assuredly not a boy, who was tall and charming, who at this moment seemed perfect in every way. It was wonderful to feel this hope again, completely unlooked for. To feel something that could actually grow into something else. It was great to feel something that was not just a momentary infatuation with youth and beauty, the type of fascination that usually didn't outlast the long weekend.

I grinned again, and just as quickly stopped, again aware that I must look like an idiot. Instead of love, I tried to call up and keep foremost in my mind all the agonies that resulted from *shattered* love. How I'd felt after Mike.

I must tread softly. Sure, I liked encompassing *these* feelings now, but I had to be careful not to risk bringing on those *other* feelings. Not again, not now. That epoch of pain after Mike had been the roughest time of my entire life.

But walking home from the bar that night, I couldn't dwell on pain and sadness, no matter how hard I tried. I marveled at my inability at that moment to call up what pain and sadness even *felt like*. Yet I realized that even the memory that I'd once felt such things had been enough to keep me cautious for a very long time.

But I no longer felt cautious. I couldn't hold even the memories of pain and sadness in my head as I staggered home on that night when the world did not end. All grim thoughts fled when I pictured Tom's dark blue eyes and that killer smile.

I no longer felt thirty-seven, or even twenty-two, like sweet Maxine. I felt sixteen, and I had no other wish in the world than a fervent desire that Tom Bastion would soon be my. . . my. . . my *boyfriend!* I'd have to tread very lightly indeed to avoid making a fool of myself this time.

How utterly ridiculous I felt myself to be at that moment. This was not at all like me, to think I was *falling in love* with some completely random dude that I'd just met, no matter how attractive he was. The very idea of falling in love was something that I didn't even think of anymore. In my mind, the high-flown, difficult and complicated concept of falling in love had been replaced by the simpler and much more straightforward idea of *falling in bed*.

I was a veteran of the war between the sexes, jaded. I was amazed at myself, fascinated by this man's effect on me. But I liked it very much.

EIGHT

Beyond the wall of sleep, I found myself in Italy, in Venice, in a gondola. The canals and ancient buildings soon gave way to a primordial swamp, complete with strangely shaped trees and odd, vibrantly colored plants. It was a swamp from one of those old natural history books, from back when they still used names like *Brontosaurus* and *Pterodactyl*. After a while, the gondolier let me off on the bank. (He came complete with striped shirt, sash and straw hat – my dreams are nothing if not stuffed with stereotypes. Perhaps they are archetypes.)

Instantly, there appeared a path through the swampy jungle, which led to a spectacular Mayan temple, lit with appropriate fires and torches. I started to climb up the million steps, then suddenly I was at the summit – you know how it is in dreams. I stood before a massive wooden door, not Mayan at all. It was a big, studded, oaken door like from the cathedral from some iteration of *The Hunchback of Notre Dame*. (*Sanctuary!*)

I pushed open the door and found myself within the Cave of Wonders from *Aladdin*, complete with golden Egyptian sarcophagi and chests full of pearls and rubies and doubloons; all the treasures of the ages. For some reason, these did not interest me. I continued on the path and soon found my way into a vast, candlelit medieval library, lined with shelves so tall that ladders were needed to access them.

I walked down the corridors of ancient books, and the medieval theme was continued when I at last found Tom waiting for me, resplendent in feathered hat, doublet and hose, *Merchant of Venice* style, all in glorious shades of blue that complemented his eyes.

He pointed to a large wooden cabinet, ornate, and shook his head, forbidding me to look in there. The mood of the dream now turned dark; a feeling of a sort of sickening inevitability reigned. I knew that I shouldn't look inside the cabinet, but still I was compelled. I just couldn't *not* do it – you know how it is in dreams. I knew that I wasn't going to like what I found in there. It was going to be something bad. But I couldn't help myself – whatever was in there was no doubt the point of the dream, after all.

So I took a deep breath and threw open the door. Sure enough, a nice juicy skeleton screamed silently back at me. My mind had delivered Tom to me as Bluebeard, and all the blue imagery was not wasted.

I tried to scream, but the phone was ringing and that snapped me awake instead.

NINE

It was Maxine. I realized that I sorely missed the resiliency of youth. Maxine had no doubt closed the bar, but here she was at – I looked at the clock – nine am, and she was just as fresh as the oft-mentioned daisy.

"Well? What did you think of Tom?"

"He was very nice." My head hurt, and my legendary eloquence and fierce command of the English language had not yet reasserted itself. Nice. He was so much more than just *nice*. I felt that I owed a better description of my impression to Maxine, seeing how it was she who, quite unbidden, had orchestrated the whole glorious thing. But I was just not up to it yet.

"Well, he thought that you were fucking awesome," she was saying. "He talked about you nonstop for the rest of the night."

I had staggered downstairs and was desperately trying to make some coffee. I paused. "Really? What did he say?"

I could picture Maxine standing in the antique shop, could see her shrug.

"What could he really say, Liz? You just met. He doesn't actually know the complete scope of your awesomeness yet. But he likes what he's seen so far. He thanked me three times for introducing you, and said you're beautiful about five times. He said he was very much looking forward to lunch today. And he told me that he wants to cook dinner for you tonight, too, if he can talk you into it."

"He cooks, too?"

"He does."

Could it possibly get any better?

"I wanted to thank you, too, Maxine. I thought he was pretty fucking awesome, his own self."

She was smug. "You're quite welcome. I knew he was just your type."

I laughed, and it made my head pound. "How did you know he was my type? As far as you know, my type is about half his age."

"Oh, pish posh." Yes, Maxine really did say *pish posh*. "Those guys were just boys. They're not really your *type*. They were all just . . . props. *To occupy your time*." Yes, Maxine really did quote REM. "But ol' Tom, he's your type, all right. I can tell. Through and through. Your soul mate."

"My *soul mate*? Really? Where's all this coming from, Max?"

"Oh, that's right. I forget that you haven't been to his place yet."

"You've been to his place?"

Long dormant, the green-eyed monster rolled over in my stomach, and I hated Maxine. What had Tom called her? *A thoughtful, intelligent child.* I hated her for her confidence, her purple-haired beauty. But most of all, I hated her for the vitality that came from only having spent twenty-two brief summers on this planet. Unbruised youth was infinitely attractive, if not necessarily to one's soul, then most assuredly to one's monkey brain. This was something that I knew quite thoroughly. Youth was something that was inimitable, as fleeting as a summer rain.

"Do you think that you're the only one who's noticed those blue eyes?" Maxine was saying. "I'm not usually into older dudes, but you can see why I'd make an exception for Tom." The monster rolled over again. "I actually noticed him standing on the street corner one time, turned around to check him out, in fact, long before I ever met him."

Then Maxine echoed my own thoughts exactly: "Goddamn, but he's fine! The first time I spoke to him, the first time he came into the shop, he bought a painting. But he couldn't take it with him at the time. So I told him I'd have it delivered, no extra charge. Delivered it myself."

I discovered that I was holding my breath, waiting to hear the details of her matter-of-fact tale of seduction, a tale that might just wreck everything before it even began. I could never compete with Maxine; her freshness, her beauty. I had to maintain some dignity.

My dignity had been a yo-yo enough, as it was, ever since I'd been in league with her. Sometimes it was up, but mostly it just walked the dog, spinning in the muck. But the string would break and my dignity would sink entirely if I tried to *compete* with her. I would not deign to even try.

If Maxine and Tom had once had a thing, even if she was done . . . I don't know, somehow that queered the whole thing for me. Besides, if Maxine was done with him, fine as he was, what was wrong with him?

I said, "What happened?"

"Well, he's no dummy, Liz. How could he be, the way he looks? He knew exactly what my nefarious intentions were. Before I had a chance to make too much of a fool of myself, he stopped me right there and said something like, 'While you're a very attractive young woman, my dearest Maxine, and I want you to know that I'm very flattered, I have regrets older than you. I would just not feel right in the morning.' At the time, I thought maybe he was gay."

If Tom Bastion is gay, I thought, *then that is proof incontrovertible that there is no God.*

"But since I've gotten to know him, I know he's not gay," Maxine was saying. "Unlike yourself, he's just not into partners half his age. And I've observed that he's apparently not into random hook-ups either, even with people his own age."

"How's that?" I exhaled, and the monster slept. I no longer hated Maxine.

"I've never seen him leave the bar with anyone, and you know what a meat market that place is. I even watched Karen – you know Karen, my boss?"

Indeed, I knew Karen. She was the owner of *Old Town Goods*. She was an exceptionally well preserved fifty or fifty-plus: one could no doubt thank a plastic surgeon for that. I'd only formally been introduced to her once, but saw her around the store sometimes. She dripped money from her tanned and toned physique, from her clunky solid gold earrings to her diamond tennis bracelets. She was one of the glitterati of our town, one of the bigger fish in the small pond of downtown small businessmen.

Still I found her brittle and phony, her smiles forced. I thought it was smart of her to allow someone as down to earth as Maxine to run her store – Karen would surely scare away all the customers, if she always looked like she smelled something bad when she spoke to them. Or maybe she just looked at me that way.

"Anyway," Maxine was saying, "I watched Karen try to pick Tom up once. They were having some kind of party at the art museum, some kind of private chamber of commerce thing. Karen always drags me along, 'cause I'm the store manager. She says it's good for me to be seen, for it to be known that I'm her representative. Whatever.

"It was so funny. I was sitting on one of the little benches, and Tom and Karen were standing a little ways away looking at some painting, drinks in hand. She said something about the painting; he cocked his head and looked at it a little sideways, gestured at it with his drink.

"Then Karen leans in and whispers something in his ear. Tom pauses. He takes a sip from his drink; continues to look straight ahead at the painting. Then he looks over his shoulder at me, smiles. All to buy a moment of time, I would imagine, to be polite, so it seems like he's thinking over whatever she said. By the expression on his face, I knew what had happened. Sure, I couldn't tell you *exactly* what she'd said, but I could tell you the general gist of it, just from the mortified but not at all surprised look on his face. I'd seen that expression before, you see.

"Then he whispered something back to her. After a moment, she slunk away. I'm sure he said something like, 'While I'm very flattered, my dearest Karen, I don't have a single regret as old as you, and I don't want to acquire any. Thank you very much, but I'm just not into bony, phony, scandalous bitches such as yourself.'"

I laughed again. "Do you think I'm scandalous, Maxine?"

I could hear the smile in her voice. "Of course you are, but you're not a dried-up, phony bitch that'll cheat on your poor, dumb, rich ol' husband with anything that breathes, now are you? And you're my friend."

"Tell me again why you think Tom and I are soul mates."

"Well, he has a garden, you have a garden. He likes to cook, you hate to cook. You like to read, he owns a bookstore. He's cute . . ." Maxine paused. "And I'm sure he'll allow *you* to seduce him, eventually."

"Let's not get ahead of ourselves, shall we?" I chewed two aspirins while the coffee brewed. "Let me make it through this lunch first."

"What are you going to wear?"

"I don't know, Max. I have a hangover. I haven't had my coffee yet. I need to have coffee before I can think about things like putting on clothes."

"Okay. Call me later and tell me how it goes. Wear something sexy!"

"Whatever you say, Matchmaker."

Maxine said goodbye, and I gratefully put the phone down.

TEN

When at last the life-sustaining coffee was brewed and poured and sweetened, I sat down to drink it, and mused over the wonderful changes that had occurred in my wonderful life over the last twenty-four hours.

The world hadn't ended; that was *all* good. Maxine had made in through her twenty-second birthday celebration apparently unscathed, or at least un-jailed. That was good.

She had introduced me to Tom Bastion. That was fucking incredible.

And then there was that weird dream. I sometimes had success in analyzing my dreams, or at least in tracing their elements back to events that had happened during the day. Of course, sometimes it was completely impossible to figure out what a dream meant. But this last one was pretty straightforward.

Ah, Italy! That was one of my long held beliefs – could there be anything more romantic and mysterious than a gondola ride through Venice? The swamp and the jungle and the Mayan Temple? All those components were easily deciphered, too, all parts of the prophesied but not fulfilled apocalypse. The Cave of Wonders and the medieval library – those visions had all been implanted in my mind by Tom's talk of undiscovered treasures and bookstores. The Renaissance garb – that was another fantasy of attractiveness of my very own. Gotta love those feathered hats.

But perhaps the Bluebeard scenario was easiest of all to divine. That was all a product of doubt. All the talk of treasures – my mind was suggesting that when something appeared too good to be true, it almost certainly was. It was suggesting that perhaps Mr. Right was not what he seemed, and what more apt portrayal than a literal skeleton in the closet?

But I dismissed the stereotyped, archetyped, at least partially gin and tonic induced dream and considered instead what Maxine had observed about Tom. Wasn't into young girls, didn't care for anonymous hook-ups. Hmmm.

I pondered the character of good-looking men. Not men in general – that was too wide a topic. Just the ones that had been gifted from birth, had been attractive their entire lives. The ones that had never had to work at it, the ones who knew, without ego ever having to enter into the equation, exactly what their effect was on women.

At the one end you had the ones that approached the whole battle of the sexes like going to a fast food restaurant. No guile or cleverness was needed in transactions there. The girl behind the counter was put there specifically to fill his order. It was just the way things were; he would be surprised, in fact, if there was some difficulty or discussion involved.

He showed up, ordered and paid, and she filled the order. Simple. There was nothing metaphysical about it. There was no need to display any particular or unusual amount of respect or even notice to the girl behind the counter. Civility was all that was called for. She'd upheld her end of the transaction and he'd upheld his. He'd shown up, she was awed and heeled over, he exercised his prerogative, then put his clothes on and went home. Thank you, ma'am, *what was your name, little girl,* and so on. These men went through life expecting women to succumb, because they always did.

If you added in some kind of religious or moral prohibition, then these were the types that actually hated women for giving in to them. If you replaced religious fervor with self-loathing, then you got the worse kind of man, good-looking or otherwise. Groucho Marx famously observed that he would not want to belong to any club that would accept him as member, and this particular breed of man lived by a similar creed. It wasn't that they *hated* the women who gave in; they just couldn't really have any respect for any woman that would sleep with them. It was twisted.

This type of man is easy to snag, if you really want one. He to whom women come easily only becomes interested when you feign disinterest of your own. All you need to do is exercise a little self control, maybe throw out *What kind of girl do you think I am?* a couple times. And then he'll pursue you, declare his undying devotion, sincerely believe that he's in love with you.

But these men are a warped breed. Their pathology is akin to Freddy Krueger from *A Nightmare on Elm Street*. Freddy couldn't hurt you unless you fell asleep. But everybody has to sleep sometime, to dream. It's inevitable, a biological imperative, you might say. And as soon as you fall asleep, Freddy has you.

This type of man finds you ravishing and ultimately desirable as long as you turn him down. But isn't the point of the battle of the sexes to eventually give in? However, with this type of man, as soon as you give in, as soon as you become as interested in him as he seems to be in you, he becomes bored and eventually annoyed, and it's soon time to move on to the next chase.

Once you're aware of this kind of pitfall, with this kind of serpent at its bottom, it's easy enough to avoid. So I left off considering these men, left them to their own unhappiness and the unhappiness they cause. It was obvious that Tom was not this type, or he surely would have made a pass at me, surely would have taken Maxine up on her offer.

Neither of us would have hesitated.

So I considered the man at the other end of the spectrum, the type that seems just a little bit embarrassed, *discomfited*, if you will, by all the women throwing themselves at him, all the women angling for random hook-ups, as Maxine had so succinctly put it.

Whether consciously or unconsciously, they seem to attach some kind of significance to the act. Maybe it's a germ thing – *Strangers and sailors, that's how you catch VD*, grandma used to say. Maybe it's a self-conscious, embarrassment thing – how *can* I do this with this person that I just met? Maybe it is an ideal of pure, bashful womanhood, that the girl for them couldn't possibly be the one that tickles their palm the first time they shake hands. Whatever the reason, the anonymous sex thing is just not for them.

I'd met lots of men like this – it's easy to spot someone who isn't interested in you, who seems unaffected by your charm. Coming from an earlier generation than Maxine, I didn't automatically think that any man who'd turn me down was gay. I simply thought him to be an uptight, goody-two-shoes. There were too many men in the world that didn't have to be chased, and good-looking men that didn't want to play were all in the same category as Father What-a-Waste to me. Pass.

It took some time for me to realize that not everyone lacked certain moral compunctions, as I obviously did. Just because a man wouldn't sleep with anything that breathed didn't *necessarily* make him a goody-two-shoes. Perhaps Tom Bastion was one of these, I thought. Perhaps he was seeking a woman that appreciated him for more than just his stunning looks. Because at our age, there could no longer be any doubt that all the beauties of the flesh will eventually fade. Perhaps he was looking for a woman that could appreciate him for himself, for that indefinable joie de vivre that I'd already sensed in him.

Perhaps I'd finally gained enough patience and maturity to take it slow and discover if I was that woman, the one that could appreciate him for more than just his looks. Maybe I could be the one that he was looking for.

This could be so much *more* than just a random hook-up. I was sure of it. So, I decided to be very, very cautious, and think about someone else's perceptions for a change. Maybe it wasn't always a good thing to not care what other people thought of you.

ELEVEN

So I didn't wear something sexy for lunch, as Maxine had suggested. I decided to adopt a wait and see attitude, to observe, to let it ride. To react, but not to act. I decided to let him be the instigator, if any instigation was to be done. That would also be a welcome change. The boys had so often been shy, unsure. Sometimes they needed a little prompting. At least at first. And that was tiresome.

I arrived at the bookstore at 12:30, in order to seem neither eager nor arrogant: noon would have been too early, and one o'clock, too late. Tom was out on the sidewalk when I strolled up, directing two young men on ladders, who were taking the sign down.

He took my hand in both of his again, and again said how glad he was to see me. I nodded at the sign. "Are you going to change the name? Is it going to be *Tom's Books* now?"

"Oh, no, that's way too much trouble. Paperwork and fictitious business name statements and the IRS and forms and more forms. I'm just having the sign re-painted, and they said it would be better to take it down and paint it then risk getting knocked off the ladder painting it while it was up there." He held the door open for me. "Let me show you what I've done with the place."

The inside of *Morry's* was basically the same, as far as the inventory went: still a lot of old books. But Tom had moved some of the shelves around and washed the ancient grime off the windows, so the place was now bathed in soft natural light. Young men and women swept and dusted, and I saw a stack of paint cans and drop cloths standing in a corner, waiting to be utilized.

I went over and stood where the drafting table and high stool had once been, looked questioningly at him at their absence.

Tom rolled his eyes. "Relics of another era."

I unrolled one of Morry's strange drawings from a stack still resting on a side table. It looked like an M.C. Escher made of gears and pulleys and cables, pipes and wires that ran up and down and across, a steampunk's dream. It was done with pen and ink, like a patent drawing submitted by Captain Nemo. It seemed to have no beginning and no end. It was quite stark, quite beautiful.

"But what *is* it?"

Tom took the drawing from me and unrolled it fully. He studied the gears and cables. "It's a representation of the glories of machinery.

From Morry's perspective. The Industrial Revolution. The wonders of technology."

"It's beautiful. Like something from another time. You should have it framed."

Tom favored me with that look of pleased surprise again, and called to one of the young men. He said, "Billy, will you take this over to that art supply place and ask them to mat it and put it in a frame for my friend here? Would you pick out a nice black frame for it? Have 'em put it on our tab."

Billy nodded, took the strange drawing from Tom, and left.

Tom said to me, "Your wish is my command." He gestured at the space where Morry's drafting table had been. "The wonders of technology from my perspective are going to be a nice counter with a nice computer and a nice electronic cash register."

"It all has to do with what age you come from, I guess." When Tom looked at me for further explanation, I added, "You know – what kind of technology seems wonderful to you? By looking at Morry's drawings, I'd say that he liked turn of the century mechanical things. And you, you like electronic things."

"I like mechanical things, too," he demurred. "I like machines, period. Electronic, mechanical. Hydraulic, pneumatic. There weren't a lot of machines around where I grew up. We might be considered a little behind the times compared to here, at least when it comes to everyday machinery."

"Did you grow up on a farm?"

Again, that look of surprise. "You could put it that way. A whole big agricultural community." He changed the subject. "What do you want for lunch? How does a steak sound?"

"A steak sounds great."

"Have you been to *Smiley's*? Down the street?" He held the door open for me and we stepped out into the December sunshine.

"I've only been there once. I found them a tad pricey."

"They are that," Tom agreed, "but money is no object when it comes to good food. I know the chef. He makes the best steak in three counties." He did the French finger kissing gesture, which made me smile at its ridiculousness.

"I'll let you order for me, then," I said.

He smiled and nodded and again held the door open for me at *Smiley's*, which was indeed just down the street.

Like *Morry's* and *Old Town Goods*, *Smiley's* was housed in one of the early 1900's buildings that made up our little burg's old downtown. I thought that this fact might contribute to *Smiley's* high prices as much as its aspirations to trendiness. The insurance premiums must be murder on an old building like this.

The clientele was light, because it was Saturday. Another problem with old downtown was that it was mostly just a ghost town on the weekends, because all of the offices and government facilities that made up its bulk were closed. The chamber of commerce was always trying to devise ways to attract people downtown after five and on the weekends. There were festivals and parades and art walks and Farmer's Markets.

The two waitresses on duty waved and said hello to Tom. One of them said, "The usual?"

He replied, "Two!" He said to me, "Do you want to sit on the terrace? I can smoke there." Then he changed his mind. "Ah, never mind. It's too cold. I can wait."

He chose a booth by the window, and the waitress came over to take our drink orders. Tom looked at me for a second, as if considering, and then said, "I suppose it's too early to start drinking. I wouldn't want you to get a bad impression of me." He looked at the waitress and said, "Just a bottled water for me."

"I'll have the same," I said, and the waitress left.

"Do you want any vegetables or bread or anything with your steak?" he asked me suddenly. "The *usual* is just a big grilled T-bone. I don't get anything else here."

"That's fine," I said, but the question must have been on my face as to why this was so.

"I try to avoid as much as possible all the chemicals in the food."

"Really?" I said, surprised that someone who smoked and drank and ate T-bones with no vegetables would be worried about chemicals in his food. The waitress brought us two bottles of water. No glasses. Trendy.

Tom said, "You'll agree that chemicals are everywhere here? In this bottle, leaching into the water. In the air, in the ground. But there are so many more, so many extra chemicals in your food here. Not only the fertilizers and the insecticides and the preservatives and the hormones. There's also all that stuff that they put in there to make it *taste good*."

I reflected that being a chemical phobe was like being a germ phobe. There are just too many people, too many germs, too many chemicals, and I'm just too lazy to worry about it.

"How can you live in the city and worry about chemicals?" I asked.

"I didn't say I was worried about them." He favored me with that killer smile. "If you *worry* about them, you'll go crazy.

"I don't eat the vegetables that they serve here because they're all cooked with rich sauces. Not only are they expensive and fattening, they're *not real*. They're full of chemicals that go straight to the pleasure centers in your brain." He pointed to his forehead. "You *think* that they taste very, very good. Real vegetables don't taste like that. So, when you taste real vegetables, you're disappointed."

He said all of this so matter-of-factly that I replied, "And how do you feel about all that?"

"I like real vegetables, how they taste, without all the sauces and chemicals. It's just hardwired into my brain. Vegetables are good for you; they're *vital*. Knowing this is just something that's second nature to me. I don't need to be bribed – I don't need ranch dressing, if you will – to get me to eat my vegetables."

The waitress arrived and set down two sizzling steaks. He thanked her, told her to thank the chef for him, then looked at me and shrugged. "But food chemical manufacturers gotta make a living, too, I guess. I just don't have to eat what they peddle." He intently watched me cut my steak and take a bite. "How is it? Isn't it the best steak you've ever had?"

It was indeed and I nodded.

TWELVE

After lunch, we walked back toward the bookstore. He didn't hold my hand or put his arm around me, but he did walk agreeably close, and I liked that very much.

I said, "Where do you live, anyway?" He told me he lived above the store, and I was amazed. "Are you zoned for that?" How east coast! He nodded. I said, "But Maxine said you had a garden."

He looked at me in surprise again. "What else did Maxine tell you?"

Now I smiled. "Nothing but good things."

He smiled back and said, "It's an aquaponic garden."

"Is that like hydroponics?" I asked, hoping that he wasn't some kind of middle-aged weed dealer.

He shook his head. "It's a self-contained system, with fish," he said. We had arrived back at the bookstore. "Would you like to see Chez Bastion? Aquaponics and all?"

I nodded and he indicated a rusted security door on the side of the building, which creaked when he unlocked it. "All this is supposed to be painted, as soon as they get to it."

I followed him up a dim flight of stairs. He paused at the top and said, *"You unlock this door with the key of imagination."* We entered the apartment, and he made that silent, encompassing gesture again, arms outstretched. "Morry used to use it as storage."

The place was tiny, just one oblong room, plus a kitchenette and a bathroom-ette. There was a table in the kitchen, with a laptop on it. There was only space for one person to sit at it. A stove with only two burners and a hotel room sized refrigerator. There was a postage stamp sized balcony ("I don't think it's very safe," Tom said) and a nook with a brocade curtain around it, behind which I assumed was the bed. It had to be a huge bed, however, because it was a long curtain. There was a little couch in front of it. No coffee table. No chairs.

But the place was incredible nonetheless, really like the Twilight Zone, *a dimension of mind, a land of things and ideas.* At the opposite end of the room from the bed nook was an enormous flat screen television. Against one wall were two large aquariums ("I had to have the floor reinforced," Tom told me sheepishly).

From out of plastic boxes atop the aquariums sprouted cucumbers and cherry tomatoes, which snaked across the ceiling, dangling from hooks. This was the aquaponic garden. He explained to me that the water was pumped from the fish tanks to the planting beds, where the vegetables grew in a kind of soil-less gravel, made from recycled glass bottles. The water then ran back into the aquarium. The fish waste nourished the plants, and the plants cleaned the water for the fish.

I asked him something I'd been suspecting ever since the chemicals-in-food conversation. "Are you a hippie, Tom?"

He rolled his eyes and pointed at a stained glass sign in the kitchen window: *Hippies use back door. No exceptions.*

"Hippies want to change this planet," he said, "in ways that are just not feasible. I prefer to adapt to what already exists." He put a cigarette in his mouth with his right hand and lit it with his left, and I was reminded of his remark the night before about lefties having to adapt.

He gestured at the wall opposite the aquariums, and said, "My treasures."

Here was a collection of outlandish objects that might have come from the sub-basement of the Smithsonian or perhaps Indiana Jones's yard sale. There was an Egyptian mummy case, sandwiched between two bookcases, over which flew a marlin. There was a weird painting of a cityscape and black birds; I assumed that this was the painting that he'd bought from *Old Town*. There was a human skull on one shelf as well as a crystal ball, and books and books and books.

"Is all this stuff real?" I asked.

"What did I tell you about real?" He smiled. "Some of it is. The sarcophagus is genuine, from the Third Intermediate Period. The sailfish is fiberglass. The painting is just strange. It's by a local artist. The crystal ball is just glass, but the skull was once an actual person. He's one of my favorites – it gives me pause to think that he was once a human being, someone that laughed and loved, and earned a living and had thoughts, had a mind that existed mysteriously within the brain that was once housed right in there." He pointed at the skull's forehead, just as he had pointed at his own when we were in *Smiley*'s. "Just like you and me."

He looked at me to see if I was in any way offended by it, and when he saw that I was not, that I found it just as fascinating as he did, he smiled and continued. "The Gutenberg Bible is a fake." He pointed at crossed swords above the door. "The rapiers are reproductions. The television is just plain awesome, but it only looks its best at night. It's really too big for this room."

"I think that it's funny that in this room full of unbelievable stuff, you like the TV the best," I said.

His smile widened, but he didn't turn the TV on. "We can go anywhere in the world with this TV. In high definition."

"It would look spectacular on my living room wall," I commented, noticing an ancient Underwood typewriter on another shelf, in museum condition. "I'm assuming that this was Morry's?"

"Oh, no, that's mine. I just had it cleaned." He rolled the blank piece of paper that was in it up a little bit and typed, *Now is the time for all good men to come to the aid of their party.*

"Do you actually type things on it?"

Again that look of surprise. "You mean, like manuscripts?" When I nodded, he said, "No. It's an antique."

"But it still works, right?" I gestured at it. "You said you'd just had it cleaned. Why don't you use it?"

"Use it?" He smiled. "It's not efficient, Liz. It's cool and all; all that workmanship. I like mechanical things, mainly because I never saw any growing up. In fact, I never saw anything even remotely like this typewriter before I came here." He brushed a non-existent speck of dust off the black paint. "This typewriter was state of the art in its day. There was never a better typewriter made, and it's beautiful to look at, shiny and black. But now, it's just not efficient. It can no longer compete, if you will. We have something better, more efficient, more *useful.* Something that does everything this typewriter ever did, plus so much more.

"This typewriter is obsolete. I just like to look at it, to appreciate all the little moving parts. Computers don't have too many moving parts." He lightly touched the keys on the typewriter again. "I appreciate the intricacy, the *precision,* of all those tiny pieces of metal moving in concert. No electricity, no plastic, no solid state. Just little pieces of metal meshing effortlessly at the touch of your fingers." He tilted his head at me, like I might be dense if I didn't understand this.

I shrugged and went back to looking at his stuff. I partially understood his appreciation for old machines, but on the other hand, if they were obsolete, why have them around? Weren't pictures on the internet good enough?

Kind of expecting to find it, I came across an old telephone, the kind where the talking part and the hearing part were separate.

"That's also a reproduction," he said. "One of those sea of junk things you mentioned. It was a gift from Max. It's not real, just a shell. There are none of the parts inside that made it work."

I nodded and poked around some more. "No record player?"

"Ah, music! *Through all the tumult and the strife, I hear that music ringing/ It sounds and echoes in my soul/ How can I keep from singing?*" He told me that these were lines from a Quaker hymn, of all things.

"But no record player?" I repeated.

45

Again, that tilt of his head. It was curiosity, I realized, like I was a strange bug. "Absolutely no record player. How you do imprint on the *absolutely* obsolete."

I said, "One time, I was in Maxine's store, and I listened to a kid tell her about his contempt for modern recording media. He was telling her about how he *loved the rich and full sound of records.* He was telling her how he still listened to his mom's old records, instead of more modern stuff, because of how wonderful they sounded.

"I felt that I had to object. I said, 'Say you like records for any other reason besides that. You can't seriously say that they *sound better.* They most assuredly do not sound better. They're scratchy and poppy and . . . just yucky.' And he insisted, saying that was all part of the sound. And *I* insisted, saying, 'No, that's all part of the *recording.*'"

"I couldn't agree more," Tom said. "That's why there's no record player here. Records and record players were never very efficient, compared to what we have now. Like you say, the sound was never as good as it could have been, as good as it is now. You could never hear all the subtleties of the performance. Once again, even the best record player ever made wasn't as good as the modern equivalent for reproducing the sound quality."

Tom reached behind the brocade curtain and retrieved a remote control. At last he turned on the giant TV. He pressed a couple of buttons and revealed a music catalogue. He scrolled down a few screens; it seemed to go on forever. He handed the remote to me.

"Do you want a drink? The sun is over the yardarm, after all."

"Sure." I immediately became engrossed in his music collection. It seemed that he had examples of everything ever produced in the English language: rock, pop, jazz, bluegrass, country, rap, ragtime, blues, techno. Pianos, banjos, guitars, drums, horns, synths. He had classical music, which I only recognized by the names of the composers. And he had recordings of American Indians, and Australian aborigines, and African tribesmen and Gregorian chants. I became quite lost in all the titles and for several seconds didn't realize that he was holding a drink out to me.

I took the glass and looked at him, astonished, speechless.

"Music hath charms to soothe a savage breast, to soften rocks, or bend a knotted oak. Someone famous said that only human beings possess a soul. Only human beings create music." He allowed me to ponder this for a moment, then said, "Zo!" again, like a dime store Freud, wiggled his eyebrows at me. "Do you have plans for today?"

Again I couldn't be sure if he was flirting with me or not. I thought he might be, but it was very subtle. *Let it ride*, I told myself.

"Nothing that can't be put off," I said.

"What would you like to do? Go downstairs and sell books?" He looked around his apartment and suddenly frowned, an expression that I hadn't seen yet. "This room is much too small for company."

"Do you want to go and visit Maxine?" I said flippantly, because I couldn't think of one single other place to go.

"A stellar idea!" he said.

We slammed our drinks, then left and walked the short blocks to Maxine's place of employ.

THIRTEEN

Just like *Smiley's*, *Old Town Goods* was dead on a December Saturday afternoon. Maxine was playing some game on her phone, and didn't even look up at us when the bell tinkled over the door.

"Uh, Miss?" Tom said. "I wonder if you might have any record players? My friend here is totally into absolutely fucking obsolete technology, so I also wondered if you might have some beepers and faxes? A mimeograph, perhaps? Or maybe an icebox?"

Maxine looked up, prepared to make some cutting remark, but when she saw that it was us, her pique faded and her smile bloomed. "Look at you guys! You look like you're on your way to the prom!"

It was three o'clock in the afternoon, so I told her it was a little too early for prom.

"So what brings you here to this mausoleum?"

"I've decided that my apartment is too small for company, Maxine."

"Since there's no place to sit but the bed?"

"I have a couch," he protested. "But the place is still too small. And the store is still being cleaned and painted. No place to hang out, so here we are."

"What do you mean your apartment's too small?" she scolded. "Didn't you say something about dinner, yesterday?"

"It didn't seem too small 'til just now." Tom paused. "Would you ladies like to have dinner with me in my tiny apartment, anyway? I have to go to the market first. What would you like me to make?"

I noticed with amusement that he didn't wait for us to agree to have dinner with him, because he naturally knew that we would. That was the legacy of being attractive: no doubt makes for no hesitation.

"I have a better idea," Maxine said. "Why don't you go to the market, and then I'll meet you at Liz's house about 5:30? You can cook dinner there. There's plenty of room. What do you say, Liz?"

Ah, Maxine, you little devil, you! This ploy had been her modus operandi on my behalf before. Why hadn't I thought of it? "Sounds good to me," I said.

"Excellent," Tom said. "I'm sure you have a table that seats three, which I do not. I'll see you later." He left to go to the market.

As soon as he was out the door, I grabbed Maxine's head with both hands and kissed her on the forehead. "You're a genius! His place really is too small."

"What do you mean? I think it's a perfect little romantic love nest."

"That it is, and that it will be, I hope, but not quite yet," I said. "Right now it's just uncomfortable for two strangers. Like you said, there's no place to sit."

"You could always sit on his lap."

"And maybe someday I will, Max, but not yet!"

"So what do you think, so far?"

"Oh, Maxine!" I said, and the years between us melted away. Women are all girls when they think they're falling in love, and are talking to their girlfriends about it. "He's just so . . . I don't even know! But I like it very much!"

"Maybe I should beg off from dinner," she said slyly. "Let you two be alone."

I was appalled. "Oh, no, it's too soon, Max! I just met him *yesterday!*"

"Since when has that ever stopped you?" she chided, and I felt an unaccustomed blush. That was shame, I thought. Not so much shame at my past actions, but shame at having them pointed out to me.

"He's different," I replied simply.

"That he is. I guess it's a good thing that I'll be there to chaperone, after all. Save you from yourself and all."

"That reminds me. I need to pick up some liquor."

"You don't have to tell me twice. Let's go."

"Don't you have to stay 'til five?"

"I have carte blanche on that," she said. "Anything after 3:30, and it's up to me. The earlier I close the place on the weekend, the less Karen has to pay me. So, let's get out of here." She turned out the lights, locked the front door and we left.

"You don't have any liquor?" Maxine asked incredulously, as we walked to the liquor store down the street from *Morry's.*

"Not anymore. What do you think I do, sit around at home and get drunk all by myself?" I replied. "Do *you* sit around at home and get drunk all by *yourself?*"

"It has been known to occur."

"Drinking is a social activity. Drinking all alone is just . . . sad."

We walked around in the liquor store, and I chose a bottle of gin, and then hesitated. "Call Tom and see if he wants anything besides gin."

"I see a cellphone in your future." Maxine spoke into her phone, then hung up. "He said gin is fine. He said to get No. 3 London Dry. No Gilbey's."

"His wish is my command." I put the Gilbey's back. I had to ask for the No. 3 from behind the counter. The man had to dust it off. This was not exactly your connoisseur's liquor store.

49

"I thought gin was gin," Maxine said.

"You don't even drink gin," I replied.

"I might start."

"Not at forty bucks a bottle. Do you really want gin? Don't you usually drink rum? Pick out whatever you want. Nothing's too good for my chaperone. Saving me from myself and all."

Maxine picked out an inexpensive rum and a liter of cola. I also got a liter of tonic water and some lime juice, and laden with liquid cheer, we paid and left.

When we got to my house, Maxine insisted on making me a very strong drink, "to make you not so nervous and to keep you from running around and tidying up until he gets here."

I sipped the drink and tidied up anyway. Just about the time that Tom was slated to arrive, he called Maxine's phone and she went outside to meet him. I reflected that this was the new paradigm in the modern world: she'd just given him the cross streets, no address or anything.

"Just call when you get to Palm and I'll come out to meet you," she'd told him.

It seemed a strange way of doing things to me. Perhaps it was time for me to adapt.

FOURTEEN

Tom carried a large cardboard box, full of groceries and pots and pans. When I looked at it curiously, he set it down on the table by the door, beside *The Maiden*, and sighed. "I suppose that you have Teflon cookware, like everyone else in the First World on this planet?"

I looked at Maxine, who rolled her eyes and smiled. I said, "Yeah, I guess so. Why?"

"Teflon is poisonous," he stated. "So I hope you don't mind. I brought some good cookware."

"You *are* a hippie!" I said, and wanted to hug him, just for being so odd. But it was too soon.

"No," he insisted with a smile. "I keep telling you, hippies have a mission to change the world. I have no mission here, no mission whatsoever. I just don't want polytetrafluoroethylene in my blood. Do you?" He looked at Maxine.

"I think I have polytetrafluoro-whatever in my soul," she replied. "What are you gonna make?"

Tom smirked at Maxine and her wit. "I guarantee you'll like it. Do you really need details?"

"I guess not. Do you want me to make you a drink? We have rum and gin."

"No, no, I'll do it, Max," I said quickly. "Your drinks are a little strong for the grown-ups. I would like to be awake past seven."

Tom picked up his box and I showed him to the kitchen.

"I'm sorry about the Teflon thing," he said. "I promise I don't have too many more eccentricities."

"I think you really are a hippie," I was delighted with his serious apology. "And anything that is healthier for me has to be a good thing, right?"

"You can live much healthier if you're just a little bit careful," he said with enthusiasm. Impulsively, he kissed me quickly, innocently, on the forehead, much as I had kissed Maxine earlier. "Stick with me and we'll live forever!"

I considered this a lovely sentiment. "Would you like to see my garden before it gets dark? It's grown over now, but . . ." I stammered to a stop and opened the back door.

The old house had a huge backyard, and I had grand plans for decks and fire pits and one of those cool outdoor rooms like you see in *Sunset* magazine. But after living there for ten years, nothing had gotten done except the garden. It was C-shaped, with raised beds and a wooden arch that spanned the legs of the C.

I was not a hippie either, but I did like to attempt to grow things. It was very therapeutic to sit out there for a few minutes in the evening and tinker with it, to weed a little or tie something up, after the drudgery of the workday and before the onslaught of the mosquitoes.

Here in Southern California, if you're industrious, you can grow stuff pretty much all year around. But I was just a single season enthusiast. I loved to prepare the plot and sow the brave little plants no later than March, but by the end of August, I was bored with it for the year. Now, three days before Christmas, my garden was quite grown over and weedy, looking like it had been abandoned for some years, instead of only for four or five months.

Tom exclaimed over it anyway, and talked about all its possibilities until I regretted that I'd shown it to him in its neglected state. I said, "Next year, I want to grow something more exotic than strawberries and tomatoes."

Tom was gleeful. "This is a great spot, perfect amount of sun. I see you have irrigation."

"That's broken." Another reason I'd given up for the year.

His enthusiasm was not dimmed. "You can grow anything you want here!"

I decided to go out on a limb, a little; it was not like I was making a pass at him, after all. I said, "Maybe you could help me pick out some plants? I figure that someone who can get cucumbers to grow out of a fish tank in the winter time could probably work wonders with actual dirt."

This idea seemed to please him, and again he favored me with that killer smile. "Whatever you want, Liz. I'll grow bananas and pineapples and orchids for you, if you want. Right here. Anything that you think might taste good."

"And cook it, too?" Maxine came out of the house and stood beside us. "Liz hates to cook."

I felt like she'd told a secret about me, then reconsidered: it was just as well that he found out now as later.

Tom, standing between us, impulsively put his arms around our shoulders and quickly hugged us both. "And cook it, too."

"How else can you be sure it wasn't cooked in the wrong kind of pan?" Maxine said.

"Indeed."

Tom took a fresh pack of cigarettes out of his pocket. He pulled the little plastic tab too hard, and wound up tearing the plastic off of the whole thing. Then he pushed the top of the box back, also too roughly, and tore the sides. Then he struggled with the aluminum foil, tugged on it for several seconds, as if it was stuck. Finally, he tore that out, too, even though I knew it would come out in one piece. Now I knew why his cigarettes looked so ragged.

He prised one out of the pack and lit it, and we stood there in silence for a minute. It occurred to me that Tom planned on staying outside until he finished his cigarette. Another modern courtesy: once upon a time, it was the very opposite – it was the hostess' duty to make sure there were enough ash trays. No one would dream of taking their habit outside.

"You can smoke in the house," I told him. "There's no need for us to stand around outside in the cold."

"Amen," Maxine said, and with a mock shiver, went back inside.

Something had relaxed in Tom, and he put his arm around my shoulder as we followed. Without a second's hesitation, I put my arm around his waist. My arm immediately felt warm and cozy under his coat, and I silently thanked Maxine for being there. Because it really was way too soon, and I already liked him way too much, and if she was not there, I might be inclined to make a fool of myself.

The dinner he cooked was delicious, and the three of us sat around and got mellowly drunk. Eschewing the lime juice, Tom had brought actual limes for our gin and tonics. Maxine tried to leave, so that we might be alone, but Tom, ever chivalrous, insisted on walking her home. She lived just this side of the freeway, and the seediness from the other side had spilled over into the apartment complex where she lived. Tom said he could allow no friend of his to be walking around in such a neighborhood in the dark.

Maxine gave me a hug goodbye, which established a little protocol that allowed Tom to also hug me. She was quite the little manipulator (seeing as she had never been much of a hugger before) and I loved her for it. It was very nice and warm enveloped in Tom's strong embrace, and I longed to linger there.

As they walked out the door, Maxine paused and said, "What are you guys doing for Christmas?"

"Just sitting by the fireplace, waiting for Santa," I said.

Maxine looked at Tom. "What about you? What are you doing?"

He shrugged. "Not a thing. I'm an orphan."

"Then you guys should come to my house for Christmas dinner! I'll even cook it." She looked at Tom with mock solemnity. "I promise not to use anything with Teflon on it."

Oh, Maxine! I thought. She was the perfect little deus ex machina to this modern love story in the making, moving it along smartly, removing all the little awkward bumps along the way. How to ask him to my house? Let Maxine do it. What do you do about Christmas when you've only known him for four days? Have Maxine invite us both to dinner.

I said, "That sounds great, Max! How very sweet of you."

We both looked at Tom. "Okay, but New Year's Eve is on me," he said. "All the painting and remodeling is supposed to be done and I'm having an open house till nine."

"One of those open bar and hors d'oeuvres, chamber of commerce things?" Maxine asked.

"By invitation only," he said and smiled. "As a matter of fact, your boss set the whole thing up for me."

"And what did she want in exchange?" Maxine asked slyly.

Tom endeavored to look mortified. "Just my gratitude for her volunteering to help get the store noticed."

"And in what form did she want you to express your gratitude?" Maxine pressed.

Tom ignored her and turned to me. "I'd be delighted if you both would attend." He turned back to Maxine. "It's semi-formal, so I'm sure you can scare up some kind of prom dress. Then, promptly at nine, I'll throw Karen and her crew out, and the real party will begin."

"We wouldn't miss it for the world." Maxine accepted for both of us.

They started down the sidewalk, and then abruptly Tom returned. "Call you tomorrow?" I nodded and thought I might cry at the cuteness of it all. "Goodnight, then!"

I said goodnight and went back into the house. I knew that the fact that I hadn't given him my phone number was not a problem. He would just get it from Maxine.

FIFTEEN

Tom and I spoke on the phone on Sunday and Monday. He came by the house to pick me up and we walked to Maxine's apartment for Christmas dinner on Tuesday. Maxine had scoped out the landscape to make sure there would be no budding-relationship, Christmas gift-giving faux pas. She made sure I didn't get anything for him and that he didn't get anything for me. I gave her a crisp one hundred dollar bill, because she expressly told me that cash was the best gift *ever*, and Tom gave her an expensive bottle of rum. I loved the fact that he always seemed to go for the finer things in life, at least when it came to food and liquor.

Maxine was a total surprise in her Christmas finery. She had her purple hair done up in a Gibson-girl that was absolutely adorable on her, and she wore a red sequined holiday dress, modest in length, and asked Tom if it was prom dress enough for his upcoming fete. He told her that she was beautiful and that she'd steal the show.

She sat us side by side on her tiny couch and handed us presents, insisting that we open them immediately. I said she shouldn't have, and sincerely thought that she shouldn't have, knowing that she worked for Simon Legree and didn't make much money.

Maxine read my mind. "Don't worry, they're both from the store. I get a huge discount. Go ahead, open yours first, Liz."

I opened the small cardboard jewelry box. Inside was a chain and a pewter, ball shaped charm. I recognized it immediately. I told Tom, "This is a replica of the charm from *Rosemary's Baby*." Maxine and I had once discussed if just such a thing existed, and damned if she hadn't found one for me. "Thank you, Maxine! It's beautiful!"

I held the ends of the chain up and Tom hooked the clasp. I was glad that it was toasty in Maxine's apartment; it was only because of this fact that I didn't shiver when he touched the nape of my neck.

"I knew you'd like it," Maxine said quickly, a little dismissively. "Now open yours, Tom."

Tom looked at us for a moment, and then silently tore open the large box she'd given him. That was another thing that I already liked about him: he didn't make useless small talk. Someone else might've said, "Oh, I wonder what it could be?" or something equally inane. But Tom didn't say anything. You could tell he was enjoying himself just by the look on his face.

Maxine's gift was a very cute ugly Christmas sweater, with giant white snowflakes on a blue background. When he modestly left the room to put it on, Maxine whispered, "This present is really for you, and me too, I guess. See if I can't pick 'em."

Maxine most assuredly could pick 'em. The blue of the not-so-ugly after all Christmas sweater perfectly accented Tom's eyes, making him appear even more breathtaking than usual. He could not have looked sexier if she'd presented him with a black silk robe with an embroidered dragon on the back. Maxine and I were both struck dumb.

Tom, not unaware of how he looked, smiled sheepishly at us. "Thanks, Max." When we continued to stare at him, he said, non sequitur, "I forgot to bring ice." She had specifically asked us to bring ice, and we'd forgotten. "I'll go get some ice."

When he moved toward the door, the spell was finally broken, and Maxine said, "That's okay, Tom. I have a few trays full. Besides, it's Christmas Day, and nothing's open. And I'm not sure if Liz would want to let you walk around all by yourself, looking like that." Again he smiled sheepishly, and she said, "Let's eat."

Her Christmas dinner, with all the fixings, was exceptional, especially for a contemporary girl who'd always claimed that she burned water. It was a lovely evening and I felt like we were almost a little family. Tom and I walked home arm and arm, and he wished me a Merry Christmas at the door. He hugged me, and again it was warm and wonderful. He smelled so good! I got the impression that he wanted to kiss me, and I certainly wanted to kiss him, but he held back. I was a little disappointed, but after all, I'd only known him for four days.

SIXTEEN

The next day it was business as usual, back to work. When the women in the office asked me how my Christmas had been, I could truthfully answer, "Very nice," for the first time in years. "Santa brought me something special," I added mysteriously.

Toward the end of our relationship, Fred had frequently called the office to beg me to give it another chance. Since I didn't have a cellphone then either, I was unable to take it all outside, so the ladies I supervised had inevitably overheard my frantic attempts to calm him down. They were aware of my proclivity for young men; they also knew that the fling with the last one had ended rather badly. It was just one more thing that they talked about behind my back. So when Tom showed up for lunch, out of the corner of my eye, I watched all their jaws drop. Something special indeed.

I stopped by *Old Town Goods* on my way home from work, and as was to be expected, it was dead. No one was buying antiques or whatever Karen was passing off as antiques on the day after Christmas. As if I was a schoolgirl, I found that I was powerless not to express my concern to Maxine about the fact that Tom hadn't kissed me yet. Somehow, in a world full of war and injustice and crime and starvation and any number of grown-up problems, this was the biggest concern on my mind. When had I become such an adolescent?

But Maxine didn't make fun of me. She was an old soul, after all. She smiled serenely. "He's waiting for New Year's Eve." She tapped her temple. "I know he is. How romantic is that? If I were you, I'd shave my legs, because New Year's Eve is gonna be the night for you guys, I just know it. And don't tell me that it's too soon.

"New Year's Eve! That's storybook stuff right there, Liz. The stuff that dreams are made of." When I didn't reply she said, "So, do you have a dress for this thing?"

"As a matter of fact I do. This isn't my first semi-formal New Year's Eve rodeo, honey." I always called her *honey* when I condescended to her youth.

She took my mild rebuke good-naturedly and replied, "But I bet it's gonna be your best!"

SEVENTEEN

The invitation to the Grand Re-Opening of *Morry's Books* said six o'clock, but Maxine insisted that we not show up until eight.

"What rock do you live under?" she asked. "Haven't you ever heard of *fashionably late*? Poor Tom has to deal with all the chamber of commerce types anyway. Let's let him do it. We'll arrive and be elegant for the last hour, and then get out of these heels."

Maxine was resplendent in her red sequined dress, and I had on a little black velvet number with glittery silver accents that always wowed them at the office Christmas party. Maxine wanted to hobble the several blocks in our party shoes, but I insisted that we call a cab. Like grown-ups, I told her. It was still early enough that we didn't even have to wait very long.

As we walked up the sidewalk to the bookstore, I spied Tom through the window, so I was able to stop and be stunned for a moment before he got a chance to see me. He'd gotten a haircut and I was surprised at the change: if anything, he looked even better with shorter hair. Smoother, sophisticated.

He was wearing a tuxedo, an *actual tuxedo*, pants with stripes and patent leather shoes, and all – not just the jacket and a pair of jeans, like some ironic, hipster bookstore owner might do. His only nod to semi-formality was the lack of a cummerbund and the fact that his bowtie was undone, as were the first two black pearl buttons on the blindingly white shirt.

He was devastating, and I remembered what Maxine had prophesied about tonight being the night. I knew that all he'd have to do was say the word.

I was not at all surprised to see Karen standing there beside him, gesturing animatedly, talking quickly, smiling winningly, all her beautiful capped teeth on display.

Maxine and I entered. There were perhaps twenty chamber of commerce types milling around in the store. The place smelled like fresh paint and was brightly lit. The new counter and cash register had been installed. Morry's strange, beautiful drawing, now framed, hung on the wall behind them. There was jazz music playing, a stylish background to the murmur of voices and clink of glasses. There was a roll away bar set up by the window, complete with bartender.

Tom was holding a drink and listening politely to Karen. But when he saw us enter, he interrupted her in mid-sentence, saying, "Will you excuse me for just a minute?"

He handed his drink to her, and without waiting for a reply, crossed the room to us. He kissed Maxine on the forehead, as was his habit, and she deftly dissolved into her surroundings, leaving us alone.

Tom gently twirled me around and whispered in my ear, "You look beautiful." He looked as good as any Prince Charming, and his attention made me feel like Cinderella at the ball.

He took me by the hand and led me back to where Maxine, grinning, was now standing next to her boss, who had morphed into one of the ugly stepsisters. She was trying to keep that *I just smelled something bad* expression off of her face, but she wasn't succeeding.

Tom said, "Karen, I would like you to meet my good friend, Liz." He put his arm around me, and I was amazed at the subtext in his voice — *it is because of this woman that I keep turning you down*, his tone said.

"We've met," Karen said, laying on her best fake sweetness.

She opened her mouth to say something else, but before any words came out, Tom asked me if I wanted a drink. Before I had time to answer, he again took me by the hand and swept me over to the bar.

"At nine, I'm throwing them all out," he told me. "I'm going to tell them that I have another function to attend."

He looked at me again and the appreciative expression that glowed in his blue eyes made me blush. *Maybe it will be tonight*, I thought.

"You look beautiful," he said again.

"Ah, it's just the dress." My mother always said that I didn't know how to take a compliment.

But Tom didn't say anything else, just slid his arm around my waist. He repeated, whispered in my ear, "I'm throwing them all out at nine."

But nine o'clock came and he didn't throw anyone out. Those chamber of commerce types that had been there only because they felt that they needed to be departed on their own (including Karen), but the rest of them stayed. The music got louder, the liquor flowed, and all of Tom's neighborhood friends and customers showed up, including all the kids that he'd generously paid to do the sweeping and the painting. Maxine didn't change out of her high heels. It was a bitchin' party. We sang, we danced, we drank. We had conga lines through the bookstore.

At midnight everybody screamed, "Happy New Year!" and Tom finally kissed me, slowly, languorously, far too completely to be happening in a room full of people, even if they were all drunk. And then we looked into each other's eyes silently for a moment, and it all just *clicked*, like something from a movie, or from fiction. But it was real and unbelievably hot.

He glanced toward the side door, where the staircase to his apartment was, inclined his head subtly, gave me a little smile. I nodded without hesitation, and it was just that easy. Not a word needed to be said.

He took my hand and we started in that direction. Halfway across the room, Maxine stopped us to give us a hug for New Year's and Tom whispered something in her ear. She held out her hand and he dropped a set of keys into it.

The security door leading upstairs wasn't locked, but Tom turned the deadbolt and locked it behind us as soon as we were inside. And then we were climbing up the dark staircase, and I was giggling. The door to his apartment wasn't locked this time, either, and when we walked in, I noticed that the place was already dimly lit for ambience, the brocade curtain around the bed tied back. He'd indeed planned this out ahead of time. He'd known that I would not turn him down.

But I didn't begrudge him the certainty. When you looked like he did, you had the right to a certain amount of certainty in such matters. I was glad that it was his idea tonight, at last. Because, truth be told, it had been my idea since the very first night when Maxine had introduced us.

As if I was some kind of virginal school girl, I came to the realization that I'd actually appreciated the little lull since then. I'd thoroughly enjoyed walking around in an exquisite daze of anticipation for the last ten days, waiting breathlessly for just this moment.

He didn't say a word, but picked me up and carried me to the bed, just like in *Gone With the Wind*.

Our encounter was simply the most intense first time of my spotted career, and that's saying something, coming from someone who has had more than the cougar's share of healthy, even athletic young men. Each at his biological peak, each so very eager to please, each possessed of the inexhaustible stamina that's actually the most attractive thing about them.

Tom kissed me like a drowning man, or like someone just rescued from the desert – but these descriptions aren't right either, because they connote a kind of desperation that wasn't there. He was most assuredly not desperate; it was more just the uniquely flattering quality of his desire. He made me feel like I was the only woman in the world, the only woman ever born. He made it seem as if he'd been waiting his whole life just to make love to *me*, as if it was a culmination that he'd longed for, for a very long time. Surely for longer than the ten days that we'd known each other.

And then, after the initial passion was spent, after all the action that *I like so much* was expended, Tom just smiled at me with a kind of glorious smugness, a supreme confidence. And then he started all over again, ever so slowly, languorously, like when he'd kissed me in the bookstore. The whole thing was incredible. *Transcendental.*

He made me feel unerringly, undeniably attractive, as if I was Cleopatra or Helen of Troy or Elizabeth Taylor. Never before had the skill meshed with the looks so perfectly; never before had the performance matched the promise so completely. For someone who can always think of something to say, I was *dumbstruck.*

EIGHTEEN

We slept spooned together, something I'd always imagined would be a very romantic thing, but something that I'd not been able to actually stand in reality, until now. There had just been too many snorers, too many sweaters, too many teeth grinders.

But it was the most comfortable, most natural position in the world in which to sleep with Tom. He slept with his arm draped protectively across my waist, his nose nuzzled into my neck. It was just the icing on an already fantastic cake.

NINETEEN

There was a bookshelf that served as the headboard to Tom's bed, where he kept his cellphone and the remote to the giant TV and an old-fashioned wind-up alarm clock and of course, more books. Promptly at nine o'clock the next morning, his phone vibrated, echoing dully off the old wood.

He reached behind him and picked it up, looked at it. "Hello, Maxine. What the fuck time is it, anyway?"

Why was I not surprised? It seemed that even the excesses of New Year's Eve couldn't reset the eternal early morning sunshine of her internal clock.

I smiled, stretched gloriously, just like Scarlett O'Hara. From Tom's side of the conversation, I gleaned that Maxine was *downstairs*, God love her, and wanted to come up and visit. Tom silently asked if it was okay with me, and I nodded.

He said into the phone, "Use the two keys on the little ring all by themselves. The blue one, then the black one. But give us just one minute, would ya, Max, for Christ's sake?"

He hung up and smiled at me, and just like that, just that completely, I knew that I would follow this man to the ends of the earth. All he would have to do was suggest it.

I felt embarrassed at the completeness of the feeling, and would've been utterly mortified if I had to speak it aloud. But it was there, nonetheless. After ten days of charm and one night of boundless, near mystical sex, I believed that he was my soul mate, just as Max had said. Exactly why I felt this way was harder to nail down. There was just something about him; he was just irrepressible.

How easily and completely, I thought again, we will believe just what it is we want to believe.

All trace of modesty gone, Tom hopped up naked and opened a door next to the bathroom, a door I'd not noticed before. It turned out to be a walk-in closet. Inexplicably, it was almost as long as the whole other half of the apartment, only narrower. It was almost big enough to sleep in.

After a minute, he threw a pair of jeans and a t-shirt out of the closet onto the bed. I couldn't help but smile when he sat on the corner of the bed and pulled the jeans on.

"No underwear?"

"Bitch, please," he said, and grinned from ear to ear. "Underwear is the most ridiculous thing ever invented."

He jumped off the bed, his bare feet slapping on the wooden floor. *I bet they'd hear* that *downstairs, if the place was open*, I thought. I lolled my head to one side and had time to admire his broad, flawless shoulders before he pulled the t-shirt over his head.

He turned around and looked at me wrapped up in the sheet. He said, "I don't imagine you want to put your party dress back on. Although I must warn you that the party has only just begun."

He picked my dress and the components of his discarded tuxedo off the floor, stepped into the closet, and hung them up. "I don't know what to offer you. All I have is sweats and shirts. Although I'd love to see you in my tux." He peeked out of the closet.

I jumped up and squeezed in there with him, hugged him. It felt very sexy to do so while I was undressed and he was fully clothed. "Sweats and a shirt are fine."

He stepped out and pulled the cord that released the brocade curtain, enclosing the bed again, then crossed his ankles and leaned against the door frame, smiling, watching me paw through the drawers set into the wall of the closet.

He pointed at a pair of deck shoes on the floor, beside which stood a bicycle. It was a great, heavy, electric-blue dinosaur of a beach cruiser, and since I imagined that it would be quite tiresome to lug it up and down the stairs, I thought that he kept it as another exhibit in his cool machinery collection, as opposed to actually riding it. I gestured at it.

He said, "I wanted a penny farthing, but it wouldn't fit it the closet." When I looked confused, he said, "One of those old fashioned bicycles with one giant wheel and one small wheel? With the seat on top? From the 1800's."

"Yeah, that wouldn't fit in the closet."

"They're rather hard to come by, too."

The shoes were a little big on me, but they would do. I put on a pair of his sweats and a t-shirt, hugging them to me because they smelled like him. This was truly the most wonderful movie cliché ever, wearing one's boyfriend's clothes, and I wondered if Maxine would recognize it.

He embraced me and kissed me with easy affection now, as if we were old lovers, comfortable with each other, instead of virtual strangers who had only celebrated New Year's Eve together in a somewhat provincially traditional way. His expression told me that he wished Max hadn't chosen just that moment to visit, and I couldn't help but agree. How much fun it would be to just take off all our clothes again.

To the ends of the earth, I thought.

Maxine knocked then, and immediately unlocked the door and walked in, like the courtesy knock the doctor gives before he enters the examining room. She arced Tom's keys through the air and he caught them, and I understood that he had left her in charge of his party and his store while he consummated his none too difficultly achieved seduction of me.

I smiled to myself. I originally had been under the impression that Maxine and I had been in this together, the orchestration of this love affair. But I was beginning to get an inkling that perhaps it was she and Tom who were in cahoots.

"What do you want for breakfast, ladies?" Tom went into the kitchen, retrieved his cigarettes off the table. "What would please you on this beautiful day that the Lord hath made?"

"Nothing cooked in Teflon," Maxine replied. Apparently, the Teflon thing was still hilarious to her. She picked a cherry tomato off of the vine that snaked across the ceiling and popped it into her mouth.

Tom smiled through a cloud of smoke, then repeated, "What would you ladies like? I could eat a horse."

"No horse, please," Maxine said immediately, and I was again struck by their casual camaraderie. They were definitely much better pals than I would've originally guessed. Again, I wondered which one of her good friends Maxine had fixed up here. Either way, it was all good.

"How does bacon and eggs sound?" Tom said, and not waiting for our reply, disappeared back into the microscopic kitchen. Soon the mouth-watering smell of bacon and coffee permeated the tiny apartment.

Maxine wiggled her eyebrows at me, and I realized that I had not yet spoken a word to her. I gave her the thumbs up.

Every time one decides to give it a whirl with someone new, one wants to think that there's at least a fifty/fifty chance that it will be great or at least good. Unfortunately, my lifetime average as far as a satisfaction rate for first times went was quite a bit lower; about twenty-five percent. So, I had recently learned to stack the deck: young men are usually always good, even the first time, just by virtue of being young.

But this one had completely, utterly, *seriously* exceeded all expectations. Tom could not have been better, I could not have been more satisfied, if I'd conjured him into flesh and blood to my own specifications. *Hot damn,* but he was fine!

The three of us crowded onto the little couch to eat our bacon and eggs. They were divine. A demon between the sheets, and he could cook, too? Could it get any better?

"Aren't you worried about whatever chemicals they put in bacon to make it taste so good?" I asked.

Tom considered me with that now familiar, surprised, curious expression. "No chemicals in bacon," he said around a mouthful.

"Yes there are," I replied, as if I thought he had to be pulling my leg. "You hear about it all the time. Nitrates or nitrites or something. Supposed to be very bad for you."

"Yeah, there's that. But not too many of what you'd call flavor enhancers." He smiled and shoveled another forkful into his mouth. "Bacon just tastes good."

"Oh!" Maxine suddenly jumped up. "How do you turn this ginormous thing on? They're having the *Ancient Aliens Marathon* today."

"Oh, yeah, that's right!" I said. "Turn it on! How awesome will it be on this TV?"

Tom rolled his eyes. He took our plates out to the kitchen, then fetched the remote, and said to me, "Not you, too?"

"What did the stoner-guy say in *The Thing*? *They practically own South America, man.*"

He looked at me with that head-tilted curiosity again. "You believe in aliens?"

I tilted my own head back at him, kissed him. "I believe that there are more things in heaven and earth than are dreamt of in my philosophy. I think that there probably aren't any aliens visiting anymore – we probably could detect them with all our technology and stuff. But I think there might really have been *ancient* aliens. Somebody had to have built all those pyramids and observatories and what have you."

"Will you two shut the fuck up?" Maxine scolded. "Giorgio is speaking."

TWENTY

The first episode dealt with some claptrap about how the aliens had left messages in our DNA, if we would only become technologically savvy enough to decode them.

Tom listened to the whole spiel, then looked at Maxine in disbelief. "Really, Max? You're telling me that the stuff of life is really just some kind of chain letter? What's it going to say when we finally get smart enough to decode it? *Kilroy was here?*"

"Look, they have to fill a lot of time, here," Maxine replied. "It's a weekly show. Some of their theories are a little more . . . out there, than others."

The next episode talked about how the aliens might have sent that comet to the earth to wipe out the dinosaurs – or maybe it wasn't a comet at all, but some kind of weapon – because they wanted the planet for themselves. Or the dinosaurs were some kind of experiment, and the aliens didn't like how it was coming along, so they wiped the slate clean and started over. Or something like that.

"This is ridiculous, Max," Tom said flatly. "Do you really believe that there are beings powerful enough, selfish enough, to wipe out an entire planetary ecosystem? Thousands, *millions* of species? On a *whim?*"

Max shrugged. "I don't necessarily ascribe to all of *Ancient Aliens'* theories, my friend. This particular one is a little ridiculous, I have to give you that. But wait till you see the one about Puma Punku."

That was one of my favorites, too. I liked the ones about all the massive structures – how could our primitive ancestors have constructed these things without help? Stone knives and copper chisels do not produce a place like Puma Punku, with its massive, weird, precision cut stone H's.

"When is that one on?" Tom asked.

Max pushed the button and paged through the hours of this first Day of Our Lord, 2013. "Not till four."

Tom looked at me. "You want to take a little walk?"

"Sure."

"What about you, Max?"

"Shush!" Maxine scolded again. "Giorgio is speaking. I'll see you when you get back."

Thus were we dismissed.

TWENTY-ONE

Tom and I walked arm and arm through the deserted downtown streets. I asked him, "Are you really annoyed with Maxine and her aliens?"

"Not at all. They have a few theories that are thought-provoking enough. A few theories that you don't have to wear an aluminum foil hat to contemplate." He smiled at me. "Besides, I'm not easily annoyed. I'm happy as a clam. Especially since I met you." He stopped abruptly and grabbed me by the elbows, and kissed me right there on the street, in front of God and everybody.

I told him that I felt exactly the same way, and we smiled at each other in our shared happiness for a moment. Then I said, "Where are we going, anyway?"

"Liquor store. Outta smokes."

"For someone who is worried about chemicals, you sure smoke a lot," I said, only half kidding. He did smoke a lot.

He featured me with that killer smile again, the one that I found so damned charming. "I told you before, I don't *worry* about chemicals. I'm just selective about which ones I assimilate. I like to smoke. Never smoked before in my life before I moved to this place, did I ever tell you that? Never had a drink, either. Never did a lot of things." He winked at me.

"Who's responsible for corrupting you so?" I asked in amazement. "Was it Maxine?"

"I've never been involved in any corruption with Maxine that you haven't already heard about. Or at least not much."

He winked, smiled, made that outstretched arms gesture again. "This world in general has corrupted me. This unapologetic den of iniquity, this carnival of strange. I fucking love it here! Tobacco, liquor. Bacon. T-bones and fast cars. Wait to you see the car I've got in storage, Liz, you will love it. The best music in the universe. Gambling. Movies. *Dirty* movies. Art. Literature. Architecture. Machinery." He stopped again and kissed me again. "A beautiful woman to love, who loves me."

This first declaration of love, delivered so soon, so confidently, so *correctly*, touched my heart. I did love him already.

It was amazing to me how I could go from six months of wallowing-in-the mud debauchery to six months of get-thee-to-a-nunnery celibacy to suddenly believing myself to be in love. How odd that thought was, how alien it felt to admit it to myself. I hadn't loved anybody in a long time, but just like that, I realized that I loved Tom. Over and above being *in love* with him, which could be an unrealistic, fleeting, momentary thing. Beyond that fantasy of romance, I just loved him. The smile, the curiosity, the *alive-ness*. How had this happened to me so quickly? It was enough to make a person start to believe in fate.

He was saying, "Life is good. *Great*. Corrupt me some more."

I said the first thing that came to my mind. "No drugs?"

His face lit up further. "What did you have in mind?"

Now it was my turn to look at him curiously, like he was a strange bug. "Where did you say you grew up again?"

He looked away, abruptly started walking again. "Big agricultural community. I'll tell you about it someday."

And with that, I realized that the discussion of where Tom was from was officially closed, at least for the moment. I thought that it was a little strange that he would be so reticent about these kind of details. We all have our quirks, however, do we not? Maybe it was unpleasant for him to talk about it. I began to suspect that maybe he had grown up in some kind of religious compound or something. Maybe he was Amish. I thought that would explain a place with little machinery and no vices.

I felt a little left out, a little bit resentful that he didn't want to tell me about it, but on the other hand, maybe I didn't want to hear about it, if it was bad enough that he didn't want to discuss it. I figured it would all come out eventually.

TWENTY-TWO

We found a liquor store that was open on New Year's Day. Perhaps all liquor stores are open on New Year's Day. He bought a pack of cigarettes, and I watched him mangle them in the opening again. Somehow he managed to tear the little strip that was designed to separate and take only the top plastic off. But the bottom plastic came off and the top stayed on instead. I was fascinated. How could someone mess this up so completely? Apparently, every time? It wasn't brain surgery, after all. He didn't tear the sides of the box this time, but again, he wound up tearing the foil instead of just tugging it out in one piece.

He noticed me watching this bizarre demonstration and offered me a cigarette. I took the box from him and shook one out. What the hell, it was a new year. I'd share another vice with him, since he was so fond of them.

"Wait, I have to show you," he said.

The cigarettes he'd bought were called *Camel Crush – menthol freshness on demand.* The good people at Camel were ever so fond of a good gimmick, and ever since they were forced to shelve Joe Camel, it seemed like they came up with a new one every week. Tom held up a cigarette, filter first. He indicated the little blue camel on the filter. "You squeeze it between your fingers to release the menthol."

There was a quite audible snapping sound, as if some tiny piece of glass was indeed being crushed inside the filter, and I immediately, irrevocably, thought of war criminals biting down on cyanide filled teeth. Unable to escape that visual, I nonetheless took the cigarette from Tom and he lit it for me. If he thought that I imprinted on obsolete technology, I thought that he was a sucker for a gimmick.

"Welcome to the party pal," from *Diehard.*

He squeezed the little button and lit himself one, then couldn't close the package because the plastic on the top was still on there and got caught at the back. He shrugged and stuffed the whole thing in his coat pocket.

This was not the strangest performance I'd ever seen, but it was in the top ten. Maybe it was a left-handed thing.

TWENTY-THREE

Maxine went MIA, starting on the twenty-fourth of January. She wasn't at Happy Hour on the twenty-fifth; not available for brunch on Saturday, nor breakfast that Sunday. Her only contact was a brief text to Tom. "Busy, my friend. Will TTYS."

We were standing in his postage-stamped sized apartment, preparing to go to *Smiley's*. Tom wanted steak for breakfast that Sunday. He showed me her text, looked perplexed.

"Our little Maxie has found a boyfriend," I explained. "Don't worry. We'll see her again soon. And him, too, no doubt."

Tom pouted at his phone. "I'm jealous."

I hugged him. "How many girlfriends do you need?"

That smile. "Just the one. Allow me to show you." He picked me up and tossed me onto his big, soft bed. The steaks were postponed until lunch.

TWENTY-FOUR

I stopped in to *Old Town* the next day after work, and found Maxine a changed woman. The ring in her nose remained, but the purple hair was a thing of the past.

"Suicide blonde?" I asked.

"Who says you old people aren't hip?"

"Who says you young people aren't hip?" I said, thinking that the name for the hair color had been around for decades before she was born. "It looks great on you."

"Thanks. I actually am a blonde. But not this blonde."

"No one is that blonde." I toyed with a Troll doll, circa about 1965, that was sitting on the counter next to the cash register. I looked at the price tag and quickly put it back down. "So, when do we get to meet him?" I asked Maxine.

"I was wondering when you were going to ask. His name is Rick. I call him Ricky; he says no one ever called him Ricky before. He's twenty-six. He came in here looking for a birthday present for his *mom*. Isn't that sweet?"

I nodded and smiled, matched her grin. I was just as happy for her as she was for me. I said, "I want to thank you again for fixing me up with Tom, Max. He's just *so* . . . we're just *so* . . ."

"I know, you're all in love and shit." She dismissed all that with a cynical wave of her hand, but smiled. "Everybody wants somebody, Liz. All the feminism in the world can't make up for that simple fact. There are just so many assholes, it's hard to find anyone that's not wasting your time. Tom's a good guy – a little odd, surely, but he's basically a really good guy. And I love you. So I knew that the two of you would be perfect for each other."

"And what about this Ricky? Is he Mr. Right?"

She grinned slyly. "I don't know about all that. But he is definitely Mr. Right Now."

"Now who's scandalous?"

"He bought his mom a pair of drop pearly looking earrings. I gave them to him at half price, and he asked me out."

"And you've been inseparable ever since."

"Almost literally."

"Tom's jealous, you know."

Maxine looked surprised. "What are we, his harem? It's not like I get any action. He'll get over it."

I said, "Indeed," and then repeated, "So, when do we get to meet him?"

And Maxine repeated, "I was wondering when you were going to ask. I was thinking that maybe you could invite us to dinner or something. You've already had my cooking. He's already had my cooking. And my place is too small for four people."

"I would be honored, Max," I said sincerely. "When is good for you?"

"How 'bout Friday?"

"Perfect."

"Have Tom cook." She smiled innocently at me.

"Of course." Then we said in unison, "No Teflon!"

TWENTY-FIVE

Ricky sported a shock of tow-head blonde hair, shaved on the sides, left long on top, so it flopped down into his eyes like the mane of a pony. Since she'd dyed her own hair a similar shade of blonde, I had the weird impression that he and Maxine looked like brother and sister. Both of his muscled arms were sleeved in intricate, expensive, very well done tattoos.

Tom asked for and received an explanation about the koi and the sparrow and the 8-Ball, and the symbolism behind each. Apparently they didn't have tattoos either on Farm World or wherever it was he was from. Sometimes he seemed like a little kid to me, when he would become fascinated with everyday things. Gimmick cigarettes. Typewriters. Some punk kid's rather mainstream tattoos.

In the kitchen, I asked him in jest if he was thinking about getting inked.

"Maybe. Why not? As soon as I can think of something that I want to have forever." He rolled up his sleeve. "Maybe your name in a heart, right here."

I was flattered by the idea, not sure if he was kidding or not. "I don't think that's necessary."

Maxine came into the kitchen to help carry the food to the dining room. She said, "I think you should get the dolphin on your ankle."

Ricky was right behind her. "It should really mean something to you," he said, stating the obvious.

"I like the idea," Tom said, "but I have to think of the perfect thing."

Maxine and Ricky carried bowls and plates out to the dining room. When we were alone again, I put my hand in the back pocket of Tom's jeans and said, "How about a picture of a typewriter, right here? Or a penny farthing?"

He took my other hand and put it on the front of his pants and whispered something obscene in my ear. Just when I started to think of him as boyish or childlike, he never failed to remind me that he was not.

"You're crazy," I said, feeling myself blushing.

He wiggled his eyebrows at me. "It's a prerequisite for living here."

TWENTY-SIX

After dinner, Ricky complimented the chef, then said, "Would anyone like to get stoned?"

Tom sat up in his chair like someone had offered him chocolate pudding with whipped cream on top and looked at me. I smiled and sighed at the same time, and raised my hand. Tom followed suit.

Maxine looked at us in surprise. "What next, old people? Skydiving?"

Tom shook his head, like the very idea hurt. "Oh, no. Gravity. Splat." He gestured up, then down. "Skydiving is for people with a death wish. So is scuba diving. Or climbing Everest. Any time you put yourself in some completely fucking inhospitable environment, like underwater, or against gravity, or where it's way below zero – anytime you do that, and then have your life depend on a string or a tube or the caprice of *the weather*, for Christ's sake, you've got a death wish. Something is bound to fail, and then you *die*. No way."

Ricky was busily rolling what used to call a *fattie* in my youth. God only knew what the kids were calling them these days. "So I get the impression that you're not much of a nature boy, Tom?"

"I like the city. I grew up around enough nature. My idea of roughing it is being at the wrong end of the hall from the ice machine."

Ricky smiled and lit the joint with a Bic that had a three inch flame on it. He passed it to me. I demonstrated for Tom. Inhale. Hold. Pass. He acquitted himself swimmingly, with nary a cough, and handed the joint to Maxine.

"Maybe someone should stay straight to look after the old people," she said to no one in particular. Ricky giggled.

"Shut up and smoke, Max," I said. "I was doing this before you were born."

"There's a visual," she said through a cloud of smoke.

TWENTY-SEVEN

Twenty minutes later we were all silent, stoned. It had been many years for me, and it was just as enjoyable as it had been when I was a kid. But I needed some stimulation for a really good high. Some music, maybe. It was just not as much fun if we were going to simply sit there and look at each other and giggle.

I glanced over at Tom, and he gave me the tilted head look, which in my present state, reminded me of the RCA Victor dog and the gramophone. *His master's voice.* This, of course, struck me as hilariously funny, and I busted up.

"You're as high as a Georgia pine, Liz," Maxine said in amazement.

"Indeed. Let's listen to some music," I suggested.

"Oh, no," Max replied, standing up and stretching. "We'll leave you old stoners to your old stoners' music. All those nine minute guitar solos. Jesus wept." She winked at me. "It's time for us to go."

"Old stoners," Ricky said and giggled.

He rose, and Tom did, too. "I'll walk you out," he said.

I remained seated, thinking it might be best for me to do so. "Later, kids."

Maxine patted me on the head, and Tom escorted them out to the gate. When he came back in, I lolled my head to one side and squinted at him. "You want some more, don't you?"

He held up the baggie and papers. "I asked Ricky if he could leave us some. He gave me the *whole bag.* What a nice kid."

"The first time is always free." I stood up somewhat unsteadily. Head rush. I took the baggie from Tom, held it up to the light. Yep, it was pot, all right. That was about all I could tell. I was not a connoisseur, but it did get a person high. I rolled another joint; it was not as fat and quite a bit more crooked than Ricky's had been, but I was out of practice. We smoked it, then smiled and giggled at each other for a minute.

Then I asked him, "What do you want to do now?"

He wiggled his eyebrows at me. It was what he always wanted to do, what I suspected he might do best, and I fucking loved it. The thought of doing *that,* stoned, with Tom, made me giggle again. Hot *damn,* but life was great! But I said, "We can do that later." Then, "You want something to eat?"

Tom thought about that for a second, his expression suggesting that it was a novel idea. But at last he shook his head.

"How 'bout some music?"

He thought about that one too, then shook his head again.

"We can do anything you want, my love. We just can't leave the house to do it." No way was I going out in public stoned.

He considered for another moment, then slapped his knee. "Let's watch *Star Trek!*"

Now it was my turn to slap my knee. "Oh, my God, Tom! Star Trek is *so dirty* when you're stoned!"

"Really?" he said in surprise. "Dirty? By all means, let's watch it then!"

"What stellar ideas you have," I said, using his expression.

We staggered upstairs and got in bed, and I summoned up *Star Trek* from the Netflix. I had watched this show's reruns my whole life; it was one of my very favorites. I had seen them all, probably hundreds of times; I knew plots and even dialogue inside and out.

But the show had never seemed dirty to me until I'd happened to catch one while I was stoned, when I was about eighteen. I searched through the episodes until I found *The Mark of Gideon.* In one scene, our indefatigable Captain Kirk is alone on the bridge with the alien girl, and starts kissing her. Cut to what would have been a commercial. In the next scene, the two of them are walking out of his cabin, arm in arm, smiling. It was subtle, but it was there, nonetheless. I looked over at Tom.

"He so totally just nailed that alien chick!" he marveled.

"I told you it was dirty!"

He giggled gloriously again, and leaned over and kissed me. *Star Trek* was soon forgotten.

TWENTY-EIGHT

The next morning I woke up with a fierce headache, which was Mother Nature reminding me why I didn't smoke pot anymore. Tom was not there beside me, but I smelled coffee and bacon. How had I come to be so lucky?

A few minutes later, he came back upstairs, all bright-eyed and bushy-tailed, with a breakfast tray. The tray contained a plate with bacon and eggs, a mug of coffee, and a tall tumbler full of something green. He set it over my lap and said, "Here. Eat. We're going to live forever, remember?"

I ate a little bacon, feeling like I might not live another fifteen minutes. Man, what a headache. He sat on the edge of the bed and looked at me expectantly.

"What did you think of the marijuana?" I asked.

He pulled the baggie out of his pocket. "I fucking loved it."

"Oh, no, Tom. Too early."

"I know, Liz, I'm just kidding." He opened the night stand drawer and shoved the baggie in it. "Drink this, it'll make you feel better."

I sniffed the green stuff cautiously. It smelled fresh and alive; a lot like grass clippings. "What's in it?"

"Burdock, milk thistle, dandelion. Green tea. Some spirulina. It'll clean all the toxins from your system." He nodded at the drawer. "For every action, there's an equal and opposite reaction."

"It's too early for physics, too."

"Drink up. I promise it'll make you feel better. This stuff is one of the reasons why I don't worry about the chemicals here. Trust me."

Trust him was something I did implicitly, so I drank the green potion off in one long gulp. It wasn't too bad, once you got past the grassy taste. He was right – I felt better almost immediately.

Tom said, "When can you get us some coke?" I blinked at him, open-mouthed. "Just kidding." He ate a piece of my bacon. "Maybe." Then he said, "Did you know that almost all ancient cultures used drugs in their religious rituals? In order to commune with their gods? Peyote, mushrooms, coca, cannabis, even tobacco?"

"Ja, Rasta Man, I have heard of that." I smiled at him. "Did you have visions?"

"*You're* a vision. My point is, you don't have to worry about me wanting to do something like that every day. It was once a *holy* thing. I think the culture here of frequent recreational use dulls the effects. But I did enjoy it."

"Good," I replied simply. I was worried for a second that all this corruption might really be taking hold. But Tom never failed to surprise me. While he seemed up for damn near anything (except skydiving), he did seem to embrace the concept of moderation.

"Let's go to the Farmer's Market. Detox day. Nothing but wholesome, healthy food today."

I picked up another perfectly cooked strip of bacon and gestured at him with it. "This isn't healthy."

"Bacon is above reproach. Bacon is just *good*."

TWENTY-NINE

The following weekend found us at the Pomona Fairgrounds for the Winternationals, at the invite of Ricky and Maxine. Here was another thing I hadn't done since before I got married: attend the drag races. When they suggested it, I was delighted. I knew Tom would love all the machinery, and I'd been quite the fan as a kid, had reveled in the bright paint and the chrome, the smell of the nitro, the long, smoky burnouts, the ground pounding acceleration.

Going to the drags was something that I'd just stopped doing after I got married, when I suddenly felt so grown up and responsible. It had seemed to be one of those childish things that needed to be put up when I became an adult.

But once the four of us began walking around, checking out all the door-slammers and funny cars and dragsters, I started to remember how much *fun* it all was, the smoke and the noise and the flames, the celebration of nothing more complicated than who made it through the traps first. No turns, no passing. Just blinding speed in a straight line.

I began to understand why I'd been feeling so old before I'd met Tom. I never had any fun anymore, never did anything, never went anywhere. Except to the bar, and then home with men far too young for me. And in the harsh light of day, that had all been nothing more than a desperate attempt to have fun in and of itself. But there was really not much fun involved – there was too much cold calculation to it, too much manipulation, absolutely no spontaneity. No surprises. Just a quick march down a well-worn, somewhat grimy path, all leading to the same end. And I always woke up feeling that the *fun* was just what I'd missed. That kind of mindless, narrow lifestyle ages a person.

In the very short time since I'd met Tom, that epoch of my life had become so foreign to me that it seemed like it was a slutty story that I'd heard told about someone else. I was always amazed when I remembered that it had been *me* out there on the boulevard doing all that stupid shit. Sure, I said to myself, all the physical perfection that young men possessed had to have had something going for it (or I wouldn't have gone for it) – but somehow, I couldn't quite remember what it was.

I never once noticed that Tom wasn't twenty-five because he always knew precisely what the fuck he was doing. In spades. I kept waiting for it not to be divinely fantastic every time, but that hadn't happened yet. Since I'd met Tom, I could no longer remember what it was that I'd once found so attractive about young men.

But besides being good in bed, Tom was smart and funny and unusual, and nothing if not *fun*. It dawned on me that I loved him more for all these qualities than for the other thing, and I slowly began to grasp that perhaps that was the point.

THIRTY

Tom gawped at all the shiny race cars in the pits. He asked intelligent questions about displacement and torque and braking, causing the mechanics to pause and actually look up at him from the gleaming engines to respond. Tom did know his machines, after all.

When the first two dragsters lined up and did a few burnouts, Tom stood by the railing as one transfixed, however, and it occurred to me that perhaps all of his technical understanding might just be entirely theoretical. I realized that he'd never heard them run before, had never *smelt* them, had never experienced an actual race.

As the two nitro-burners began to stage up, Ricky hurriedly gave us all ear plugs. He and Maxine and I stepped up onto the bleachers for a better view, but Tom stayed by the railing, leaning forward eagerly, watching intently. The lights on the Christmas tree signaled that the dragsters were pre-staged, then staged. Then the amber lights went off, one, two three. Then the green lit and there was nothing but the deafening roar as they thundered down the track. It was just as cool as I remembered it.

Tom turned to us in wonderment.

"First time to the drags, Tom?" Ricky asked.

Tom nodded, unable to speak.

Ricky stepped down from the bleachers and slapped him on the back. "It's awesome, isn't it? The way all that power travels up through the ground, through your body? The pistons thudding counterpoint to your heartbeat?"

Maxine, standing on the bleachers behind him, looked at him in complete surprise. "Aren't you the poet?"

Ricky turned and smiled at her, then looked back at Tom. "Am I wrong?"

Tom said simply, "It's awesome. Just like you said – I can feel all of that horsepower hammering up through the pavement."

Ricky turned to look at Maxine again. "You know, I've been told that some women become aroused from being exposed to all this raw vibrating power." She giggled to indicate that she was not one of them.

Tom looked at me hopefully, and I rolled my eyes at him. "Horsepower is not a prerequisite," I told him.

"Come stand by me," he said and took my hand so I could step down from the bleachers. "I want to hug you when the next ones go by. So we can feel it together."

Before the next pair started doing burnouts, he said, "I wanted to find one of those places, like in the movies – somewhere where you can be close to where airplanes take off. I wanted to hear it, to *feel* it. But this is so much better."

At dusk, they rolled out the jet-powered funny car, and I knew he was going to get the chance to feel what it might be like to *stand next* to an airplane as it took off.

First there were enormous clouds of white smoke and the ear-splitting, brain-piercing whine of the turbine. Then came the booming belches of yellow flame, longer than the car itself. The light staged and Tom pulled me to him in anticipation, then kissed me hungrily while the ground shook and the funny car with its giant flaming tail streaked by at two hundred and sixty miles per hour. I don't know about women becoming aroused at the drag races, but it was working for Tom.

THIRTY-ONE

I had to work on Valentine's Day, and Tom promised to have a special dinner waiting for me.

But he had another surprise in store when I got home. With help from the kids that he'd hired to paint the store, he'd cleaned out, repaired, and replanted the entire garden, all while I slaved away diligently at my boring office job. It was like something out of one of those home improvement shows – the garden was totally transformed while I was gone.

This was the most wonderful Valentine's Day surprise ever – fixing up the garden was planning for the future, wasn't it? Planning for *our* future?

And he came through with the promised romantic dinner, also, served al fresco in the middle of the newly raked and refurbished garden, complete with table and chairs and candles and flowers, and appropriate mood music in the background.

I told him how wonderful it all was, and he looked sheepishly at me across the checkered tablecloth. "Like George Washington, I cannot tell a lie, Liz. I got the idea for all of this romantic dinner stuff from the internet. To tell you the truth, I've always been a little shaky on the whole idea behind the significance of Valentine's Day dinner."

I made his own tilted-head gesture of curiosity at him. "What *are* you talking about?"

"Well, don't I make you dinner almost every night?"

"But that's not how things are, traditionally. Traditionally, the woman does all the cooking. You're a fucking Renaissance man." *Unlike anyone I've ever known*, I thought. "Usually, a man takes his girl out for dinner on Valentine's Day, because he's doing her a favor by relieving her of the responsibility of cooking." I tilted my head the other way. Why was all this news to him?

"So what you're telling me is that the whole making dinner or going out to dinner on Valentine's Day thing doesn't really have anything to do with the meal itself, so much as that he's showing how much he loves her by doing something nice for her. The significance is in the gesture, not the meal itself."

"In most cases, yes. Besides, almost everyone likes to go out to dinner." Sometimes he was just so fucking weird it defied description. "Does this firm things up for you on the whole Valentine's Day dinner thing?"

He looked at me blankly, gestured with his fork, maybe a little bit piqued that I was making fun of him. "There are a lot of traditions involving cooking and eating, Liz. The hunters bring in the game and there is a big communal sharing and cooking and eating and celebrating. Everybody gets their portion when the hunting is good, and everyone starves when it's bad."

I loved it when he got all anthropological. I just couldn't understand why a person who knew so much about ancient things sometimes had so much trouble with modern things.

"And since the advent of agriculture, there have always been harvest festivals. Again, everyone contributes, everybody shares. Human beings come together and eat during all the milestones in life – when they get married, when they have a baby, when they die. Picnics, festivals. It's always a community or at least a family thing. I could never make the connection between the community thing and the couple thing for Valentine's Day."

I pictured a caveman bringing a big roasted leg of something to his cavewoman, but when Tom continued to look blankly at me, I realized that he really didn't ken how taking your sweetie out for dinner on Valentine's Day could be construed as some large declaration of love.

"It just seems such a pedestrian gesture," he said.

"Not everyone can build the Taj Mahal, Tom."

He smiled. "Have I adequately expressed my love?" He indicated the restored garden.

I got up from the table and came around and sat on his lap, hugged him. "You most certainly have. This demonstrates that you're willing to take the trouble to grow things to cook for me. You're willing to cook healthy things for me, so we can live forever, like you always tell me. What greater love is there than that?"

"That was exactly my intention," he said solemnly. "You understand completely. All this other stuff," he indicated the candles and the flowers, "all this is just cultural window dressing."

"Let me go get your present." I went into the house and brought out the box. He unwrapped it and made over the complicated, exposed gear clock that I'd chosen for him. I thought that he could hang it in the bookstore, that maybe it would prompt him to think of me every time he looked up to see what time it was.

When I'd picked the heavy, loud-ticking thing out, I'd been thinking of Tom's appreciation for all things mechanical. But my selection was also prompted by that lovely sentiment, how he was always telling me that he was going to see to it that we would live forever.

If only that could be so. It was a truly beautiful idea, and when I saw this clock, it had put me in mind of a verse. I recited it for Tom. *"Ah! Let us love, my Love, for Time is heartless; be happy while you may!"*

Tom responded with a poem. *"Time is too slow for those who wait, too swift for those who fear, too long for those who grieve, too short for those who rejoice; but for those who love, time is not."*

THIRTY-TWO

On Saint Patrick's Day, our local bar went full Irish. They also went full Mexican on Cinco de Mayo: Tecate and Corona and Dos Equis at half price. The people who owned the place were neither Irish nor Mexican. It was all just a way to make money.

Tom felt compelled to go over there and drink, wallow in all the kitschy symbolism of a holiday celebrated by Californians far removed from anything remotely like a cultural source. To me, shamrocks and leprechauns and green beer were not so much Irish as they were an outsider's stereotype for being Irish. But since I'd vowed to myself that I would follow Tom to the ends of the earth, I figured that the least I could do was to go out to the bar and drink with him on St. Paddy's Day, if that was what he wanted to do. No matter how ridiculous I felt.

In my opinion, America has at least three official drinking holidays: St. Patrick's Day, the Fourth of July, and New Year's Eve. Sometimes you can throw Thanksgiving in as a drinking holiday. But mainly, it's drinking and greenness, and pretending you belonged to a proud and storied people; drinking and barbequing and fireworks; and drinking and trying to ignore all the mistakes that you had made during the past year. Followed by the next day of hungover and the realization that, *God, green is just not my color*; hungover and sunburnt; and hungover and facepalm: *Who did I kiss at midnight last night?*

I'd always thought that, with a little effort, one could do New Year's with sophistication and the Fourth with patriotism. But St. Paddy's Day had always just seemed to me like an outrageous excuse for people who were not even vaguely Irish to go out and get falling down drunk.

When Tom opened the door of the bar, the wall of noise from within nearly knocked me down, and I hesitated. They were all so far ahead of us already, and there is absolutely nothing less fun than being the only sober person in a packed crowd of wall-to-wall drunks.

I said to him, "Let me see your phone for a second."

He took it out of his shirt pocket and handed it to me. I walked a few paces away from the door so I could hear, and dialed Maxine's number. She answered immediately. I said, "So you're not already here?"

"Tom said three. It's not three, yet."

"Damn right it's not three, yet. It's only the two of us, and nine hundred drunks, pretending to be Irish."

"Ah, humor. I'll be there in a minute."

"Are you at home?"

"Yeah."

"Is Ricky coming with you?"

"Uh . . . no. Ricky won't be coming with me anywhere, any more."

Damn. "Ah, Max! I'm sorry to hear that."

"Que sera, sera, my friend. Next!" she said, not at all upset.

"I'll walk up there and meet you half way. I hate crowded bars." I walked back up the street and handed Tom's phone to him. "I'm going to walk up and meet Max. She just broke up with Ricky."

Concern filled his eyes. "Is she okay?"

"Bitch, please," I said, and smiled at him. "This is Maxine we're talking about. She was the one who originally said, *a woman without a man is like a fish without a bicycle.*"

He tilted his head at me. "Really? How clever! Maxine said that?"

I hugged him and put my mouth next to his. "No, not really. That's a famous feminist proverb." I kissed him quickly. "What kind of an anthropologist are you?"

"I didn't major in Women's Studies."

"Somehow, I doubt that." I nodded at the door to the bar. "Go on in, see if you can find us a table, which I doubt. I'll be back with Max in a few minutes."

He nodded, squeezed my hand, and opened the door. The tsunami of noise flowed out again, and I shuddered. I hated crowded bars. Someone always got something spilled on them. Sometimes there was a fight.

I sighed and turned up the sidewalk toward Max's apartment. I'd only walked three blocks when I spotted her coming the other way. She smiled and waved, and I quickened my pace.

"So," I said, "do you want to tell me about Ricky?"

One side of her mouth curled up. She said, "I just became so *bored,* you see," like John Malkovich in *Dangerous Liaisons.* She sighed. "Does Tom have a younger brother?"

I was a little surprised and disconcerted to discover that I didn't know. I shook my head and said, "He never talks about his family."

"Good. Then there's a chance he does. I'd like to meet another one like him. Maxie is getting tired of the locals."

I touched her arm, so she would look at me. "Has Tom ever told you where he's from, Max?"

"No. You?"

I shook my head.

"All I know is, it's got to be somewhere not anywhere near *here.* He's a strange one. But in a good way."

88

I couldn't help but agree. We'd reached the bar. I took a deep breath and opened the door.

It took us a minute to make our way through the crowd. At last we spotted Tom across the room, standing at the bar. Maxine and I watched as a diminutive blonde in a skimpy leprechaun costume, green tam and all, with a bunch of green t-shirts slung over one arm, walked by him. We watched as she noticed him out of the corner of her eye, and immediately changed direction and went back. She laid her hand on his arm to get his attention. He looked at her hand, then at her face. She smiled.

Now Maxine touched *my* arm, indicating for me to stop. She quickly took out her phone and typed, "Hold on. This oughta b good." I looked at her curiously. She typed, "Just watch."

The blonde was holding a t-shirt up to Tom's chest, trying to gauge if it was the right size. It read, *I'm not Irish, but kiss me anyway.*

I rolled my eyes and looked at Max. She held up her phone again, pointed at the last thing she'd typed. "Just watch."

The blonde tossed the t-shirt over Tom's arm. Apparently, she thought it was his size. I watched him reach for his wallet. The blonde put her hand on his arm again, shook her head. Her fingers were crowned with long green fingernails, which I noticed because she crooked one at him, indicating that he should lean closer so he could hear what she was going to say next.

Tom obliged, and she put her hand lightly on the back of his head, and said something into his ear. I watched Tom's eyebrows go up, watched him smile. Then he said something into *her* ear. She released him and looked at him questioningly, and made what looked like a peace sign with her long-nailed fingers.

He nodded, then glanced around the bar. When he saw us, he smiled guiltlessly, waved, and pointed us out to the blonde. We waved back. She looked at us in amazement for a second, then turned abruptly on her dominatrix-style high heel and stalked away.

Maxine pushed a button on her phone, typed, "What did u tell her?"

Across the room, Tom took his phone out of his pocket. He typed something, and Max looked at her phone.

She showed it to me. It read, "I told her that I already had 2 girls lined up, but she could wait her turn if she wanted 2. Told her it might b a minute, tho."

Maxine laughed and I rolled my eyes again.

We made our way across to where he stood at the bar. Tom put his phone back in his pocket, kissed Maxine on the top of her head, and put his arm around me. He caught the bartender's eye, pointed at his empty glass, held up three fingers. The bartender nodded.

I held the t-shirt up to him, just as the blonde had done, and kissed him, then put it back over his arm.

Maxine typed, "What would u have said if we hadn't been standing here?"

Tom took his phone out of his pocket again. He typed, "I would've pointed at 2 other girls."

After three or four more glasses of curiously brand-unidentifiable, fairly flat, dyed beer, Tom decided he'd had enough of the wearin' o' the green, and we started working our way toward the exit. Just inside the door, the blonde passed by again, and she made the mistake of looking at Tom. He smiled and yelled over the noise, "Thanks for the t-shirt!"

She glanced briefly at me and Maxine, then flipped Tom off and again stalked away. Maxine laughed and pushed the door open. We stepped out onto the sidewalk and I was sure I was deaf.

I looked at Tom. He looked back at me with a little smug smile on his face, an amused twinkle in his eye, both of which were entirely adorable. He said, "What?"

As always, I couldn't help but smile back at him. "You're such a bastard, Tom Bastion. *Such* a bastard."

"What?" he said again. "She asked me if I'd . . . if I'd like to . . ."

Maxine said, "If you'd like to what?"

Tom's eyebrows shot up in surprise. "I'll give you three guesses, Max, and the first two don't count."

"I'd probably guess that Miss Lucky Charms there asked you the same thing that Karen asked you."

Tom closed his eyes and put his hand to his forehead. He grimaced. "Ah, Karen. Karen wanted *me* to . . . to . . ." He grinned helplessly at me, dropped his hand. For someone who could so skillfully *do it*, he had a delightfully difficult time *verbalizing it*, at least when he was trying to describe what some other woman had said.

I said, "We just can't leave you alone for a minute, can we?"

"Like moths to a fucking flame," Maxine said.

Tom shrugged, put his arm around me. "I see no other woman on this planet but you." He kissed me, and somehow I knew it to be true.

I hadn't even felt the slightest jab of jealousy while watching the blonde proposition Tom. He couldn't help the way he looked. I believed in his faithfulness implicitly, like the sunrise. It was just something about the quality of his desire, as I've said before. Because he made me feel like I was the only woman in the world, it only followed that I'd believe that he thought I was, too.

He put his other arm around Maxine, "And of course, I see you, too, Max."

"Fat lot a good that does me," she replied.

I saw an opportunity. "We were just wondering if you might have a younger brother for Max," I said.

Tom closed one eye, squinted, as if he was trying to remember if he had a brother or not. I thought it was an odd response to so straightforward a question. Finally, he said, "I'm my mother's only son, but I've got two half-sisters. Haven't seen them in decades. My dad might have other sons."

I thought this a strange statement, and again wondered if he might be the product of some weird religious cult.

"Story of my life," Maxine said. Then she burst into *I Need a Hero*: "*Where have all the good men gone/And where are all the gods?/Where's the streetwise Hercules to fight the rising odds?/Isn't there a white knight/Upon a fiery steed?/Late at night I toss and turn/And dream of what I need . . .*"

"Wow, Max," Tom said, "I didn't know you could sing."

"Shut up, Tom," we said in unison.

THIRTY-THREE

When we arrived at the house, Tom said, "Since I figured that you ladies were getting tired of green beer, I have another St. Paddy's Day potable for you." He disappeared into the kitchen, and Maxine and I sat on the couch. A few minutes later, he reappeared with three steaming mugs, complete with whipped cream.

I sniffed it, smelled the whiskey. Irish coffee.

Tom sat in the chair across from us. He said, "I bet you didn't know that today is actually an official holy day. I try to celebrate all the holy days I can. I like to mingle with the people on holy days."

"You just try to celebrate, and you like to mingle, period," I said. I sipped the Irish coffee, tasted the brown sugar and heavy cream, felt the whiskey warm my belly.

"I just thought it was an excuse to get drunk in public," Max said.

"Google it," Tom said.

Sometimes Maxine flat out refused to believe some of the off-the-wall shit he came up with, so she took out her phone and did just that. After a moment, she read the Wikipedia entry to us. *"Saint Patrick's Day was made an official Christian feast day in the early seventeenth century and is observed by the Catholic Church, the Anglican Communion (especially the Church of Ireland), the Eastern Orthodox Church and Lutheran Church."*

Tom smiled at us smugly, then leapt up and went back to the kitchen to make himself another Irish coffee, because he'd slammed his.

I looked at Maxine. "Do you ever wonder if . . . do you think Tom is an alcoholic?"

Max looked up from her phone, looked toward the kitchen, paused. "An alcoholic? Tom? Nah. That word makes me think of a bleary-eyed, unshaven, just all around loser. Tom's no alcoholic. He's always bright-eyed and bushy tailed. I've never even seen him with a hangover."

Those first-thing-in-the morning, grass-clipping potions never failed to take care of that, I thought. And then there was also the homemade bread that he concocted. It didn't matter if we'd been drinking all night, if I had a big piece of this soft, dense, delicious bread before I went to sleep, I would not have a hangover the next day. It was like fucking magic.

"Sure, he likes to drink, but he never gets falling down drunk, does he?" Max was saying. "Besides, alcoholics drink because they're trying to kill something. They drink because they want to forget something, to remember something; something they did to somebody, something somebody did to them. Alcoholics are always trying to bury something.

Tom's the happiest person I've ever known. He's not an alcoholic. He just likes to get his buzz on."

Daily, I thought. But I had to admit, Max was right. Tom never got sloppy drunk, and his drinking never prevented him from getting up and going to work; never prevented him from getting up for *anything*.

So I figured maybe he was just making up for lost time, and again wondered exactly where it was he was from. Somewhere with no vice, no machinery. Somewhere where they even had polygamy, maybe. I couldn't even begin to hazard a guess where that might be.

THIRTY-FOUR

On an achingly bright day in early April (or so my father once told me), Mr. and Mrs. Allen celebrated the birth of their first and only child. As the thirty-eighth anniversary of this momentous happening approached, I was a little miffed at the complete lack of importance that Tom and Maxine were attaching to the event, their complete lack of anticipation as it impended.

On St. Paddy's day, Maxine had said off-handedly, "Oh, we should have a party for your birthday!" But then she'd not said another word about it again. I thought that perhaps Maxine was at a loss as to who she would invite. I'd slept with most of her friends, as easily as Deucalion throwing rocks over his shoulder. I'd not repopulated the earth, but surely Maxine wouldn't want to invite that crowd to any birthday party of mine, not with Tom around. She knew better.

I told her about a nightmare I'd had recently, where I'd inexplicably found myself an unwilling bystander at just such a party. There they all were, gathered in my living room, drinks in hand – Terry and Sonny and even psycho Fred, and the busboy from *Applebee's,* as well as my ex-husband, and Mike, and everyone I'd ever slept with in my entire life. And there was Tom, mingling in among them, talking to them.

In my dream he stood out; he was the only one in color, so to speak. Even in my dreams he was luminous. The rest of them were pale, indistinct, blurry, compared to him. Yet still he talked to them, like a living being conversing with shades. He smiled and laughed with them, asked them questions. I stood there, unable to move – you know how it is in dreams. Unable to run or hide, I was forced to witness my wonderful Tom hobnobbing with all the mistakes I'd ever made.

Every now and then, from across the embarrassingly crowded room, Tom would turn around and look at me curiously. Then he'd turn back to whichever one of my appallingly long string of worthless boyfriends he was talking to and ask something else, as if for clarification. Then he'd turn back and look at me again. Sometimes he'd grin; sometimes, he'd look perplexed. Once, he even feigned shock. On more than one occasion, he elbowed my ex-boyfriend, ex-husband, ex-boulevard conquest, and the two of them had a good snicker together at my expense.

Maxine guffawed mightily when I told her about this dream. Ha, ha, ho, ho, hee, hee. Affronted, I said to her, "It was most assuredly not funny. It was horrible."

"If it really happened – God, that *would* be horrible. Hell, just seeing Fred again, by himself, would be *horrible*. But it's just a dream, Liz. You put too much stock in dreams. And because it *was* just a dream, it's hilarious. What do you imagine Tom was asking them? What do you think they were telling him? You don't think they could tell him anything about you that would surprise him, do you?"

I shook my head. *O shame! Where is thy blush?* I thought. Why it was right here, so charmingly manufactured and whimsically displayed for me by my own unconscious mind. Tom, who was so different, so perfect – yukking it up with all my old boyfriends, none of which could hold a candle to him on any front. Yeah, that was hi-larious.

In real life, such a conclave would never occur, could never occur, thank Christ. So, if her friends were out, who else could Maxine invite to a birthday party for me? The women I worked with? Pffft. Maxine knew better than that, also. What I did outside of work was none of their uptight, gossipy, back-stabbing business.

So maybe this was the reason why Max had dropped the idea of a birthday party for me: she'd discovered my total lack of desire for any other friends besides her. And Tom.

Tom, on the other hand, had no trouble whatsoever throwing a successful party. He could fill a room in twenty minutes. He knew every business owner downtown, and most of their customers, as well. Not to mention having his own thriving clientele at *Morry's*. Tom knew people from all walks of life, bikers and bankers, punks and pols, artists and actuaries. He talked to everyone who walked into his store, and remembered their names and their stories whether they bought anything or not.

Tom had lots of acquaintances, and I thought that was surely all one needed to throw a great big, loud birthday party for one's not getting any younger girlfriend. You couldn't term these people Tom's friends, but they'd do in a pinch. I'd never known Tom to pursue a single friendship, except the one he had with Maxine. Enough people surely attempted to pursue friendships with him – he was always getting invites to go to this event or that event, this party or that party. Sometimes he accepted and we attended, if it was something that intrigued him, like an art show or a concert. But he avoided receptions and open houses and fund-raisers like the plague.

Tom seemed to be perfectly happy just hanging out with me and Maxine. At least for the moment.

This did not absolve him of his failure to plan a birthday party for me, however. Maxine might have trouble filling an appropriate guest list, but Tom didn't have her excuse. I was beginning to feel a little sniffly, a little sorry for myself, as if I should be joining the *Friends of the Friendless*, like Lucille Ball. Could it really be possible that they had forgotten my birthday?

Fuck it, I thought. I don't want a house full of people, anyway, spilling things on the floors, trampling my garden.

Did they really forget, though?

THIRTY-FIVE

On Friday, the day before my birthday, Tom, Maxine and I arranged to meet for lunch at *Smiley's*. I expected the wait staff to surround us at any minute and sing *Happy Birthday*, but it never happened.

"Will you meet me at the store before you go home after work?" Tom asked as he paid the check. "There's something I want to give you for your birthday." He didn't look at me, and I found this curious. He looked at Maxine, and then she looked out the window.

"My birthday's not 'til tomorrow," I said, with just an edge of irritation. The *in case you forgot* went unsaid.

Tom tilted his head at me, as if trying to figure out what I was angry about. After a second, he seemed to give up trying to figure it out, seemed to give up caring about it entirely. He shrugged, looked away. This wasn't like him either. He always asked me intently if something was wrong, if he thought something was wrong. Wouldn't let it go until I explained myself.

"We might not live to see tomorrow, Liz," Maxine said, apropos of nothing. "Then you would have missed out on your birthday present."

I didn't know how to reply to this, so I told Tom, "I'll be there."

We stepped out onto the sidewalk, paused; we would all be going back to work in separate directions. Tom lit a cigarette.

Maxine said, "Well, I'll be seeing you," and bumped fists with him. It was not an unheard of gesture between them, but it was more something of a congratulatory thing when they did it. Not a farewell thing. I was immediately suspicious.

Maxine said goodbye to me, and walked away.

I looked at Tom, scrutinized him. He looked back at me blankly. There was something up with him and Max, I thought. Why did he want me to go to the shop after work? If he had a birthday present for me, why couldn't he just bring it over to the house? And Maxine – why had she gone out of her way to encourage me to go over there?

I began to get the idea that they were planning some kind of everyone jump out and yell, *Surprise!* kind of thing. It would be necessary for them to get me away from the house to pull such a thing off. Tom could lure me away with tales of birthday presents at the store, leaving Max time to take his key and go let all the guests in, hide them.

I saw through the whole set-up, but decided to go with it anyway. They seemed to have planned it out so much; I thought that it would be mean for me to ruin it by not playing along. And in the back of my mind there lurked the idea that perhaps I was imagining it all — they were not in league, there was no surprise party, they really had forgotten about me. If that was the case, then I'd just look stupid if I didn't go over to the shop to receive my mysterious present.

I gave Tom a hug and a kiss and told him I'd see him after work.

THIRTY-SIX

I took my time locking up the office and walking over to the bookstore. I didn't want Maxine to be rushed gathering all the guests together. I wanted to allow her plenty of time for this important task.

I paused on the sidewalk outside the bookstore, looked in the window. I could see Tom inside, behind the counter. He'd just finished ringing up a young woman, and I watched him smile at her, tell her thanks. I watched him consult his watch.

On some kind of a schedule are ya, Tom, my love? I thought. Then he looked right at me through the window, as if he'd heard my thought, and I jumped a little bit. He came outside and put his arm around me. "Let's go upstairs, birthday girl."

"My birthday isn't until tomorrow," I replied churlishly.

Tom looked at his watch again. "Oh, it'll be tomorrow soon enough."

We walked around the side of the building and when he opened the security door, I was a little disconcerted to see the key to my house still hanging off his key ring. How was Maxine going to get in, if he hadn't given her a key?

Once inside his tiny apartment, Tom surprised me by immediately pushing me up against the wall behind the door and whispering something dirty in my ear about what exactly it was that he wanted to give me for my birthday. It was sexy and hot and totally unanticipated, and I enjoyed it very much. But I suspected that his ardor might not be entirely spontaneous, when, in the middle of kissing my neck, I caught him checking his watch again.

But it was all right with me. If this was what he wanted to do to kill some time before the surprise party, I was down. *I was always down.*

But seconds later, before we'd even had the chance to start taking off our clothes, there was a knock at the door, and Maxine did her little pause-before-entering-the-examination-room shtick. Tom still held me pinned against the wall, and he looked over his shoulder incredulously at her.

She walked past us and said indifferently, "You people need to get a room. Seriously."

Tom pushed himself off the wall. He straightened his shirt a little bit, shook his head, cleared his throat. At last he said, "This *is* a room, Max."

"Better that I caught you before you started instead of coming in in the middle, eh? And if you're planning on doing these things every *single* fucking time the opportunity . . . *arises*, then you should be more careful about locking the door." She winked at him. "When do we eat? I do believe it's your turn to cook, Tom."

"I always cook, Max."

"Then it *is* your turn!" She punched him in the arm. "What do you want for dinner, birthday girl?" she asked me. "Tom has volunteered to cook."

"My birthday isn't until tomorrow," I repeated.

THIRTY-SEVEN

Tom said he needed to stop at the market, and the two of them laughed and chatted while we walked down the aisles. I followed behind them morosely, but they were totally oblivious to my silence. I considered that this apparent stalling could all be part of the set-up, but as the time wore on, I imagined that a houseful of people waiting around to jump out and yell, *Surprise!* would be getting pretty bored by now, pretty tired of waiting.

I even wondered peevishly if that little interrupted grind against the wall was all Tom intended to give me for my birthday.

When at last we were walking up my street, I cast around, looking for extra cars that might indicate that there were people hiding inside the house. Try as I might, I could identify no cars that weren't always parked there. When we walked up on the porch, the house was dark, quiet as a tomb.

I sighed. There was no ruse, no conspiracy between Tom and Max, no surprise party. It had all just been wishful thinking on my part.

Tom unlocked the door with his key, but before we could enter, he reached in and flipped the lights on in the living room. "Surprise, Liz," he said conversationally, and nodded into the house.

I stepped inside. There was a seventy-two inch flat screen television attached to the wall, where there had only been blankness and an old thirty-six inch tube television before. Tom picked up an enormous remote that was sitting on the table beside *The Maiden*, and pointed it at the TV. An instrumental version of *Happy Birthday* swelled, and *Many Happy Returns, Liz!* appeared on the screen.

I looked at them, dumbstruck. They grinned back at me smugly.

"The party's tomorrow night. At the store," Tom said. "I figured that you wouldn't want a bunch of people trudging around in the house."

"Spilling things on the floor," Maxine added.

I was still speechless. They knew me so well. I'd thought I knew them just as well, yet somehow I'd allowed myself to doubt them.

The enormous TV was the best gift ever, but not because I'd ever coveted such a decadent thing. It was the best gift ever because Tom was giving me a part of himself. Nobody loved big TVs more than *him*. To an observer, this might seem like an entirely selfish gesture, but I knew there was no such obvious artifice to it. Tom didn't give me a giant TV just because *he* wanted to watch it; he bought it for me because he wanted us to watch it *together*. With an almost child-like glee, he was always telling Maxine and me, "Hey, you guys gotta see *this*." There was nothing that pleased him more than sharing the things that he loved with us.

"Maxine picked this out for you, too," Tom said, and handed me a small box, wrapped in blue paper.

I opened it. It was a cellphone.

"It's a simple one," Maxine said. "Nothing fancy. You can always upgrade." She hugged me. "Welcome to the twenty-first century!" Then she looked at Tom and said, "That scene at your apartment, that was great."

"You almost missed your cue."

This time they engaged in a congratulatory high-five.

Maxine said to me, "You were sure that we were stalling for some reason, huh? A surprise party, maybe? The look on your face!"

"All fucking week," Tom added. "I thought I was going to bust up. You've had this hangdog, poor-me look, all week. It was so hard not to comfort you."

"You people!" I said, and hugged them both. "You fucking bastards!"

"I've got an idea!" Tom said. He pushed another button on the remote, and the Netflix queue appeared. "Let's get stoned and watch movies on Liz's awesome new TV!"

"The simple pleasures are the best ones," Maxine agreed, and sat down on the couch. "Happy Birthday, Liz!"

"You fucking bastards!" I repeated. "I love you!"

THIRTY-EIGHT

By the time Tom's birthday rolled around at the end of the month, his garden had become a flourishing riot of unstoppable healthiness.

Cherry tomatoes and cucumbers twined and intertwined over the arch. Regular tomatoes threatened to o'er top their cages. The tender greenery belonging to potatoes and onions and carrots shot ever upward. Stalks of sweet corn climbed toward heaven. Sunflowers, already thick stalked and tall, turned their yellow heads and tracked Apollo's progress across the sky. There were strawberries and bell peppers and snap beans and sweet peas. He'd planted a large lime tree off to one side — so we'd always have a fresh garnish for our gin and tonics, he'd explained. Beside the lime tree, he'd planted some large-fronded thing that I couldn't identify.

"Banana tree," he said.

As I've mentioned, I'd long been a garden dabbler, starting my brave little soldiers with great expectation and anticipation every spring. But by August, my army had always become dead, dying, or just plain sadly wizened veterans, exhausted, producing nothing any longer but stunted, withered fruit. It was always around that time that I never failed to lose interest until the next year, leaving the troops to fend for themselves, unmourned.

But Tom's garden was already stupendously healthy and producing, and it was only the end of April. It seemed as though the whole thing had sprung up overnight, like a World War II Bugs Bunny Victory Garden cartoon. I'd never seen anything quite like it. The size and variety and overall perfection of his produce put the garden magazines to shame. Everything was already juicy and succulent and delicious, ripened to perfection, picked at the height of flavor and all that.

I asked him how everything had come to be so luxurious, so soon, and he said it was all about balance. Then he started in on a lengthy diatribe about pH and nitrogen and companion planting and compost and beneficial insects and proper sun and water.

He looked at me and smiled that beloved smile. "It's really incredibly easy. This place has evolved to be bountiful; the Earth *wants* to produce. You just have to provide the necessary ingredients, and then stand back." I mimicked his tilted head, curious look, and he realized that I could not possibly care less about all the technical aspects of agriculture. "Let's just say that I'm blessed with an inordinately green thumb, then. You could say it's hereditary."

THIRTY-NINE

"He's a witch," Maxine opined, gesturing at the incredible profusion. I looked at her in surprise. "Male witches are called warlocks."

"Whatever." She picked one cherry tomato after another until she had a large handful. It didn't even make a dent in the overall abundance. "He can obviously control the forces of nature. I've never seen a garden like this outside of a Martha Stewart spread. And she doesn't do any of that shit all by herself. I'm telling you, Tom is some kind of hippie nature witch. This much, in so short a time? It's fucking supernatural."

I remembered the stained glass sign hanging in the window at Tom's apartment: *Hippies use back door. No exceptions.* He always objected when I called him a hippie. And if I really thought about it, there was nothing too hippie-ish about him, really, past his ability to grow things and his desire to avoid all unnecessary ingestion of chemicals. I even had to remind him to recycle.

And Tom was certainly no nature lover. The whole concept of camping totally baffled him. "If I wanted to sleep in the dirt, I'd just sleep on the sidewalk in front of the shop," he'd say. He could simply not understand why anyone would want to leave the comforts of home and go out where you might not be able to get any cellphone service; where there was no internet; where you might not be able to summon help if you got hurt; where there were plenty of things that could hurt you, like poison ivy and cliffs and wild animals and serial killers dumping bodies and other desperate criminals on the lam.

"It's dark! I could fall into a precipice!" he said, doing his best Ace Ventura impression.

As long as he had a little patch to cultivate for his own use, Tom could dispense with the wide open spaces. As long as he could obtain the freshest possible food, he reveled in the confines of the city. He *appreciated* the city. He liked to walk around downtown about five o'clock in the morning, listening to the hum of the transformers, watching the timed signals turn from green to yellow to red without there being any traffic yet for them to guide. He didn't mind the noise, the poison pumped into the air by too many cars, the crowds. He waxed poetic about curb, gutter and sidewalk, believed that there were few perfections to equal a newly paved thoroughfare.

"The city is the apogee of mankind's achievements," he would say. "You can get anything you want in the city. Have that shit delivered."

FORTY

"I've got the perfect thing here for you to give Tom for his birthday, Liz," Maxine told me when I stopped by *Old Town* after work the day before the anticipated event. We'd decided that one pretending-to-forget-someone's-birthday-play was enough for any one year. Tom knew that we were scoping out presents for him.

"Oh, yeah, why don't you give it to him yourself?" I asked, a little bit jealous that she could so easily decide on something for him, when I was still having a hell of a time making up my mind. And his birthday was *tomorrow*, for Christ's sake.

"I got him a carton of cigarettes."

How entirely practical, I thought. "What is it?" I asked, thinking that perhaps I should just stop being stupid and allow Max to solve my dilemma for me if she could do so.

She brought a small box out from under the counter and removed the lid with a flourish. Inside was a large red pocketknife with a white cross insignia. I looked at her doubtfully.

"It's a Swiss Army Knife," she explained. "It's got like eleventeen different little tools on there. Look, there's a church key and a corkscrew and a screwdriver, and some kind of little hooky thing. And there's a little pair of scissors. Who could use a little pair of scissors more than Tom? He can open his Power Bars with them."

Tom was inordinately fond of Power Bars. If he wasn't eating something he picked from the garden, or a grass-clipping smoothie, or a T-bone, or bacon, or magic hangover-cure bread, it would be a Power Bar.

Tom had the ability to remove the peel from an orange in one piece. It was quite the trick. He'd just insert his thumb in the top and give it a little downward jerk and the peel would split open and fall away. He could similarly crack the stem on a banana and extracted the insides, unbroken, after only putting a single split in the peel. He did these things unconsciously, without even looking. It was quite the experience to watch; I'd never in my life seen anyone peel fruit as effortlessly as Tom did. Maybe it was a left-handed thing.

But he was completely flummoxed when it came to opening Power Bars. He would try to pull the seams apart, first at one end, then at the other. When that didn't work, he would try to stick his fingernail in between the seams and open it that way.

If Maxine was on hand, she would watch him struggle for a minute, then just take the Power Bar away from him and tear it from top to bottom, not along the seam at all. She'd just rip it open down the side and hand it back to him.

I looked at the knife. I thought it wasn't a very romantic birthday present, but everything didn't have to be about romance, did it? I thought that he'd like it and that he'd use it. There was something to be said for practicality, wasn't there?

I sang The Fabulous Thunderbirds to Maxine. *"Wrap it up, I'll take it."*

"There you go with the oldies again," she replied.

FORTY-ONE

Maxine and I sat on the front porch on Tuesday, sipping our drinks, waiting for Tom to come home from work so that we could give him his birthday presents. Maxine had taken off early so she could prepare her world-famous stuffed peppers for him, selecting two fat shiny green ones and one red one from the garden. She cooked them in a Teflon-free pan.

The harsh blat of motorcycle exhaust suddenly filled my ears, shattering the early evening stillness. Tom rode up effortlessly on a huge black and chrome bike, like he was born to it. He stopped in the middle of the street, revved it up and grinned at us from under a shiny black half-helmet.

I spilled my drink.

I didn't need to see the V-Twin to know what it was. The roar of the exhaust was unmistakable.

We walked down to the curb. Tom took the helmet off and tossed it to Maxine. He shut the bike down. "Happy birthday to *me*."

"*You bought a Harley?*" I asked in astonishment.

"Borrowed it, actually. Or maybe it's a rental. I traded Johnny the Biker a boxed set of turn-of-the-century porn for it. He said I could keep it 'til tomorrow. Quite the connoisseur is our Johnny, of that sort of thing. Said it's not easy to come by." Tom undid the leather saddlebag on one side and fished another helmet out. "Who wants to ride bitch first?"

"Oh, me! Me!" Maxine squealed in delight. She and Tom traded helmets. She put hers on and climbed on the back of the big Harley. "Take the peppers out of the oven, will ya, Liz? We'll be back in a minute."

They roared off down the street, and I went back into the house to save Max's special birthday dinner from burning. I marveled that no other person I knew could talk a biker out of his hog overnight, all in exchange for some black and white Daguerreotypes of nineteenth century prostitutes. No other person but Tom Bastion.

We ate Maxine's delicious dinner, and Tom made over his Swiss Army knife and thanked Max for the carton of cigarettes.

"How old are you, anyway, Dad?" Maxine asked.

Tom blinked blankly at her for a split second. "*Let's find out*," he said, like the owl from the old Tootsie Pops commercial. He took his wallet out of his pocket, looked at his driver license for a second, seemed to make a quick calculation.

He looked at Max. "I am forty-two today."

"And you are so odd," she replied, giving me a *what the hell was that?* look.

Not long afterward, Maxine gave Tom a hug and wished him happy birthday; then, ever considerate, she made some excuse about having to see a man about a horse, and left.

He nodded in the direction of the Harley parked at the curb. "Let's take a long ride."

FORTY-TWO

The summer after I turned fifteen, I was a junior counselor at an all-girls camp in the mountains. Only little girls, teenage girls, and women populated that camp.

Except for the camp director's son.

He would pull up to the main building on a Harley not unlike this one, helmet-less in those days, long, black, curly hair streaming over the collar of his leather jacket. I would forget, literally *forget*, whatever I was doing and just watch him walk by. Once I poured an entire pitcher of water onto the table when he strolled through the chow hall, because I'd forgotten that I had it in my hand when he came in. He was all of seventeen.

His name was George, and he could have been a teenaged version of Tom: the same black hair, the same blue eyes, the same killer smile. I walked into the office one evening when he was there talking to his mom, and he smiled at me on his way out, and I just knew that I was in love.

When I walked outside again, he was leaning against the side of the clapboard building, smoking a cigarette, waiting for me. He asked if I wanted to take a little ride with him, and I did not hesitate for a second, didn't think of the trouble I could get in, didn't think I might get kicked out of camp, didn't think that I might get sent home to my mother in disgrace.

I simply nodded wordlessly and climbed onto the back of the Harley. He fired it up and I wrapped my arms around his waist, felt the hard, flat muscles of his abdomen through his t-shirt. We rode out onto the darkening mountain road, and at first I could only smell the pines and the hot oil scent of the V-Twin. But soon the vibration of the bike traveled up my legs, along my spine, until I felt every nerve in my body awaken, every cell come alive. I laid my cheek against George's back and reveled in the warm, animal, *male* smell of him. I was sure that I was in love. Nothing could be better than this.

George drove the Harley to the bottom of the long hill that led away from the camp, then we rode cautiously across the rickety old bridge at the bottom. He stopped for a moment on the other side; he looked over his shoulder and smiled at me. I would've been happy to sit behind him on that bike all night, just hugging myself to him. I would've been happy to hold on to him *forever*, but he turned the big bike around and drove back. We rode through the flat, grassy center of the camp, and the dew steamed out behind us in a mist as it hit the hot exhaust.

George pulled up in front of my cabin and waited for me to climb off the bike. I looked at him with no little expectation – it had indeed been just a *little* ride. He put his palm on my cheek and gave me a sloppy, hesitant, boyish kiss on the mouth. Then he smiled fondly at me and turned the bike around and rode away.

I stood there in the dewy grass until long after he was gone, until some girl inside the cabin called my name, breaking the reverie. It was the first time I'd ever been aroused, the first time I'd ever mistaken those aching physical sensations for love. It was one of the most erotic experiences of my life. Although I'd think about George for years afterward, I never saw him again.

Now I settled in behind Tom on the throbbing Harley, put my arms around his waist, laid my cheek against his back. We rode out of the city, to the foothills of the mountains. Tom stopped in a secluded spot in a grove of trees. He found a blanket rolled up in one of the saddlebags, and laid it down in the tall grass. We made love under the waning gibbous moon in the crisp spring air. It was another one of the most erotic experiences of my life.

I will follow this man to the ends of the earth, I thought again. Happy birthday to *me.*

On the ride back home, I laid my cheek against his back again, molded myself against him. Nothing could be better than this. The rumble of the engine reminded me of a bass line and I sung The Fabulous Thunderbirds softly to myself. "*No more will I shop around, now, baby/I know I got the best thing in town, now, baby/I've seen all I want to see, now, baby/Bring your lovin' straight to me, now, baby/Wrap it up, I'll take it.*"

FORTY-THREE

On Memorial Day, Tom decided that he wanted a carnivore's feast. Maxine and I sat on the front porch and watched him while he barbequed ribs and steaks and pork chops and hamburgers. By the time he was done, we would have enough cooked meat to last for a week.

The weather was already becoming good and toasty, the precursor to the blazing California summer heat to come, which I loved so much. I might not have liked it so thoroughly if I worked outside; then it might just be miserable. But I worked in an air-conditioned office, and the ladies I toiled beside kept it like the arctic in there. To me there was nothing better than stepping out into the sun in the afternoon and feeling the heat consume me on the walk home. I'd always reasoned that because Hell was sizzling, they might not take me. I'd like it too much.

Maxine fanned herself like a southern belle. She looked at Tom. "Isn't he hot?"

"He most assuredly is," I immediately replied.

"Ah, humor. Ha." She called across the yard to Tom, "Aren't you hot with all those clothes on?"

He looked up from the grill in surprise. "What?"

"I said, aren't you hot in that shirt?"

Tom looked at himself. He was wearing the same long-sleeved, collared kind of button-up shirt he always wore. He had it unbuttoned, with the sleeves rolled up; he wore a wife beater for an undershirt. He had on a pair of jeans. No underwear, which Maxine could not possibly know. Deck shoes. No socks.

Tom shrugged at her, made a *what the hell are you talking about?* gesture with the spatula.

Maxine arose and crossed the yard. She said, "It's summertime. I think you should lose the shirt. Get some sun." She held her hand out to him.

Tom tilted his head at her, nonplussed. Maxine wiggled her fingers, indicating that she wouldn't take no for an answer. Tom glanced at me. I just shrugged.

He said slowly, "Okay, Max, you fucking lunatic." He set the spatula down on the corner of the grill. "Anything for you." He removed his shirt and handed it to her.

She considered him for a minute in appreciative silence. At last she said, "Much better. It's summertime. I think you should wear as little clothes as possible."

Tom's eyebrows rose in surprise. "I think you've been out in the sun too long, Max."

"Maybe. But I think you should dress just like this for the entire summer. In fact, I think you should *always* dress like this." Max turned around and grinned at me. "Can I get an amen?"

"Amen," I said conversationally. Tom did look good in just his undershirt, but then he *always* looked good. Dressed, undressed, semi-dressed.

"I think I'm being objectified, here," he said, and tried to get his shirt back from Maxine. She held on to it for a second, making him tug at it before she finally let go.

"You are most definitely," Max replied with a grin.

Tom shrugged into his shirt; picked up the spatula again. "If I don't wear a shirt, where am I going to carry my phone?"

"If you don't wear a shirt, I'll carry your phone *for you*." Maxine winked at me and came back up onto the porch.

I knew that this was just the simplest excuse that Tom could come up with. He was basically a very modest person, clothing-wise. He wasn't someone you looked at twice because of how he was dressed. Women didn't notice what he was wearing; they noticed *him*. He knew he had it, and had no desire whatsoever to flaunt it *by showing too much skin*, as my mother used to say. Tom didn't have to be conceited, because he was convinced. Too many little blonde leprechauns, and conniving antique store owners, and young purple-haired beauties had convinced him. And those were just the ones that I knew he'd turned down.

"Seriously, Max. You need to get out of the sun," Tom advised, and went back to flipping burgers.

Max sat back in her chair beside me, and tilted her head, considering Tom, mimicking his trademark gesture. "Ah, Liz, what a lucky woman you are. He's just fine all day long and three times on Sunday. It's a crime that he doesn't have any brothers."

One part of my luck, I reflected, was that I didn't have to be worried or jealous that this beautiful young woman was so enthusiastically admiring my good-looking boyfriend. She didn't mean anything by it.

I knew it wasn't the sun that was getting to Maxine, but the season, and a certain lack of male companionship that she'd been experiencing lately. Whenever she started to get a little too appreciative of Tom, I knew it had been too long. He was like some kind of hormonal yardstick for her. When she had a boyfriend, she disrespected him just like she would a beloved big brother. It was only when she was going through a dry spell that she again started noticing out loud how fine he was.

As if reading my mind, she said, "I need to find a date."

Only tired aphorisms came to mind, lame reassurances that she'd find someone eventually. So, I didn't say anything. Maxine didn't need any reassurances from me. She knew that she could have any man she wanted with just a wink. Any man but Tom.

FORTY-FOUR

Several weeks later, the three of us were again sitting on the front porch. Max was going on her first date with a new beau, someone she'd met online. Ever the modern girl, Max knew that this was a little bit dangerous; that added to the adventure for her. Still, she didn't want him to know where she lived yet, didn't want to meet him at the bar. She wanted someone else to meet him at the same time she did. Maxine wanted witnesses. So she'd asked if she could have him pick her up from my house.

"Do you know what tomorrow is, Max?" Tom asked.

Whenever Tom would ask her a simple question such as this, Maxine would look at him carefully for a moment, trying to figure out ahead of time what the bigger explanation was going to be. His simple questions always got her attention, and she would always answer slowly, simply, and directly.

"Tomorrow is Friday, Tom." She glanced at her phone. "The twenty-first of June."

Tom smiled at her perfectly logical, perfectly obvious answer. If he wanted philosophy from Maxine, he needed to ask a more in-depth question. "Okay, do you know the significance of Friday, June twenty-first?"

Maxine looked at me. I saw her checking off birthdays, anniversaries, holidays in her head. Finally, she said, "Nothing significant comes to mind."

"Never mind then."

She would not let him off that easily. "Am I forgetting something?"

"Tomorrow is the first day of summer. The summer solstice. The longest day of the year. I'm surprised to hear that you don't celebrate the solstice, Max." He winked at me. "Sacrifice a chicken or something. It's a big *Ancient Aliens* kind of day."

"The day when the snake shadow runs down the side of that pyramid in Mexico?" Max replied eagerly. "What's it called?"

"*El Castillo*, the Temple of Kukulcan at Chichen Itza. The return of Quetzalcoatl." He nodded appreciatively at Max's *Ancient Aliens* recall, then gently corrected her. "But no, Quetzalcoatl returns on the equinoxes, not the solstices. The shadow of the serpent descends the pyramid in March and September. The first day of spring and autumn, when the day and night are equal. It happens in the afternoon." Tom turned and looked innocently at me. "I forgot all about the vernal equinox this year, in March. I was doing something else that afternoon. Must've slipped my mind."

"I hope you are similarly occupied in September," I replied.

Tom smiled, pleased that I remembered what we'd been doing on the first day of spring. It had actually been just a shot in the dark on my part, what one might call an educated guess: we did it so gloriously often, that I'd just assumed that sex was what he was referring to.

He looked back at Maxine and blinked. "What was I saying? Oh, yeah. The solstice. Big *Ancient Aliens* day. At the Temple of Kukulcan, when the sun casts its shadow over the pyramid, the light and shadow cut it in half, at the exact moment of the solstice.

"At Stonehenge, there's a stone that lies outside the main circle. If you're standing within the circle, and you look through the entrance, you can see the sun rise directly over the stone on the solstice. A shadow is cast into the central circle of stones.

"There is a carving called the Sun Dagger, atop a butte in Colorado. It's a coiled petroglyph, and on the summer solstice a shaft of sunlight pierces it." Tom paused.

"And?" Maxine prompted.

Tom shrugged. "I was just thinking about making our own summer solstice sunrise celebration. Our own *hierophany*, if you will."

"Is that one of those anthropological terms?" I asked.

He smiled at me, again with my favorite expression of pleased surprise. "A *hierophany* is the sacred made manifest."

"Like a miracle?" Maxine suggested.

Tom shook his head. "No . . . a miracle is somewhat unexpected, or something necessary to solve a crisis. *We need a miracle*. A hierophany is just the opposite; it's something that's *expected*. Foretold. In whichever peoples' mythology, the god said, *This is going to happen, at this moment, on this day*. And damned if it doesn't."

"And you can make such a thing happen?" I asked doubtfully.

"I can." He seemed surprised at my skepticism. "I can do a lot of things that you don't know about, yet, my love. Both holy and profane." He smiled at me and I may have even blushed, thinking that some of the profane things he could do *were* holy. He looked at Maxine. "But you have to be here at sunrise to see it."

"We've got to work tomorrow, Tom," she replied. "Not everyone is an independent business owner, like you."

Tom looked at his phone, pushed buttons. "Sunrise is at 5:39 tomorrow, Max. What time do you have to be to work? Nine?" He looked at me. "What about you? Eight?"

"I'm actually off tomorrow. Gotta sacrifice a chicken." In reality, the boss was out of town, and had given the whole office the day off. He did it a couple times a year.

Tom looked back at Maxine, and she said, "Nobody can deny you anything, can they? And you know it. I'll be here."

He smiled. "I'll need a few things. Do either of you have a compact you're not using?"

"Look in the junk drawer," I told him. "In the kitchen."

Tom retrieved my old compact from the junk drawer, as well as one of those two-sided sticky things that you use to hang pictures, a tape measure and a black Sharpie. He went outside into the garden and we followed him. He made some calculations on his phone, made a couple measurements, then looked at us.

"This part is secret. I have to say some words." He looked at us blankly, and I was sure he was having us on. "You people aren't initiated. You can't watch."

Maxine opened her mouth to say something, changed her mind. She turned and went back into the house. Tom winked at me. I couldn't think of anything to say either, so I followed Maxine.

Completely intrigued now, we watched Tom through the window. He made further calculations, further measurements. He snapped the bottom half off of the compact, then taped the mirror part to one side of the arch with the picture hanger, measured again. He fiddled around with it, measured again. He found a little stick on the ground, pushed it behind the mirror so it stuck out at a little bit of an angle, measured again. Then he went over to the other side of the arch, measured one more time, and wrote something on the arch with the Sharpie. I noticed that he didn't look up at the sun once, nor did he raise his arms heavenward, chant, or say any words.

Then he turned and looked right at us through the window. I knew he couldn't see us, because the kitchen was in shadow. But he still knew we were watching him. Tom knew that Maxine and I didn't believe that he could be doing anything even remotely magical. We just didn't believe in that kind of stuff.

You people aren't initiated. Indeed.

Twenty minutes later, a nice-looking, clean cut young man pulled up in front of the house in a nice-looking, clean-cut sedan.

"This would be Sammy," Maxine said and smiled fondly.

"Good job, Max," Tom said *sotto voce*, before Sammy made it up to the porch from the curb. "He's wearing a tie."

"You just shut the fuck up, Tom Bastion," Max whispered, not looking at him. "Don't you dare embarrass me."

116

Sammy introduced himself as Sam. I thought it was an insight into Max's feelings towards these young men, or maybe men in general, that she always called them by the diminutive of their names. Ricky. Sammy. *Jose-baby.*

He was not quite as tall as Tom, rail thin, with short, reddish-brown hair, enormous brown eyes and a shy smile. He couldn't be a day older than Maxine. I made up my mind on the spot that I wouldn't call him Sammy like Max did. It would make me feel like I was his mother.

When Tom offered him a drink, Maxine looked at him, shocked, as if he'd offered the kid a line of coke. "Sammy's driving, Tom. In fact," she looked at her phone, "we need to be going if we're going to catch the previews."

Sam told us politely that it had been nice meeting us, and they left.

"Wow," Tom said. "Max sure seems intent on making a good impression with this one. I thought she was going to punch me."

Maxine always wanted to make a good impression when she met a new man, I thought. She was always enthusiastic at first. Hope always sprang eternal within Max; she never even entertained the thought that the new one might also turn out to be a dud like the last one had been. And she remained enthusiastic, right up until the moment that she decided that she was bored. Then it was, "Next!" like turning off a light switch. Max never agonized over whether or not this could still be Mr. Right after she discovered his clay feet. She just changed her shoes and moved on.

I wished her luck, hoped that Sam was the one, hoped that Maxine would be as happy with him as I was with Tom.

I looked at Tom, who was watching their taillights disappear down the street. I said, "So . . . are there any pagan *pre*-solstice rituals that I should know about? Anything into which you might have to . . . initiate me?"

He put his arm around me and we went back into the house. "I'm sure I can think of something."

FORTY-FIVE

Maxine arrived the next morning at 5:15 with Starbucks for us, and a side order of her cheerful early morning attitude. I asked her how her date had gone, and she gave me the thumbs up, but then would say no more. It was undoubtedly too early to tell.

I wasn't quite as cheerful as Maxine, not as happy at getting up so early on one of my rare extra days off. But just like she'd said, the two of us couldn't deny Tom anything, so I was not that put out. Just a little cranky, and a lot skeptical.

Tom took a flashlight outside with him, and positioned three lawn chairs in the garden, facing east, facing the section of the arch that he'd written on. It was still dark, and I couldn't have read what he'd put there, even if I'd tried.

He sat us down in the chairs and we waited, sipping our Starbucks. I had to admit that there was a sort of anticipation in the air, anticipation to see this *hierophany* – what he'd called the sacred made manifest. Maxine felt it too, and was silent.

Then with a suddenness that took me by surprise, the sun broke over the horizon. A shaft of light struck the mirror and bounced, reflected to the other side of the arch. A round circle of light appeared there in the still-darkness. It revealed a heart-shape drawn on the wood, in which Tom had written, *I love you, Liz and Max.*

It seemed like such a simple trick, but I sensed that Maxine was as awestruck as I was. It was like the scene in *Raiders of the Lost Ark*, where the sunbeam shines through the headpiece to the Staff of Ra, and all that. It *was* a hierophany, something sacred made manifest, even if we knew that there was nothing supernatural about it.

After a few moments, Tom smiled smugly, then arose and silently went into the house. After another moment, Maxine and I looked at each other.

"He is so *odd*," she said. "How does he know how to do this stuff?" I shook my head. We sat there in silence and enjoyed the sunrise for a while, until the smell of bacon cooking drew us back into the house.

As Maxine was walking out the door to go to *Old Town*, Tom asked her, "Do you have to work on the Fourth of July, Max?"

"Oh, yeah," she said without hesitation. "Always gotta work on the Fourth. It's a huge money-maker, with all the people downtown for the street festival, waiting around for the fireworks. Karen keeps the place open 'til dark."

"What about Sam? Does he have to work?"

"I just met Sam last night, Tom. But he works for a title company, at an office like Liz. I'm sure he doesn't have to work on the Fourth of July. It's a national holiday, for Christ's sake. All the cubical worker bees get national holidays off."

"That's why they call them national holidays," I opined.

They both looked at me. Then Tom said, "You can't work on the Fourth, Max. We're going to Lake Havasu. With this." He pushed a button on his phone and showed us a picture of a slick, red boat.

I looked at the picture. "When were you going to tell me about this?"

Tom smiled innocently at me. "I'm telling you right now. Surprise!"

Maxine sighed. "It's great, Tom. But there's no way Karen will let me off on the Fourth of July."

"I got us a little place, right on the water," Tom insisted. "It's got its own little dock and everything." My mouth fell open in disbelief, and he explained. "You know Jerry? He works at the bank?" When I continued to stare blankly at him, Tom shook his head. "Never mind. Jerry's a customer. His daughter is getting married on the Fourth of July. In Sacramento. Then they're all flying out to Havasu on the seventh. Trouble is, Jerry's boat and his truck are here, so we made a little deal. I drag his boat to Havasu on the third, and we get to use it and his place until they arrive on the seventh."

Once again, I marveled at his ability to come up with the most incredible, off-the-wall plans. "How are we going to get back home?"

Tom looked at me in surprise, as if he couldn't believe that I'd think that he'd overlook such an important detail. "Cadillac. It's already reserved." He showed me the text confirmation from Avis of Lake Havasu City on his phone. Tom looked at Max again. "What do you say?"

"It sounds like a blast, Tom. But I'm telling you, Karen won't let me off. It's a big sales day for her, like Black Friday." Then a thought struck Maxine. "Unless *you* ask her." She winked at me. "I'm sure she'd do *anything* for you."

Tom hesitated, made a little embarrassed look of distaste. But Maxine was engrossed with the idea now, thrilled that she'd thought up a way that she could get to go with us.

"Come on, Tom." She looked at her phone. "She's in by now. If anyone can talk her into it, it's you. Let's go. Use that charm for something besides making Liz weak at the knees."

Tom looked at me and I kissed him. "Go for it."

"All right, I will. The sacrifices I make for you, Max. The indignities I suffer. Let's go."

"Maybe you should take off your shirt," Maxine suggested. Tom rolled his eyes and they walked out the door.

FORTY-SIX

Maxine told me how it went down that evening after work, because I couldn't get anything more out of Tom than, "It's a go."

"But what happened?"

"Let Maxine tell you. She'd be disappointed if she didn't get to tell you."

I waited with no little impatience for Max to show up after work. I asked her what went down, and she grinned from ear to ear.

"So we walk in the store, and Karen sees Tom, and just stops talking to the customer she's with. *Just stops talking to the guy,* and stares at Tom. The guy's in a hurry, he's gonna be late for work, and he just mumbles to a stop, too, 'cause he realizes suddenly that the proprietor is ignoring him. Now they're both looking at us. Without missing a beat, Karen says, 'Good morning, Maxine. Could you write Mr. Maxwell up for me, please?'

"She doesn't even wait for me to reply. Now I'm being ignored, too, because she's smiling at Tom. You've seen her smile at him, that big shark's grin, showing all her teeth. I look at Tom for a second, then walk over and start ringing Mr. Maxwell up. Then he takes his purchase and leaves in rather a huff, without saying another word.

"Karen crosses the room in three big steps and says, 'Good morning, Tom. I haven't seen *you* in a while. What can I do for *you*, today?'

"Tom doesn't look at me, because he knows if he does, he'll bust up. This shit is really just too easy for him. He smiles at Karen and says, 'As a matter of fact, there is something you can do for me. It's kind of a big favor, though, and nobody can help me but *you.*'"

"I did not say that," Tom objected.

"Whatever. You did tell that you had a favor to ask her. Then she was all ears."

"But you make it sound like I asked her something . . . *untoward.*"

"She wants you to ask her something *untoward*, Tom! And you fucking know it! As soon as you said, 'There *is* something you can do for me,' Karen already had you undressed and was on her knees. In her mind, anyway. She already knew she'd say yes, before you even asked her anything, because she knew what she *wanted* you to ask her, and couldn't think of anything past that."

Tom tried not to grin, failed. "I appealed to her business sense. I told her that my store manager was scheduled to have a Caesarean Section on the third, and that her doting young husband, who also worked for me, would be there at the hospital with her. So I was going to be entirely short-handed on one of the biggest retail days that occurred in our little downtown business community. I told her that I knew she had trained Maxine so well; I told her that because of her influence and guidance, I knew that Maxine could perform professionally and efficiently, could handle the pressures of such a busy retail day. So I asked her if I could please borrow Maxine to work at my store on the Fourth of July."

Max said, "Karen just blinked at him for a minute. Then Tom said, 'I'm sure you can think of some way for me to make it up to you.'"

"I did not say that!" Tom protested. "I told her that I'd make it up to her by coming in and helping her, the next time she did inventory. I told her that I knew how tedious taking inventory can be, and I said I'd be more than happy to lend her a hand with it."

Maxine grinned evilly at me. "Karen's never taken inventory in her life. But I could read her fucking mind, Liz. She was thinking about how she'd summon Tom some night; how he'd show up and she'd lock the doors. She was thinking about how she and Tom would be there in the store all alone. She'd finally have him right where she wanted him. She was thinking of the dusty old four-poster on the second floor, about how she would go about taking *his* inventory."

Tom put his hand to his face, peeked through his fingers. "It was a perfectly innocent suggestion."

"It was a perfectly *suggestive* suggestion, at least in Karen's mind. She said, 'I guess I can part with our Maxine for one day, even if it is one of the busiest days of the year.' She looked over at me, and I blinked, trying to pretend that I hadn't been listening. But Karen wasn't concerned with me. I was just a bargaining chip in her new plans for *taking inventory*. She looked back at Tom.

"He said, 'Thanks, Karen, I really appreciate it. I might need her for a few days. The whole weekend, now that I think about it.'

"She paused at that, but then she just shook her head. In for a dime, in for a dollar, I guess. Inventory and all." Maxine giggled. "Then she said, 'That'll be fine.'

"Tom said thanks again and gave her a little grateful smile. Karen said, 'Oh, don't mention it, Tom. It's my pleasure. Anything for *you*.' And before he could move, the nervy bitch stepped up and *hugged* him."

I looked at him in surprise. "Did you hug her back?"

Tom closed his fingers over his eyes.

"Of course he didn't hug her back!" Max said. "That would only encourage her. He just stood there. Took one for the team, so to speak. She clung to him for way too long, I thought, and I grinned at him over her shoulder. Finally, she let go, and said, 'I'll call you about that inventory,' and I thought, *I bet you will.*"

Tom said, "I told her to be sure to do that and thanked her again."

"Then he looked at his watch and told her that he was late for work," Maxine continued. "Then he backed out of the store like a rat from a sinking ship, before she could hug him again."

"I thought I made a rather dignified exit," Tom said.

Maxine shook her head. "You didn't."

"How easily you'll become a whore for Maxine!" I laughed. "My boss is gay, Tom. Do you think you could get me out of work at tax time?"

His eyebrows shot up in surprise. "I don't know about *that*. But this was worth it." He smiled at Maxine. "We couldn't go to Havasu on the Fourth of July without you. What about Sam?"

Max nodded. "He's down. It might just be his lucky weekend."

"What I want to know," I said, "is what is Karen going to think if she goes by the store and sees that it's locked up tight? In case she decides that she wants to *take inventory* sometime that weekend? Make her own fireworks?"

Tom shrugged. "Power failure. Plumbing backed up."

"She won't stop by anytime that weekend," Maxine said. "She'll be too busy making money. And besides, she'll be short-handed." She giggled.

"What about on Monday morning, when you roll in there all tired and sunburned?" I said.

"I'll tell her that Tom decided to have a sidewalk sale, and he's such an evil boss, he made me sit outside in the sun and oversee it." She winked at Tom. "I'll tell her how mean you are. I'm sure she'll like that."

FORTY-SEVEN

After work on Wednesday, the third of July, Tom told us, "Jerry said to bring everything with us. He told me that the traffic is murder in Havasu on the Fourth, and it takes an hour to get to the liquor store and back. He said to try to make it so that we don't have to drive around in town too much once we get there. He also said that the place has been locked up since April, so we might want to bring food."

Sam drove Tom to the south side of town, where the money lived, to pick up the truck and the boat. When Tom pulled up in front of the house, I couldn't see much of the boat, because it had a cover lashed securely to it. But the truck was a giant red monster, the same color as the hull of the boat, a Ford F-150 Lariat SuperCrew. It was huge, massive, with a chrome grill and bumper a mile wide, headlights as big as the eyes of a humpbacked whale. It couldn't have been more than a year old.

It was right up Tom's alley.

We walked out to the curb when he got out of it, and Maxine whistled. "Jesus. I didn't know that they still made beasts like this. No wonder we're so dependent on foreign oil."

Tom was lighting a cigarette, and he opened his mouth to retort. I whispered in his ear, "Do not say *bitch, please* in front of Max's new boyfriend."

Tom looked down the street to where Sam was just pulling up behind the boat. He smiled at Max. "Bitch, please. This truck is state of the art. Loaded. Jerry doesn't fuck around. It's awesome. Power everything. It's like driving your living room."

Maxine looked down the length of the truck, taking up about three parking spaces, what with the boat attached to it and all. "It's bigger than my living room." She laid her hand on the warm, shiny red hood. "What kind of gas mileage does this living room get?"

"Jerry said it's rated for a combined nineteen. Pulling the boat, he said we should get about fifteen."

"Fifteen? Miles per gallon? Christ on a crutch, Tom! I thought there were some kind of government guidelines about gas mileage, nowadays. My grandma's deuce and a quarter got better mileage than fifteen miles per gallon!"

Tom tilted his head. "Your grandma's what?"

"My grandma's *deuce and a quarter*. It's a car, a big old dinosaur of a car. A Buick Electra 225. She had a white 1970 convertible. And I know it got better than fifteen mpg."

"I bet this truck is just as comfortable, Max, and I know it's safer," Tom replied. "It's not a convertible, but it's got a sunroof. A *power* sunroof."

Maxine just shook her head, turned and walked down the street to where Sam was locking up his nice, clean-cut, no doubt fuel efficient sedan. She knew it was no use arguing with Tom about the evils of gas burners. He couldn't possibly care less about their impact on the environment. He wasn't quite sure if he believed that we were, indeed, dependent on foreign oil, and if we were, he didn't care, either way.

The big Ford was powerful and comfortable and thrummed quietly, yet was still capable of generating an astounding four hundred and eleven horses out of its not fuel-efficient, rather anachronistic 6.2 liter V-8. All Tom had to do was put his foot to the floor. The truck was an immense, luxurious, entirely *useful* machine. That was all that mattered to Tom, and he relished the opportunity to put it through its paces.

The four of us packed the red Ford with everything necessary for a road trip across the county to Arizona, as well as everything we thought that we might need for the Fourth of July weekend beneath the London Bridge at Lake Havasu. We raided the garden, the grocery store, the liquor store. We filled three coolers.

Then we hit the road and got the hell out of Dodge. East through Moreno Valley and Beaumont; past the bright lights of Palm Springs, then skirting Joshua Tree National Park. Then through the miles of uninhabited desert, then north to the lake. The miles sped out smoothly and silently behind us. It *was* like riding in your living room.

There was already traffic in town when we arrived, but the truck's GPS led us to Jerry's vacation home on the lake as quickly as possible under the holiday circumstances.

Tom turned off the truck and smiled at me. *"Thus with imagined wing our swift scene flies, in motion of no less celerity than that of thought."*

I smiled back at him. I loved it when he dropped the occasional Shakespearean quotation. It reminded me that he was so much more than just an accomplished sex fiend and avid gear head.

"What the hell does that mean?" Maxine called from the back seat.

Tom closed his eyes. "It means we're here, Max. We have arrived. Get the fuck outta the truck."

FORTY-EIGHT

Jerry's vacation house was small but comfortable, nothing like the McMansion Tom had described on the south side. But it was his *vacation* home, after all, so it was okay with me that it was modest. My regular home was modest, and I didn't even aspire to a vacation home. It was a little bit dusty, but as cold as an icebox.

"Does he let the air run when he's not here?" Max asked. "That must cost a fortune."

"What are you, new?" Tom asked and winked at me. It was Max's favorite question to me when I was having trouble with my cellphone, or the computer, or the remote for the big TV.

Maxine looked at Tom. He held up his phone. "I turned the air on when we stopped for gas. Jerry gave me the code. Modern technology, my little Luddite. It's a wonderful time to be alive."

Maxine took out her own phone, typed something. Tom's phone lit up. Her text read, "I've got your Luddite. Right here."

FORTY-NINE

Tom made his trademark mouth-watering breakfast the next morning, all the while humming to himself and dancing around in the kitchen. I smiled to myself. He was just so fucking *odd*.

"Why the extra bonhomie this morning?" I asked.

He stopped dancing and came over and kissed me. He pointed out the window, then he actually *giggled*. "If Max thought the truck was too much, then she's gonna have a tiny litter of carnivorous kittens when she sees the boat."

So *fucking odd*, I thought.

A few minutes later, Maxine and Sam appeared, holding hands. Sam was completely tousled, looking a little sheepish because he knew that we couldn't help but know what the two of them had been doing.

Oh, I thought, *Maxie's caught herself a shy one*. How out of character for her.

They sat at the counter that separated the little kitchen from the little dining room and left off holding hands. When Sam turned to look out the window, Maxine winked at me and mimed, "Happy birthday to *me*."

Tom noticed it and opened his mouth to say something, but Max scowled her *don't you embarrass me* face at him again. He blinked innocently and said, "Breakfast, kids?"

FIFTY

"Are you on something?" Maxine asked Tom. "Speed, maybe?"

Tom had already finished his breakfast and was sitting at the counter, watching us eat, drumming his fingers on the granite. He nodded out the window. "It's ninety-two degrees, already, Max. I want to get that red bitch out on the water."

"Sounds like a plan," Sammy said and quickly cleaned his plate.

Tom lit a cigarette and squinted at us through the smoke. "Come on, my darlings. We're burning very hot daylight."

Max and I finished up quickly, because, after all, we could deny him nothing. We walked outside and the heat hit us like a solid wall. Maxine made a face.

"Welcome to the desert," Tom said. He pushed a button on Jerry's keys and the garage door opened. A large, expensive cooler sat on the dusty concrete, not one of the ones we'd brought with us. Sam moved to fetch it, but Tom stopped him. "Hold on a second, my friend. Why bring it out into the sun any sooner than we have to? You have *got* to see this awesome boat first."

We walked down the driveway. Tom had been busy that morning. In addition to making breakfast and packing the cooler, he'd already unhooked the cover from the red boat. I suspected that it was only his love of sharing that had prevented him from removing it completely and stowing it in the garage.

He said, "Voila!" and pulled the cover off in one smooth motion, revealing the jet boat in all its glory. The tiny picture of it on his phone had not done it justice. The cover had been on it there, too. It was about eighteen feet long, and it turned out that only the sides of the hull and the gunwales were painted that bright, arrest-me red. The long bow was as black as an oil slick. There were two bucket seats in front, and a curved bench seat behind them, upholstered in red with black accents. On one side, near the stern, a drop-shadow, *Raiders of the Lost Ark* style font spelled out *Radioactive*.

And then there was the engine. The unrelenting sunshine winked off the chromed valve covers, the chromed intake, the chromed headers pointing back out over the stern.

"Hot damn!" Sam exclaimed. "Is that a 460 Ford?"

"That it is," Tom said. They grinned at each other, and I was witness to the birth of a friendship. "Jerry says it'll do eighty on flat water."

And then they stood there in the blazing sun for five minutes looking at the boat's motor, talking specs, displacement and horsepower and all that kind of thing. Maxine finally whistled, and they stopped and looked at her.

"Hey, men people! Can we get this show on the road? I'm melting here."

Tom nodded wordlessly at the garage, and he and Sam brought the cooler out and put it in the boat, behind the bucket seats. Tom opened the back door to the truck, and said, "Ladies?" I noticed that we were now relegated to the backseat, while the men sat together in the front. I smiled.

The boat ramp and dock were at the end of the driveway, but even for that short distance, the heat inside the truck was suffocating. Tom had the air on, but it didn't have time to cool the interior down. Max and I got out and walked up onto the dock while Tom and Sam slid the boat off the trailer and tied it up. Then Tom arced a set of keys through the air to Sam. "Fire her up, my son. I'll go park the truck."

Sam stepped gingerly into the boat. He sat down in the bucket seat, made sure the boat was in neutral, stuck the key in the ignition and turned it. The boat roared to life, the settled down to a burbling idle. Max and I were forgotten.

Tom came back down the driveway, hopped up on the dock. He and Sam grinned at each other, wordlessly appreciating the sound of the engine. Then Tom made a quick little throat cutting gesture, and Sam shut it down.

He turned to Max and me, and said, "Okay, ladies. I'm going to assume that power boating is a new thing for you. I've only been once myself, down San Diego way. But I'm a quick study." He winked. "Here are the rules. Do not stand up the boat. If Neptune himself flops up on the bow, tail and flukes all a'glistening, *do not stand up in the boat.* Stay away from the motor —"

"It's hot," Sam interjected. He said to Tom, "I had a buddy in high school. He got drunk and fell right across one of these. One arm on each header." He loosely raised his arms to shoulder level. "Burnt the fuck out of himself."

Maxine and I looked at each other. Apparently, this was the first profanity either of us had heard out of Sam. She winked at me.

"Can you think of any other rules?"

"Don't stand up, stay away from the engine." Sam considered. "Sunscreen?"

"In the cooler."

"Earplugs?"

Tom patted the pocket of his shirt. He handed us each a pair of earplugs. "Shall we about it then?" He hopped down into the boat and held his hand out to me. I stepped in and immediately sat.

Maxine went to the front of the boat and was about to step onto it. Sam shook his head. "No, Max. Don't step on the bow. You *never* step on the bow of a boat like this."

"That's why they painted it black, Max," Tom said. "So it'll burn you if you step on it. You only have to learn that lesson once, eh, Sam? Which parts'll burn you?"

Maxine flipped them both off.

Tom gestured for me to scoot over, then held out his hand and helped Max into the boat. She sat down next to me.

Tom jumped out and untied the bow line, then stepped back into the boat again and pushed us off. He vaulted gracefully into the other bucket seat. "Take her out, Sammy, my boy. Jerry says we have to maintain idle speed until we get out onto the lake, but after that, she's all yours."

Maxine and I were invisible for the first two hours that we were on the water. Tom and Sam ran the boat back and forth, taking turns, talking about the engine, laughing and joking. They didn't get a chance to see if the *Radioactive* could really do eighty miles per hour, because the lake was wall-to-wall with other boaters. But they got it going fast enough, bouncing over wakes and generally having one helluva good time together. They didn't say a word to either me or Maxine.

Tom found a nice beach that wasn't already completely filled with other boaters, and maneuvered the craft gently into the sand. Then he and Sammy *high-fived each other*. It was adorable.

Tom and Sam leapt over their respective sides of the boat in tandem, and waded behind it, pushed it farther up onto the sand. Then Sam unexpectedly reached into the boat and picked Maxine up bodily and carried her to the beach. She squealed in delight.

Tom waded around to my side of the boat and kissed me. Then he really *kissed* me. Then he said, "Do you want me to carry you, too?"

I shook my head and whispered, "Just kiss me again."

Maxine yelled from the beach, "Hey, old people! Get a room!"

FIFTY-ONE

Tom and I carried the cooler up to the beach, and set it on the sand. Maxine said, "Oh, thank God. Beer me, would you, Liz?"

I opened the cooler. First, there were large Zip-Loc bags filled with fruits and vegetables. Then a king-sized bottle of sun screen. I moved them out of the way, and dug through the ice. I found nine bottles of water, a bottle of gin, a bottle of rum, a bottle of whiskey, and a bottle of tequila. No beer. I looked at Tom.

"It's like a fucking Easter egg hunt, eh?" He dug around in the cooler and came up with a shot glass, shook the ice out of it.

"No beer?" Maxine asked in shock.

"Beer takes up too much space," Tom said. "You can't drink beer, here, anyway. It's too damn hot. You just sweat it out."

Sam reached for the shot glass.

FIFTY-TWO

The four of us spent the day alternately drinking, running into the water to cool off, and sitting on the beach. It was too hot to do much of anything else, and there were just too many and various watercraft of all shapes and sizes on the lake to really do justice to the red jet boat. We talked, and got to know Sam, and Sam got to know us. And we all got sunburned, despite the sunscreen. You just sweated it off.

As the sun started slanting lower in the west, Tom suggested that we go back to the house and barbeque, and watch the fireworks from there. Sam pronounced it a stellar idea (he'd already picked up Tom's idiom) and we went.

When we arrived back at Jerry's little vacation home, Tom fired up the barbeque, and Maxine went inside to take a shower, claiming that she had sand in places that she hadn't even realized that she had places before. I went inside and made drinks for Tom and Sam and myself, proper drinks, with ice and soda and no sand.

When I came back out, Tom and Sam were standing by the barbeque talking. They stopped when I came up to them, and I handed them their drinks. Then Sam said abruptly, "So, yeah, Tom, about that 460."

Tom smiled at me, and I walked back across the little grassless yard, away from the heat of the barbeque, away from the boring conversation about the glories of the internal combustion engine. I sat in a lawn chair. I was sunburnt and more than a little bit drunk, and I was happy with just watching them. Tom looked over at me and smiled every now and then. I waved.

The ice in my drink seemed to melt almost before I knew it. I went back into the house to get some more, and was met on my way back out by Tom and Sam and a plateful of hamburgers. Tom set them on the counter.

I set my drink on the counter beside them, then turned to look for the bag of buns in the cabinet where he'd stuck them. When I turned around again, Sam had disappeared.

"He went to get Max," Tom explained. He gestured for me to toss the bag of buns to him. "They might be a minute."

We constructed hamburgers and stood there in the blessed arctic air conditioning and ate them in silence. Max and Sam's absence became more and more obvious. Finally I said, "They're going to miss the fireworks."

Tom shrugged. "Could be."

We walked hand and hand down the driveway, then onto the little dock. Tom took off his shirt and shoes and trunks and dove into the water naked. I looked around to see if anyone could see me, and satisfied that no one was around, I doffed my own clothes and joined him.

The water was as warm as blood. Tom swam over to where it was shallow enough to stand and motioned for me to follow him. He put his arms around my neck and whispered that unlike the beach, there was no sand here. I smiled and wrapped my legs around him. He kissed me, bit me on the neck. I looked up at the waning crescent moon and pitied Max and Sam inside in the air conditioning.

When the fireworks started, we recovered our clothes and squeezed together onto the curved bench seat of the boat, spoon-like, and oohed and ahhed over the light show, as was its due. Tom fell asleep, his breath soft on my neck. I drifted off soon afterward, thinking that I had never in my life been more happy, more *content*, than when I was wrapped in this man's arms.

FIFTY-THREE

I smelled bacon cooking and opened my eyes. The sun had just started to climb above the horizon, but it was already at least eighty degrees. I sat up gingerly and looked behind me at Tom, thinking he might still be asleep. But he was already awake, just waiting for me to be awake, too. Now that I was sitting up, he smiled and took off his shirt, then immediately leapt up off the curved seat and dove over the gunwale, making the boat bump against the side of the dock. He broke the surface of the formerly glasslike water and tilted his head at me, inviting me to join him for another . . . *swim*.

I considered it for a moment, then glanced back at the house. The lights in the kitchen were on, and I thought I could see Maxine moving around in there. I reluctantly shook my head and said, "Come on. Apparently breakfast is served."

I stepped onto the dock, then met him as he walked up the ramp out of the water. I carried his shirt, and we strolled back to the house, arm in arm. Tom's skin was wet and slick against mine, but not cold. Nothing was ever cold here, I thought, unless you went indoors. Or perhaps underground.

Maxine was perched at the counter, dressed only in an over-sized, knee length t-shirt. There was a huge pile of bacon on a plate in front of her. She nibbled a piece of it, musing. But as soon as Tom entered, she flew out of her chair, ran over and threw her arms around his neck. If this was not unexpected enough, she then pinned him bodily to the wall and kissed him right on the mouth.

She said, "Thanks, Tom. Now I get to have my cake and eat it too." She nodded over her shoulder at the plate of bacon. "You guys have breakfast. We'll be out . . . later." She released Tom, winked at me, and fled to the back of the house.

"Wow," I said. "That was sexy." I handed him his shirt.

Tom shrugged into it and said nothing. He didn't seem at all surprised at Maxine's strange behavior. Well, maybe a little surprised, but not nearly as much as I was. After a moment of silence, it became apparent that he was not planning to enlighten me. I asked, "What's Max thanking you for?"

"Oh, that." He strolled over to the counter, idly picked up a piece of bacon and stuffed it into his mouth. He looked blankly at me.

"Oh, that," I repeated back to him. "Yes, that." I smiled.

Tom took a deep breath, chewed his bacon, looked at the ceiling for a moment. He exhaled. "You remember yesterday, when Sam and I were talking out there by the barbeque?"

"Yes. You were talking about engines. Boats."

Tom laughed. "No, Liz. We were talking about *women*. Sam was asking for my advice, about Maxine, about . . ." he gestured toward the back of the house. "I was surprised."

You are frequently *surprised*, I thought.

"So, I said, 'You've come to the right man, Sam, my son. I do know a little bit about women.'" Tom grinned smugly. "Certainly a little bit more than he does, it turns out, so –"

"You know a little bit about what women *like*," I corrected him. "I don't know how much you know about women in general."

"But that's all I need to know, isn't it? What women *like*?" He hugged me. "What *you* like? You tell me, my lover, what else do I need to know besides *what you like*? Are you unamused with me in any way?"

"Not in any way," I answered immediately. I couldn't think of a single additional thing to say.

Tom continued. "So, Sam asked me if I knew any –"

"*Tricks?*" I said, finding my voice again. "Sam asked you if you knew any *tricks?*"

Oh, my God, I thought, no wonder Max was thanking him. Tricks. Treats. Tom knew 'em all. *The things he could do.*

He considered me in mock annoyance for a moment, chewed his bacon. "Sam asked me if I there were any *pointers* that I could give him."

Maxine and Sam didn't reappear until lunch time.

FIFTY-FOUR

Jerry drove us to the Avis on Sunday morning to pick up the slick black Cadillac XTS that Tom had rented for the drive home. They shook hands and clapped each other on the back when they said goodbye, and I again marveled at how many "friends" Tom had, people that he hardly knew, yet who trusted him completely with their most prized possessions: Harleys and trucks and jet boats and vacation homes.

He never brought any of these people home to dinner, never met them at the bar and had a drink with them, never went over to their houses to hang out and watch the game. As far as I could tell, Tom didn't seek any other companions besides me and Maxine. And now, perhaps his boat-engine, sex-talk buddy Sam.

The XTS was amazing. Like the big Ford truck, it was like riding in your living room, if your living room was very *expensive*, very fast, temperature controlled, quiet, and bound in leather. I cursed the exceptional, pressure mapped bucket seat, because the console that ran next to it prevented me from sitting closer to Tom.

He shook his head and said, "You *do* imprint on the obsolete, my love. They don't much make bench seats any more. Certainly not in rides like this." He gestured at the Cadillac. "This is a *luxury* car, Liz. State of the art in individual passenger comfort. We don't have to all slide in together like in grandma's deuce and a quarter."

Maxine's description of her grandma's Buick had apparently intrigued Tom, and he'd therefore taken the time to Google it; or else he wouldn't suddenly know that Electras came with bench seats. Earlier in the weekend, he'd never even heard of a deuce and a quarter.

I'd wager a week's pay that nobody his age, outside of people immersed in the computer industry itself maybe, just flat out *enjoyed* the internet as much as Tom. Whenever he was sitting still, if he wasn't reading, he was surfing. He claimed that he never left his personal information anywhere, but I wasn't so sure. The internet was Tom's playground. He was always saying, "Well, would ya look at that."

After a few unexpected shocks, a few things I could never, ever *unsee*, I learned to ask, "What is it?" before I looked. Occasionally it was a car wreck. Sometimes it was a two-head snake, or cats or little babies doing cute things. More often, it was something else entirely.

And any time I had a question, or anytime Maxine would just wonder out loud about *anything*, Tom would rub his hands together, grin and say, *"Let's find out,"* like the owl from the old Tootsie Pops commercial, and take out his phone.

"It's a wonderful time to be alive on this planet," he would always say. The only thoroughfare he appreciated more than a curvy, nicely-banked, well-paved, two-lane blacktop was the information superhighway.

FIFTY-FIVE

Tom piped some kind of classical music through the Caddy's impeccable stereo system, and Max and Sam were asleep before we even got out of Havasu City. They slept for the entire trip home, curled up together like puppies. They reminded me of napping children, worn-out, sunburnt, exhausted from too much holiday fun. Except that the fun they'd been having had been of the grown-up variety.

Pointers. I looked over at Tom, and he smiled at me, like he always did. Pointers, indeed.

Nestled in the extraordinary leather seat, I felt inordinately proud to be an American. Surely, nothing was as wonderful as the ageless joy of a sunburnt, delightful Fourth of July weekend, spent with people you love.

FIFTY-SIX

When I got home from work on the following Friday, I found Sam and Tom sitting on the couch waiting for me, all smiles. When I came in the door, Tom leapt up and gave me a big sloppy kiss; one of my favorites. He said, "Is it okay if Sam and I use the shed in the back yard, Liz? My love?"

"Certainly . . . What for?"

"So we can work on engines," Sam said.

"I don't think you can even get a car into the backyard anymore. Not with the garden." The driveway portion of the backyard was just a shade over nine feet wide, and the garden encroached on that.

"We're not going to work on cars, Liz," Tom said.

"How pedestrian," Sam said.

"Just engines," Tom said and they high-fived.

I smiled at their adorable friendship. "Whatever you desire, gentlemen." I accepted another sloppy kiss from Tom. My favorite.

FIFTY-SEVEN

Maxine and I sat in the backyard, sunned, picked cherry tomatoes off the vine, and watched Tom and Sam, shirtless, as they cleaned out the large shed that had sat in the corner of the backyard, unused and neglected for all the years that I'd owned the house. Maxine had the time of her life all afternoon, giggling and making not unflattering, but still somewhat off-color comments about their state of undress. I may even have blushed a couple of times. I was thankful that they were out of earshot.

By the time the sun started to dip in the west, they were done. A small army of trash bags and various other unidentifiable pieces of debris stood on the curb awaiting garbage pick-up on Monday. Tom and Sam stood there admiring their labor for a moment, then high-fived each other again.

"Goddamn, but we're good!" Sam said.

Maxine said to me, "Ain't they, though?" and winked.

The two of them approached where we sat in the garden, and Tom said, "You want to go fire up that barbeque, my son?"

"Oh, dinner and a show," Maxine said.

Tom looked at her curiously.

"Never mind," I told him. "Maxine's in a mood."

Sam said, "What are we gonna cook? I could really go for grilling a couple big salmon."

Tom made a face. "Salmon? Like fish-salmon?"

Sam nodded. "Is there any other kind?"

Tom shook his head. "I've got steaks."

"Like fish-steaks?" Max said.

"Like cow-steaks. And I also have cow-burgers." Tom smiled at his friend, shook his head again. "I'm sorry, Sam. I never eat fish anymore. Not since I came here. Growing up, I ate enough fish to last for the rest of my entire life." He shook his head a third time. "No fish."

"But fish is good for you," I said.

"*Variety* is good for you." He looked at me, maybe just the slightest bit annoyed, which surprised the hell out of me. He repeated, "I've had enough fish to last for the rest of my life."

"Steaks it is then," Sam said, and they high-fived again.

FIFTY-EIGHT

On Sunday, I woke up to the sound of the birds chirping. It's not the most bothersome sound in the world, but it's definitely in the top ten. I only heard the birds chirping on the weekend; it seemed as though I was already gone for work before they began their infuriatingly cheerful racket during the week.

I only heard them because the bedroom window was open.

My house was built in 1909 and had not been retrofitted with central air. I was the only hold out on the block. I didn't have the wiring for it and besides it was not necessary downstairs. Apparently, the old-timey builders had known something about insulation, because it stayed nice and cool on the first floor. We might need a little fan in August, but that was about it.

Upstairs, directly under the roof, was another story. My bedroom would reach surface of the sun temperatures in the summer, so I had a little air conditioner in the wall. But the first morning that I turned it on, Tom said, "What are you doing?"

There he went again, questioning the obvious. I answered, "I'm turning on the air. It's going to get like an oven in here."

"The air's already on," he gestured at the air all around us, and smiled. "And we're not going to be here. Let it get hot."

"But we'll be here later —"

"Not till tonight, right?" Tom described for me how houses in ancient Sumeria were built facing inward toward an open courtyard. "This courtyard was called a *tarbusu*," he said. "All the rooms opened onto it because it provided a cooling effect by creating convection currents."

I smiled at him. "What do ancient Sumerian houses have to do with my air conditioner?" I asked.

"Sometimes we can go back to ancient times and find a better solution. If we can change the convection in here a little bit, the air flow, we can cool things off considerably. Naturally. Well, almost naturally." When I looked at him blankly, he said, "Do you have a box fan? I'll fix it so we don't need to even turn on that filthy little container of germs." He nodded at the air conditioner. "At least not at night. Just like in ancient Sumeria. A little air flow goes a long way. Trust me."

Trust him was something I did implicitly, so I gave him the box fan and watched him rig it up in the doorway, with a couple of beach towels blocking the rest of the space.

"It's still going to be too hot," I said.

"Trust me," he repeated. He put the fan on a timer, so that it came on automatically. The temperature usually dropped considerably after the sun set, and the fan sucked out the hot air and drew in cooler air through the open window. By bedtime, the bedroom was cool. It was not ice-truck cold like it would be with the air conditioner going, but it was pleasant enough. It seemed a little primitive to me, but it would be significantly cheaper than running the air all day in an empty room, just so it was cool enough when we finally went up there to sleep.

"Sleeping under an air conditioner is bad for the respiratory system," Tom said. "*Really bad.*"

"You smoke too much to worry about your respiratory system," I replied.

He looked at me in surprise. "Why compound it if I don't have to? We're gonna live forever, remember?"

FIFTY-NINE

I was sitting up, cursing the birds, when Tom said, "I'm going to run to the store. You want eggs for breakfast?"

Every time he leapt out of bed, talking about making breakfast, *every time*, I was again amazed at my incredible luck. "Eggs sound great," I said. I watched him step into his jeans and shrug into a shirt. He rolled up the sleeves and smiled at me.

"I'll be right back," he said.

"Kiss me first, before you go," I replied.

SIXTY

Tom surprised us all by cooking salmon for lunch. He ate a leftover steak.

Sam looked at him is disbelief. "This is the best salmon I've ever had!" he exclaimed.

"I said I didn't eat it. I didn't say I didn't know how to cook it. I come from a long line of fish eaters, but if I can help it, I will never eat another . . ." Tom paused. A back-up warning beeper was sounding harshly in the street. Tom looked at Sam.

"That would be Artie," Sam said. He stuffed the last bite of salmon into his mouth and the two of them hurried out to the street.

Artie turned out to be a tow-truck driver. Tom and Sam waved him around to the driveway at the back of the house, but Artie parked on the street anyway. The wrecker was too wide for the driveway. Maxine and I stood in the yard and watched with interest as the newest episode of the what-the-hell-had-Tom-come-up-with-this-time show unfolded.

Artie was a short bull of a man, balding, with the remainder of his hair tied in a pony tail. His eyebrows reminded me of wooly-bear caterpillars. He wore an immaculate blue uniform, and I imagined that this must be his first stop of the day for it to still be so clean. The shirt was short sleeved, and I could see that his arms were mottled black from the elbows down. This bothered neither Sam nor Tom. Both enthusiastically shook hands with Artie and slapped him on the back. I watched as they unloaded several large, heavy, chipped and rusted steel components. I could still almost make out the red paint through the age and wear. I sighed.

"What is that thing?" Maxine asked.

"That's called a cherry picker, Max."

"They're going to climb trees, now?"

"No. Not that kind of cherry picker. It's an engine hoist."

The trio had the ancient hoist assembled now. An engine was strapped down on its side in the wrecker, looking puny and naked without its car around it. Tom undid the straps, and they chained it to the cherry picker and lifted it off the wrecker.

"This is not going to be a clean hobby," I said to Max as I noticed oil dripping out of the corner of the engine.

The three of them pushed the cherry picker up the driveway, the filthy engine swinging gently back and forth. They had a little bit of trouble getting it across the short unpaved portion between the end of the drive and the shed, but after a little effort, they succeeded in shoving the whole thing inside.

The three of them came over, and Tom told Artie to sit down at the table in the garden, said that he would be right back. Artie smiled at me. He had no front teeth. In a refined, cultured voice, so out of sync with his appearance, he said, "You must be Liz. I've heard so much about you." He looked at Max and identified her, also.

I felt like I was at some kind of surreal garden party. Instead of the Mad Hatter, I felt like I might be sitting next to the Mad Mechanic. I asked, "And how do you know Tom, Artie?"

Before he could reply, Tom reappeared. He set a sizzling plate of salmon in front of Artie, and handed him a knife and a fork and one of my best linen napkins. The feeling of unreality was intensified when Artie took the napkin and stuck it into the front of his shirt with one apparently permanently grease-stained hand.

Tom said to me, "We have lunch at *Paul's* a lot."

I took this to be any explanation for Artie's bib. Then I looked back at Tom in astonishment. *Paul's* was the most expensive restaurant in town. This greasy pit-bull of a man with no front teeth was a gourmet? I watched him saw into the salmon, one pinky extended, and again I thought I might be in the *Twilight Zone*. Sam and Tom both watched expectantly as Artie chewed.

"Well?" Tom asked at last. "How is it?"

Artie made the French finger-kissing gesture, and I exchanged looks with Maxine. Where did Tom find these people?

I asked him again, "How do you know Tom, Artie?"

Artie held up one finger to indicate that his mouth was full. Tom spoke for him. "I located a bunch of engine manuals for him on the internet."

"Impossible to find," Artie said at last.

Tom smiled at me and shook his head, almost imperceptibly. "Just had to Google it, my friend."

Artie chewed another bite of salmon before replying. "Whatever. I'm not too good with computers."

"What did you bring us, Artie?" Sam asked.

"It's a '98 Subaru Outback. Double overhead cam." Artie watched Tom and Sam grin at each other, then also grinned. "Knock yourself out, boys. Have fun."

SIXTY-ONE

Once every other month or so, Tom would either cook a fabulously complicated gourmet dinner for us and Artie, or the five of us would go to *Paul's*. I could tell that the mechanic was a regular there, because only the other customers stared at him. The wait staff treated him like any of their other snooty clientele. Not long after, Artie would drop off another engine for Tom and Sam to dissect, and they would give him the previous one to dispose of. Sometimes, it would be reassembled; more often, it would be in a couple of grease-stained cardboard boxes.

Tom and Sam were not really building engines in the shed. They were mostly just taking them apart and putting them back together again. When I went out there to see what they were doing, I was always subjected to combustion engine dissertations that I could not possibly care less about before I was able to make my escape. Artie brought them all kinds, the weirder the better: pancake motors, rotary engines, old two stroke motorcycle engines. They even had a headless outboard motor in there once.

Tom liked to take them apart. He liked to clean the crud off the worn-out cams and crankshafts and rods and pistons with little metal brushes and study them. Sam liked to put them back together again. When they were finished, the motors didn't run. The two of them didn't expect them to run. It would have been really too much trouble to make them run anyway; they would have needed to provide fuel and a spark. Making them run was not the point. The whole adventure was just an exercise in the enjoyment of seeing how things worked.

Tom wallowed in the filthiness of the whole endeavor. He'd get oil on his face, in his hair, all over his clothes. Not to mention getting saturated from the elbows down in it. He didn't mind it one bit. For most of the rest of that summer, Tom's beautiful hands were seldom clean. They were always caked with engine grease, stained with old oil, the pink nail beds blushing at the filthiness of the black crescents of his fingernails.

I went out there once to fetch him inside, after Sam had gone home. I opened the door and he turned around and smiled at me. "This is the coolest thing, Liz. Check it out."

He gestured for me to come closer, to give him my hand. I held it out and he took my wrist, leaving a black thumbprint on either side.

"Okay. Do this." He stuck his thumb and two fingers into a little metal bowl half full of fresh motor oil. Then he rubbed them together. I hesitated for a moment, then followed suit.

"What do you feel?" he asked.

I looked at the thick tan fluid running over my fingers and thumb, rubbed them together. I looked back at him. "I don't feel anything, Tom." *I feel a little stupid, maybe,* I thought.

"Okay, stick your other hand in this one." He pointed at the oil pan from one of his old engines. It was caked and smeared with the grease and road dirt of however many hundreds of thousands of miles.

"Like this." He wiped his fingers across the bottom of the inside of the oil pan, held his hand up and rubbed his fingers together. The old motor oil, black as tar, ran slowly down his palm and dripped onto the floor. I did as he did.

Tom closed his eyes. "Okay, what do you feel now?"

I rubbed my fingers together. The used oil felt gritty, sharp, sandy. "It's dirty," I said.

Tom opened his eyes. "Isn't that the coolest thing?"

I blinked stupidly at him. "What?"

"You can actually feel the dirt in the oil." He ran his fingers along the bottom of the oil pan again "You can't see it, but you can feel it. That's why engines wear out. All that dirt scours the parts."

"What is so cool about that?" I asked, looking for something to wipe my hands on.

I watched Tom fondly touch a camshaft that was lying on the workbench. He ran his finger over the rougher metal; rubbed the smooth surface of one of the cams with his thumb. It was like a caress.

He shrugged. "I don't know. I just like to fuck around with the insides. Stick my hands in the oil. Feel the texture of the metal, the sand and dirt in there. I like to take them apart, *feel* how all the parts mesh together. It's awesome."

How odd *he is,* I thought again. He sounded almost like he was talking about a woman, instead of a filthy old engine that would never run, never *mesh,* again.

"I bet you'd like to work on one of those virgin-clean race car engines," I said and moved closer to him. "No grit in that oil. Metal all shiny. Oil like honey." I dipped my fingers idly into the bowl of clean oil again.

Tom stuck his fingers up to the knuckle in the oil pan again, then rubbed them together. "I don't know. This one has some personality. You can tell it's been somewhere." He gave me that little half smile.

"You don't have a whole lot of use for virgins, do you?"

147

Before I thought to stop him, Tom put his palm on my cheek, drew me to him, and kissed me. I could feel the grit on my skin, could smell the ancient petroleum stink of the dirty oil. He put his other hand on the side of my neck, caressed my cheek with his thumb like he had the smooth metal of the camshaft, leaving another black streak on my face. I ran my hand up the side of his face, smearing it with clean motor oil.

This went on for some time. Finally we emerged from the shed, looking like chimney sweeps. I smiled at him and said, "Now I know where the term *grease monkey* comes from."

He tilted his head at me. "I haven't heard that one."

"Wait till you look in a mirror. You won't even have to Google it."

SIXTY-TWO

While he still climbed the stairs to feed the fish and harvest the aquaponic vegetables, Tom never stayed at his little apartment for more than a few minutes at a time anymore. The fridge was empty, the big TV dark, his treasures dusty. Every now and then, I would get nostalgic for his big soft bed with its tie-back brocade curtain, and we would spend the night there together. It was always a little like a pilgrimage to me, returning to that tiny room, the place where I'd first discovered to my delighted surprise just how amazing he was. But Tom never slept there by himself anymore. He was always at my house, which I'd begun to think of as *our house.*

And that was deliciously okay with me. Besides being Mr. Right in his own right, Tom was also the perfect roommate: he cooked, he picked up after himself, did all the yard work, fixed things. And of course there was absolutely nothing I enjoyed better than curling up and falling asleep next to him every night.

Besides, my television was bigger than his, and Tom liked him some television. As the summer wore on, I became a bemused witness to his strangely eclectic preferences. He didn't sit in front of it for hours at a time, but when he decided that there was something playing that he wanted to see, Tom watched television with the avidness of a fat kid bound to the couch by bullies and childhood obesity. If the internet was his source for popular culture information, television was his source for popular culture entertainment. It was his window to all the aspects of the world that he'd not yet seen, he told me.

But his tastes were a mixed bunch.

He would make a salad or light a cigarette and settle in to watch anything about any ancient civilization, the more remote or lost to the sands of time, the better. It didn't matter if it was a documentary about Atlantis, or an Indiana Jones movie, or *King Solomon's Mines*; Tom could entirely suspend disbelief for a good archaeological yarn.

Also along these same lines, he would watch anything about history, mythology or religion. *Anybody's* history, mythology or religion. I learned all about those people in India that worship rats; the Mormon practice of baptizing the dead; *Kaparot*, the practice of transferring one's sins onto a chicken; and various and sundry other bloody or otherwise just damn strange religious practices from around the world.

But Tom was interested in religion only in the abstract sense, in an *informational* sense. Actual religious programming, shouting preachers and hand-clapping choirs, or anything that even remotely touched on any religion as if it was – you will pardon the pun – *the gospel truth*, immediately annoyed Tom. He was not easily annoyed, but catching the faithful and their leaders on television qualified, and he changed the channel immediately, every time.

I knew he could quote the Bible extensively: he was always dropping a psalm or verse on Maxine, usually when she least wanted to hear anything of that nature, which was undoubtedly what amused him. I believed half of the fun of their lives was fucking with each other. The devil can quote scripture, too, it's been said, so I knew that this ability didn't make him a believer. And the swiftness with which he changed channels on the believers confirmed it for me.

Tom was also bored entirely with politics or political commentary or political comedy. He wouldn't listen for even a second to any kind of protest, or hippies whining about the environment in general or global warming in particular, or the plight of the Third World. "They'll catch up," was his only comment on that thorny issue.

Nor would he sit still for *Ghost Hunters* or anything even remotely paranormal. Haunting was simply not dreamt of in his philosophy. He was convinced that there was nothing incorporeal left behind when we died. And if there was, he was just as sure that such an aspect would not in any way desire to hang around on this plane.

It amused me to think that so diverse a group – preachers and protestors and hippies and clairvoyants – would be surprised to find themselves all lumped in together, and even more surprised when they were all summarily dismissed as bullshit.

He didn't watch true crime stories, what my mother called *murder shows*, tales of passion and deceit, cheating husbands and wives offing their spouses for no other reason than the belief that they could get away with it. He accepted man's inhumanity to man, but had no interest in wallowing in true stories about it.

But he could get into any account about a bank robbery or a jewel theft or an art heist, whether true or imagined. *The Thomas Crowne Affair* was one of his favorites.

Tom actually fell asleep if I would put on anything about nature. The glories of the national parks or the Serengeti or the rainforests literally *put him to sleep*. But he would snap awake again if there was something on about *cryptozoology*, such as a search for Bigfoot or the Montauk Monster or Chupacabra. Animals that *were* bored him, whereas animals that *might be* intrigued him.

He never missed a *How It's Made*, or a *Mythbusters,* if it was about physics or they were blowing stuff up. He loved travel shows, unless

150

they were about visiting natural wonders. Tom was Anthony Bourdain's biggest fan, because ol' Tony was a great cook, just like Tom was; and he was a world traveler, like Tom wanted to be. And Tony never failed to demonstrate gleefully how much he relished being an eater and a drinker and a traveler. He was just as unapologetic about his enjoyment of his vices as Tom was.

Tom was ambivalent about basketball, but the mere mention of golf or baseball would send him into entirely delightful giggles. He considered golf and baseball right up there with underwear in their ridiculousness. He liked boxing, but not MMA, deeming it graceless. Since he'd been to the drag races, he was totally turned off by the sterility of watching auto racing on TV, because he couldn't feel it or smell it, or even really hear it.

When he discovered the horseracing channel, he just looked at me and said, "Really? This rates its own *channel?*" until I told him that he could bet money on it online. The idea of gambling on a bunch of big animals running around in an oval suddenly piqued his interest. He liked harness racing best. Trotters were so much better to him than regular thoroughbreds, because there was a truck involved (it pulled the gate away from the contestants), and they had drivers instead of jockeys, and little wheeled buggies called sulkies. Simple machines, but machines, nonetheless.

This blending of animal and man and machine fascinated him. Then I got a *Would ya look at that,* and an eyeful of disturbing You Tube videos showing flying horses and disintegrating sulkies. Ever curious, Tom had Googled *harness racing accidents.*

He lost a significant chunk of change in one afternoon betting on the races, but before I had time to worry that he might become a compulsive gambler, his interest waned. There were too many other things on.

Tom loved *Star Trek*, especially the original series, and any really ancient science fiction, like the old black and white *Buck Rogers* and *Flash Gordon* from the late thirties. But the juggernaut that was *Star Wars* left him unmoved.

And Tom loved movies. He said that he enjoyed being immersed in a different world for two hours. He said that a movie, of whatever genre, made him feel as though he could forget who he was. It made him feel that he was an actual bystander to the story. I said that was precisely the point. I could never hope to achieve his level of absorption, however. Tom allowed himself to become completely captivated by his movies, while any inconsistency or unlikelihood always popped me right back out into real life.

He gave them all a whirl: comedies and horror movies, dramas and period pieces. He enjoyed the effect on his emotions – the ridiculousness or the fear or the seriousness or the history. He was fond of violent adventure movies – think anything with Bruce Willis in it, because he could actually *feel* the adrenaline. Yet he found Tarantino over the top, violent just for the sake of being violent. He loved a good mechanized war movie. He could take or leave westerns.

But the kind of movies that Tom absolutely dug the most were romances. Personally, I don't like romances, for just the reason that he enjoyed them so thoroughly. I don't like my heartstrings tugged, don't like my emotions to be toyed with by fictional characters and situations. Life is sad enough without having to feel for imaginary people.

But I sat through all of them with him. The sad ones: *Casablanca* and *Gone With the Wind* and *West Side Story*. And *The Way We Were* and *Love Story*. I think he was the only person on the planet that thought *Sunset Boulevard* was a tragic love story. Yet, to Tom, *A Streetcar Named Desire* wasn't a love story at all.

"A study in human brutality," was his only comment.

Titanic had a tragic love story *and* massive machinery, and I was sure I caught him wiping away a little tear at the end of that one.

I also had to endure the happy ones, but it was all a first time thing for me, because I had up to that point successfully avoided *When Harry Met Sally*, and *Sleepless in Seattle*, and *The Princess Bride*, and *50 First Dates*, and (Jesus wept) some execrable fluff called *Along Came Polly*.

Tom was possessed of a completely sentimental, idealistic love-conquers-all streak which I could not ken. The movies he liked best were just so sappy to me, so pandering to the happily ever after ideal. No couple is ever that happy, I thought, that perfect for each other.

Then I looked at him and thought about much I loved him, how desperately, how completely I loved him. How ridiculously beyond all belief was my love for him. And I considered that maybe *we* were that happy together. I immediately stopped making fun of his fondness for love stories.

SIXTY-THREE

When I stopped by *Old Town* on the second of August to visit Maxine, out of the blue, she asked me if she and Sam could come over on Sunday to watch the kickoff of the NFL pre-season on the big TV. It was the Hall of Fame Game, she explained, the Cowboys vs. the Dolphins.

I said, "Of course," and she rubbed her hands together gleefully.

"It's going to be so awesome on your giant TV!"

"I didn't know you were a fan, Max." I was surprised again by the truth of the expression *you learn something new every day*. Who'd a thunk it?

"Oh, yeah. I love me some football, Liz. It's the only sport I can stand, actually. It's like all my sportiness is used up in just that one. What about you?"

I told her that I had been a football fan on and off over the years, usually commensurate with the tastes of whatever man I'd been dating. "I love a good game, but to me, watching one alone is like drinking alone. It's just sad. So, when there's no man around, I don't usually follow." I said again, "I'd never have figured *you* for a football fan, though, Max."

"Oh, yeah. Whistle to whistle, my friend."

"Funny that I never heard about this before."

Maxine shrugged. "It doesn't usually come up in girl talk. Nice dress, girlfriend; how 'bout dem Raiders? See? It doesn't go together. Does Tom like football?"

"I guess we'll find out."

SIXTY-FOUR

It turned out that Tom was ambivalent toward football. He echoed my own sentiment, that it was something that was no fun to watch by one's self. And since Tom was not even remotely the bro type, he'd never even seen the inside of a sports bar.

But when Sam and Max showed up and turned an otherwise forgettable exhibition game into a drunken, screaming party, Tom caught their enthusiasm like a cold. By halftime, he was already on the phone ordering the *Sunday Ticket*. If it was something that the four of us could enjoy together, he was down.

SIXTY-FIVE

Like some debutante retiring her whites, on Labor Day, Tom dutifully retrieved his long coat from the dry cleaners, where he'd left it since spring. It was still too hot to wear it during the day, but the nights would start to cool off soon enough.

On the autumnal equinox, he made hot apple cider, complete with allspice, cinnamon, cloves and nutmeg. And of course, rum. I hadn't used the fireplace in the living room for years, but he insisted on building a raging fire, even though it was still a little warm out for such things. We opened the windows so it wasn't like a furnace in there, and settled in with blankets and pillows on the floor in front of it, and did the same wonderful things that we'd enjoyed on the vernal equinox. I couldn't help but agree with Tom: this *was* the very best way to mark the change of the season.

SIXTY-SIX

As Halloween approached, Tom became musing, pondering; quieter than usual. We were walking home from work in the gathering dusk one evening, and I mentioned his uncharacteristic contemplation. "What's on your mind?" I asked him.

He tilted his head at me, as if I'd noticed something about him that he'd not himself noticed. Then he shrugged, noncommittal. "The year is dying, my love. It's harvest time," he reflected. "Winter impends. The death of all life."

How dramatic he can be, I thought. Nothing much died in Southern California in the winter. Unless we had a frost, and that only killed a few overly ambitious tropical plants, and even then, usually not permanently. The weather was the main reason that I continue to live here. There are really only two seasons: gloriously, stupefyingly hot or mildly, annoyingly cold. If you blinked, you missed anything that might be called the transition seasons of spring and autumn. But the blazing summers were far more likely to kill you than the winters.

Tom said, "Now is the time when mankind is confronted with his own mortality. Now is the time that he begins to bargain with death. Since the days have started to get colder, I can't seem to stop thinking about all these death-related cultural aspects."

"Bargain with death?" I repeated.

He gestured at all the pumpkins on the doorsteps of the houses on our street. "Halloween. All Hallow's Eve. The next day is called All Hallows, or All Saints' Day. It's really about more than little kids begging for candy. In the Christian canon, it's a day for the commemoration of the deceased faithful; in some churches, the departed are remembered specifically, by name. The feast day was ordained by Pope Gregory, for *all the just made perfect who are at rest throughout the world.*

"Halloween also has roots in the pagan observations of Samhain and Lemuria. In addition to being harvest festivals, on these days, the malevolent and restless spirits of the dead were propitiated." He gestured at our neighbor's yard, with its tombstones and animatronic monsters. "Ghosts, goblins. Halloween is about negotiating with death, Liz. Trying to get the dead to leave us alone."

I knew that Tom had no use for ghosts. I asked him softly, "What do you think happens after we die?"

"Are you asking me if I believe in heaven or hell? *The undiscover'd country from whose bourn no traveler returns?*"

I nodded.

He sighed, again uncharacteristically. "Humanity fears the unknown of an afterlife, because the majority of religions have invented an all-seeing God to judge what the faithful have done in *this* life. Jesus is coming, and is he pissed." He grinned a little, then sobered again. "Damn near everyone is made to feel sinful about something, sometime during their life. Religious dogma regarding sin and morality, and what a frowning God has in store for you after you die is pervasive here; it's inescapable. Even if you don't believe in it, you still *know* about it. You still have an occasional thought about it."

He again quoted Hamlet. "*For in that sleep of death, what dreams may come when we have shuffled off this mortal coil, must give us pause.* People fear what may come after death, because they fear an eternal punishment for the real or imagined transgressions that they may or may not have committed. Hellfire and pain, forever." He shook his head. "It makes no sense. How can you feel pain if you're dead?"

"What about heaven?"

"A belief in heaven allows you to be your brother's keeper. You're so good and wonderful and are going to heaven, so you want to make sure your brother toes the line and gets to go too. It allows people to have a feeling of superiority about their own imagined goodness; allows them to feel they have the right to instruct others in the true path. *And if requiring fail, they will compel.*" He fell silent and looked at me, seeming to be a little self-conscious about all this sudden seriousness.

I asked him again, "What do you think happens after we die?"

He considered me in silence for a long moment. "Where I come from, we think of ourselves as members of what could be considered a great big hive. Life is very easy, and therefore, there isn't a lot of hope that things may be a lot better after we die, or fear that they may be a lot worse. Everything is okay now, and it'll be okay later.

"So the prevalent belief is that when one dies, one's essence, one's energy, one's *spirit*, for lack of a better word, simply melds with the greater energy, the greater nothingness of all the others that have died before. There is no reward, no punishment. Just an anonymous blending of energy. Peaceful oblivion. I guess you could say that they believe that when one dies, one simply becomes one with the universe, another particle in the great void."

"But that's not what you believe."

"No. Not anymore." He lit a cigarette, exhaled smoke. "To me, their philosophy has become almost as menacing as the threat of some

157

physical pain. I now believe that there *is* a reward or punishment once we die, but it's not based on adherence to or violation of any prevailing morality of the moment. The only reward after death is to be reunited with the one we loved in life, in whatever form we might take, energy or light or whatever. The only punishment is to be deprived of that other person, that other energy. To me, it *would be punishment* to become, indeed, just another undifferentiated particle, instead of again existing as one half to that whole that you were in life, with that other person."

"So your philosophy could be said to be completely at odds with what everyone else believes? Where you come from?"

He shrugged. "I guess you could put it that way."

I thought I saw a breakthrough in our relationship looming; I thought that he might finally be going to open up about his upbringing. I said, "Is that why you left? Because you didn't agree with what everybody else believes?"

Tom grinned then, that same old delicious killer smile, and it was like the sun scattering thunderheads. Whatever blue mood he might have entertained was instantaneously vaporized.

He shook his head. "I left because I wanted to have fun, Liz." He looked at me with that familiar curious expression again. "Hell, I didn't even have a philosophy of an afterlife until I came here. To tell you the truth, I was rather underdeveloped in a lot of ways, philosophically speaking. I've expanded my perceptions of life exponentially since my arrival in your little town.

"I've kind of just discovered this idea of an afterlife since I've been here, sort of drew my own conclusions. Now I believe that whoever makes us happy in life must also be there to share in our happiness after life."

That was a simple enough philosophy, I thought. "You were freaking me out a little bit with all this talk about death and bargaining with death and the great void," I told him.

"Ah, I'm sorry, Liz. I've just been feeling a little pity for mankind's fear of death and a possibly unkind afterlife, since it's started to get colder, since the days are getting shorter. I was just thinking that when the nights are longer and colder, it's easier for people to fear what might come next. That fear – it's the one outgrowth of mankind's history that I find truly unfortunate, lately."

"Because you have the ideal *don't worry, be happy* attitude?"

"I believe implicitly in the philosophy of an afterlife that I've developed since I came here. Besides, we're gonna live forever. Or at least for a very long time."

I smiled at Tom's resurrected smile, as I'd always been powerless not to do. He put his arm around my waist, and all dark thoughts were forgotten.

SIXTY-SEVEN

Tom and Maxine decided that they would team up to cook Thanksgiving dinner. Preliminaries were squared away before the Lions game started at nine-thirty; dishes were all settled in and starting to cook right before the Cowboys game commenced at one twenty-five; thanks had been given, and the excellent meal consumed and already cleared away by the time the prime-time game came on at five-twenty.

In other words, the holiday was all about the football at our house this year. Football and drinking and yelling at the seventy-two inch flat screen television. The meal was secondary.

It delighted me to observe the strengthening of Tom and Sam's friendship since that weekend in Havasu. There was none of the feigned disrespect that one might expect from two so different in age. They were like brothers. They picked up each other's bad habits: Sam started smoking, and Tom affected wearing a baseball hat backwards. I thought it looked adorably ridiculous on him.

I walked in on conversations between them that died suddenly at my appearance, so I suspected that Sam still occasionally consulted Tom for *pointers*. Or maybe they were just talking about sex in general, or women in general, or Maxine and me in particular. Whatever the specifics, I was convinced that whenever they stopped talking abruptly and looked at me innocently, this was indeed the subject matter under discussion.

Women had the same kind of conversations with their girlfriends, and I believed that these kinds of things should be kept separate. I never asked Tom what they'd been talking about when they'd both clam up so quickly. I was pretty sure that if I asked him, he'd give me the unvarnished truth. And just as when he would say, "Would ya look at that," about something on the internet, I was pretty sure I didn't really want to know any specific details about what they were talking about. In fact, I was *completely* sure of it. Grandma had always told me to make sure I really wanted to hear the answer before I asked the question. So I didn't ask. A little mystery was enjoyable.

Tom and Sam had a mutual respect for each other's knowledge of cars and motors and boats and bikes and anything that was fast and loud. And if I imagined that Sam might still defer to Tom's been-around-the-block knowledge about the opposite sex, Tom definitely deferred to Sam's encyclopedic knowledge of football. Tom understood the rules and penalties and stuff like that, but since he'd only really started paying attention to the game this season, he counted on Sam to provide tales about how much tougher it used to be in the old days; to give hushed, awed descriptions of historic great plays; to tell stories of the team dynasties of yesteryear.

They enjoyed the violence of football as only men can, although I doubted either of them had ever taken a tackle in their lives. Sam was too slight of build, and Tom had apparently only recently escaped from whatever weird religious compound he was from.

When they would jump up and scream at the TV at the same moment, or exuberantly high five each other, Maxine would make some remark about our having created a monster when we introduced them. But she was actually just as delighted at their friendship as I was. It was a rare and wonderful thing when two women could even stand being around each other's boyfriends, let alone actually *enjoy* their company. Maxine loved Tom, and I found Sam to be a clever and intelligent, thoughtful young man, who treated Maxine like the queen she was. Rare indeed.

SIXTY-EIGHT

For the third year in a row, I celebrated Maxine's birthday with her. Tom had announced that he'd be treating us to dinner at *Paul's* this year. Not only was it Maxine's birthday, he said, it was also the one year anniversary of the first time he and I had met, as well as the sixth month anniversary of the first time Maxine and Sam had met. Only the best restaurant in town would due for such a multi-faceted celebration.

"How do you remember this shit?" Maxine asked him.

"You guys went out for the first time the day before the summer solstice, Max, don't you remember? And your birthday is on the winter solstice this year. That's six months.

"Come to think of it, your birthday was also on the winter solstice last year." He looked at me. "Except somehow, marking the solstice slipped my mind last year."

I wrapped my arm around his waist. "You were too concerned that the world was going to end to worry about the solstice last year."

"The world was supposed to end because it *was* the solstice. And I knew that the world wasn't going to end, solstice or not. So it couldn't have been that. Must've been something else." He kissed me lightly and smiled.

SIXTY-NINE

While we were getting ready for our glamorous, dressed-up night at the finest restaurant in town, and the men were out of earshot, Maxine reflected on what a long way we'd come since her twenty-first birthday.

"Look how respectable we are!" she said and grinned evilly, not respectably at all. "I've had the same boyfriend for six months, and you, for *a whole year!* That has got to be some kind of record!"

The dinner was excellent, but I got the impression that Tom and Sam were in collusion to get it over with as soon as possible. I didn't want to reflect on how late I'd stayed up on her twenty-first birthday (nor did I want to reflect on what I'd been doing), and Maxine and Tom had closed the bar on her twenty-second birthday the year before. But at the impossibly early hour of eight forty-five, this year, the four of us had already concluded dinner and were standing outside of the restaurant on the sidewalk. Tom kissed Maxine on the forehead and wished her happy birthday, high fived Sam, and they went their way and we went ours.

Sometimes the most memorable revels are conducted between two people alone.

SEVENTY

The *Ancient Aliens* Marathon was scheduled to start at ten o'clock in the morning on Christmas Eve this year, instead of on New Year's Day. As far as this scheduling change was concerned, I imagined that the network probably thought that, since people would be winking at the impossibility of Santa visiting the homes of every child on earth that evening, they might also be willing to entertain *Ancient Aliens'* own special brand of fairy stories during the day. Perhaps the television executives realized that people were less amenable to being gulled on New Year's Day; they were less likely to buy outrageous extraterrestrial theories when they were hungover.

Maxine had hit the party supply store a few days before, and purchased Roswell themed party favors. She made some kind of delightfully sweet yet healthy cupcakes from a recipe Tom had given her, and stuck little plastic aliens and spaceships in them. Tom made Irish coffee, declaring that he couldn't sit through an entire day of *Ancient Aliens* sober. Sam was unable to attend the gala event because his kid sister had been taken in for an emergency appendectomy in the wee hours of the morning, and he found himself spending the day with his family at the hospital.

But an unforeseen event occurred when Maxine and I and Tom (still protesting) sat down to watch the first episode. When Max hit the power button on the remote, she got only the DirecTV logo, and some message about a lost signal. After pushing many other buttons and following many directions, after checking all wires and connections, and even after making a phone call to a very harassed sounding woman who said she was in Mississippi, it was determined that someone would have to come out and look at our set-up before the TV would work again.

"Did ya'll have some wind recently?" the woman in Mississippi asked. "It appears that your dish might have shifted." She made a service appointment for me for the day after Christmas, said she was sorry for the inconvenience, and hung up.

Maxine pouted. She said to Tom, "Can't you go up on the roof and make some measurements and point the dish in the right direction? Like when you did the *hierophany?*"

Tom blinked at her in surprise. "That involved the sun, Max. I knew where the sun was going to be." He gestured upward. "The sun is big. *Ubiquitous.* I have no idea where the satellite is. It's . . . invisible."

"Well, hell," Maxine said in disappointment. "Can we go to your place and watch it there?"

He shook his head. "I had the cable shut off there months ago, Max." He again gestured upward. "My TV's upstairs now."

It was in my bedroom, taking up an entire wall. I thought, not for the first time, that if we ever got burglarized, the thieves would think that they'd hit the jackpot indeed, when they discovered not one but two giant screen televisions in one little modest downtown home. We checked and discovered that the cable was out upstairs, too.

Then Tom said, "All might not be lost, Max." He picked up a cupcake and removed the little plastic flying saucer. "I have a little story that I've been thinking of – about all this *Ancient Aliens* crap." He removed the paper from the cupcake and ate it in two bites.

"Are you thinking about becoming a writer, now?" Maxine replied. "You could sell your own book in your own bookstore." She brightened a little at how convenient that would be.

"I'm really just more of a storyteller, Max. I don't know if I'd ever write any of it down. It's just since you guys have been subjecting me to *Ancient Aliens*, I've been thinking up a little story that would explain it all. Kind of tie up the loose ends, eliminate some of the inconsistencies, like that. A sort of history. About how it actually might have been. What do you think? Do you want to hear it? I know I'm not Giorgio, but he's kinda trapped on the invisible satellite right now, and can't beam down."

I could just listen to the sound of Tom's voice and be happy. It was music to me, if he was reading the phone book, so I was down. Maxine nodded; she also liked to listen to Tom talk, and it was better than no *Ancient Aliens* at all.

Tom retrieved a fresh, unopened pack of cigarettes from his coat pocket and tossed it onto the coffee table. He sat down on the couch, and sipped his coffee, no doubt composing his thoughts for the recitation of this story. When he went to reach for his cigarettes, Maxine snatched them up first.

"Now I want you to watch carefully, Tom."

With slow, exaggerated movements, Maxine grasped the little tab between her thumb and forefinger, holding the other three fingers up as if she were holding a delicate tea cup. She gently tugged, removing the top half of the cellophane. Then she delicately folded back the top of the box and tugged out the foil. She pulled out a cigarette with her fingernails and handed it to him, then closed the box and tossed it back onto the table.

"See how easy that is? You just have to do it slowly."

Tom lit his cigarette, grinned at her through a cloud of smoke. "Thanks, Max. Now you just have to always be on hand to open all my Power Bars. And cereal boxes." He looked at me. "Potato chip bags."

"You don't eat potato chips," I said. He shuddered.

"Don't you use the scissors on your Swiss Army knife?" Maxine asked. "And then just put everything in Tupperware like I told you?"

"Yeah, I use the scissors. But not the Tupperware." Tom wrinkled his nose. We didn't own any Tupperware. "I don't like plastic for food storage, Max. It's not as stable as you think it is. It leaches into things. But I did want to let you know that I've finally mastered that can opener." He winked at her.

When I looked at him in surprise, he smiled and said, "I'm just kidding, Liz. You know that I can use a can opener. A can opener is just a machine, after all, is it not? You know how much I like machines."

Tom put his cigarette down in the ashtray and said, "Okay." He splayed his hands out in front of him, imitating a movie director. "First, I want you to picture the other planet. No need to stretch the imagination too much — it's a place a lot like this one: same kind of atmosphere, same gravity, stuff like that. A little warmer maybe. But so much like Earth, in fact, perhaps it would be easier to describe it *as Earth*, just reconfigured a little, geographically. An almost parallel evolution occurred there, producing parallel species. Some just got the chance to evolve a little bit further there than they did here, and one species evolved in a different direction, but I'll get to them in a minute. They would become the dominant species on this other Earth.

"So imagine if our Earth, instead of breaking up into the continents that we have today, through tectonic movement and all the grinding ages of time — imagine, if instead, there were only two major continents. Let's say that one of them was similar to North America and South America, like the Western Hemisphere, say. The shape doesn't matter, really. If it helps you to picture it, just imagine one vast continent, just like our North and South America, stretching nearly from pole to pole. This is where the Dino People dwelt." He picked up his cigarette.

Maxine unconsciously mimicked Tom's tilted head gesture at the cartoonish name. "Dino People?"

Tom squinted at her through a cloud of smoke. "You don't like Dino People? How about Reptile People?"

"Reptile People? I don't think I like that, either."

"How about Herp People? Like *herpetology*, the study of reptiles and amphibians?"

Maxine shook her head. "No, that sounds like an STD. Go with Dino People."

"As you wish." Tom smiled at us and continued. "So, on the Western Hemisphere of this planet so much like the Earth," he gestured with his left hand, the one with the cigarette in it, "on this hemisphere, live the Dino People. Now, I want you to imagine what could have happened here if that comet had never hit."

"You're talking about the comet that wiped out the dinosaurs?" Maxine asked.

Tom smiled at me. "Who says this generation isn't hip?"

"They certainly don't," I replied.

"Yes, Maxine, the comet that wiped out the dinosaurs. It was an asteroid actually. But we could discuss that event itself for hours, and it's not really germane at this point. We're not talking about Earth right now.

"What do you suppose the world would be like today if that asteroid hadn't hit here? What do you suppose the world would be like if the dinosaurs hadn't been wiped out? That was what happened on this other planet."

"They had dinosaurs on this other planet?" Maxine asked.

Tom nodded.

"Does this other planet have a name?" I asked.

"Let's call it Sirius, shall we?"

"Oh, no, Tom, not Sirius," I said. "Every alien story ever told starts with Sirius. Think up some other planet, some other name. Besides, Sirius is a star." No astronomer I, but I did know that much.

"Yes, Sirius is a star, the brightest star in the night sky. There are actually two stars, a binary system, Sirius A and Sirius B. Sirius, the Dog Star, *Sopdet, Tishtrya*. What's in a name?"

"But it's not a planet," I insisted.

"This is a long story, and there are a lot of names. I'm trying to make things as simple as possible. Let's just say the planet of which we speak is in the Sirius star system, so we'll call it Sirius, *just like in every alien story ever told*," he mimicked my criticism. "Agreed?"

Maxine and I nodded.

Tom continued. "So, there were dinosaurs on the Western Hemisphere of this planet we'll call Sirius. But no asteroid ever collided with Sirius. No blotting out of the sun by dust, no vegetation die off, no mass extinction. No wiping out of the Terrible Lizards.

"So what happened instead? The dinosaurs evolved. And as you may be aware, evolution favors bigger brains and more compact sizes. Smaller, faster, smarter. No tails. So, after appropriate millennia, there were no more Terrible Lizards, no lumbering Apatosaurus, no giant-headed, giant-toothed Tyrannosaurus. Not anymore. They evolved into Dino People instead."

Tom paused for a moment to let us consider that. He snuffed out his cigarette, then continued. "They were humanoid in shape, two arms and two legs. A big head, with black, almond-shaped eyes."

Maxine grinned slyly and gestured at a cupcake with a plastic alien stuck in it. "Like a Gray?"

Tom grinned back at her. "More like a Sleestak. Big, robust, scaly. Only the babies looked like Grays."

Sleestaks were the lizard people from the 1970's era children's show *Land of the Lost*, and they were resurrected in 2009 by Will Ferrell in the movie of the same name. I found it to be hilariously funny, and I don't even like Will Ferrell's movies. But critics and fans alike panned it.

The Sleestaks were, just like Tom said, green Dino People with big black eyes. They had lots of teeth, but only two or three claw-like fingers. And they were slow.

Tom addressed these drawbacks. "The Dino People were not cumbersome like Sleestaks. They had evolved five fingers and toes." He looked thoughtfully at his large hands, those hands I loved so much. "Five fingers and toes are the perfect amount, you see. They work well with the brain." He tapped the side of his head. "The Dino People were sleek and fast. And smart. At the point in their history where I'd like to begin my story, their civilization had advanced to the point of perhaps the Dark Ages here."

I felt the need to interrupt on this point, before I could bust up at the picture of Sleestaks in Renaissance costume, the image that had sprung immediately to mind when Tom said *Dark Ages*. "So there had been a Rome and a Greece filled with Sleestaks on Sirius? And then Rome fell, and the Dark Ages commenced, and all that?" I asked, deadpan. "This is after the Golden Age of Sleestak civilization? Sleestak Egypt, Sleestak Greece, Sleestak Rome had already risen and fallen?"

Tom shook his head. "No, that's not right. No Golden Age. Let me start over. The Dino People's history was linear, a straight climb of progress. No starts and stops. No rising and falling. This was a continent wide culture, not little kingdoms and customs and different rates of development, as occurred here. No oceans separated one Dino People from another.

"At the point where I want to begin, they were somewhat primitive, in the sense that they were just above hunter-gatherers. No agriculture, no giant cities. Agriculture was not needed, because game was plentiful.

"There had not been an agricultural revolution among the Dino People, because they were not omnivorous, like primates. They were almost entirely carnivorous, like snakes. Or alligators. Suffice it to say that the continent supported a population of what we would term hunter-gatherers, but their civilization was more advanced than that. They were organized, had writing, religion, history; cities, but not large cities. They possessed nothing that we would term *technology*, in the modern sense. They had just developed a sea-faring culture on the eastern coast of the continent, and they were on the brink of setting out to explore, to conquer the other half of the world."

Tom looked at us to see if this explanation was sufficient, and Maxine and I nodded. I pictured Sleestaks on tall ships, dressed as pirates with eye patches and bandannas and peg legs. I suppressed a giggle.

"Now, a different evolution had occurred on the other continent, in the Eastern Hemisphere, if you will." Tom gestured with his right hand. "This continent was just as large as the one where the Dino People reigned, but the configuration was different. Upon this continent there existed a vast inland sea. A lake, really, fresh water — hundreds of thousands of square miles. Imagine a sea as big as the continental United States in the middle of an even larger continent. The land around this lake was marshy and swampy. Only in the sparse highlands would you find much of what you would term *dry land*. Rivers fed the sea from higher elevations, and other rivers led out into the ocean that separated the Dino People from this continent.

"Now, evolution on this continent had proceeded differently. There were no Dino People here. There hadn't even been any dinosaur *types* here, because the ground was infirm, marshy. On this continent, the dominant species was what we would have to classify as a hominid species, except that they were also amphibious, in that they spent some time on the surface of the water, or just on the banks, but most of the time under the water. They were mammals, breathed air; nursed their young, just like we do. But their cities were half sunken, they swam from place to place . . ."

"So they were mermaids?" Maxine asked.

Facepalm. Tom sighed. "Yes, for lack of a better word, they were mermaids. But that term, it's so . . . *undignified*. I prefer Fish People."

"But that isn't exactly accurate, is it?" I asked. "You said they were mammals, breathed air. That would be like calling whales or dolphins fish. Did their tails go this way?" I indicated vertically, like fish. "Or this way?" I indicated horizontally, like aquatic mammals. Tom gestured that their tails were horizontal, like a whale, just as mermaids had always been depicted.

He said, "Okay, we'll call them Mermaid People, because that's the most accurate term. Let's just dispense with all the fairy tales that we associate with mermaids, shall we? Ariel and her hoarding and all that?"

We nodded.

"Because here," Tom said firmly, a shade of that Shakespearean cast to his voice, "here was a valiant, brilliant, dignified people. And beautiful. They resembled a race of god-like human beings, with large, clear blue or gray eyes, and long, luxurious hair. The men generally wore beards. If you saw a group of them all sitting around in the pool, you might think that you had wandered into a party of Hollywood's most beautiful Beautiful People."

"Until we saw their tails?" I asked.

He nodded. "Their tails were also lovely, however. They ranged in colors from silver to blue to green to tan to brown to red. Exquisite."

"With scales and all?" Max asked. "Like a fish?"

"No, not like a fish," Tom replied. "Their skin was the same as ours. It just changed color on their tails."

Maxine and I reflected upon the beautiful Mermaid People for a moment, then Tom began again. "In the same stretch of ages that had produced only ignorant, peasant Dino People on the Western Continent, the Mermaid People had flourished on the Eastern Continent to the point where they had all the technology that humanity has on this planet. Cities, medicine. History, culture. The capacity for space travel."

Maxine smiled. "Here it comes," she said.

Tom held up his hand. "Not quite yet. Before a civilization commences with space travel, there must be a motivation for space travel. The motivation here on Earth was a certain greed, and a certain political desire from one culture to dominate another culture.

"But things were not exactly the same on Sirius. I have to explain a little about the Mermaid technology, contrast it with technology on this planet, as this difference is really the crux of so many things.

"Briefly. The first major step toward what mankind has become here on Earth started when man discovered how to work metals. After that, it was all progress. The ability to make tools out of metal defined this planet, right up until the invention of plastic."

I looked at him in surprise. "Isn't that a little simplistic, Tom? What about stone construction? Wooden ships? Concrete?"

He tilted his head at me. "It's not simplistic at all, Liz. Everything here developed based on metallurgy, either directly or indirectly.

Buildings couldn't be constructed out of stone until metal tools were invented to cut and dress it. Wooden ships got around, but once they were made out of metal? And there weren't even many long distance wooden ships before metallurgy, anyway. You need metal for rudders and stuff like that. The Romans had metallurgy, and they invented concrete. And concrete was great, but after it was reinforced with rebar? The entire Industrial Revolution was based on a prior metallurgy. And everything since the Industrial Revolution, well . . . progress has been just an onward and upward continuation of it."

I still looked skeptical.

"I'm not talking about cultural expansion, Liz. Knowledge and power and politics." He gestured with his hands, to encompass everything. "I'm talking about the basic thing that allowed everything else to happen here. First there was metallurgy. Mankind flourished. The next major leap was electricity, which has a metallurgical basis in conductivity, does it not?"

I had to admit that it did.

"And then plastics and solid state and all that, until you have this wonderful world that exists today. But none of it could've happened without metal. There was a burst of expansion after stone knives and bear skins gave way to metal tools, and that eventually led to stone construction and wooden ships and concrete. Then electricity and big giant metal machines that have given way to tiny hand-held machines. Is that not an accurate assessment of the state of the First World today?"

I nodded reluctantly.

"I have to contrast how things evolved here as opposed to how they evolved on Sirius. Mankind dragged their future kicking and screaming out of the bowels of this planet. Man transformed the Earth into his own image, mashing and bending and blowing things up. Sometimes the Earth rebelled and reasserted its dominance, like when the San Francisquito Dam failed above Los Angeles, or when the wind reclaimed the Tacoma Narrows Bridge, or a thousand, a million other engineering disasters throughout human history. My point is that mankind has always attempted to conquer the Earth, to control it. To mold it in his image."

I coughed and said, *"Hippie,"* under my breath.

Tom smiled his glorious smile, then leaned across the coffee table and kissed me. "I'm not passing judgment on human history, Liz. There've been mistakes – there continue to be mistakes. Great, horrible, cruel, greedy, just-not-right mistakes. But overall, the history of mankind is just fucking *epic*, an incredible story of the overcoming of

171

all odds to tame a basically unforgiving, uncooperative place. And through mankind's blood and sweat and tears, it's turned out to be a pretty awesome place, I must say."

"At least in the First World," I said.

Tom shrugged. "Do I not choose to live in the First World?" He dismissed the rest of the disadvantaged world with a short wave of his hand, as was his wont, and repeated his standard line on the subject. "They'll catch up someday."

Maxine smiled bitterly. She was young and keenly felt the travails of the oppressed, or at least she thought she did. She said, "Yeah, it's a great place, Earth. What with the wars and disease and poverty. And mankind is wonderful, treats his home so well, with all the horrible pollution and devastation that we have wreaked upon it, in that drive to tame it."

Tom held up his hand. "I'm not going to get into a discussion of the evils of mankind with you at this point, Max. I said that there've been mistakes. Some quite monumental. But I'm maintaining, for the moment, that mankind has come a long way since stone knives and bearskins. Mankind has done a pretty good job, when you consider that it's always been a struggle, when you understand that they've had to dig everything that they've had to work with out of the ground. Will you give me that point for a second?"

Maxine nodded.

"But an amphibious people can't do a whole lot of excavation, now can they? It takes more than upper body strength to *dig*. It takes *legs*, an ability to stand up. They possessed none of this. So the Mermaid People didn't invent metallurgy on the scale that it was utilized here. Sure, they had a few metal and even stone tools, but they were all small, handheld, delicate – the equivalent of dental tools and styluses. Maybe a few knives and little saws. But there would never be any giant smelters overflowing with red, molten steel on Sirius.

"The Mermaid People didn't pull the basic materials of First World civilization out of the ground. Not only was there never any massive metallurgy, they didn't invent plastic, or conductive electricity in the way it's known here, or even solid state." Tom paused.

We waited. At last he began again. "I want you to think of a totally alien technology. A technology based on life itself, on genetic manipulation. And before you say *hippie* again, Liz, I'm not saying that their technology is superior to ours, at least not in its basic tenets, although it is vastly superior in its scope. I just want you to imagine a technology that is organic. *Grown*, if you will, as opposed to *built*." Again he paused to let us imagine that.

172

Maxine finally said, "You're going to have to be a little bit more specific, Tom."

"Let me explain a little about genetic manipulation, then. First of all, let's not use that term. It's rather Hollywood, summoning up pictures of science gone awry too much. *Jurassic Park* and *Gattaca* and all that. Clone monsters and armies comprised of trained primates. Gorilla armies, if you will." He scratched the top of his head in parody of a monkey to indicate that he meant *gorilla* and not *guerilla*. "Let's use a more sedate term, a more accurate one. Instead of *genetic manipulation*, let's call it *biological modification*.

"Now there are three types of biological modification. The first is called *selection*."

"Like *natural selection?*" Maxine asked.

Tom smiled. "Yes, my little Darwinist, like *natural selection*. Survival of the fittest. The individuals with the characteristics most adapted to their environment live long enough to reproduce, passing on those survival benefits to the next generation. The ones that can't adapt, don't get to reproduce, die out. That's natural selection."

"That's why skunks and opossums still get hit by cars," I interjected. They both looked at me. "And cats and dogs, too. The ones that are still too dumb not to get run over still get to reproduce. If only the ones smart enough not to get run over got to reproduce, then the next generation would be smart enough not to get run over, too."

"I suppose," Tom said, unsure. "But I'm not talking about natural, Darwinian selection. I'm talking about planned, controlled selection, for the traits that someone wants in a creature. Controlled selection is how man made wolves into Chihuahuas. To not put too fine a point on it, the smallest and rattiest products of each generation were bred together until the little dog resulted.

"A common part of dog breeding is also the elimination of wolfy tendencies by breeding dogs that in their mature state still retain puppy characteristics. In make-up, they have the rounder, less pointed muzzles, like puppies; in behavior, they're less vicious. They never really grow into adults, behavior-wise.

"So, if you have one creature, and you want to create a similar one, you select the characteristics that you want and only breed the creatures with those characteristics. Then you wind up with basically the same *species*, but a different *breed*. This is a long process, taking many generations, right? And still you'll never make a dog into a cat, or a cat into a bird through selection."

"Or a mermaid into a man," I said.

173

Tom smiled, leaned over and kissed me again. Apparently, it was my reward for a correct response. "Exactly. Man has been using selective breeding since time immemorial. That's how we came to have Chihuahuas, after all.

"But the next type of biological modification is much more complicated, more modern. It's called by a rather poetic term: *transgenesis*. Since all creatures on Earth are made up of the same basic units, it's possible to take a gene from one creature and insert it into another creature. Then the new gene will be passed on to the creature's offspring.

"Through transgenesis, mankind has produced such parlor tricks as cats that glow in the dark, mice that carry human antibodies, silkworms that make spider silk. It's a difficult process, and it's made that much more difficult due to wild science fiction type speculation that secret government agencies are already producing hybrid monstrosities. Montauk Monster, anyone? Chupacabra, maybe?" Tom smiled.

"The third type of biological modification is called *atavism activation*. An atavism is an ancestral characteristic that appears unexpectedly again, such as when a person is born with a tail. Our ancestors had tails, and sometimes that gene is reactivated for some reason. Other results include snakes with legs, chickens with teeth. Genetic engineers can turn the genes on that produce these things.

"On Sirius, the ability to use all these forms of biological modification developed over the eons. Instead of a metal structured, steam and gas powered industrial revolution, they had a biological one. Eventually, the Mermaid People were able to grow whatever they needed. Buildings. Light and power sources through plasmas and bioillumination."

Tom picked up his smokes again. He tilted his head curiously at the pristine box for a second, not shredded and destroyed because Maxine had opened it for him. Again, I wondered what it was that made him have so much trouble with opening them correctly. He shook out another cigarette and lit it, then threw them back on the table and continued.

"Through the ability to manipulate the genes of various plants, and thereby to manipulate their structures, the shapes and sizes that they would eventually attain, the Mermaid People were able to grow anything they needed. To their precise specifications. Dwellings. Packaging, to protect whatever small metal and stone tools they fabricated."

"You mean, they grew some kind of vegetable-matter bubble wrap to protect their tools?" I asked.

174

"It goes like this. A certain seed starts to germinate. Then a little stone knife or a metal stylus, or whatever tool, is then inserted into the nascent fruit. Then the fruit is induced to grow around the tool, encasing it. When you needed a new tool, you can just pick it and peel it."

"Like a banana?" Max asked.

Tom nodded. "Just like that, only without the actual banana growing inside the peel. This process makes it easier to store and transport small, delicate instruments."

"The peel would just grow around the tool without the fruit part?" Max reiterated.

Tom nodded, and we just looked at him for a moment. What comment could be made about banana-peel encased tools?

Tom continued. "So, the Mermaid People had the capability to grow anything they needed. Food. Medicine. Spaceships."

Maxine squinted in disbelief. "Spaceships? Really? How does one grow a spaceship?"

"Let me see your phone, Maxine," Tom said. When she handed it to him, he unlocked it, and summoned up his name on the contacts list. "What happens when I push the button?"

"It calls you."

"How exactly does that happen, Max?" He studied her phone as if *it* was a piece of alien technology. "How exactly does this thing work, anyway?"

"I don't know exactly how it works, Tom. But I know nobody *grew* it."

"Do you?"

"That's a science fiction kind of cop out, don't you think, Tom?" I asked.

"Is it, Liz? Max can't explain how something works that she carries around in her pocket every day. That she believes she cannot live without." He handed Maxine's phone back to her. "Yet you want me to explain how a biologically modified, organically grown spaceship comes into being. I'm not an engineer."

"That's right. You're an anthropologist. You're more concerned with the social development and hierarchies of the Mermaid People than their *amazing* organic technology." I smiled at him.

He smiled back. "Indeed. And even if I could explain it, none of us would probably understand it. It has to do with first inducing a plant to grow a gigantic, fibrous, hollow shell. Something that is tough enough to withstand the rigors of intergalactic travel."

175

"Like the pods from *Invasion of the Body Snatchers?*" Maxine exclaimed. "Are your aliens gonna turn out to be pod people, Tom?"

Tom shook his head. "No, they're not that alien. They're mammals. Hominids. Primates, just like us. Arthur C. Clarke famously observed, *any sufficiently advanced technology is indistinguishable from magic.*" He gestured at Maxine's phone, then featured me with that killer smile. "Besides, this is only a story, remember? Suspend disbelief for me for a minute. On Sirius, they *grew* their technology, through biological modification. Imagine that they were all *hippies*, Liz, if that makes it easier for you. One with nature and all that."

"Mermaid hippies," Maxine said. "Growing spaceships."

"Exactly," Tom said.

"So, if everything was so wonderful there, and they grew everything they needed, what did they need spaceships for?" Max asked. "I'm assuming that there were no hardships, if housing and lights and everything was just *grown*. I assume that they ate fish and they grew any other food they needed. Why did they want to leave this natural paradise?"

"Why, indeed. Like I said, just having the technology for space travel doesn't automatically create a *need* for space travel. There has to be a motivation. You've forgotten about the Dino People."

"How could you forget about the Dino People, Max?" I asked, and winked at Tom.

"Actually, there was another factor, something similar to what may be happening here. Let me tell you about that first, then come back to the Dino People.

"You have to understand that both cultures on Sirius had unbroken histories. There had been no rises and falls of societies, no Enlightenments followed by Dark Ages, followed by new Enlightenments. Nobody burnt the Library of Alexandria on Sirius. No knowledge was lost and then needed to be rediscovered.

"So at about the time the Dino People were about to take to the sea in search of conquest, the Mermaid People ascertained that their way of life was not only endangered by this immediate threat, but by a threat that would creep up on them slowly. Sirius, you see, was drying out."

"You're telling us that Sirius had global warming?" Maxine said.

Tom nodded. "It would still be thousands of years, millennia maybe, but eventually, the giant inland lake that had spawned the Mermaid People's culture would evaporate. Their learned and scholarly figured this out from consulting their thousands of years of records.

"The seas that surrounded their continent were filled with predators and an almost toxic level of salinity. Add to this the imminent threat of an invasion by the Dino People, and it was decided that some action had to be undertaken. It was decided that it was high time for the Mermaid People to stop being the Mermaid People. It was decided that it was time for them to finally crawl up onto dry land." Tom paused, snuffed out his cigarette. "They already had the capability of flight, had possessed it for centuries. They used it to spy on the Dino People. They knew about the Dino People, you see, but the Dino People didn't know about them. Not yet."

"They had water in their grown spaceships?" Maxine asked, before I could.

"Yes. They were very heavy. And these were not spaceships, per se, that they used to spy on the Dino People. More like heavy duty aircraft.

"Dino mythology was rife with descriptions of sightings of these angelic flying beings, and godlike abilities were assigned to these unknown creatures, mostly because they were so strange and different from the Dino People themselves."

"Just like in damn near every mythology *here*," Maxine observed.

Tom nodded. "And just like in Earthly mythology, there were Dino stories of these god-like beings taking Dino People away, bringing them back."

"Just like alien abductions?" I asked.

Tom smiled. "Exactly. The truth was that the Mermaid People had indeed visited Dino villages, and had taken samples from some of the Dino People, just to see how these creatures worked. They were so very different from the hominid mermaids, so they were curious about them, you see.

"And since the Mermaid People had decided that it was time for them to conquer the dry land, before invasion and climate change made such an effort an imperative instead of a pre-emptive plan, they stepped up their tissue gathering from the Dino People. Perhaps the scaly ones could hold the key. *They* had evolved legs, had they not?

"But all the transgenesis in the world proved fruitless. It wasn't possible to hybridize a Mermaid Person with the legs of a Dino Person. There were just too many characteristics to be exhibited across species that were just too incompatible.

"So the Mermaid People tried a little atavism activation on themselves. Can you guess what happened?"

"That wouldn't work either," I replied. "If they'd always been amphibious, then there would be no genes for legs to be re-activated."

"Exactly! So what do you think the Mermaid People did?"

"They came here," Maxine said immediately, without hesitation. "They came here and got *our* DNA."

"That's it in a nutshell. Yet, it's a little more complicated than just that. Do you want to hear the whole story?"

We nodded, just like he knew we would.

"The first traveler from Sirius set out alone. Call him *Enki*."

"Enki?" I said. "Not the fish god Dagon?"

"What a Lovecraftian bent you have," Tom said. "Another reason why I love you." He leaned across the coffee table and kissed me again. "Dagon was a god of fish and fishing, from a later time. Enki was the Sumerian god of creation, intelligence, mischief; as well as fresh and saltwater."

"So you're telling us that Enki was a real person, an amphibious space traveler from Sirius, who actually called himself Enki?" Maxine asked.

Tom spread his arms and intoned, "*And out of the ground the Lord God formed every beast of the field, and every fowl of the air; and brought them unto Adam to see what he would call them: and whatsoever Adam called every living creature, that was the name thereof.*" He dropped his arms. "I'm just giving you the names that you'll recognize, Max. From history. From mythology. From *Ancient Aliens*."

SEVENTY-ONE

The being that would later be known as Enki cleared a bit of debris from around a valve and relaxed. The biosphere in which he traveled cruised along, humming softly. Not with the sound of machinery or electronics, but with the sound of life itself. The warm water in which he swam lapped softly at his movements. It keep him alive, nourished him – it nourished him and all the other myriad life forms that made up the ship. Some of the components were microscopic, like the little algaes and molds that multiplied in the water, that produced the integral parts of the air he inhaled, cleaned up the waste gases that he exhaled, fed the larger creatures on which he fed, as well as sustaining all the modified mollusks and bi-valves that provide propulsion, the bioluminescent creatures that gave him light. Those little creatures were the basis of everything.

And then there were the bananas.

But Enki was lonely, even though his ship mimicked home, reproduced everything that he needed. He missed company; he missed his wife, she of the red, curly hair and the long blue tail, with its wide, delicate, nearly transparent flukes.

Enki sighed. If everything went as planned, he thought, his descendants – they would have neither tails nor flukes.

He longed to splash down, to swim and be free for a time in the great waters of the alien world. Not so alien after all, he thought, since it had water. No place with water could be entirely alien.

The ship sped on through space and time. Enki relaxed and smiled, thinking of his wife. He slept.

At last the biosphere arrived, entered the alien planet's atmosphere. After a few low orbit passes, Enki decided on a large lake and gingerly set his craft upon its surface, far enough from the shore so as not to be in danger from any of the place's native land creatures. He left the ship and swam, exalting in the fresh water, a little bit colder than that which had sustained him within his ship. But water was water, universally, and he rejoiced in the bracing coolness.

Enki opened a large leaf-shaped bag and took out a braided net (it had been grown that way). He caught some fish in it and approached the shore. He flopped up none too gracefully onto the sand, and with other components found in his bag, he built himself a fire on the beach. It was a chemical fire, created by mixing various extracts, and would burn until he dropped another chemical into it to put it out. He removed a long, yellow-colored, fruit-looking thing from his bag, and peeled the rind from it, to reveal a delicate, very sharp metal knife. It was so sharp that the tough organic covering had been induced to grow around it, just to keep it from slicing right through the bottom of the leafy bag.

Enki cleaned and roasted the fish, although he needed to do neither of these acts in order to eat them himself. But the fish were not for him. They were for the monkeys.

He mustn't think of them as monkeys, Enki chided himself. He watched as three individuals approached, sniffing the air, entranced by the new, strange, delicious smell of the roasting fish. They were not really monkeys anymore, he told himself. They had actually been out of the trees, walking upright, for some millennia by now.

When the trio that had been attracted by the smell of the cooking fish got close enough for Enki's comfort, he stuck a piece of driftwood into the chemical fire and held the branch out toward them in warning. They stopped and looked solemnly at him. There was little intelligence behind the muddy eyes, yet, but there was curiosity, and that animal desire engendered by the smell of cooking food.

Enki took a bite out of one of the fish, chewed it, his eyes never leaving those of his three curious visitors. Then he threw the half eaten fish at the feet of the nearest watcher. The three of them scattered, but not too far, and they came back immediately. Enki munched serenely on another fish. The nearest individual picked up the one at his feet, looked at his companions, looked at Enki. He sniffed the fish, found that it smelled good, took a tentative bite. He made a guttural sound of pleasure at the taste of the warm, juicy, cooked flesh, and his companions stepped closer. But the first one pushed them away and selfishly devoured the rest of his fish.

They would learn to share soon enough, Enki thought wryly.

The one that had wolfed down the fish looked again at Enki, and would have stepped closer if it hadn't been for the strange, hot thing that he held out in front of him.

Enki then threw the rest of the cooked fish to them, and they gobbled this strange new treat greedily. *Monkey see, monkey do*, Enki thought. Then he amended himself again. These were not monkeys, and it would not do to think of them as such. These hairy, smelly, curious creatures were the future of his race. And he had a lot more stops to make, a lot more fires to build, a lot more fish to fry.

SEVENTY-TWO

"So Enki did a fly-by about a million or so years ago and taught *Homo erectus* how to cook. And he planted some bananas."

When we looked at Tom silently at these revelations, he smiled and offered further explanation. "The ability to cook one's food led to a larger brain, ladies. Harvard primatologists postulate that cooking one's food makes it easier to absorb calories. Less energy is expended in digestion. More time for thinking." He tapped the side of his head. "Someone teaching *Homo erectus* how to cook his food – it led to a major step in evolution."

"And the bananas?" Maxine asked.

Tom held his hand up, fingers splayed, thumb crossed over the palm. "There are four staple foods on this planet: wheat, rice, corn, and bananas." He lowered his fingers, one at a time. "And unlike the first three, you can cook and eat every part of a banana. It's a perfect food."

When Maxine still looked skeptical, Tom said, "Do you really want a fucking dissertation on bananas right now, Max? It's just part of the story, this story *I am making up*, remember? Accept this element. Enki brought fire, and taught the cavemen how to cook their food so that they could evolve some smarts a little bit faster. And Enki brought bananas."

"Wasn't it Prometheus that gave fire to mankind? To, uh . . . cook with?" I asked. "Or are you going to tell me that he was a later god, too?" I ignored the bananas thread altogether. I'd already heard the *bananas are from outer space* spiel somewhere before.

"All mythologies spring from the same well," Tom said. He pointed upwards. "From Sirius." He smiled and repeated, "Remember, it's just a story." He stood. "I'm going to make myself another Irish coffee. Anyone else want one?" He unwrapped another cupcake, removed the plastic alien, and stuck it in his mouth.

Max and I both raised our hands, like we were in school.

I was thinking that another drink or five could only help with the suspension of disbelief at Tom's ridiculous story. But like I say, I just liked to hear him talk, so it was not that much of a hardship to me. And what else were we going to do on Christmas Eve with no television? Still I hoped that this narrative would start getting a little more believable pretty soon. Growing spaceships, yet. Bananas are from Sirius. Indeed.

Tom reappeared moments later with fresh Irish coffees for us, whipped cream and all. He sat down and resumed his far-fetched story. "*Zo*. Enki gave proto-man the gift of fire, taught him how to cook. He left some bananas, then returned to Sirius.

"Time passed. Things got dryer on Sirius, slowly, as had been predicted. The Dino People discovered the Mermaid People, discovered that they were not gods after all. They slaughtered thousands in those first days, harpooning them, dragging their wriggling, not yet dead bodies onto the shore. Filleting and eating them right there, as if they were so many bluefin." Tom paused, to let us picture the carnage that he was so casually describing, I thought.

"The Dino People were mostly repelled, however, at least along the shore. The Mermaid People could throw a spear, too. There's no more apt archetype than Poseidon and his trident. But like the Vikings, the Dino People kept coming back. They were primitive, but persistent. They established footholds in the dryer highlands around the inland sea, and would make raids along the shoreline. A food source as large and abundant as this was not to be passed up. Plus they caught smaller fish, and ate the various little land animals that lived on the Eastern Hemisphere. These were all easily exploited, unaccustomed as they were to any similar apex predator.

"The Dino People bred and multiplied in the highlands of the Eastern Hemisphere. They became a constant threat along the shoreline of that great inland sea that had spawned the sophisticated underwater culture of the Mermaid People. Then they became still more of a threat, as they built boats and set out to explore the sea itself. The Mermaid People had not developed too much weaponry to defend themselves, even in their technological sophistication."

"It's difficult to grow guns, I imagine," I said.

Tom ignored my gentle derision. "The Mermaid People developed a chemical not unlike magnesium, that could burn underwater. But they were slow in developing a way to propel it, to deliver it to the target more accurately than by simply attaching it to the end of a trident. They would perfect these weapons eventually, but something had to be done to stem the dino threat as soon as possible.

"So about the time that *Neanderthals* and *Homo sapiens* were running into each other in field and stream here, the Mermaid People decided to send another expedition to Earth.

"The mission of this expedition would be to work on that thorny problem of acquiring legs, ASAP. It had become agonizingly apparent to the Mermaid People that the only way to combat their ever-menacing foe would be to meet him on his own ground. The actual *ground*, in this case.

"Things were starting to get a little out of hand; the Mermaid People were in danger of losing their dominance of the great lake that comprised most of the Eastern Hemisphere. They were in danger of being subjugated by a race that really consisted of nothing more than smarter than average lizards. They were in danger of being wiped out entirely, eventually, if they didn't act now.

"So, one lone Enki wouldn't cut it this time. This mission involved an armada of ships, almost the entire undersea fleet. It would have been called an invasion force, really, had there been anyone here intelligent enough yet to recognize it as such.

"This group would come to be known as the Annunaki that Giorgio is so fond of, Maxine. But they just didn't land in Sumeria; our Sumerian friends were just better record keepers. And they didn't come for gold, either, as it's been said."

"They came for *us*," Maxine said. "For our DNA."

Tom nodded. "They landed in different bodies of water all over the planet, set up outposts. Along a sort of a gridline pattern, where the topography would allow.

"There was one place that'll be familiar to you, Max. One ship splashed down in a lake in Bolivia later called Titicaca. The leader of this band would come to be known as Viracocha. His name means *sea foam*. You're familiar with Viracocha, Max? And his city? They did your favorite episode of *Ancient Aliens* on it."

Maxine smiled. She knew nothing if she didn't know her *Ancient Aliens* episodes. "Puma Punku, right?"

"Yes. Puma Punku is part of Tiahuanaco. Incan tradition says that Viracocha created the world right there, and in a way, it's true.

"In Incan tradition, Viracocha himself is the substance from which all the universe is created. He is intimately associated with water. The sun, which he created, he wears for a crown, and the tears descending from his eyes are the rain. He is responsible for the creation of the moon, the stars. Time itself.

"It's told that Viracocha rose from Lake Titicaca and made mankind by breathing upon stones. *And when he had created the world, he formed a race of giants of disproportioned greatness painted and sculptured, to see whether it would be well to make real men of that size.*

"But these first creatures turned out to be mindless, brutish. Disrespectful. Viracocha destroyed them by calling forth a massive flood called *Unu Pachakuti, the water that overturns the land*. Then he breathed onto smaller stones to create mankind as he is now.

"It's said that Viracocha fathered the first eight enlightened human beings, two of which founded the Incan civilization. *He it was, showed men how to bring streams of water to their crops, and taught them how to build terraces upon the mountains where crops would grow.* Like Adam, his sons are said to have named all the trees, flowers, fruits and herbs.

"Eventually, Viracocha and his sons reached the coast. Then they're said to have walked west across the water until they winked out of sight. Legend has it that Viracocha, like King Arthur, will return to his people in times of trouble. *But he told those whom he had left behind that he would send messengers back who would protect them and give them renewed knowledge of all he had taught them.*" Tom lit another cigarette and looked at me to see if I would interrupt with some snide remark. When I remained silent, he smiled and continued. "I forgot to mention the Grays. All this reciting of Incan scripture, and I forgot them entirely."

Maxine clapped her hands together. "I want to believe, Tom!" she said, quoting the *X-Files*. "Tell us about the Grays!"

Tom grinned at her enthusiasm. "Remember I told you how mankind has bred dogs so that even when they're grown, they maintain puppy-ish characteristics? Rounded faces, playful dispositions, stuff like that?"

We nodded.

"The Grays are something along those lines. They used to be full, robust, Sleestak-looking Dino People. When the Dino People began raiding, the Mermaid People were able to surprise and net a few of the marauders and maroon them on tiny islands in the inland sea for study. A good many of them unfortunately drowned in either the netting or the marooning, or in trying to escape from either or both, but these things happen. They weren't very strong swimmers."

"The Mermaid People observed them and found them to be too difficult to handle, to control, in their natural state. Impossible to *tame*, if you will. So, the Mermaid people just took the ones they'd captured and bred them and genetically modified them until they were small and compact, with the big eyes and the big heads – how the Dino young look, before one of the last of their growing-into-adulthood molts, or skin sheddings, or whatever they're called. They also kept the characteristics of Dino young – they were not aggressive (at least not to their masters). They didn't eat much; they were engineered to be omnivorous, to be able to digest almost any plant or animal material; including a kind of Sirian freshwater kelp, which could be dried and stored indefinitely. The Mermaid People found their new creations to be quite useful as –"

"Slaves?" Maxine asked.

"I was thinking more along the lines of *servants*, Max, or even *soldiers*." Tom slurped the whipped cream off his coffee, stirred it with one of the little plastic spaceships. "But *slaves* will work, too, I guess. When they came here, the Mermaid People brought some of the Grays with them. They were better suited for terrestrial work here, having legs after all, so the Mermaid crews brought them along to build what needed to be built on dry land, to use the native materials. To clear the vegetation, to cut and dress and move the stones."

He paused when another thought struck him. "The Mermaid crews also brought them along for food. They found that they didn't have to eat them once they arrived, but they would have, had food not proved plentiful here. That was the other reason they brought them along."

Tom grinned at our wide-eyed, shocked reactions. "That's why the Aztecs bred Chihuahuas, you know. If they didn't find enough game while they were out raiding for human sacrifices, they'd just eat one of their Chihuahuas. They're really just sandwiches on legs. They learned this practice from Sirians."

He let us reflect on the utility of that. The brutality of *that*. Then he continued. "So, Max, you're familiar with some of the theories about what Puma Punku was? The big H-shaped blocks?"

"Giorgio said that they could've fitted together to make some kind of gigantic door, complete with mega-hinges and all that. Another guy thinks they could have fit together in such a way as to have made some kind of launch pad, rising up at an angle so the spaceships could get some acceleration as they took off."

"Forget all that misguided bullshit." Tom dismissed these theories with a wave of his hand. "Puma Punku was the equivalent of a giant holding tank. The H-blocks fitted together and held water, so Viracocha and his crew could work there. So they could start melding their DNA with ours. He built Puma Punku because he felt a little exposed on Lake Titicaca, you see."

SEVENTY-THREE

Viracocha and Abra, his wife, had quarreled before they had splashed down on the lake, and they had quarreled after, and they continued to quarrel. Abra was absolutely furious that he had decided to build the stronghold at Puma Punku. She was outraged, incensed that he would waste all that time and all those resources to build what amounted to an enormous swimming pool. It was ridiculous, it was insane, it was arrogant, it was unnecessary. Abra fumed, she raged.

It would be so much easier to just stay in the lake, work from there. She couldn't understand why he insisted on building an artificial structure when the wonderful lake was right there.

But Viracocha remained steadfast. He believed that there was going to be a flood, and anything that they were using, anything that they had built in the lake would thereby be swept away. His lieutenant, Caridad, agreed with him. They had studied weather patterns, geology. A flood would engulf the lake before their mission could be completed. Their diligent research had convinced them of it, and no objection would be considered, whether it came from Abra or any other member of their party.

And so Viracocha designed the plans for an artificial lake, for the interlocking blocks that would form it.

In the bowels of their biosphere slept the giants, the *Igigi*. These were the workhorse slaves, huge, bioengineered past even the brutish prime of their Dino forebears. Although they were all sprung from the same genetic base, they were as different from the Grays as a Clydesdale is from a pony. They were necessary for the heavy lifting; even with the assistance of the nautilus-based anti-gravity creatures that Viracocha and his crew had brought along with them, it would be difficult for the big-headed, spindly-limbed Grays to fit all of those massive blocks of stone together by themselves.

And so construction commenced. While Viracocha and his crew frolicked in the lake, swimming in and out of the ship as it floated at anchor, the Grays cleared and leveled the area, this holy place where the historic melding of Sirian and Earth essences was to occur.

Then the *Igigi*, some seven of them, were slowly brought out of their slumber by the Grays. Using a highly accurate tool that combined caustic chemicals and power from a creature that could best be described as a fresh-water version of an electric eel, they cut, dressed, and fitted the H-shaped blocks into place. With the smaller Grays acting as foremen, the vast pool was not erected overnight, as subsequent legend may have told, but it didn't take much longer than that.

Then the great biosphere hovered over the vast artificial pool. There was a clap of sound as power from the ship was applied to hydrogen and oxygen in its hold. The ship dipped; then millions of gallons of the pure stuff of life gushed from the sky into the pool. This sterile water was augmented with the living soup from the ship, and soon all the myriad little creatures who were essential to life were multiplying with abandon in their new home. All the finny crew flopped gracelessly into the water from the sky; only one crewman was necessary to return the ship to the surface of the lake and remain with it.

Viracocha had only two other men with him; one stayed with the ship. The other fifty members of his crew were women. What genetic material that was necessary from the males was abundant and easily enough harvested; the two specimens in the pool could supply more than enough. But the women were necessary to grow and incubate the new hybrids, one each.

One moonless night, the experiment commenced. Viracocha sent out a specialized band of Grays to collect sufficient human subjects from the hunter-gatherer tribes that dwelt in the surrounding countryside. These Grays glowed in the dark through a special gene for bioluminescence that had been introduced into their mothers while still aboard the ship, during the trip from Sirius.

The humans were such easy prey; the ones that didn't flee in terror, stood their ground and threw rocks and other primitive projectiles at their ghostly pursuers. When they saw these puny weapons bounce off the Grays' energy shields, they too, fell to their knees in fear and wonder.

It wasn't like they needed to be killed. Just stunned and . . . borrowed for a short time. Necessary cells and tissues were appropriated, eggs and sperms and gametes. Then the subjects were released, freed to return to their compatriots, none the worse for the inestimable contribution they had unwittingly given. Around the fire, they regaled their brethren with hushed, awed stories about the time they had spent with the gods.

Sirian/human zygotes were manufactured and surgically inserted into the brave female crew member volunteers. During the nine months that the new beings were gestating, their mothers swam, ate, relaxed, and meditated upon the future in the great pool that Viracocha had caused to be erected. They were treated with all due deference by the two men present. Their names would be remembered on Sirius, as progenitors to a fresh and superior lineage.

To keep the *Igigi* and the little Grays occupied while the new race gestated, Viracocha set them to work building a landing pad for spaceships at Tiahuanaco. A large plaza was cleared and leveled, and many-tonned sandstone blocks laid flat. On some not-too-distant day in the future, Viracocha imagined, ships from Sirius would land here. They would not have to splash down in the lake anymore, because the crews that would step off the ships would *step off the ships* – they would have feet and legs instead of tails and flukes, all as a result of the work that was nearing fruition now. *His* work.

But the construction of the landing pad was not to be completed. One morning, three Grays scrambled up to the top of the great artificial lake and cried out in fear and panic for their masters. When Viracocha and a very pregnant Caridad and a very pregnant Abra broke the surface of the still pond, the Grays gibbered and gesticulated. The tale they told was a bloody one: two of the giants had become involved in a confrontation with five or six of their small Gray brethren and had killed them all, smashing their little bodies, rending their spindly limbs, devouring them in a last act of savagery.

Viracocha stroked his beard and considered.

Abra said, "These monsters must be dealt with swiftly."

Word had not long ago reached them from another Annunaki outpost in what would someday be called Sumeria. The communiqué stated that the *Igigi* under the command of Enlil had become disgruntled after he had commanded them to construct a drainage canal. They had balked at the task, for reasons not mentioned in the message. They had rebelled; set their tools ablaze.

"The Lord of the Storm was sudden in his wrath," Caridad reminded her captain.

Viracocha was still thoughtful. "Enlil was not building as massive a structure as we are."

Abra slapped her tail on the water, her old anger returning. "You build structures to your own vanity, my husband." She gestured at the pool. "Nothing else is really needed here. Take these brutes in hand before they endanger our true mission." She patted her belly.

Viracocha instructed the still panting Grays to bring him one of the chemical-power tools that were used to cut the stone. From his vantage point in the tall pool, he could view the *Igigi* as they labored on the landing pad. He noted several large splashes of blood on the sandstone – all that remained of the six unfortunate Grays.

Yet, Viracocha's *Igigi* were not entirely rebellious – even after such a murderous interlude, they had gotten back to work. He sighed, wishing that there was some other way. But Abra was right. The importance of any stone construction project disappeared in comparison to what Abra and Caridad and the other women were constructing inside their bodies. All avenues that might jeopardize that in any way had to be cut off. The *Igigi* had outlived their usefulness.

Viracocha took aim at the first giant, and a stream of corrosive, stone-melting plasma erupted. The *Igigi* fell over dead.

Abra and Caridad took turns eliminating the rest of them.

SEVENTY-FOUR

"I heard that Annunaki story with Enlil and the *Igigi* differently," Maxine said.

I looked at her in surprise, amazed that she could keep all these ancient deities and demi-gods straight in her head. Especially when I knew that she could only name four dwarves, three reindeer, and no apostles at all.

Tom smiled. "You heard that the Lord of the Storm negotiated with the *Igigi*? That they didn't like manual labor, so Enlil created man to relieve them of it?"

Maxine nodded.

"That's *folklore*, Max. Mythology. The holy scriptures of a thousand cultures are what people made up to explain what they believed the "gods" had in mind for mankind when they arrived here, and after they left." He sipped his whiskey-laced coffee.

"I'm telling you the real story. Viracocha and Enlil, Isis and Osiris, Zeus and Prometheus. They were not gods, arrived here to lead the monkeys to enlightenment. They were *scientists*, for lack of a better word, here to take something from you that they needed.

"Viracocha didn't create a race of giants and then destroy them and create man. That's all just mythology. The *Igigi* were servants, slaves, if you like, that he'd brought with him from Sirius. Once he judged them to be loose cannons, a possible threat to the central mission, he wiped them out. Nor did Enlil let the *Igigi* out of their labors by creating people to replace them. He wiped his out, too. Almost all of the *Igigi* that accompanied the Annunaki crews as labor forces wound up being wiped out."

I sensed bait, and not entirely unwillingly, I bit. "What happened to the rest of them?"

Tom looked innocently at me. "*Sásq'ets*. Yeti. Yeren, Yowie. Wendigo."

"Are you saying that Bigfoot are descendants of the *Igigi*?" Maxine asked.

"That's exactly what he's saying," I replied and shook my head.

"But Bigfoot is a monkey, a *hominid*, like you say," Maxine countered.

Tom's eyebrows shot up in surprise. "Is he, Max? How many Bigfoot have you seen?"

Maxine opened her mouth to say something, then snapped it shut again.

"Worldwide reports from time immemorial seem to suggest that there's something big lurking in the woods," Tom said. "But no one has ever really seen it, now have they? They may think they have, but how many sets of corroborating witnesses have there really been? So maybe it's not a hominid after all. Maybe it's the descendant of a big lizard, bioengineered once upon a time to be clever and resourceful and self-sufficient. Able to eat damn near anything.

"And maybe these creatures have been avoiding mankind all this time, because someone that looked a lot like us cut their ancestors in half with stone-cutting energy tools turned into weapons."

"They looked a lot like us, except that they had tails and flukes," Maxine said.

"Or maybe it's all bullshit," I said.

"It's just *a story*, my love. A little of the *Ancient Aliens* oeuvre for Max on this eve of our Savior's birth. On this day when we ourselves are like Mary and Joseph on their way to Bethlehem." Tom gestured at the dark television. "In that we are technologically challenged, I mean."

He began his tale again. "The thing that happened in that pool at Puma Punku happened all over this planet, Max. Annunaki bands extracted DNA from humans; then mermaid women carried the hybrid babies to term. Then the babies grew up and mingled with the natives, passed the hybrid genes on. It's all right there in the Bible.

"*And it came to pass, when men began to multiply on the face of the earth, and daughters were born unto them, that the sons of God saw the daughters of men that they were fair; and they took them wives of all which they chose.* Except the sons of God were human-Sirian hybrids.

"This went on all over the world. *And he brought him forth abroad, and said, 'Look now toward heaven, and tell the stars, if thou be able to number them,' and he said unto him, 'So shall thy seed be.'*

"All the lists of begetting in Genesis? Why should all those boring verses about who went over and married who, the hairy men and the smooth men — why would such apparent nonsense even be considered important, nonetheless *holy* enough to keep in the scripture? All that stuff is really just a garbled history of a breeding plan. Keeping track of the hybrids in the general population." Tom lit a cigarette and considered us through a cloud of smoke.

"Viracocha and the other Annunaki aged a lot slower than those whom they begat, those who worshipped them. Their women were great grandmothers by the time the flood in Bolivia finally occurred, the *Unu Pachakuti, the water that overturns the land.* Just as Viracocha had predicted it would. He didn't cause it, Max. He simply predicted it,

191

through the study of the geology of the area, of weather patterns and what have you.

"The actual flood and the myth of the flood also served to mask another part of the real story. Legend tells us that Viracocha, in his great anger at mankind's failings, had summoned a flood and wiped them all out, worldwide, except for a fortunate few. This was such a great story, that it was spread to all Annunaki outposts and disseminated to the worshipping populations. It still exists in the holy books of dozens of faiths.

"It meshed so well – it was a perfectly logical explanation for what the primitives would soon experience. For even in all those locations where there hadn't been any flood at all, the people would soon notice that their gods, yea, verily, had caused a great deal of their friends and neighbors to disappear.

"Viracocha and Enlil and all the rest had enough hybrid specimens to take back to Sirius, you see. Viracocha didn't walk across the western sea with just his sons, Max. Viracocha didn't walk anywhere. He had a tail and flukes. Viracocha flopped back into his biosphere with the rest of his crew and took a couple of cohorts of human-Sirian crossbreeds back home. And so did all of the Annunaki legions. Each filled up their ships with their new creations and returned with them to Sirius. The new hybrid peoples, you see, had just been press-ganged into the fight against the Dino People."

Tom unwrapped and ate another cupcake, waiting for some reaction from us. When we offered none, he continued. "In addition to the hybrids themselves, the Annunaki took back with them all the foodstuffs that the bipeds would need to thrive and multiply on Sirius. All the bounty of fruits and vegetables of this world, all the insects needed for pollination. They already had bananas on Sirius, so –"

"Just like Noah?" Maxine asked. "Two of every animal and all that?"

Tom smiled his glorious smile at her, pleased at just how completely she was going along with his tale. "Not exactly, Max. The Sirians didn't know a whole lot about terrestrial animals, being from the water. There wasn't a lot of big game on their marshy continent, anyway, and they had never bothered to try to catch and eat any of the little animals that came down to the shoreline to drink.

"They'd always gotten their protein from consuming fish, and planned on continuing to do so, even after making the transition to land life. They did have one fairly large animal, a mammal, a lot like a harbor seal. They were good for meat in a pinch, but mostly they were kept around like pets.

"So, they didn't bring back any earth animals, at least nothing more than the insects needed to pollinate the new plants. The Sirians were very selective about what they decided to introduce onto their planet."

I noticed that Tom had left off calling his aliens *Mermaid People*, and simply called them *Sirians* now.

He was saying, "They only brought palatable plants; beautiful, fragrant flowers; beneficial insects. They took apples but no crabapples. Bees, but no wasps. Butterflies, but no cockroaches. Every imaginable edible plant, but no weeds."

"No weeds? Like, no *weed?*"

"No weed. No tobacco. No poppies. No coca. No cacao for chocolate. No juniper for gin." Tom smiled at me.

"The first crossbreeds, the ones that the Annunaki brought back with them, adapted immediately. Though they were vastly outnumbered, they drove the Dino People back into the highlands of the Eastern Continent, away from the shores of the inland sea. At least temporarily.

"With that threat overthrown, at least for the moment, life was easy; food was plentiful and grew without a whole lot of cultivation. *And out of the ground made the Lord God to grow every tree that is pleasant to the sight, and good for food.*

"Sirius was beautiful, like the Garden of Eden. Anything that the Sirians didn't bring back from Earth with them, they just bioengineered, so that the environment was perfect for the new hybrids.

"And the Mermaid People lined up to have their embryos bioengineered so that they would be born with legs. It was a bittersweet choice; they were deciding to let their way of life die out. They were deciding to embrace an entirely new way of life. The offspring would mostly be created out of their own genetic stock; they would just have this rather major mutation. The only difference between the new babies and the old babies was that the new babies had legs instead of tails.

"And there was one other curious offshoot of the procedure." Tom held up his dominant hand. "About ninety-eight percent of the new babies would turn out to be left-handed."

"Why was that?" Maxine wanted to know.

Tom shrugged. "An unforeseen consequence. No one ever wasted much time trying to figure it out." He sipped his coffee and considered us for a moment. "Have you ever noticed that Adam was left-handed?"

When we looked at blankly at him, Tom took his phone out of his pocket, and accessed a copy of Michelangelo's *The Creation of Adam* from the Sistine Chapel. He held his phone up so we could see it. Sure

193

enough, God is reaching toward Adam with his right hand, and Adam is reaching back with his left.

"That's just the way the painting is composed," I scoffed. "If Adam was reaching out with his right hand, the pose would be awkward."

"Maybe." Tom looked at the picture again. "*So God created man in His own image; in the image of God He created him; male and female He created them.*" He pushed a button on his phone and put it back into his pocket.

After a moment, he continued. "Another reason that the Mermaid People were willing to give up their way of life so easily was because the rearing of their new bipedal offspring didn't differ very much from the way they'd raised their tailed offspring. They'd always raised their children communally, in schools – like schools of fish." Tom smiled at his own pun. "The children all lived together in centralized parts of the communities. Adults lived in their own parts. Those members of the community that loved children the most raised them, and their parents visited whenever they wanted.

"This set up was just moved onto the shore. The first child centers were always near the water, so Mom and Dad could just swim up and play and visit with their strange new offspring." Tom smiled at the convenience and wonderfulness of *all that*.

I said, "I think I need another drink."

Before I could make a move to get it myself, Tom arose and went to do it for me. Even though this yarn that he was spinning was patently ridiculous, I couldn't help but be captivated. What other man would tell space alien stories on a television-less Christmas Eve, just to amuse his friends?

I looked over at Maxine. She smiled, shrugged. "He's easily as entertaining as Giorgio."

Tom called from the kitchen, "Who wants a ham sandwich?"

Maxine and I arose to go out and watch him make sandwiches for us. It was the least we could do.

Twenty minutes later, Maxine and I were once again seated in our chairs, munching our ham sandwiches, as childlike as Cindy-Lou Who with her cup of water, waiting for Tom to finish his own sandwich so he could continue his story.

Maxine said, "So let me see if I got this so far. Here is Sirius, populated by a shrinking population of mermaids. Their new offspring are a bunch of happy, healthy, two-legged, left-handed vegetarians."

"They ate fish, too," Tom said. "Fish were and continue to be the main source of protein on Sirius. But in those days, there were also the occasional dino-croquettes."

I couldn't comment on the concept of *eating your enemy*, so I said, "I'm picturing the population from *The Time Machine*." I added, "The old one, with Rod Taylor."

Maxine shook her head. "How old is that? Was it even in color?"

"It's a classic, you Philistine," I said. "The humans in the far future are beautiful, but indolent. They're called *Eloi*. They just sit around in the ruins of the old civilization all day, eating fruit, doing nothing. The climate is mild, food is plentiful. They don't have to work, they don't learn, they don't create. They just sit around and wait to be picked off by the smarter *Morlocks*."

Tom squinted. "That's not even remotely right. Surely, Sirius was a natural paradise, everything engineered to be perfect for the new bipedal population. But they still had to plant and harvest. They still had to do whatever bioengineering had to be done to induce things to grow the way they wanted them to. They still had to work. They still had a sense of purpose. There was meaning to their lives."

"They still had to grow spaceships," Maxine added. "Fight off the Dino People."

"Right. And grow dwellings, and everything else." Tom seemed a little miffed at my opinion of the Sirians. "They still had to work. They just didn't have to work very hard.

"Just because there's plenty – that doesn't necessarily make a people indolent. Plenty makes it so people don't have to go to war, don't have to hate a more fortunate other. Everyone was equally fortunate on Sirius. There were no haves and have-nots, Liz.

"And because their culture was not the product of a constant struggle, as it would come to be here, Sirius didn't develop any of the ills that are the products of deprivation, like we have here. There was never any need for escapism, because everything was just bitchin' there. So there was no alcoholism, no drug addiction. Alcohol and what we term drugs of recreation never even developed on Sirius."

"It sounds boring," Maxine said.

Tom smiled at her. "It most certainly does, doesn't it?"

"What finally happened with the Dino People?" I asked.

"Ah, a good question." Tom unwrapped another cupcake, removed the spaceship, took a large bite, spoke with his mouth full. "A perfect question, actually, because it allows me to segue back here to Earth. It allows me to finish my explanation for all the mysterious ancient civilizations and their unexplainable mega-monoliths. It lets me solve the *Ancient Aliens* conundrum once and for all."

Tom sipped his spiked coffee and rubbed his hands together. "Zo, here goes. On the Eastern Continent, you have Mermaid People, bipedal crossbreed imports from Earth, and Dino interlopers." He gestured to his right. "More bipeds are born there every day, and they are loved and cherished by their amphibious parents. The dinos still mock, still raid, still slaughter and eat any hominids they can catch, whether amphibious or terrestrial.

"And there is that whole giant continent of dinos across the sea, billions of them." Tom gestured to his left. "The mermaids don't want to sacrifice their new and precious bipedal offspring to the toothy maw of further confrontation with the lizards, yet this is a problem that cannot be ignored. The Dino People already outnumber the mermaids and their new terrestrial children by a staggering amount, worldwide, because they reproduce quicker."

"Did they lay eggs?" Maxine wanted to know.

"No, they were live bearers, like snakes. But, like snakes, and unlike people, they usually gave birth to no fewer than three or four young at a time, with a shorter gestation period. So the hominids were outnumbered, and would continue to be outnumbered, unless something was done. What do you think it was, Max?"

"They came back here and got more people."

Tom nodded. "They came back here and crossbred more people, inserted a little more Sirian genetics into *Homo sapiens*. They returned to Earth and expanded centers in all the places originally begun by the Annunaki. In South America, In the American Southwest, in the British Isles, in Egypt, in Greece, in Turkey, in the Middle East.

"And in a very short time, they raised what had been simple hunter-gather bands to that level of societal sophistication that produces the highest population: the city. The Sirians taught them how to grow enough food to support large populations. They taught them how to farm in terraces in South America. Taught them how to make chinampas in Mexico. Taught the Mayans how to irrigate. Taught the Asians the finer points of rice cultivation. Taught the Egyptians how to take advantage of the Nile's flood.

"The Sirians taught these people mathematics and geometry; helped them to lay out and build all the great monumental cities of ancient times.

"Because it was now written among the Incas that Viracocha had *created the world* there, the landing pad that he'd envisioned at Tiahuanaco would later be built upon, turned into a place of pilgrimage by the puppet kings of later –"

"Invaders?" I said.

"*Visitors*. All the great ancient cities can be found along a vague grid pattern: along flight lines, you might say. Some cities themselves are laid out based on celestial bodies; usually the constellation of Orion. This was so visiting Sirians could fly over and look down on the lights of a city – the Pyramids on the Giza Plateau, the Thornborough Henges in England, Anasazi villages in the Southwest – and know which leader from Sirius they were visiting."

"Lights?" I said. "You mean fires?"

"Not fires, my love. If you were to fly along these gridlines in ancient times, you would behold these cities lit up through the use of bioluminescent sources. They might have seemed like fires to the locals, but they were actually a combination of chemical and bioluminescent elements – fires that would burn indefinitely, smokelessly, with very little heat, until they were extinguished with other chemicals. *And the angel of the Lord appeared unto him in a flame of fire out of the midst of a bush: and he looked, and, behold, the bush burned with fire, and the bush was not consumed.*

"The stone ley lines that encircle the Earth also transmitted bioluminescent energy, once upon a time. Think of telephone poles. A signal travels along the wires strung from one pole to the next, until great distances are covered. Similarly, energy traveled from one stone to the next. They were used for light and communications between outposts.

"On Sirius, the new bipeds needed room to flourish, and what better place to do so than the considerably dryer Western Continent? This, coupled with the fact that, if left to survive, the dinos would always be a threat, convinced the newly terrestrial Sirians that it was high time for a little inter-continental invasion of their own.

"But it would take a lot of manpower to conquer the entire other side of the planet. The Sirians needed *soldiers*, for lack of a better word, to help annihilate the Dino People.

"So here on Earth, the Sirians taught the people how to feed large populations, because they needed large populations for export. As these populations flourished, Sirians taught their charges how to use their stone-cutting tools, and set them to work building all the great stone monuments that still exist today. The ones that you're so familiar with, Max: the pyramids, the observatories. Gobekli Tepi, Easter Island, Nemrud Dagi, Saksaywaman, Teotihuacan, Machu Picchu. Stonehenge, Mesa Verde. Tenochtitlán.

"All these places were constructed for two simple reasons. The first was to give these large, well-fed populations something to do, to keep them occupied. Keep their minds off invading their weaker neighbors, as fortunate peoples invariably want to do on this planet. The second

197

was to create unique signposts, so that other visitors could know where they were on the globe.

"It's as simple and as uncomplicated as that. No great holy underpinnings, no trying to leave messages in stone for future generations to decipher.

"Sirians and their puppet kings ruled in Egypt and South America, Assyria and Mexico. All over the world. They built cities and funneled people to Sirius to fight the Dino People. People born here went there; people born there came here. They intermixed, until we were all one race."

"How could we all be one race, Tom?" Maxine said. "We're not even one race, here on Earth."

"Racial distinctions are literally skin deep, Max," Tom replied. "They're a product of climate, mostly. But as far as our basic components go, we're all the same. Our internal organs, our blood, are all identical. You can get a blood transfusion from anyone that's the same type as you, no matter what their race. You could get a blood transfusion from someone from Sirius, if he was the same blood type, because at the level below skin tone and eye color, we're all the same. Most of the races here are also represented there. You could have a little Sirian baby and no one would be able to tell that his daddy wasn't a local. Not even a geneticist."

Tom again paused for a response. Again we remained silent. He considered us for a minute, then a new thought seemed to hit him. "You might be interested to know that some of the characteristics that you think *make you human*, that separate you from the rest of the animal kingdom – some of these characteristics came down to you from Sirian handiwork. Not learned or evolved, per se, but inserted, engineered."

I couldn't help but notice that Tom had at least twice now referred to humanity as *you* instead of *us*. Mostly he would say *us*, but I noticed the *you* this time. I got the impression that this apparent slip, this little inconsistency, was going to be part of some big reveal at the end of his story. Surely, he was doing it on purpose.

"Such as?" I asked, biting again at this new bait.

"Well, music, for one thing, or at least rhythm. In the brief period of Sirian history when her people were warlike – that is, in this period we're talking about, when they were importing soldiers to fight the Dino People – during this time, the ability to appreciate rhythm was hard wired into your genes."

There it was again – *your* genes, not *our* genes. Where was he going with this?

"Rhythm is good for marching, you see, for organization of troops. You can't get monkeys to march, now can you? Not on their own. The ability to appreciate rhythm was engineered and inserted into the crossbreeds' genes, so that they could be organized, so that they would march. On Sirius, this never progressed much farther than just that, an appreciation for simple rhythm. There's a little drumming on the summer solstice, but that's about it.

"Music in all its myriad, amazing incarnations is an Earth invention. That simple appreciation for rhythm evolved and was refined to the most sublime degree here. Nowhere in the universe is music even remotely as awesome as it is here. But it would never have occurred without that little Sirian addition."

Maxine was not concerned with Tom's paean to human musical ability as much as she was with his mention of what happened on his mythical planet on the summer solstice. "Drumming? Like a celebration of some kind?"

Tom smiled. "I guess I forgot to mention that little important tidbit also. My bad. Especially since it's so important in our *Ancient Aliens* context.

"The reason that all the ancient cultures celebrated the summer solstice in stone was because it was a significant date in Sirian history. It's the only date that merits a worldwide day of feasting and celebration, and yes, drumming, on Sirius.

"It was on Earth's summer solstice that Viracocha and the other Annunaki returned to Sirius with their cargo of hope, that first group of Sirian-human hybrids, Max. And then that cargo, of course, commenced the fight to save the planet from the dino menace.

"Later, homesick Sirians here on Earth remembered the date, and had the natives incorporate it into their many monuments as a remembrance, here, of those brave first mermaid visitors. The very ones who'd made it possible for these later Sirians to be walking around down here, giving orders and building monuments in the first place."

Tom paused. He sighed. "A darker aspect of humanity that came down from Sirian tinkering is the human capacity for addiction. A desire for some kind of routine was manufactured, the *habit* of regimentation. Again, such a desire was useful for a fighting force. After the dinos were eventually overcome, this need faded on Sirius. It's not like there's anything to become addicted to there anyway. Sirians *need* nothing that they don't already have, you see.

"But here on Earth, the desire to escape the rigors of a hard life has been present throughout her long and difficult history. And the desire for something better, a different routine, if you will, can sometimes translate itself into bad habits. And something addictive is present on every side." He smiled and lit another cigarette. "Such a need can take a person over, here."

"You can't say that only people become addicted, Tom!" Maxine objected. "Only people might make music, but they did those experiments with rats. The rats would push a lever and they'd get coke, and the scientists discovered that the rats would keep pressing the levers until they died. Isn't that addiction?"

Tom squinted. "I don't think that's exactly how the experiment went, Max. I think that's just how an over-zealous, anti-drug press reported it." He brightened. "But for the sake of argument, let's say that it did go that way. What you have to ask yourself is this – do the rats know they're going to die if they keep pushing that lever?

"No." Tom answered his own question. "They don't have the capacity to know that. Maybe they just like how it makes their little ratty brains feel. Maybe that's physical addiction, but not psychological addiction, like people acquire, because rats aren't self-aware, now are they? If you remove the cocaine, I doubt if the rats try to climb out of their cages looking for a dealer. But people have the capacity to know that they're going to die. But they push their levers anyway. That's definitely addiction."

Maxine said, "So you're saying that we got this capacity for addiction from the Sirians, and they've got the same capacity, but there's nothing there to get addicted to?"

Tom nodded. "You could indeed put it that way. This capacity for addiction, it's an outgrowth or side-effect of an embedded desire for regimentation. There's no military on Sirius anymore, so Sirians no longer have any need for regimentation, so thereby, the desire for it has faded. No need for addictions either, even if there were addictives. Life is just too wonderful on Sirius.

"Here, you can't get by without some kind of structure, some kind of routine in life. When this Sirian-implanted desire for regimentation goes awry, here, the result can be obsessive compulsive disorder, where a person is helpless not to do the same action over and over and over again.

"But this characteristic also allowed for the development of the assembly line, here; eight hours a day, five days a week, year in and year out, the same thing, over and over – repetitive motion tasks drive the global economy. You can't get monkeys to work on an assembly line. People can do it because they unknowingly have an embedded desire to do the same thing repeatedly. Get up. Fall in. March to the front.

Point." Tom closed his right eye and aimed at an imaginary target on the wall. "Shoot. Kill lizards."

Maxine wasn't concerned with OCD or assembly lines. She grinned. "So if we bought us a couple hundred kilos and hopped the next biosphere to Sirius, we could addict us the whole planet? Maybe pick up a few bucks?"

Tom's eyebrows shot up in surprise and he smiled. "I absolutely love the way you think, Max! *Addict us the whole planet?* That would be a definite possibility!"

I couldn't even begin to think of a response to any of this.

Tom said, "You know that vague idea, that *why are we here?* question that bothers some people, that desire to assign some larger purpose to everything?" He made that world encompassing gesture with both arms.

We nodded.

"One could say that one of the driving forces of mankind is the search for that missing link of *purpose*, right? What were you put here for? What is the meaning to existence? That vague feeling that they might not be fulfilling their purpose is something that some people can never quite shake. But the question of just *what that purpose might be* is something that they can never quite answer, either. That's because it's a question that was asked and answered through a little bioengineering a long, long time ago. The question continues to be asked, in your genes – but the answer is long forgotten.

"You're not what you think you are, Max. You think you're a product of evolution, or the whimsical creation of some god. But you're actually only partially an evolved creature, and partially a rather complicated science experiment. If you were simply an evolved product of this planet's environment, you'd be a lot hairier. Where do you think you get your naked skin? Why do you think your nostrils point downward, instead of outward like a great ape's? These are all characteristics of a being that evolved in the water."

"So, you're saying that the hairier you are, the less Sirian you have in you?" I asked.

Tom nodded. *"And Jacob said to Rebekah his mother, 'Behold, Esau my brother is a hairy man, and I am a smooth man.'*

"You're not you at all, but what the Sirians created, for their own use. And that purpose you desire, that unknowable purpose? It was an inserted imperative to return to Sirius and fight lizards. An inserted imperative to do what you were told, to do what your Sirian overlords wanted you to do. Addiction, OCD, the ability to work at a repetitive task job your whole life, that search for purpose – these are all the result of Sirian tinkering."

"If we're all the same, us and them," I pointed upwards, "then what is *their* purpose, if the dino threat was eventually overthrown?"

Tom shrugged. "Their purpose is to maintain the status quo. That's why I say that they're not indolent. They're always busy, like bees in a hive. Their purpose is to grow more things. Raise more children. They don't long for an answer to the question *why are we here?* They know why they're there. To continue."

"It sounds boring," Maxine said again.

Tom sighed again and smiled at her. "Indeed." Then Tom snuffed out his cigarette and leaned forward conspiratorially, as if he wanted us to know that the next part of his tale was something that he didn't share with just anybody. I reflected that he really was a good storyteller, even if the material was just silly.

"What I want to discuss next touches upon the reasons why the Sirians left the Earth, why they promised to return. Why they never did. Or at least why they never did en masse, like in the old days." He wiggled his eyebrows at us. "Actually, they return all the time.

"The names of the Sirians in this part of the story won't be familiar to you, Max. They didn't make it into human history or many mythologies, although there may be a very much garbled parallel in Egyptian mythology. And the idea that exists in many religions, that women are basically evil and not to be trusted, and therefore, men must always be in charge? That concept could have arisen because of the actions of these Sirians that I'm going to tell you about now."

When we looked at him dubiously at this declaration, he shook his head and said, "You're familiar with the story of Osiris and Isis and Set?"

Maxine considered. "Refresh my memory."

"Set kills and dismembers Osiris, and disperses the pieces of his body all over Egypt. It was the Egyptian belief that one couldn't be resurrected unless the body was whole. Isis reassembled all of her husband's body parts, except for one of the most important ones, which had been eaten by a fish. She later fashioned a golden one for him, from which she conceived Horus."

"There's a visual," Maxine replied.

"Anyway, that part isn't important," Tom said. "What's important is that Set is not identified as a man, as such, in Egyptian mythology. He's identified as *male*, but he's always depicted as the *Set animal*, with a curved nose, forked tail, long ears, and so on. Set doesn't look like any real creature, so I've always thought how much more of a jump could it be to make him female instead of male? Why does the bad guy have to be a man? Why couldn't Set have really been a destroying *female* entity?" Tom shook his head again. "The Egyptian connection is just my own personal pet theory. Anything's possible in mythology."

He paused, lit another cigarette and began again. "The part of the story that I'm going to tell you about next concerns two women and one man. They were like the dark and the light, the good and the evil, the passion and the mind – these women. And caught between these forces of nature was one man." Tom blinked for a moment, as if he was realizing for the very first time that we were two women and he was one man. Then he shook his head again as if to clear it, and continued.

"Allow me to introduce our actors. Bianca was a crossbreed Sirian sprung from the Aztec race, and was their most beautiful specimen at the time. Maybe of all time. She had a full-lipped, red mouth; large, tilted black eyes, and smooth, flawless mocha skin. She was compact and athletic, *Mexica* perfection, except for a little scar on her right cheekbone." Tom paused, thoughtfully rubbed his own right cheekbone with his left hand.

I'd never heard him describe a woman in such glowing terms before, and was disconcerted a little at his appreciation this time, I must admit. Even if he was speaking of some mythical creature. I looked over at Maxine. She frowned. She didn't like it either.

Tom suddenly continued. "You're familiar with the Aztecs and their gruesome human sacrifice rituals? The Aztecs believed that their sun god, Huitzilopochtli, had directed them to found the island city of Tenochtitlán; He was the patron deity of it, and of the people themselves. His name has been translated as *left-handed hummingbird*, I kid you not – although not everyone agrees on that translation.

"Huitzilopochtli was also the god of war. The Aztecs believed that He was in a constant fight against the forces of darkness, and in order to keep Him healthy and always up for this struggle, they believed that the war god needed nourishment in the form of human blood. From sacrifices.

"The Sirians didn't teach them that shit, I'll have you know. Earlier priests and kings had come up with that bloodthirsty philosophy all on their own. When the Sirians arrived, when these new gods fell from the sky, the Aztecs simply adapted their practices to the new reality as they perceived it. The Aztecs were always adding deities to their pantheon, anyway, from other peoples and regions.

"Some of the new deities were hardly gods at all, but Sirian captains. Any new god that was dedicated to exuberance or intoxication – riots, banquets, sports – was probably just a Sirian captain. Upon arrival here, these crossbreeds had learned to appreciate some of the pleasures of the flesh that didn't exist on Sirius, and were not at all above partying with the natives.

"But even though they had not been the original inspiration behind them, the Sirians encouraged and exploited the Aztecs' most brutal beliefs, because familiarity with *human* sacrifice translated seamlessly into mercilessly slaughtering lizards on the home front. The Sirians didn't really care what the Aztecs did to each other; no one was overly concerned when they sacrificed each other to their ancient gods. Especially if this gruesome practice made them all the more battle-ready when they were taken to Sirius.

"The Aztecs were the commandos in the war with the dinos. They were the Marines, if you will. Also prized were Viking Berserkers.

"And Bianca was sometimes right there with all these fierce warriors, knee deep in gore. That's how she got the scar on her cheek, dodging some dino spear on some bloody beachhead on the Western Continent.

"When she wasn't on Sirius, fighting, she was back on Earth among her Aztec brethren, running through the jungle hunting jaguars, picking out prospects for transport back home, giving witness to human sacrifice, side by each with the primitives. Bianca was like a jaguar herself; wild, dark, deadly. Merciless."

Tom paused again. He'd developed a sort of faraway look in his eyes that I had *never* seen before. After a moment of this, Maxine clapped her hands together, making both of us jump.

"Did you know this woman, Tom?" Max asked suspiciously, completely forgetting that this woman was just another part of the story he was making up. I'd forgotten that fact myself, what with his in-depth description of her.

"No, Max. Bianca lived thousands of years ago, at the time when Sirians were still building monuments here, taking soldiers back home. We don't live *that* long."

Max and I exchanged glances. *We?*

Tom lit another cigarette from the one he was putting out and continued. "As I say, Bianca was wild, vicious. She took her sport with the warriors as she wished. She was known to play *ōllamaliztli* with them at Tenochtitlán. You know, the ancient ball game? She liked to go out at night in the moonlight with someone who struck her fancy, and challenge him to a round, just the two of them. If he pleased her, he might be fortunate enough to enjoy her company a little more completely. If he displeased her, there might be a fresh trophy on the

204

tzompantli – the skull rack – beside the ball court in the morning. And that warrior would be seen no more."

Tom paused, took a drag on his cigarette, considered us for a moment. "Then there was Eydis. Eydis was everything that Bianca was not, though she was equally as stunning. While Bianca was petite, Eydis was tall, nearly six feet. Bianca was black-haired and black eyed; Eydis was blonde, with pale blue eyes, blue like ice, like an Arctic sky. She had a little pointed chin, a delicate, patrician nose, and a small, pink mouth.

"Where Bianca reveled in the chase, the hunt, Eydis was a thinker, a planner. Though it must be mentioned that she could be just as ruthless in her ambition, in the carrying out of her plans. She was a captain of the crew in charge of the ley lines and their energy, that bioluminescent light and communication system that more or less encircled the globe. Her mind was lively and quick, and her smile could warm the very stones she worked with."

I noticed that Tom had not lost himself in contemplation while telling us about this fair-haired woman, as he had while describing the Aztec Bianca. Somehow, it didn't surprise me at all that he would favor the *wild, dark, deadly* one over the thinker with the nice smile, no matter how pretty he said she was.

"And these two exceptional Sirians," Tom continued, "these two beautiful, intelligent, resourceful crossbreeds would probably have never met, and certainly never would've clashed, had it not been for one man."

Tom held up his index finger, and again I was struck by his ability to hold our attention with his silly fairy tale of Sirians and dinos and crossbreeds. Now it appeared that it was about to turn into some kind of three-sided love story. I found that I was looking forward to hearing more about *that*, because now it might become interesting.

I'd gone along with the grown spaceships and the alien invaders nonsense all morning, with minimal protest. So I figured that I could certainly listen to Tom's low, enticing voice tell us about mythical alien sex and intrigue without further complaint, for the rest of the afternoon, or for however long it took him to finish this epic.

"Basheer was a hybrid born in the ancient city of Ur, in southern Iraq," Tom was saying. "He was tall and strong, but not generally respected by his peers. He tended to be a little arrogant, and his Middle Eastern heritage gave him bushy black eyebrows that were always trying to meet in the middle. His underlings found this comical, and would often speculate behind his back that he was a throwback to an earlier Earth species. There was too much monkey in Basheer, they would say, and not enough mermaid.

"But despite this tendency toward hirsuteness, something that is not a Sirian characteristic, Basheer was said to have been irresistible to women. It was said that one look from his unusual tan eyes was more than enough to put them under his spell. One appraising smile from the soft, cruel, bow mouth, and women could deny him nothing, even if they knew that doing what he asked would be to their own detriment."

Tom favored me with one of his own little half smiles, one of those that made it so I could deny *him* nothing. *My addiction to that smile had not been to my detriment,* I thought. Not yet. I wondered if I'd be able to stop myself if I knew that it would be. I doubted it.

I would follow him to the ends of the earth, I thought again, whatever the cost, as long as he smiled at me sometimes. What a totally ridiculous *thing* I'd become because of him, I thought, not unhappily.

"But a way with the ladies does not a Sirian commander make," Tom was saying. "In addition to the snide remarks about his eyebrows, his detractors pointed to the much larger, much more unfortunate story of the complete failure of a dam development that he'd been in charge of in Egypt.

"It was a massive project, encompassing thousands of tons of earth and rock, shored up by two rubble and rock-fill walls facing the banks of the Nile, and two walls created by stepped limestone blocks on the upstream and downstream sides.

"Basheer had been young when he was assigned to this project; perhaps too young. Construction went on for ten years, but before the dam could be finished, a Nile flood – just the thing that it was being built to control – crested and destroyed it. Had this dam ever reached completion, it would've been the first project of its kind on this planet. But after its destruction, the idea it represented was pretty much abandoned. The Egyptians wouldn't attempt another such dam for eight hundred years.

"Basheer was sent to Mesoamerica in disgrace. His failure and the ridicule of his peers – always just out of earshot – turned him bitter. He was consigned to some low level construction overseer position in Tenochtitlán, which was an affront to his ambition, adding to his bitterness.

"Basheer knew that he'd never find the validation he craved through this assignment. So he sought it through the adoration of a woman." Tom blinked those big baby blues at us blankly, innocently.

"Bianca's beauty and warrior's prowess were legendary in Tenochtitlán, and Basheer was not in town for three days before he heard tell of it." Tom's innocent expression evaporated, replaced by an entirely devious, curled-lip grin. "The whispered snickers that she was just as likely to *fillet you* as she was *to lay you* especially intrigued him.

"So when Basheer heard that Bianca was slated to meet another warrior on the moonlit ball court, he arranged for that particular warrior to be otherwise occupied at the appointed hour. He arranged for two other young *Mexicas* to waylay and entertain him. They were not as beauteous as Bianca . . . but there were *two* of them.

"Basheer melded with the shadows of the back wall of the ball court, and watched Bianca's slow descent down the many steps. He watched her glance up at the stars, gauging the hour, gauging that her paramour was late.

"Just when she was becoming annoyed enough to consider leaving, Basheer stepped out into the light and said, 'He's not coming.'

"Bianca sneered slightly. 'Then tomorrow he will die.'

"Basheer shrugged. At least that unsuspecting warrior would enjoy himself tonight, he thought. 'I anticipate that you might take my challenge instead,' Basheer said. He approached until he was standing beside her. Bianca, small and compact, had to look up to see his tan eyes.

"The *Mexica* warrior smiled. 'Ah, Foreigner, I don't think you want to play this game with me.' She gestured at the court. 'The stakes here can be high indeed.'

"Basheer looked around him at the moon-washed stones. 'It's true that I don't know much about this tiresome native game. However, I have seen it played, and I've discovered that it bores me.' He stepped closer to Bianca, laid his hand upon her cheek, the expression in his eyes daring her to flinch. 'I have a far more interesting game in mind for you.'

Bianca didn't flinch, so he leaned in and she allowed herself to be kissed. But Basheer knew that this warrior wouldn't just *give in* so willingly. So, when she endeavored to flip him over onto the ground, he anticipated the maneuver, and using her own body's momentum against her, he chucked her roughly onto her back. He knelt astride her, casually pinned both wrists above her head with one hand.

"He said, 'Now I can play whatever game I wish with you.'

"Bianca smiled. She enjoyed a man that was stealthier than her, stronger. There were so few of them. She thought that this tan-eyed stranger was fearless indeed, to attempt such a seduction.

"'Kiss me again, Foreigner,' she said. 'I am not unfamiliar with *this* game.'

"When Basheer leaned forward to comply, Bianca knocked him off balance with her knee, arched her back. Basheer was rolled to one side.

Fast as lightning, their positions were reversed, and Bianca now knelt across *him*, holding a short obsidian dagger to his throat.

"'Beg for your life, Newcomer, and I might consider allowing you to leave this place.'

"Basheer smiled. 'Be careful what you demand of a man who has nothing to lose, *Mexica*. Sacrifice me, if you must. But first allow me to pay homage to she who bested me.' He slowly raised his hand to her cheek again, and Bianca hesitated in distrust, pushed the dagger harder against his skin. 'I am unarmed for death, *Mexica*. Yet the weapon I possess will still induce your surrender.'"

Maxine and I looked at each other in surprise at this clever dialogue, a witty ending to Tom's otherwise predictable love scene. He grinned devilishly at us.

"Heedless of the dagger, Basheer pulled Bianca's head down and kissed her again, savagely. He knew that she was intrigued, that she wouldn't kill him. At least not yet. Not until her curiosity was satisfied. And by then, well . . . Basheer was confident that Bianca would want to keep him around for further such *games*.

"Bianca returned his rough kiss. Basheer was right – she was hooked. He would've been surprised had it turned out otherwise." Tom snuffed out his cigarette. He picked up another cupcake, looked at us questioningly.

"Go ahead," Maxine told him. "They didn't come out sweet enough for me."

"They're sweet enough. Unless you've got your fingers stuck in a honeycomb, sweetness is mostly a chemical illusion, Max. Too much sweetness isn't good for you."

He stuffed half the cupcake into his mouth, and again resumed his tale with his mouth full. "You couldn't really call what Basheer and Bianca shared *love*. Although she did save him from getting sacrificed three times. The Aztecs didn't like foreigners, even if they might be gods. Like the Mayans, they never did have much of a sense of humor." Tom winked at me.

He ate the other half of his cupcake, looked at us for a second. "No, it certainly couldn't be called love by modern standards, not the way we think of love, with monogamy and all that. Sirians are not monogamous even on Sirius, and on this planet it was never even a consideration. Too many fellow Sirian crossbreeds, too many healthy, willing natives. *The sons of God saw the daughters of men that they were fair.*

"But Basheer and Bianca were only unfaithful to each other, if we even want to use that word, when they were separated by continents or oceans or the void of space. And even then, it wasn't that often; more of a reflexive gesture, a way to pass an evening.

"Whenever it was possible for them to be together, there could be no others, then. Bianca was sprung from a people not known for a developed sense of romanticism; Basheer was ambitious, and had had that ambition slapped down because of his own shortcomings. He was watchful and suspicious. Maybe because both of them were emotionally stunted in these ways, they didn't aspire to any lofty concepts of happily-ever-after. All that mattered was their all-consuming physical passion. The brutality of his desire for her and the ferocity of her appetite for him were all that were required, and when they came together all other realities were blotted out. Small talk was unnecessary.

"Basheer slowly climbed up a few rungs on the ladder of construction supervisors at Tenochtitlán. He really was an excellent builder. The Egyptian dam project had just been too ambitious. For him. For the Egyptians. It was not entirely his fault that it'd been a disaster."

Maxine giggled. "You make it all sound so *municipal*, Tom. The Aztecs engaged in human sacrifice, for Christ's sake, and you make them sound like a Caltrans crew, hanging signs on an overpass."

"The stability needed to maintain a large population over an extended period of time requires a bureaucracy, Max. Even in ancient times; even with a culture that gleefully slaughtered its captives and sometimes its own people."

"I have trouble imagining a people running around in feathers and loincloths, tearing out the still beating hearts of sacrificial victims on one day, then turning around and doing their taxes on the next," Maxine said.

"Yet a fairly intricate bureaucracy existed, nonetheless, Max. Worldwide. There were Sirians who acted as *advisors*, for lack of a better word, in all facets of life. Food production; food distribution. Irrigation, sanitation. Transport of soldiers to the front on Sirius. Building projects. Bread and circuses.

"While Sirians were here, they ran *everything*. You have to remember that. They and their puppet kings ruled all of the ancient societies that Giorgio is so fond of discussing on *Ancient Aliens*. Mesoamerica, Egypt, Mesopotamia. And while they were in control, everything ran like one big Elgin watch. Smoothly, efficiently.

"It was only when the local populations were left to their own devices that things started to fall apart. That's probably why you have trouble picturing a bureaucracy in ancient times, Max. You don't raise an entire world population to that level of complexity, take them, in a very short time, from hunter-gather tribesmen to the sophistication of the most-in-the-know New Yorker or Chicagoan or Angeleno, and then leave them all behind and expect that they'll be able to sustain themselves."

"Why *did* the Sirians leave us behind?" I asked.

"I'm getting to that," Tom said. "Remember, I said I'd explain everything?"

We nodded, and he continued. "So, Basheer slowly climbed up the bureaucratic ladder of construction advisors in Tenochtitlán. He even finally went back to Sirius to take his lumps for the dam debacle. But when his higher-ups saw what a fine job he was doing among the Aztecs, they sent him back and even promoted him.

"Eydis had been on Sirius at almost the same time as Basheer was there. She missed him by mere days. He left to go back to Earth, and she arrived *from* Earth. She was looking for additional engineers for her ley line crews, and soon heard all about his triumphs and tragedies. He sounded like a likely candidate to her, and she was frustrated that she'd missed him.

"So Eydis returned to Earth to locate him. She splashed down spectacularly in *Lago de Texcoco*, skipping the biosphere gracefully off the surface of the water as if it were just a giant flat rock. Eydis was an excellent pilot; there were few things she enjoyed more than being at the helm, making the big transports sing and dance. Water landings, terrestrial landings – each was equally effortless for her.

"Then there were the smaller, sub-orbital, terrestrial flyers. They arrived on Earth stored in the bellies of the biospheres, in those holds that had once housed *Igigi*. Eydis liked to put them through their paces as fast as Earth's gravity would allow. She called it *shaking the leaves off of them*. She was fearless, and like the best pilots, she was confident enough to be a little reckless.

"'You only die once,' she was fond of saying, because there was little chance of surviving a mishap in one of the sleek terrestrial craft, especially at the speeds and altitudes she favored.

"Eydis anchored her giant transport on the lake, and stood in the open hatch, serenely gazing out at the calming waters. Her gaze fell upon a local fisherman, and she beckoned to him. The fisherman was dumbstruck with fear and awe and love. While he'd seen his share of spacecraft splashing down in and taking off from the lake, he'd never beheld such a goddess as this before, had never seen blue eyes or blonde hair. Eydis spoke gently to him, persuaded him to take her across to the waterfront. The event would live in the lore of his family for generations, the day that *Abuelo* served a pale goddess by rowing her from her sun barque to the Tenochtitlán shore.

"Once set respectfully upon the beach by the dazzled fisherman, Eydis walked into Bianca's island city like she owned the place, in search of the Sirian that she'd recently heard so much about back home.

"Basheer was not hard to find. With his strange tan eyes and light skin, he didn't look like an Aztec, and besides, Eydis knew precisely who it was that she sought. She had a detailed picture of him in her mind. While on Sirius, quite by accident, Eydis had overheard two young women discussing Basheer. She had befriended them and had wound up paying far more attention to their giggling off-the-record portrayals of him than she had to all the eloquence of the council's official reports.

"Sure, there'd been the dam thing, but his record in Tenochtitlán was stellar, blah, blah, blah. The breathless accounts from the young women were far more riveting to an engineer and biosphere pilot who'd been unable to find any male companionship that amused her lately. This disgraced-though-recently-redeemed engineer sounded like he might be just the ticket, according to these girls. Eydis would offer him a new position and then hope that he would offer her one." Tom grinned at his own off-color humor.

"Eydis found Basheer as he was overseeing the setting of the last cornerstone for some pyramid. She observed him for some time, took in the tall, lean physique. She had surveyors and builders aplenty on her staff, at her . . . *disposal*, but none who looked like *this*. Yes. He would definitely do.

"When he turned around and their eyes met, she felt as though a bolt of energy had passed through her, like what happened when she touched two live ley stones at the same time.

"Such energy was not deadly like electricity; it was actually quite pleasurable. Being originally a water-based people, electricity had always been rather problematic to Sirians. They'd never considered attempting to harness the energy of electricity any more than they would've attempted to harness the energy of earthquakes. Electricity was just not their thing."

Tom took a drag on his cigarette. "Eydis had tracked this man down on a whim. They didn't even use ley stones here in Mexico; the living jungle interfered with the process. Here they communicated with flags and bioluminescent light signals. Yet Eydis felt the same bolt of pleasure from looking at this tan-eyed foreigner that she felt when she stood between two of her stones and connected with them.

"Basheer turned over the supervision of the pyramid to a native for a moment. The priests wanted to sacrifice a few prisoners and install a few hundred pyrite orbs and make a few blessings before any further construction would commence, before the next course of stones could be set.

"Basheer approached Eydis, but didn't smile at her – he no doubt wondered what bad news a blonde Sirian woman, so out of place here, might be bringing to him now. The petulance apparent in the set of his mouth thrilled Eydis still further.

"She smiled. 'Fear me not, Engineer.'

"Basheer didn't return her smile. 'I fear no one, Sirian.' He gestured around him. 'And I'm not an Engineer any more. Just a foreman.'

"'I've just come from home, and –'

"'How goes the war?' Basheer interrupted her. It had been almost six Earth months since he'd been home to make his final report on the dam. It had taken Eydis that long to track him down."

"Their communications weren't very good, were they?" Maxine said.

Tom shook his head. "Not compared to us, to modern Earth communications."

Now he was *us* again, I noticed. It amused me that he kept switching sides.

"'Things were at a stalemate when I was last home,' Basheer said.

"'Fortunately, it seems that the tide turns in our favor,' Eydis replied and smiled at him again.

"Basheer still didn't return her smile. He just continued to gaze at her expectantly, maybe with a small tinge of annoyance now. Eydis wondered if this pout was permanent, or if, under the right circumstances, he could be induced to smile.

"She ignored his rude interruption, and said, 'It is I who bring *you* good news.' This was an attempt on her part to be artful: his name meant *the one who brings good news*.

"When his expression still didn't change at her wit, Eydis continued. 'I come to take you to the islands in the Cold Sea, where the climate is temperate, and the natives friendly.' She nodded at the Aztecs working around her, some of whom had ceased their tasks and now stared humorlessly at her. 'Your expertise is needed there.'

"Basheer studied Eydis for a moment – this striking blonde Sirian who'd just shown up out of nowhere, offering to take him out of the jungle, out of his shame. It took him only that moment to detect that familiar hunger in the light blue eyes. He immediately knew what she was looking for, and it wasn't another engineer for her crew.

"'And what expertise would that be?' he asked. The recognition of another supplicant to his affections at last made him smile. Where *did* they come from? How *did* they find him?

"Eydis didn't realize how much she had craved that smile until she finally saw it."

Tom paused and lit another cigarette off of the one he was preparing to put out, and I realized that I felt a certain kinship with this Eydis, this ice princess that Tom had invented. I knew what it was like to crave a man's smile.

As if he read my mind, Tom favored Max and me with his own killer smile. He said, "Eydis was silent for a moment. She considered Basheer, looked him up and down – thoroughly, as if he was on sale.

"'I think you will enjoy the climate there much better than here,' she replied at last, and slapped a mosquito before it could make a meal of her Viking-sprung blood. 'And in gratitude for my removing you to those infinitely better conditions, I believe that you will allow me to avail myself of any and *all* forms of expertise that you might possess.'

"Surprised by her self-assurance, Basheer laughed. Again Eydis felt that little thrill of pleasure. He repeated to her what he'd once said to Bianca: 'Be careful what you demand of a man who has nothing to lose, Sirian.'

"'I demand nothing of you, my cautious friend. I offer you the opportunity to call yourself *Engineer* again. I offer you a chance to contribute to the energy fields that gird this planet, instead of continuing to build these stone monuments to death.' Eydis gestured around her. 'I offer you the opportunity to stop worrying that at any moment you might become the main event at the summit of one of them.'

"Basheer stepped forward and grasped her chin in his strong hand. 'And do you also offer yourself as part of this bonanza, Sirian? Because I need no fresh overlords. They are all the same, regardless of the climate.'

"The attraction Eydis felt toward him almost overwhelmed her. Basheer seemed like he might be a little bit more that she'd bargained for, but that was even better. Eydis liked to be in control, but the only thing she liked better than being in control was surrendering to a more dominant force. Like Bianca, Eydis found it difficult to find many men to fit *that* bill. But she recognized one when she saw him, and it thrilled her to the bone.

"Eydis swallowed, quite aroused now. 'I invite you to take advantage of whatever aspects of this *bonanza* that you desire, Engineer. Take advantage as you dare.'

"Basheer left Tenochtitlán that afternoon, without a backward glance. Bianca was in another part of the vast Aztec empire; he paused only long enough to leave word for her as to where he had traveled. He was confident that she would follow him to the other side of the planet, whenever she returned here and found him gone. He knew that she'd have to slaughter a whole cohort of warriors before she'd find another like him, another that made her feel alive the way he did.

"And if she didn't follow . . . well, Basheer knew that he already held Eydis under his thumb, without ever having even touched her yet. He decided to make her wait a little while for that event. Then she would be in the palm of his hand."

Tom paused. Maxine and I were leaning forward avidly now, hanging on his every word. He tilted his head curiously at us and smiled faintly.

After a moment, Maxine said, "Well, hell, Tom! Don't stop now!"

"It's just starting to get good!" I added.

"Aren't you guys hungry?" he said.

"Here." Maxine handed her phone to him. "Order a pizza. Just finish your story."

"Who orders pizza on Christmas Eve?" I asked.

Maxine looked at me. "A lot of people. People who have something else to do besides cook. People who want to hear the end of dirty stories about aliens."

Tom was already on hold with the pizza place. When he finished ordering, he handed Maxine's phone back to her and said, "Zo! Where was I?"

"Your boy Basheer had just found himself possessed of two women," Max replied. "One who couldn't get enough of him, and one that he wouldn't give any play to." Maxine glanced at me, and then thought about what she'd just said. She narrowed her eyes suspiciously at Tom. "Do proceed."

Tom lit a cigarette and smiled at us through the smoke, just as pleased as he could be that he had our undivided attention. "For about six months, in every corner of the place that would someday be known as the British Isles, Basheer had been setting up stones in straight lines to conduct bioluminescent energy. He was ambivalent about the new assignment; almost daily he weighed the pros and cons. The natives were friendly and respectful, helpful and intelligent. As Eydis had said, Basheer no longer had to worry that he might be abducted at any moment and flayed alive with an obsidian knife, just because the Aztecs' had decided to pay their humorless devotion on that day to the greater glory of some or another new god. Someone who was really just another crossbreed commander – someone that Basheer himself may have had lunch with on Sirius the season before.

"The weather was nice at the moment, but it would soon be getting on to winter, and Basheer hoped to be somewhere else when that happened. He longed to be somewhere where it was hot again. It didn't matter whether it was a dry heat like Ur or Egypt, or a wet one like Tenochtitlán. As long as it was hot.

"Basheer counted himself lucky that he'd so far successfully avoided any climate on this planet that featured the ordeal of a real winter, and he had absolutely no desire to experience any aspect of snow and ice now. Snow and ice were unknown on Sirius. The temperatures cooled down in the winter, but nothing so drastic as snow and ice."

"Kind of like here in Southern California?" I asked.

"Exactly. Only this Southern California-like climate was planet wide. You don't evolve a lot of amphibious hominids and cold-blooded, smart lizards in a place where things freeze over." Tom took a drag on his cigarette, then continued. "Basheer hadn't yet achieved the prominence that he desired, and this cutting off of his ambition was hardship enough for him to bear; he didn't want to suffer the weather also. He liked to think that he could imagine the cold well enough from looking into Eydis ice-colored eyes, touching her white skin. He deigned that he'd experienced winter quite thoroughly enough, just from listening to her talk about it.

"The work itself was fairly mindless. He'd built pyramids in two hemispheres; had attempted to build dams, for Christ's sake! So he felt that laying out rocks in straight lines was below him, no matter how important their function might be.

"But Eydis amused him well enough. She taught him how to fly. She had a grasp of Sirian history and a feel for the direction in which their people should go after the dinos were overthrown that delighted him. She also had a few ideas for what could be done with *this* planet. They spent many nights discussing these and other topics until the cock crew. Discussion, on any subject, had never been Bianca's long suit, and Basheer relished the intellectual gymnastics that Eydis put him through, surely as much as he savored her pale body.

"Basheer also enjoyed that certain kind of adoration for him that lived and breathed behind Eydis' clear blue eyes. Bianca had always given him the impression that her need was *for him* only because he was so proficient at satisfying it. Basheer knew that if ever someone came along that could satisfy her better, he'd be a memory. This thought never troubled him overly; he was confident that nonesuch other existed. But, on the other hand, there was always the possibility that he could sustain an injury or something like that. Basheer knew that if he could not perform for some reason, Bianca would be gone. The satisfaction in his encounters with her came from achieving her surrender. This never failed to be a challenge, yet was always utterly worth the effort.

"But Eydis appreciated him for himself, for his mind and thoughts, certainly as much as she appreciated him for what he could do for her. And she took no effort at all; Eydis would surrender at a smile. It could be said that Eydis *loved* Basheer, and this quality of the blonde's worship alone had kept him on the windswept heath for some time longer than he'd originally intended.

"Basheer found himself on the coast of Cornwall when the sun rose on the autumnal equinox. It amused him to see that, while the natives danced and prayed for he knew not what on this day when the seasons changed, they fled in terror when a small terrestrial craft streaked across the sky like a comet and splashed down in the bay.

"Basheer was delighted. He knew it had to be Bianca. Anyone else would have conveniently set the little craft upon the ground. Basheer knew that Bianca was uncomfortable with her landing skills and always preferred the certain safety of a splash down. So he knew it could be no one else but her.

"He commandeered a local boat and rowed himself out to where the flyer bobbed at anchor. Bianca stood in the hatchway and smiled fondly. As he approached, she shouted, 'I have searched high and low for you in this climate, foggy, raw and dull, Foreigner.' A wave broke over the bow of the little vessel Basheer piloted and Bianca laughed. 'See how you struggle! This place has made you as weak and pale as these light-eyed worms who serve you!'

"Basheer pulled beside the hatch and stepped onto the flyer, leaving the boat adrift. Eydis had taught him how to deftly put one of these terrestrial craft down on the ground. He'd just use it to return to the shore. No need to travel by boat like a primitive.

"The interior of the flyer smelled like home to Basheer: a tiny taste of Sirius, mixed in with the muddy vegetation smell of Tenochtitlán, all overarched by Bianca's heady *Mexica* scent. Before he could speak a word, she leapt into his arms, wrapped her legs around him. She held his face in her hands for a moment, then laughed and bit him hard on the neck.

"'Come, Foreigner!' she purred. 'Show me what good news you have for me.'

"The sun had begun to sink into the cold water when Basheer took the controls of the little flyer and piloted it up the coast, then up into the air. After a few finesse flying lessons for Bianca, he not unskillfully landed it.

"Through the viewer, he was unsurprised to see Eydis approach immediately. After all, he'd been missing from his tasks all day.

"But when he opened the hatch, he *was* surprised to hear her say, 'It's about time you arrived, Israfil! How can we energize this field in a timely manner if you remove our tools to places unknown . . .?'

"The good-natured smile with which Eydis chided the tardy Israfil faded as she beheld Basheer and Bianca. Bianca was sitting on his lap, so that he could . . . show her how to better work the controls.

"Bianca smiled slowly at the blonde pilot and said, 'Hail, Sirian,' paying deference to Eydis' rank. But there Bianca's respect ended. She leapt lithely from Basheer's lap, then out of the flyer and onto the ground. She said, 'I come to carry your Engineer to warmer climes. Winter impends on this dreary isle, and *my* isle of blood and stone beckons him. His tastes are far too refined and his constitution far too delicate to remain here and slog through the mud and cold with you any longer this year.'

"Bianca turned and grinned at Basheer and he grinned back. He made no move to disembark from the flyer.

"'He is free to take his leave, if the weather frightens him,' Eydis replied, and looked coolly at Basheer.

"He just continued to grin silently, not in the least affected by her insult. He was so glad to see Bianca, so glad that she was going to take him back to Mexico. He was willing to brave marauding Aztec priests before he was willing to suffer through the winter in Britain.

"'I'll keep you no longer then, Sirian,' Bianca said and hopped back into the flyer.

"Eydis leaned into the hatch and looked directly into Basheer's happy face. 'See that you return about a month ere the anniversary of Viracocha's triumph, Engineer. I carry your son, and he should make his appearance about that time.'

"Before Basheer had a chance to reply, Bianca told Eydis, 'I will bring him personally,' and closed the hatch."

"Oh, no she didn't!" Maxine exclaimed.

Tom and I looked at her. He said, "What's wrong, Max?"

"How could Eydis allow this woman to just drop out of the sky and take her man away? Especially when she'd just said that she was going to have his baby? And what a bastard he was for leaving!"

Tom said, "Wait a second, Max. You're applying your modern sensibility to an ancient, *alien* culture."

"What are you talking about, Tom?" she asked. "Are you saying that Basheer *wasn't* a bastard for abandoning his woman and her unborn child to go have sex and do human sacrifice with this Aztec chick?"

Tom smiled. "You've got it all wrong, Max. Basheer wasn't abandoning her, not in the way you mean. He was just going back to Mexico with Bianca because he didn't want to winter in England."

"But he should've stayed there with her . . . to *help her* through the winter. He shouldn't have left with the other chick once he found out that Eydis was pregnant. He had a responsibility to her then."

Tom laughed. "This wasn't Small Town, USA, Max. Sirian ideas of child-bearing and responsibility were a few millennia ahead of their time, even a few millennia ago. Eydis became pregnant because *she wanted to*. It wasn't an accident or a mistake. She didn't do it in an effort to ensnare Basheer, to chain him to her with feelings of responsibility toward his young. 'Cause that ain't how things work on Sirius.

"She simply decided that she wanted to mingle her genes with his; she made up her mind that any child they produced together would be strong and beautiful, and that she'd be proud to be mother to such a child. If your mother believes that you'll be strong and beautiful before she even makes up her mind to conceive you, how could you turn out any other way? This is one reason why Sirians are a proud and beautiful people.

"I told you before: on Sirius, children are raised communally, in special sections of the city established just for that purpose. Why would Eydis want or need Basheer to remain with her through her pregnancy, when she was going to just deposit the boy on Sirius to be raised, eventually?"

Maxine frowned. "I don't know, Tom. Just to be with her and help her through that time?"

Tom grinned gleefully at us. "I thought you were a feminist, Max! Do you think you'll *need a man* around to help you when you're pregnant? You don't *need* a man around now, do you? Fishes and bicycles and all that?"

Maxine grinned back at him. "No, Tom. I don't *need* one, but it's still damn nice to have one around. Can I get an amen?"

"Amen," I said.

"Suffice it to say that Sirian women decide when they want to have children, and how many, and with whom," Tom continued. "There's no need for the man to stick around and care for her or them, because everything is accomplished on a community level. Food is provided communally – the concept of *the breadwinner* is strictly an Earth construct.

"Sometimes the woman drops the baby off at the child center as soon as he's born, but usually she keeps him with her until the time he'd be about ready for pre-school here. She keeps him until he can walk and talk; until he's potty trained, if you will. Then she takes him in, and there he remains until he's deemed an adult, at about twenty. Mom and Dad visit if they want. They go to the park, on vacations, et cetera. But the kids don't live with Mom and Dad.

"At any one moment, Mom might be there visiting one or two kids; Dad might be there visiting considerably more. This was how things were on Sirius before the advent of bipedalism, and this was how things continued.

"Eydis didn't feel abandoned, Max. She knew that Basheer would be back to witness the birth of his son – even on Sirius, such a thing is an important event in a man's life. As I've told you, Sirians are not usually monogamous, so Eydis didn't begrudge him Bianca anymore that Bianca begrudged him Eydis.

"But it must be noted that Eydis did have that streak of devotion to Basheer that isn't generally a Sirian trait: *Eydis loved Basheer*."

Maxine said, "I don't understand what you're saying, Tom. If Eydis loved him, how *could* she allow him to leave with another woman? How could she not be jealous of this other woman?"

"Jealousy is not a Sirian trait. Jealousy is an outgrowth of possessiveness, Max. Sirians are not possessive, not in the least. Eydis didn't feel that she *owned* Basheer. He was free to share himself with others, as she was; as Bianca was. She couldn't deny him this freedom; the idea would never have occurred to her.

"Remember, he wasn't going to fly back to Tenochtitlán and settle down and raise a family with Bianca. Bianca was not the settling down and raising a family type, but more importantly, *Sirians* aren't the settling down and raising a family type. *There is no settling down and raising a family on Sirius*. If a woman wants to reproduce, she does, but there is no tying the man down to the whole process. The woman herself is not even tied down for too long. The children are not raised by their parents, so their parents are free almost immediately of the burden of being parents.

"Look at it this way. If your dad goes over here and has kids with this other woman, and then takes care of them too, he's essentially taking food out of your mouth and your mom's mouth, and giving it to them. He's dividing his resources, spreading them pretty thin, having responsibilities all over town. It isn't like that on Sirius. A man is not individually responsible for feeding his children, so it doesn't matter how many he has, with however many women. One of his women and

219

her child doesn't benefit more than the other. Again, there are no haves and have nots."

"But you said that Eydis loved him," I said.

Tom smiled and leaned across the table and kissed me. "And love is a wonderful thing, isn't it?"

"But what does that mean?" Max insisted. "What does it mean to love someone in a society where everybody is doing everybody else, and nobody cares about it?"

Tom smiled. "Love is love, Max. Just because everybody is available to do everybody else, doesn't mean one *has* to do everybody else. Love – monogamy, if you will – doesn't abound on Sirius, but it does happen sometimes."

"But how do you define love there?" Max insisted.

"The same as anywhere else, Max. Love is when you just want that one person. In this case, Eydis was satisfied with just Basheer. She loved him. She didn't feel the need to seek out others. But she didn't mind that he did, because that's just how things were. Just because Eydis was willing to share Basheer with Bianca doesn't mean she had to like her, however."

"That's jealousy, then," Maxine said in vindication. "If they were all just one big happy family, completely okay with sharing Basheer, then they'd all like each other, like on those reality shows about polygamy."

Tom tilted his head at her. "Do you watch that shit, Max?"

"Oh, hell, no. The very idea of the ego of some man thinking he can handle two or three women – and the complete *lack of ego* of these women who are willing to share him – it all just pisses me off. But I have seen the previews."

Tom said, "Once again, you misunderstand me, Max. I'm not saying that Sirians were never jealous of each other. Basheer, himself, was sometimes nearly consumed by jealousy, when some underling was assigned a better position than he was. There's just not a whole lot of jealousy associated with sex.

"Eydis and Bianca didn't like each other – you could say that they were jealous of each other, if you want. But they weren't jealous of each other regarding Basheer. Neither felt that the other was better able to keep him, because neither sought to *keep him*. Both were confident that he would come back.

"Here's an analogy. What do you call that mangy cat that you feed at the store?"

"Big Head."

"Right. So if you feed Big Head today, and he goes across the street and someone at the bar feeds him tomorrow, are you jealous?" Before

Maxine could answer, Tom said, "No. You're not jealous. You know he'll be back when he's interested in whatever food you have for him. It was the same with Eydis and Bianca, at least as far as Basheer was concerned.

"But still you might say that they were jealous of each other, because each felt that the other possessed qualities that she wished she possessed. They hated the differences that they saw in each other – differences that each perceived as strengths. Bianca secretly admired the pilot's height, her strange clear eyes and her honey-colored hair. Eydis admired the warrior's flawless mocha skin, her physical stamina and agility. Bianca wished that she could discourse like Eydis could; Eydis wished she could fearlessly slaughter the enemy, hand to hand, like Bianca did.

"But again – none of the things they hated or admired about each other had anything to do with Basheer. The most they felt about each other on that score might have been a mild annoyance – a mild annoyance *with him*, really, that he was not there with her at the moment, because he had chosen to be with the other one at that moment. But that was about it."

The pizza arrived, and we divvied it up and devoured it in silence. When there was nothing left but crusts and orphaned pepperonis, Tom clapped his hands together, making us jump. "Who wants a drink?"

Maxine and I both raised our hands, and Tom leapt up to go make cocktails. He also took the pizza box out to the kitchen and disposed of it. He was such a wonderful roommate.

Maxine nodded after Tom. "Would you ever share him? With someone you didn't like? *With anybody?*"

"I wouldn't even share him with you," I replied and smiled.

"I'm hip. This part is getting more far-fetched than growing spaceships."

"I think maybe Tom's typical male fantasy might be leaking out a little into this story," I told her. "Seriously – what man wouldn't love to invent a planet where you could do anyone you wanted, and if she got pregnant, she wasn't going to bother you about it?"

Maxine nodded. "It is entertaining, though."

Tom brought a rum and coke for Maxine and a gin and tonic for me. For himself he had concocted a tall tumbler of his newest invention, what he called the good-for-you Bloody Mary. It consisted of V-8 Juice and a good two shots of vodka. Then he spiced it up and sliced cherry tomatoes and pearl onions and celery and God-only-knew-what-else and threw them in there. It was delicious, and it took a spoon and a straw to consume it, like a malted milkshake. I didn't know how good it was for you, but it would get you drunk.

Tom began again. "You don't need to feel for Eydis and her cold loneliness on the English coast, anyway, Max. Since Basheer was on the other side of the planet, she decided to return to Sirius until her son would be born. While home, she became involved in a program to equip the biospheres with a newly developed weapon.

"The tide was turning in the war with the dinos, and this weapon promised to finally help the Sirians to defeat them permanently. It was similar to the caustic chemicals and plasma tool that they used to cut stones – but on a spacecraft sized scale. And they had added the magnesium-like substance from earlier hand-held weapons. The result was kind of like Greek fire. Deadly. Devastating.

"Eydis became so fascinated with it that, before long, she found herself in charge of equipping a transport and its flyers with the weapon and taking it back to Earth, just to have such a vessel on hand there. Besides, it was much more fun and definitely more acceptable to be napalming forests and shattering granite cliff faces here than on Sirius. Eydis barely noticed that the time was passing, and didn't have time to pine for Basheer, not even once."

"That was because she had a part of him with her," Maxine said and patted her flat belly.

Tom nodded, shrugged. "Before she knew it, it was time to return to Earth and present him with their son."

"'I will return for you again on the equinox, Foreigner,' Bianca promised. 'If I am not otherwise amused.'

"Basheer nodded, smiled. He knew that she wouldn't be. He watched the flyer take off, then walked across the green grass to the shelter where his son would soon be born. He'd located Eydis at the site of the latest ley stone erection project, in *Bretagne*, near a town that would someday be known as Carnac."

"Why would she chose to have her baby here instead of on Sirius?" Maxine asked. "What if something went wrong with the delivery?"

Tom squinted at Maxine for a moment, then looked at me. "Call it a *hippie thing*, maybe. Delivery would've been the same either place. It's a more . . . *natural* thing on Sirius, than it is here. Always has been. No hospitals and all that.

"It was a little boy, as Eydis had promised. Basheer named him Akil, which means *intelligent* in Egyptian."

Tom smiled suddenly. "That's another phenomenon that comes down to you from your Sirian forebears, Max. All babies here might not be born left-handed like they are there, but they all look like their daddies at birth, here, just like they do there. That's so Dad can identify his child himself, in case Mom got it wrong."

"I thought you said that Sirian women decided when they wanted to get pregnant?" I said.

Tom grinned, threw up his hands. "Right, but sometimes mistakes can be made when it comes to identifying the dad. Maybe Mom didn't care which man was Dad this time." He shrugged, communicating mystification at the minds of Sirian women. "When babies are born they generally look like their daddies, here and on Sirius. They might grow to look like Mom later, but at that moment of birth – that's so Dad can look at them, and be sure which ones are his.

"Anyway. Akil looked like Basheer, in that he had black hair and light tan eyes; but he had Mom's fair skin. It warmed Eydis to see Basheer smile; his frowns and pouts were all forgotten, at least for the moment, when he looked at his son."

Tom sipped his vegetable lollapalooza, spooned out half a cherry tomato and ate it. "This situation went on for five years. The only difference was that after the first year, Eydis would arrive in Tenochtitlán and pick Basheer up, instead of waiting for Bianca to bring him back. The seasons now varied when she would arrive, although he never did spend a winter anywhere but Tenochtitlán.

"This arrangement arose because Eydis had now become the commander in charge of outfitting all of Sirius's transports and flyers with the new weapon. It was discovered that it was easier to outfit them here and then return them home afterward. Like I say, it was thought better to wreak devastation here in testing out the new weapon than on Sirius. So at the time of which I speak, almost the entire fleet was, for lack of a better word, *parked* here on Earth, in Mexico, awaiting their retrofits, or if they were already done, awaiting their return home. There were maybe only a total of three transports and maybe twenty flyers, already weaponized, on all of Sirius.

"The transports and flyers were parked in Mexico, but the crews that actually weaponized them were in Europe. So Eydis would do a flyby across Mexico, and drop off a newly weaponized transport and take an unweaponized one. On the way, she'd pick up Basheer and head back to Europe.

"In those five years, Eydis and Basheer had three children. Akil and two little girls."

"Just like you," I said. "Didn't you say you have two sisters?"

"Half-sisters," Tom corrected. "I'm my mother and father's only child, my mother's only son. There are no doubt other half-brothers and half-sisters that my dad sired, but I don't know any of them."

Again, I thought that Tom must be sprung from some strange religious sect, and that their odd marital practices had obviously informed his story.

"This random showing up of Eydis in Tenochtitlán began to become an annoyance for Bianca. The blue-eyed Sirian was known to disrupt festivals with her arrival, drawing unwelcome attention to herself and Basheer at times when sacrificial victims of any unusualness were highly prized.

"Eydis had been warned to never show up with Basheer's children in February or May, times when the Aztecs sacrificed their offspring to the rain god. Erring on the side of caution, Basheer advised her to never bring them at all. Bianca agreed with a grin, saying that it was probably best for her to leave her strange, light-eyed, white-skinned children on Sirius, or even in Europe. There they might be revered as the seed of gods – while in Tenochtitlán, they might be sacrificed as unique tributes to Tlaloc, a more ancient and much more bloodthirsty deity.

"It would have been so much easier, so much safer for everyone, if the golden Sirian would have just allowed Bianca to bring Basheer to her whenever winter ended. But Eydis insisted on making her grand entrances, drawing the attention of various priests and their minions. This angered Bianca. Even though she loved this brutal people from whose blood she had sprung, Bianca knew that undue attention from priests could get anyone sacrificed atop the *Templo Mayor*, including Bianca herself, not to mention the light-eyed foreigners.

"When Eydis made the mistake of arriving in Tenochtitlán on the night of the vernal equinox, Bianca had already had enough. It was the festival of *Xipe Totec*, the Night Drinker, the Flayed Lord.

"Priests danced through the crowds of spectators, wearing the gory, flayed skins of sacrificial victims. They would touch the bystanders with the freshly disarticulated and defleshed femurs of these victims. *For fertility.*" Tom grinned.

"Why did they do these horrible rituals?" Maxine asked, appalled.

Tom's grin widened. *"He that eateth my flesh, and drinketh my blood, dwelleth in me, and I in him."*

Maxine said, "What?"

Tom shook his head. "Never mind, Max. Legend said that the god *Xipe Totec* flayed Himself to feed His people. He was a god of agriculture, and scholars speculate that this removal of the skin represents the way that kernels of corn lose their outer skin before they germinate. *Xipe Totec's* priests would wear the flayed skins of the sacrifices for twenty days, and when they at last emerged from these putrid coverings, it was a symbol of rebirth. Renewal.

"The Aztecs also gave *Xipe Totec* the credit for having invented war. That was convenient, because most of the victims flayed in His honor were war captives. But not all of them.

"Despite the mobs of onlookers, despite the bloody priests dancing through the streets, Eydis somehow managed to locate Bianca in the crowd.

"Bianca was amused to see her walking up the street, the horde parting before her and then congealing in her wake, the onlookers pointing and whispering. Bianca was amazed at her foolhardiness, and for once didn't envy the pilot's stature, her white skin, her honey-colored hair. Tonight was not a night to stand out. Tonight was a night to blend in with the faithful.

"'Hail, Sirian,'" Bianca greeted her with a grin.

"Eydis glanced about nervously, nodded absently at the sign of respect. Bianca was pleased to note that perhaps at last the pilot had realized what a mistake she'd made by landing here tonight.

"'Where is the father of my children?' Eydis asked. 'Where is Basheer, *Mexica*?'

"'He serves the god in *Yopico*,' Bianca replied.

"'I am unfamiliar with the native tongue,' Eydis replied in annoyance.

"Bianca nodded at the Great Pyramid, lit with fiery torches as well as bioluminescent ones. 'It's the name of the temple of the Red Smoking Mirror, within. It's the sanctuary of He whom the natives honor tonight. *Xipe Totec*.'

"Eydis nodded, still annoyed. It was not in her to understand why Bianca wallowed in these gruesome rituals alongside the natives. 'Will Basheer return soon from this duty?' she asked.

"Bianca laughed. 'This is *Tlacaxipehualiztli*, Eydis. The *flaying of men in honor of Xipe*.' Bianca nodded at the dancing priests. 'Basheer will not be returning. He has been sacrificed.'

Maxine and I both covered our mouths with our hands at this horrifying turn of events. Tom had us now; his story suddenly didn't seem quite so silly anymore. We both felt Eydis's sudden, complete, inexplicable loss.

Tom continued. "Bianca looked serenely at the tall blonde, whose mouth now hung open in speechless disbelief. 'Such things often happen to foreigners here, Sirian. I warned him. And you. Unfortunately, I was not on hand to save him this time.'

"Eydis covered her heart with her hand, then put her hand on Bianca's shoulder to steady herself. Bianca looked at her hand, and Eydis removed it quickly.

"Bianca gestured at the crowd. 'Mourn not, Sirian. There are many more captains in this throng, and natives, too. Younger, stronger flesh. Although, I would advise that you wait a few days before auditioning any. In fact, I would advise that you take your leave as soon as possible, lest you share Basheer's fate.'

"Eydis took a deep breath and composed herself. She would not allow this brutal *thing* of a Sirian to ken how much the loss of Basheer affected her. People died. It was a fact of life. People died and returned to the great energy of the void, to peace."

Again I recognized the viewpoint of whatever weird cult it was that had produced Tom, because he'd told me at Halloween that this was their philosophy. *What is fiction,* I thought, *but an extrapolation of one's own beliefs, a projection of one's own thoughts and desires onto imaginary characters?*

"Eydis exhaled and said, 'Indeed.' She willed herself to be completely calm, the ice in her eyes a reflection of the ice in her heart, in her soul. Basheer was returned to the great energy. There was no cause to mourn him. Mourning wasn't a Sirian trait.

"'I will take your advice, *Mexica*. I bid you farewell. I doubt we will meet again.'

"Bianca dismissed Eydis with a wave of her hand as she knelt to receive a light plunk on the head from a thighbone, a blessing from one of the dancing priests. He paused and looked curiously at Eydis. She turned away quickly and melted into the crowd."

Tom paused, sipped his tomato-soup-colored drink and looked at us. Maxine thought about the full tragedy of the story he'd just told us and unconsciously returned him his own gesture, tilting her head at him in bruised wonderment.

He smiled. "You want to know what bearing this heartbreaking tale has on . . . on anything, right, Max?"

"I hate it when you read my mind, Tom," Maxine replied. "It's annoying as hell."

"Simple deduction, my friend." Tom tapped the side of his head. "I can't read your mind, but from the look on your face, I can tell that you want me to get to the fucking point."

Maxine nodded.

"Okay." Tom set his drink down and lit a cigarette. "Eydis knew that she shouldn't mourn the death of Basheer. He was returned to the great energy, at peace, and all that shit. But she couldn't help herself. He hadn't died of old age, or in honorable battle, fighting dinos on Sirius.

Such ends she could have accepted. But not this way. The awfulness of his end *assailed* her. Sacrificed, flayed alive by primitive crossbred monkeys, on this backwater planet! She could not accept it, couldn't stomach it.

"While she was still standing beside Bianca in the crowded street, Eydis had decided that she must avenge Basheer's death. She would slay the black-hearted *Mexica*, if not for him, then for the honor of his children. When she put her hand over her heart, she'd removed a little seed pod that hung there on a braided grass chain. When she touched Bianca's shoulder she had surreptiously mashed the seed, placing the bug on her, and –"

"*The bug?*" I said in disbelief. "As in, a tracking device?"

Tom smiled his glorious surprised smile. "Exactly! Except it was an *actual bug*. A tiny, bioengineered creature of the genus *Siphonaptera*, I believe. I'm not exactly sure. It's an Earth creature, not something that we have on Sirius, so I'm not too familiar with it. I think –"

"*Fleas?* Eydis gave Bianca *fleas?*" Maxine was looking at her phone

Tom smiled, impressed with Maxine's quick Google. I noticed that he'd taken ownership of Sirius again, saying *we* instead of *they*.

"Not fleas, Max. Just one flea, a tiny bioengineered bug that emitted a tiny but very strong, very unique signal. Something in its little microscopic heartbeat, I think."

"A bug," I said. "Literally and figuratively."

"Actually and idiomatically. Eydis went back to her transport, riding at anchor in the lake. She consulted the tracker for this bug, by now securely clinging to one of the *Mexica's* luxuriant black hairs. A green light bioluminesced on the . . . *dashboard*, if you will, of the transport. All was in order with the bug. Eydis would be able to locate Bianca, no matter where she attempted to hide. She waited."

"I thought you said that their communications weren't very good," I said. "But you keep coming up with new stuff that they had."

"This is a history, Liz. It's not that I keep coming up with new stuff; it's that I just remember stuff when it's germane to the story." Tom winked at me. "This story that I'm making up."

"This story that you're making up as you go along," Max suggested.

"Does it seem that way?" Tom asked in surprise.

"Sometimes," I replied. "First you said that their communications weren't very good, yet now you say that they used bugs, *actual bugs*, as tracking devices."

"Okay, let me digress a minute and discuss Sirian communications. They never developed voice communications of the type that later developed here on Earth. That kind of thing involves too much electricity, I guess. Sirian communications, like transport to transport and transport to ground, were energy pulses, like Morse code, if you will. It was all dependent on the ley lines girding the planet. It was weak at best."

"What about communication with Sirius?" Max asked.

"Another energy pulse deal. A beam was aimed, sent; took a few weeks to get there. That kind of thing. But they did have the bugs, which produced a unique energy signal that could be tracked planet-wide. If Eydis would've planted a flea on Basheer, she would've known that . . . but I'm getting ahead of myself." Tom picked up his drink, plucked out a pearl onion and chewed it. With his mouth full, he said, "Are we good on the communications, then? Not a lot of snappy repartee ship-to-ship, okay? Just the equivalent of dots and dashes."

Maxine and I nodded.

"At the height of the celebration of the Flayed Lord, on a whim, Bianca decided to fly to Puma Punku. Maybe she wanted to see Viracocha's vast, now still pool by moonlight. Maybe she wanted to –"

"Maybe she wanted to mourn Basheer in her own way," Maxine opined.

Tom grinned. "Maybe."

"Maybe she just wanted to get the hell out of human sacrificing, skin-flaying Dodge," I suggested.

Tom said, "Maybe Bianca was just in the mood for a long ride. She liked flying over water best anyway, and the most direct route to Tiahuanaco took her mostly over the ocean." He sipped his drink. "Anyway, when she lifted off in her little flyer and headed south, Eydis was waiting for her."

Tom paused and looked from one of us to the other. He leaned forward again, again seeming to let us know that this was not a part of the story that he told to just anyone. "Bianca set the craft down not far from the pool, and barely had time to disembark before Eydis attacked."

He paused again, letting us picture magnesium-laced Greek fire erupting out of a giant, *grown* spaceship. "Bianca ran. Eydis fired again and again, making that big transport walk and talk, but still the pale green signal continued to bioluminesce on the dash. Bianca lived still."

Maxine smiled slyly. "So it was *Eydis* that destroyed Puma Punku?"

Tom grinned in delight. "Blew the shit out of it."

"So much so that, to this day, all the king's horses and all the king's men haven't been able to put it back together again enough to figure out that it was once a giant swimming pool," I stated.

Tom nodded, still grinning. "Yet even amid all this carnage, Bianca was able to get back to her flyer and lurch it into the air. She guessed what was going on, that the fair-haired Sirian blamed her for Basheer's sacrifice, and was trying to kill her. So she pointed her little craft toward the place where the bulk of the transports were parked, hoping that she could outrun the enraged pilot and land there. She figured Eydis would not fire on the transports, all parked together like battleships at Pearl Harbor. Bianca figured she'd be safe from Eydis's wrath there." Tom took a drag on his cigarette, exhaled and grinned at Maxine through the smoke. "She figured she's be safe from Eydis . . . *in Mapimi.*"

"Oh!" Maxine exclaimed, making me jump. *"The Zone of Silence!"*

"Up the coast of Peru, over Guatemala, then inland again, over Tenochtitlán, Bianca flew her small craft, with Eydis hot on her tail in the slower transport. North, straight up the gut of Mexico. Bianca was only seconds ahead of Eydis when she clumsily set the flyer down amid the transports. There were probably twenty of them, nearly all of the Sirian fleet on earth, each with its little flyers all nestled in its belly.

"But Eydis didn't care about the fleet." Tom spread his hands out in front of him. "She was incensed, utterly single-minded now. Nothing mattered to her anymore, nothing – not her children, not her mission. Basheer was dead. All she cared about now was annihilating Bianca. It was Bianca's fault that her children were fatherless. She fired, again and again.

"Paying heed only to the green signal, Eydis ignored all the frantic dots and dashes now sounding in the cabin from the ground crew. Bianca ran between the transports and Eydis fired on her again, fired on *them*, turning transport after transport into smoking, irreparable piles of ash. The fires produced by the chemicals in the new weapon destroyed the organic material of the ships in their entirely."

"Nothing was left but strange magnetic forces that disrupt radio signals, right Tom?" Maxine asked eagerly.

"That's more a by-product of the geology of the *Zona Silencio*, Max." He speared a half of a cherry tomato with his straw. I got the impression that Tom might be getting more than just a little bit drunk. I smiled.

"As the ships burned, the desert became temporarily alien to the rattlesnakes and tortoises that lived there – it suddenly was filled with gray-white smoke and a smell like burning leaves, leaves that had never grown in the desert. Leaves that had never grown on *this planet.*

"Another Syrian pilot was able to save one of the transports, limp it into the sky, away from the destruction raining down from above. His name was Israfil – a young man who had once worked for Eydis in

Europe. He had no idea what was going on, only that the *base*, for lack of a better word, was under attack. There was no way to identify who piloted the attacking craft, unless the pilot replied to his signals.

"He formulated the idea that the pilot must be a dino leader who'd somehow commandeered a transport, had somehow piloted it across space, and was now proceeding to attack the source of all the troops that were slaughtering his people on Sirius. It was a ridiculous scenario, but Israfil couldn't conceive of any reason why *a Sirian* would be attacking and destroying damn near all the transports that they had on Earth.

"He fired repeatedly on Eydis, but she dodged his shots. However, her mindless hunt for Bianca was interrupted by Israfil's defense; he succeeded in running her off from the base. Valiantly, doggedly, Israfil chased Eydis. He chased her across the Gulf of Mexico, across the peninsula of Florida, across the vast expanse of the cold North Atlantic. He got a few light hits in, but still the big craft stayed in the sky. Eydis gazed down in fond nostalgia as she flew over the southern corner of her beloved British Isles.

"But then Israfil had her, and he fired for the last time. Eydis was the better pilot, but Israfil was the better gunner. Eydis's ship sputtered, crippled now, and fell. It augured down into the cold waters of what would someday be called the Baltic Sea."

Tom grinned mischievously at us. I was sure of it then. He *was* drunk. "In 2011, a boatload of treasure seekers discovered Eydis's ship at the bottom of the Baltic, between Sweden and Finland, under two hundred and eighty-five feet of water." He took his phone out of his pocket, typed; he showed us a grainy photo of a strange circular object on the ocean floor. If you used a little imagination, it almost looked like the *Millennium Falcon*.

"If it was one of their grown ships, why didn't it rot?" Maxine asked skeptically.

Tom looked at the picture, shrugged. "Maybe the water's really cold there. Preserves things." He put his phone back in his pocket. "Who needs another drink?"

You most assuredly don't, I thought. As if reading my mind, he left his glass sitting on the coffee table, collecting only mine and Maxine's.

I said to her, "I think Tom's getting a trifle tipsy."

"I think it's adorable."

I didn't know about *adorable*, but it was amusing. We were usually always drunk ahead of Tom, suddenly finding ourselves to be all sloppy and slurry, while he still seemed as fresh and uncorrupted as a preacher on Sunday. It was a change for Maxine and me to be the ones more in control of ourselves.

He returned and set our fresh drinks down. "Allow me to draw this epic to a close now, while we're all still young.

"Eydis's homicidal rampage caused history to take a hard left." Tom closed one eye, tilted his head, and made an abrupt turning gesture with his left hand. "The fleet on Earth was destroyed. Maybe five or six Sirian transports still existed in the entire galaxy: two or three here, two or three there. There would be no more transporting of vast numbers of Aztec warriors or Viking Berserkers to Sirius to handle the dirty work.

"Earthside leaders still had no idea what had actually occurred; Israfil's crazy idea that maybe somehow it was the dinos that had attacked even seemed almost possible. Leaders back home didn't even know that *anything* had occurred. Communications with Sirius were weeks behind. The Sirians on Earth sent a report out; even though no response was expected, no response being received suddenly seemed ominous.

"So the day after Eydis's destruction, in what may be termed to have been a little bit of a *panic*, a decision was reached. The Sirians would leave Earth, en masse, and return home, just to see what the situation was there, just to see if their planet needed them.

"The three remaining transports flew along the gridlines and stopped in all the major cities. A call went out, alerting all Sirians that they had best be gettin' while the gettin' was good: we're going home now, and we don't know when we might be coming back. If you don't want to get left behind on this backwater rock, it's high time to report to the ship."

Tom quoted Toy Matinee, *"Here's a concept you can't dance to/A deal you cannot hum/There may not be an empty seat when all is said and done."*

I leaned across the table and kissed him, supplied another line. *"This party is addictive, self-destructive no doubt/so I hope that someone saves a seat for me on the last plane out."*

Maxine just shook her head at us, unfamiliar with the tune. "And then . . . ?"

"The transports went around and collected everybody that wanted to go. Like I say, it was kind of a panic; the attack on the base had rattled the Sirians. Worldwide, their energy fields vibrated with unease."

I pictured lines of nervous Sirians snaking up the steps of the Great Pyramid of Tenochtitlán, hurriedly boarding giant pods, like the people on that iconic ladder, trying to flee the fall of Saigon in 1975.

"There were many Sirians that elected to stay, worldwide, however. Many were leaders – kings placed here to rule and guide the natives, and they enjoyed the prestige and adoration of their biddable, monkey-crossbred peoples. Why go back to Sirius and just be another pea in the pod? They figured that it might not be so bad to live out the rest of their long lives here, revered and worshiped.

"Most of them didn't actually believe that anything was amiss, anyway. They mostly all put it down to some kind of accident with the new weapon, some kind of equipment failure. They didn't really believe that their Sirian brethren would not be returning for them." Tom paused, drained his drink, and started picking the remaining, thoroughly vodka-infused vegetables out of it with his spoon.

"They never did come back, though, did they?" Maxine said. "The great religions all say that the gods promised to return, but they never did, did they?"

"You're getting ahead of me, Max. There's one more part. While all this stuff was going on, the festival of *Xipe Totec*, the destruction of the fleet, all that, there were three Sirian captains who'd known better than to be in Tenochtitlán on such a festival night. So they'd flown out to the jungle to hunt jaguars with spears; to let this month's orgy of blood and death and sacrifice pass them by.

"The hunting had become boring almost immediately, however, so they'd made camp, started a nice little chemical-slash-bioluminescent fire and settled in to drink *octli* and tell raunchy stories." Tom picked another pearl onion out of his almost empty glass.

"*Octli?*" Maxine asked.

"*Pulque*. It's made from the agave plant. Like tequila or mescal."

"So these guys are sitting around in the jungle getting drunk while Eydis is shooting up the fleet?" I said.

"Yep. But they got the message when they got back to their flyer the next day. And they reported to the nearest transport for passage back to Sirius, immediately, without pause. None of these three wanted to be stuck on Earth. One of them, a certain tan-eyed, light-skinned individual, wondered vaguely about his women as he was jostled in the packed hold of the transport. He knew that one of them would definitely elect to go back home, but he was not so sure about the other one. He was pretty sure that she would elect to stay in Mexico, and he –"

"*Basheer wasn't sacrificed?*" Maxine exclaimed, as if she knew Basheer personally. I thought maybe Maxine was getting a little plastered also.

232

Tom smiled. "Of course not. He was too smart to allow that to happen, but more importantly, *Bianca* was too smart to let that happen. She'd suggested it, and he and his two buddies went jag hunting."

"But why would Bianca tell Eydis that he was dead?" Maxine asked emphatically. "That is so fucked up!"

"Bianca was convinced that Eydis was endangering all their lives with her constant visitations, so she wanted all that to end. She figured that she'd give Eydis a good scare, then she'd just tell Basheer to fly over there to Europe to let her know that he wasn't really dead, as soon as he got back from hunting. How was Bianca to know that Eydis would flip out? Destroy the *fleet*, for Christ's sake? Alter the course of history?"

"It was still a fucked up thing to do," Maxine maintained.

"History is full of fucked up things, Max." Tom shrugged, picked the last cherry tomato half out of his glass, chewed it up.

"When the three sole surviving transports returned to Sirius, they found that the war was at its apogee, at the very turning point. They joined forces with the other three transports, now warships, and within six months, the dino threat was finally eliminated. Completely. The lizards were wiped out, more thoroughly than that asteroid had wiped them out on Earth. The only thing that looks even remotely like the Dino People on Sirius anymore are scattered groups of Grays, that the Sirians keep around for research, and as servants. Just the little spindly fellas. No *Igigi* that could possibly rise up and rebel."

"Do the Sirians send them back to Earth sometimes? To do research *here?*" Maxine asked. "To do abductions and cattle mutilations?"

"Sirians almost completely lost interest in Earth, once the war was over, Max. There was no need to import any more sometimes problematic cross-bred monkeys to fight for them. They had the entire, vast, *immense* Western continent to subdue and populate; they had a lot of dwellings to grow, a population to feed.

"Sirians were concerned with Sirius, now. They were concerned with the happy work of making the whole planet into the same natural paradise that had once existed only on the Eastern Continent. In their zeal to begin, Sirians pretty much forgot all about this primitive, backwater planet.

"Here on Earth, those that had opted to remain behind tried to keep things operating smoothly. But their technology began to run down; bioluminescent lighting and tools, which received their chemicals and fuels from Sirian sources, eventually ran out of them and went dark, quit working. The energy that once made the ley stones seem as though they were almost alive dissipated into the atmosphere. The various Sirian cultures across the globe lost touch with each other.

"As this entropy accelerated toward oblivion, the native populations began to notice a distinct lack of miracles happening anymore. There were no more amazing flying craft, no more levitating stones, no more monoliths erected overnight.

"So, the locals began to tell tales of earlier miracles that they'd heard about, or had seen personally, or had even participated in. Some groups, such as the stonecutters that had worked closely with the 'gods' on the construction of all the great monuments, suddenly considered themselves special, above their peers. They believed that they possessed a superior knowledge that the rest of the rabble did not, because the now decamped 'gods' had once supervised them directly. They began to set down secret traditions to remind themselves of this specialness, to never let their posterity forget that they'd once been the favorites of these 'gods.'

"Unfortunately, what they chose to remember didn't have too much to do with geometry and construction. All that's come down to us now are a few 'secret societies,' feared and suspected by their friends and neighbors, who have a bunch of secret handshakes and code words, but who've forgotten all about whatever technical knowledge the 'gods' left them." He twisted the Masonic ring on his pinkie and smiled.

"The Sirian kings and leaders that had remained behind attempted to assuage the natives' uneasiness and loss of religion by disseminating tales about how the now-absent gods had promised that they would return someday."

"But they never did," Maxine said again.

Tom nodded, but held up his finger. "Hold on a second, Max. The 'gods' never returned, not en masse, as they once had. There were no more transports, no more flyers slicing through the air. As I said before, it was impossible for a basically very primitive population to maintain all the glories of civilization. All the glories that they had not earned, had not discovered, had not struggled to produce on their own. Humanity had essentially just been plopped down in a world of technology and sophistication that they couldn't understand, and as such, couldn't hope to reproduce or even maintain. As the years passed and the remaining Sirians died out, the artificial civilizations that they'd installed here fell apart. The stories that they'd told to the locals, and the events that the locals had witnessed and remembered, became garbled; eventually they became myth and scripture.

"Mankind had to essentially start all over again. He had to now learn on his own everything that the superior culture and technology of the

Sirians had once just handed to him. And so he did, taming this planet all by himself. The only thing that remains of the Sirians here are a bunch of confusing stone edifices and some far out mythologies. And a whole lot of biomodification.

"But that's not the end of the story."

"Somehow I didn't think it would be," I said suspiciously.

He leaned across the table and kissed me. "So, our buddy Basheer and his two compatriots are back on Sirius. Don't get me wrong, Sirius is a great place. It's stunningly beautiful in its natural, bioengineered perfection. There were women aplenty, welcoming their heroes.

"They drank in the beauty of home: trees and crops and grasses and lakes and oceans. Imagine the most pristine natural vistas here, unmarred, as they were before man left his mark. Everything on Sirius was green; there were no ugly stone edifices, blood-soaked. No marauding Aztec warriors eager to sacrifice them to agriculture gods. No agriculture gods were necessary there.

"In fact, there had never been any gods at all, nothing that could be termed *religion* on Sirius. Viracocha and his crew are honored once a year, on the day of Earth's summer solstice. Not as gods, of course, but simply as great men, as heroes who saved their people. Similar to how Americans honor Lincoln and Washington and King.

"Basheer and his friends were certainly glad that they'd been lucky enough to get back; they were certainly glad that they hadn't been among the unfortunates trapped on Earth. But still, they found that they missed it. No *octli* on Sirius, no jaguar hunts, no noisy festivals, bloody or otherwise, no fawning natives awestruck at their apparent godhood. Nothing but fresh air, good food; women that can take or leave you, depending upon their whim. Women who don't care if you feel the same way.

"Sure, Sirius was a paradise, but it was definitely a *serene* one. Basheer discovered that he missed Eydis, even though he could see her face whenever he looked at his children. He wondered why she'd opted to stay behind when they were here, waiting for her. He wondered why she'd opted to stay behind when she should've known that he wouldn't have considered staying behind for a second.

"But Basheer found that he missed Bianca most of all, and all her fiery ways. He discovered that he missed her more than he ever would've guessed, actually dreaming of her blazing eyes and curving red smile. Sirian women are utterly lovely, but *fiery* is not an adjective that applies.

"Basheer and his friends made inquiries – maybe they could take one of the remaining transports back to Earth for a little visit, just to see how things were progressing? But they found that the transports had all been decommissioned; had been turned into vast rotting piles of compost, to be spread upon the crops necessary to feed the growing populations. There were still flyers, but flyers were not interplanetary. Basheer and his friends were summarily told that there would be no more Sirian resources devoted to carrying Sirians back to Earth.

"But Basheer and his friends weren't daunted. They discovered that there were quite a few former visitors that missed the Earth and her sometimes dark distractions. Things were too calm on Sirius after the orgiastic worshippers and decadent abundance of Earth. Basheer and his compadres uncovered a veritable *streak* that existed in the population, in fact, of Sirians that would like to visit Earth, and not only ones that had already been there. Tales had spread and there were many eager tourists ready to go.

"So Basheer and his friends invented a system which allowed *individuals* to return to Earth. He came back himself; the *portal*, for lack of a better word, is in Mapimi, where the fleet had been destroyed. He even found Bianca, and learned the whole story."

"Portal?" I said.

"Yes, though that's really not a very accurate word. It's not like it's a door or a vortex or anything like that. There are just certain places where . . . we *arrive.*"

I caught the *we* again, but Max took no notice.

"There are several, all over the world, depending upon which continent you want to arrive on," Tom was saying. "There is Mapimi, in Mexico, and Aokigahara in Japan. There is —"

"There's a portal in the *Suicide Forest?*" Maxine exclaimed. "Giorgio did a show on that! It's this place in Japan where everybody goes to kill themselves. It's a suicide *destination*, like jumping off the Golden Gate Bridge!"

"That's just an unfortunate coincidence, Max," Tom said. "It doesn't have anything to do with —"

"Right. Where else are these portals?"

"There's one in China. There used to be one on the Great Plains, I think. There's one in Russia, and —"

Maxine held up her hand, took out her phone. "Would that be near *Russia's remote Mt. Otorten, "Mountain of Death" where in 1959, nine hikers were found burned and mutilated by an undetermined cause?*" She handed me her phone, and I saw that she was quoting from Wikipedia's *Ancient Aliens* page.

"I don't know where the one in Russia is, Max. I don't speak a lot of Russian."

I handed Max's phone back to her. "So, you're saying that some Sirians liked it here?"

"Especially right after the war. The desire faded significantly over the centuries, after those veterans that had actually spent time here died out. But the legend lives on, and some people on Sirius still enjoy tales about their ancestors' influence on the monkey-planet. They enjoy the idea of that epic love story, between Basheer and Eydis and Bianca. They like to think about what could've happened if Eydis hadn't destroyed the fleet, if travel on a large scale had continued between Earth and Sirius.

"The idea of Earth is kind of like the Wild West to them, or even Las Vegas – full of every self-indulgent thing that doesn't exist on Sirius. Sirians who decide that they would like to visit Earth – maybe they have a little bit more imagination than the rest of the population. They want to find out what they might be missing. They come here all the time."

"People like . . . you?" Maxine asked.

Tom grinned. "Maybe."

We all were silent for a moment. Then I said, "That's a helluva story, my love."

Maxine squinted at him. "Have there been any famous aliens that have visited here? More famous than *you?* Anyone we might've heard of?"

Tom smiled innocently, and said, "Perhaps. And some not so famous ones. But still, they altered your history."

"Like who?" she asked.

"Well, on Sirius, the bacteria that causes *Yersinia pestis* was originally carried by a Sirian animal not unlike a harbor seal. Remember? I mentioned that the Mermaid People once kept them as pets; they would cooperate in the herding of schools of fish, kind of like a sheep dog."

I thought that Tom's story had reached its conclusion, what with the big reveal that he was one of them, and all. I'd seen that coming from early on. But apparently there was more.

He looked at us blankly. "Anyway, these Sirian seals carried this bacteria, and since they'd lived side by each for so many millennia, sometimes the bacteria would jump to a member of the Mermaid People. It wasn't virulent or deadly in the seals or the people; it just caused a little swelling around the lymph glands. It was no more of a deadly zoonotic disease on Sirius than is ringworm here."

Max screwed up her beautiful face in revulsion. "Okay, I was grossed out by the bioengineered fleas, but *ringworm?* What the hell is *ringworm?*"

237

"Ringworm is not really a worm at all, but a circle shaped fungal infection. It's native to this planet, not Sirius. You can get it from cats or sheep or cows. It's harmless; you put a little cream on it, it goes away. A *Yersinia* infection is treated similarly on Sirius, with herbs and compresses. In fact, the infection is a rarity nowadays, because no one spends that much time with seals, anymore, so —"

"What does this *yeastina* thing cause here?" I asked.

"*Yersinia,*" Tom corrected me. "*Yersinia pestis.*"

"What does it cause here?" I repeated.

Tom grinned sheepishly. "On Earth, this relatively harmless Sirian bacteria causes —"

"Bubonic plague." Maxine looked up from her phone. *"Bubonic plague is from Sirius?"*

"Near as we can figure, a visitor from Sirius arrived in China in the early 1300's. He had a mild *Yersinia* infection; probably didn't even realize it. After he arrived in China, he got bit by a flea. A regular Earth flea, not a Sirian bioengineered one. The flea bit a rat, and then other fleas bit that same rat, then those fleas bit some other rats, bit some people . . ."

"And the Black Death ensued."

Tom smiled at me and shrugged. "Oops."

"Anything else?" Maxine asked.

"Well, there was a visitor to Kansas in early 1918. He had a little bit of what you might call a cold . . ."

That one I recognized without further description. "You're telling us that Sirians caused the Spanish Flu Pandemic, too?"

Tom shrugged helplessly; said, "Oops," again.

Maxine was apparently not concerned with the deaths of an estimated fifty to one hundred million of her formerly healthy fellow human beings as a result of some alien germ. Maybe she was unfamiliar with the Spanish Flu, because she asked no more about it.

"What about actual historical figures?" Maxine wanted to know. "Was Hitler from Sirius, Tom?"

"No, Hitler was from Austria. But it's rumored that Lanz von Liebenfthatels may have been from Sirius. He came up with some of the theories of racial superiority that later influenced Hitler." When Maxine looked at him blankly, Tom nodded at her phone. "Google it."

Tom stood up and stretched. I stood up too, and hugged him. I said, "So you're from another planet? That explains a lot."

He kissed me on the forehead. "It's just a story, Liz."

"So if you're not from Sirius, then where are you from?" I asked.

He looked at me in surprise for a split second, then said, "Ah, that's another really long story, my love. I think Max has had enough of my long stories for one day."

Max was consulting her phone and didn't look up.

Tom disengaged himself from my hug and walked toward the kitchen, calling over his shoulder, "What would you ladies like for dinner? Something . . . *absorbent*, maybe? I think I drank too much today."

SEVENTY-FIVE

Tom and Maxine cooked another turkey for Christmas dinner the following day. Sam showed up in the early afternoon, and we were all happy to hear that his sister would make a full recovery.

For a change, there was no rampant, all-day alcohol consumption; no one had a drink at all until after dinner, when we had a nice glass of wine. This was because Tom wasn't saying, "Who needs a drink?" every ten minutes. He sipped eggnog all day, un-spiked. I found him to be unusually quiet again, as he'd been on Halloween. Introspective. I wondered if he was contemplating the Savior's birth and whatever dogma he'd been taught about it.

But he was back to his regular gregarious self when we opened presents after dinner. Sam bought Maxine a bottle of her favorite perfume; she gave him a very lovely powder blue tie. Tom bought me a Blu-ray player and a surround-sound speaker system for the flat screen.

"You're never getting rid of him now," Sam said.

Like I would ever want to, I thought.

I gave Tom a plastic model called a *Visible V-8*. It was a one quarter scale model of a combustion engine, clear, so you could see how everything worked together. How everything *meshed.*

"This is so cool!" Sam said. "I put one of these together when I was a kid. When it's finished, it actually runs!"

Tom looked at the box, looked at me, looked at Sam. He tilted his head curiously. "It's so small. What does it run on?"

"It runs on a battery," I told him. I nodded at the back yard. "Now you won't have to get all greasy so often." We grinned at each other.

"And it'll actually run," Sam reiterated. "You want to put it together now?"

SEVENTY-SIX

That night I dreamed of a desert. Tan sand and pebbles and surprisingly healthy looking green scrub. Dark brown, rocky hills in the distance, seemingly free of vegetation, their peaks humped and worn. A cloudless, cinematically blue sky, like from *Lawrence of Arabia*. Heat. Somehow, I knew I wasn't in California anymore. You know how it is in dreams; you just *know* things.

I saw a purple Nopal cactus, with what looked like a yellow rose growing out of it. That was a curiosity. Then, behind the cactus, I beheld a gnarled little man, brown and ancient, perched expectantly on a battered aluminum lawn chair. His hair was white. The worn straps of the lawn chair that showed along the edges were a jarring electric blue, interspersed with dirty gray stripes. A plastic cooler that might have once been red sat beside him in the sand. A stack of clothing was neatly folded on top of it, pointy cowboy boots and all.

The whole scene had some sort of bizarre Southwestern peyote trip vibe to it. Brightness. Vibrant, living colors: blues, greens, purples, yellows.

The old man said something to me in Spanish. I shook my head, uncomprehending. Why had I not paid more attention in high school?

But suddenly, I remembered the little humiliation that our 11ᵗʰ grade Spanish teacher would inflict upon us. When he rattled off something, and if we stood there looking stupidly at him, too caught up in the joys and agonies of high school life to have learned the lesson, he would not pass on to the next unfortunate until we said, *"Lo siento. No entiendo."*

I'm sorry. I don't understand.

The old man tilted his head curiously at me, the same familiar gesture Tom always made. He said, *"No se arrepentirá. Él ha llegado."*

He pointed a twisted, arthritic finger, and I turned to look behind me. There was a clap of thunder in the clear blue sky, and some kind of strange ball lighting writhed and struck the ground. I looked back at the old man, but he nodded, still gestured. I turned again, and now I could see a figure approaching from the distance. After a moment, through the shimmering heat waves, I was able to ascertain that it was a tall, dark-haired, white man. After another moment, I was able to ascertain that it was a tall, dark-haired, *naked* white man, his gait strangely familiar.

At about twenty yards, I realized that it was Tom, his hair longer and curlier and shaggier than I'd ever seen it. This, coupled with his incongruous, delicious nudity, made him seem more beautiful than ever. My mind whispered, *Now this is my kind of hippie.*

Tom was striding lazily across the desert toward me, like it was something he did every day, walking around in the burning sand naked, looking just as fine as ever.

He smiled at me, said, "Hello, Liz," matter-of-factly, but didn't stop, didn't kiss or embrace me. Instead, he passed me by and shook hands with the old man, who was now standing. The man held out the stack of clothing, and Tom said, "*Gracias, mi amigo.*"

He shook out a pair of jeans and stepped into them, sans underwear, as I knew was his habit. Then he sat in the lawn chair and the old man held out a crisp pair of socks and the cowboy boots to him. Tom brushed the sand off his foot, pulled on one sock, then one boot.

Then he paused and squinted up at me. He said, "What do you suppose this weird ass dream means, anyway, Liz?"

I snapped immediately awake with an audible gasp. Tom slept beside me, his face buried in my neck, as was his endearing custom.

Oh, my God. I knew exactly what this weird ass dream meant. It was all true. *Tom was a fucking alien.*

I stealthily slid out of his embrace, out of bed. I dressed quickly, silently, wanting sincerely not to wake him up. I had to get out of there. I had to talk to Maxine.

SEVENTY-SEVEN

I burst through the door of *Old Town Goods*. As was to be expected on the day after Christmas, the place was empty. Maxine sat behind the counter, playing with her phone. She set it down and smiled at me.

"Aren't they coming to fix your cable today?" she asked me.

"Not 'till this afternoon." I paused, then asked without further preamble, "So how exactly did you meet Tom?" I tried to make my voice even and blithe. "Did he say that he'd been . . . here . . . uh, here, *in town*, long? When you first met him?"

Maxine was entirely oblivious to my upset. Her phone beeped and she looked at it, typed something, said, "The first time I saw Tom, he was standing outside of Morry's. He looked like an extra from some Sergio Leone flick. Like if Clint Eastwood had needed a sidekick in *A Fistful of Dollars*, it would have been Tom. All that was missing was the serape. He actually had the hat and the cigarillo.

"I just happened to be walking past Morry's, and the two of them were standing outside, gesturing at the shop. Their backs were to me, and from that angle, Tom looked like a regular *charro*, with the boots and the hat and the tight pants and all that riot of black hair. You know that Maxie likes her some Mexican boys, so I turned around to look at him as I passed. He smiled at me and I saw those blue eyes and I realized that he wasn't Mexican at all."

"You mistook Tom for *a Mexican*?" I asked incredulously. Tom was the whitest person I knew, but it made sense when I considered my dream. Hadn't he told us that there was a portal in Mexico?

Maxine shrugged. "He had a *dark* tan. Not like a sunburn, like you get from one day, but an actual *tan*, like he'd been out in the sun for a *minute*. And it was also the get-up. He looked like he might be leaving to ride in a Mexican rodeo at any moment."

I paused and thought about Tom looking Mexican. I couldn't imagine it. He'd been just as pale as usual in my dream. Not even any tan *lines*, not to mention a tan. But then again, he had just a-fucking-rrived, had he not?

I changed the subject. "What about the packaging thing?"

"The what?"

"You know, how he has trouble opening everything? Doesn't that strike you as odd?"

"No one said he wasn't odd, Liz."

"But why do you think he has so much trouble opening everything?"

"He doesn't have trouble opening *everything*, Liz. Just . . ." She thought. "Just cigarettes. Cereal box liners. Power Bars. Anything that's wrapped in plastic, stuff with a seam. He has trouble figuring out where to pull on things with seams. If that's the only handicap you've found him to have, I'd give it a pass."

"Have you ever known anybody else to have trouble like that?"

"What's this about, Liz? All that talk about biomodification and growing spaceships getting to you? You think Tom's really not of this world now, that he's from Sirius? Just because he tells a good story?"

The story wasn't even that good, I thought. I took a deep breath, made a conscious effort to calm my voice. How astute she was. She made me feel stupid for even considering such a thing.

"It's nothing like that, Max," I said and laughed a little breathlessly, maybe just a shade hysterically. "I'm just feeling a little curious. Wondering what Tom was like when *you* first met him."

"Like I say, he looked like he'd just breezed into town from somewhere south of the border. I've mentioned the first time I saw Tom to you before. I don't think that you pay attention to me sometimes, Liz." Maxine snapped her fingers. "I can even tell you the exact day it was, because I remember standing in your kitchen and telling you about it. It was on my birthday, the same night that you made the mistake of taking Fred home."

It never ceased to amaze me how Max felt not one scintilla of responsibility in the whole Fred episode. The fact that it was she who had introduced us made no impression on her conscience at all.

She said, "The next time I saw him was when I actually met him for the first time, when he came into the store and bought that painting. It was a couple of months later. The tan had faded by then, and he looked about the same as he did when you met him. He'd gotten a haircut. Not Mexican, but fine nonetheless."

The bell over the door tinkled, and the man himself walked in. He said, "So here you are," and I realized that he'd no doubt texted Max, looking for me, since I'd bolted from the house like a crazy person, not saying anything.

"Isn't the cable guy coming today?" he asked.

"Not 'til this afternoon," I said again.

Tom kissed me lightly and smiled at Maxine. Maxine and I considered him for a moment. Nobody spoke. Tom finally said, "Am I missing something here?"

"No, *El Gallero*. You're not missing anything," she replied, smiling.

Tom's eyes widened in surprise, the same expression he might have if she'd called him a *son of a bitch* in church.

244

Maxine continued, "Liz was just asking me about when we first met. What you don't know is that I saw you a long time before you saw me. The first time I saw you, you were standing in front of the bookstore talking to Morry, looking like a *vaquero*. In fact, I thought you were Mexican until I saw your eyes."

"I do remember that, actually," Tom said and favored Maxine with his killer smile. "I remember you walking by."

"I'm hard to forget," she replied. "Where *had* you come from, *El Gallero*, that you were dressed like that?"

"*Por qué sigues llamándome El Gallero?*" he asked Maxine.

Maxine shrugged. "*No es nada, amor.*"

Tom looked at us, a little perplexed. Now I, too, was perplexed. Maxine speaking Spanish was surreal, after the dream I'd just had. Who'd a thunk it? But then she did like Mexican guys, had probably just picked up a few words and phrases along the way. Or, I thought vaguely, maybe I was still asleep, still dreaming. Either way, I again wished that I'd paid more attention in Spanish class.

"I'd just made it up here from Mexico when you saw me," Tom said after a moment.

"What were you doing in Mexico?" I asked too quickly.

He looked at me curiously. "I was assimilating. Why the third degree, ladies? Are there some chickens missing, Max?"

"I told you. Liz was asking about the first time I ever saw you."

"But why *el gallero*? Did I look like a cockfighter to you? Have you ever even *seen* a cockfighter, Max? Or even a cockfight, for that matter?"

Maxine shrugged. "Maybe. You never know."

Facepalm. "You called him a *cockfighter?*" I asked. No wondered he'd looked like he'd been slapped.

Maxine grinned at Tom. "Got your attention, though, didn't I?"

Tom looked away from her craziness and said to me, "Right after I arrived here from Mexico, I left town again. I spent a month or so in Vegas with Morry. Then Morry went home and I came back here. That's about the time Max and I officially met."

"The hell with Mexico," Maxine said. "What did you do in Vegas?"

Tom favored her with a crooked half smile. "What do *you* do in Vegas?"

The two of them shared an evil little chuckle for a minute, then Tom looked innocently at me, realizing that he probably shouldn't be standing around grinning about past Vegas exploits in front of someone who hadn't been along at the time. That kind of thing could play on the outsider's imagination. *What happens in Vegas, stays in Vegas,*

245

and all that. But I really wasn't concerned about Vegas at right that moment, although I figured that was probably where he'd learned to drink and smoke and perhaps some of that other stuff that he was so good at. I blushed at *that thought*, and Tom tilted his head curiously at me.

He said, "Morry wanted to have one last adventure before he returned to the *auld sod*. I'd never been to Vegas, so he felt it was his duty to show me a good time. Pass the torch, so to speak."

"An adventure? *A good time?*" Maxine rubbed her hands together. "*Do tell* us about that, Tom! Were there women?"

"Goddamn, Max! Are you trying to get me trouble?" He tried to be angry with her, but failed, grinning.

Maxine giggled. "Liz came in here all freaked about out something." So she *had* noticed. "Started asking me all this stuff about the first time I met you. I think she has come to the conclusion that you really are an alien!"

Tom looked back at me and smiled from ear to ear. "Is that a fact?"

Now I felt even more stupid, silly. It was just a dream, after all. Still, I felt the need to defend myself. I said, "Why do you have so much trouble opening things that are wrapped in plastic?"

Now Maxine was giggling uncontrollably. "It's because he's . . . because he's an alien! No plastic on Sirius, right Tom? Everything comes wrapped in banana peels!"

I don't usually mind being laughed at – if you take offense at being laughed at, people will laugh at you every chance they get. But they were pissing me off, now. I'd *dreamed* about Tom in some not-California desert, all speaking Spanish and shit, and then I come in here and Maxine starts talking about how he'd looked like he'd just come across the border the first time she'd seen him. Then he fucking admitted that he'd been in Mexico before he'd come here. And he'd told us that *they arrived* in Mexico. All the pieces fit together so perfectly. Dream or not, it still suddenly seemed so real, so plausible.

Tom realized that it was rude for him to be laughing at me, and tried to stop. Maxine had no such compunctions, and kept right on giggling. Tom almost had himself under control, but he made the mistake of looking at her, and busted up again.

"Fuck you guys," I growled, turned around and walked out of the store.

Tom caught up with me on the street, still wrestling gamely with his composure. He tried to put his arm around me, but I shrugged it off. "Did I not just say fuck you guys?"

Tom stepped in front of me, walking backwards. "Wait a second, Liz."

I stopped and looked up at him, feeling stupid. Stupid for taking so much from such a laughable dream, for allowing myself to be so influenced by something that was really just random electrical signals firing randomly in my sleeping brain. Which my sleeping mind then tried to interpret, tried to assign some meaning to. It was just a reaction to the outrageous story he's told us. A silly story to pass a television-less Christmas Eve. Tom wasn't an alien. It was just a dream.

I felt stupid for getting mad about being laughed at, for storming out of *Old Town* like a petulant child.

He put his arms around me, and hugged me to him. I melted against him, all anger forgotten. This was the man I loved, the man I would follow to the ends of the earth. The perfect man.

Then he whispered in my ear, "What if I told you that it was all true, Liz?"

I backed up so I could see his face, prepared to be instantaneously angry, and even more so than before, if he was having me on. But he wasn't laughing at me now. His expression was watchful, solemn, challenging. Yet still a little curious.

He said, "You had a dream, didn't you?"

My mouth dropped open in surprise, and I took another step back. He was now holding me at arm's length. People were stepping around us on the sidewalk.

He favored me with that smile, that absolute *killer* smile, the one that I'd fallen in love with the first time I'd seen it, that night at the bar when the world hadn't ended. That night at the bar when the world had begun. He slowly took my hand and enfolded it in his, tilted his head at me, and tugged a little on my hand, so that I'd walk with him.

He said, "I guess I've got a little bit more 'splaining to do."

We walked the rest of the way home in silence.

SEVENTY-EIGHT

Tom hung his coat up, then sat on the couch, and I sat across from him in the same chair I'd been sitting in when he'd started his ridiculous story about the Dino People and the Mermaid People. I was still not sure I believed all *that*. But the fact that he, himself, was not from around here was inescapable.

I waited patiently.

"You want a drink?" he asked.

"It's nine am, for Christ's sake, Tom."

He held up both hands in a little warding-off gesture. "None for me, thanks. I was just thinking of you. It can't be easy suddenly coming to believe that someone you . . . that someone you *know* is an . . . is from another place."

He didn't want to say *someone you love is an alien, from another planet.* Which was just fine, because I didn't want to say it either.

I said, "Let's start with the dream I had. How do you . . . what do you know about that?"

Tom considered. "Let's see. There was a desert. There was a big flash. I was naked. You, unfortunately, were not. There was Martin. Is that about right?"

"*How do you know what I dreamed?*" I thought I could probably put up with aliens that couldn't open things, but I had to draw the line at mind control.

"It's not like it's mind control or anything."

I flinched when Tom said *mind control*, and he flinched at my flinch. "Oh, shit, did you just think that? It was just a coincidence, I promise." He made that warding-off gesture again. "I can't read your mind, Liz, I promise. At least not by virtue of any extraterrestrial means. Sometimes I can guess, because I know you, and I can make certain deductions, but —"

"*How do you know what I dreamed?*" I repeated.

"It's because I dreamed the same thing, at the same time. Sometimes, when . . . people . . . are close, there can be that kind of sharing between them when they're asleep. To be completely accurate though, *you* know what *I* dreamed, not the other way around. Unless we try to actively cultivate it, it's kind of a one way street. Like I say, I can't read your mind."

"But I can read yours?"

"Let's see. Give it a try." Tom gave me his best sexy smile, wiggled his eyebrows at me. "Tell me what I'm thinking right now."

I wanted to be annoyed with him, but I failed. "Yeah, just like you said, it doesn't take anything extraterrestrial to know what you're thinking right now. I can tell by the look on your face."

He smiled at me for another moment, then said, "It's just something that happens sometimes when two people who are simpatico sleep together. I mean, literally, when they *are asleep* together."

"So you were dreaming about . . ."

"I was dreaming about my very first day on your glorious planet." He made that world encompassing gesture, then dropped his arms. "Why do you all of sudden believe me, Liz? I tried to spell it out for you, tell you the real story. But you just laughed at me." He smiled to let me know that he hadn't been offended. "Hell, I thought Maxine believed me more than you did."

"Max didn't believe you either. It's all just too ridiculous."

Why had I decided that something so insane might really be true? Why did I suddenly *want to believe*, like Maxine? It was the dream, and also the fact that Tom was just so completely unlike anyone I'd ever known.

"You are just *so odd*, Tom," I told him. "So different. You've just got to be from somewhere else, and I've often speculated where it might be. Some place with agriculture but no machinery, no vice. Some kind of polygamy, maybe. I used to think that there might be some kind of off-the-wall religious underpinning to it, like you might be Amish or something."

His face lit up in delighted surprise. It was my favorite expression. "And this is my *Rumspringa*? Here on Earth?" And then that so familiar tilt of his head. "You could almost term it that, if you really think about it. The Amish youth get a chance to act up before they decide to settle down and be baptized in the church. Or not. Most of them do. We get to act up also, but we don't generally ever go back. I know I'm never going back. I like it way too much here."

He paused. Then, "Morry went back. After his wife passed away, it kind of took the joy out of this place for him. Better to return to the green, green grass of home than to continually be assailed with the memories of a lifetime, suddenly turned sad, all around you.

"But Morry deciding to return home – that was one of the reasons I got to come when I did. There's something of a waiting list, you see. Can't have the whole planet coming here. Might seem like an invasion. Someone would talk. But because Morry was a relative, I shot right up to the top of the list."

"Morry was a –?"

"Did I not say Morry was a relative?"

I tried to think back and remember if I'd ever noticed Morry being left-handed. I shook my head. I couldn't remember.

"And his wife?"

"No. His wife was . . . like you. From here." He said again, "Why have you decided to buy it all now? Today? But not on Christmas Eve?"

"I don't know, Tom. We were all drunk on Christmas Eve. You most of all. Maybe I give too much credence to my dreams. And I guess that being from another planet is as good an explanation as any as to why you are so fucking odd." I couldn't really explain any better than that, because I just didn't know. I said, "How many of you are here?"

"A few. A bunch. I don't really know. It's not like we can tell us from you, any more than *you* can tell us from you. And it's not like we're looking for each other, like we have a secret handshake like the Masons or something." He glanced at the ring on his pinkie. "We're not here to organize, Liz. Or invade, or anything like that. We're tourists."

I tried to riffle through a lifetime of memories, tried to recall if I'd known any other lefties that had trouble opening things; lefties that had an inordinate fondness for machinery; left-handed profligate drinkers, smokers, stoners, T-bone eaters. Any left-handed sex fiends. Exceptionally green-thumbed lefties. But I couldn't really place any lefties at all, except for my dad. And Tom.

"You don't suppose that my dad . . .?"

"Probably not." Pause; a heartbeat. "But it's not out of the realm of possibility. We've been coming here for a very long time."

"Is there any way to . . . I mean, are there records? Could we find out?"

"Nah. No records. Like I say, it's usually a one way street. There's a lot of arriving here, not a lot of going back there. To go back, first you send a request to do so via energy pulse message – Morry cobbled the necessary apparatus together from stuff he had lying around. He sent his request to Sirius right from the center of your little town.

"He didn't want to go all the way to Mexico first, and then have to wait around for a response. Morry's response from Sirius was *me*, showing up on his doorstep, telling him that I was here to take his place, so to speak, that it was a green for him to go back home. Then, to actually travel back to Sirius, you have to go to Mexico. You leave from there."

250

"You really do speak Spanish," I marveled. "And Maxine, too."

Tom looked dubious. "I might be a little bit more fluent than Maxine. I don't know where she picked up the term *el gallero*, but I have a hard time believing that our little Max has ever been to a cockfight."

"Absolutely nothing surprises me anymore," I said, and it was the truest thing I'd ever said in my entire life. If I was game to buy that my boyfriend was an alien, how much more of a stretch was it to think that Maxine had watched chickens fight to the death?

"Have you ever been to a cockfight, Tom?" I asked.

He smiled at me, a trifle warily, I thought. "I've been to a lot of things, Liz."

"Tell me." I gave him one of those *I want the truth* looks.

Apparently deciding that I could handle the truth, Tom took a deep breath, exhaled. "Well, I haven't really been here that long. There's a whole world yet to see."

"You're stalling."

"Okay." He reflected. "Yeah, I've been to a cockfight. And a couple bullfights. And more than a few fist fights, both organized and extempore. I went to a donkey show in Tijuana, once."

"*A donkey show?*"

Tom blinked rapidly for a moment. I got the impression that he wasn't ashamed of having attended, so much as he was embarrassed that he was going to have to explain what it was to me, now that he'd brought it up.

"It's a —"

"*I know what it is!*"

Now it was his turn to look surprised. "Really?"

"Yes, I'm a big girl, Tom. I've heard of a donkey show before. But I can't believe you actually *attended* such a thing."

Tom shrugged, not at all ashamed. "I'd just arrived here. Someone took me along with them. It's not something that I would necessarily want to see again. Hell, Liz, it's not like I *participated* —"

"Okay, I don't want to talk about *that* anymore. You were saying that you speak fluent Spanish?"

"Yeah. And Nahuatl. And Quechua." That killer smile. "*We practically own South America, man.*"

"How did you learn all those languages?"

"You know the part in *The Matrix*, where they plug the thing into the back of their heads and they learn things?"

"*I know kung-fu.*"

"*Show me.*" Again he smiled. "It's kind of like that. But without any holes. Without any computers or machinery." He ruffled the back of his head. "It's related to the sharing-dream thing. Just more in-depth."

"Do you know kung-fu?"

"No. But I do know quite a few languages. I'm an anthropologist, remember? I know a little about Earth history, customs. I know enough to fit in here."

Oh, yeah, you blend, I thought. I said, "Where in Mexico, exactly?"

"You really want to know all my secrets, don't you?" Tom smiled, still a little warily, I thought.

"Yes, I do, now that I've found out you're not Amish."

"I told you already. *The Zone of Silence.* Mapimi. Like Max said, Giorgio did a show about it."

Then it hit me. I had not thought past my own personal situation until that very second. But now I realized that this whole thing had global implications.

"So they're right!" I said in amazement. "The *Ancient Aliens* people. *They're right.*"

Tom's expression was doubtful again. "I wouldn't go so far as to say that. Their perceptions are too much like the blind men and the elephant. They have some things down pretty much correctly, but most of it is just wild, totally off the wall conjecture. Everyone has a pet theory that they want to be true, you see. They *want to believe,* like Max says, but they only want to believe what it is they want to believe, whether it's the truth or not. And if my theory contradicts your theory, then I'm not going to listen to you, and you're not going to listen to me, and so on.

"A lot of people want their theory to fit into human history and religion in a way that's just not going to happen. We were here first, Liz; we did this and that. After we left, mankind reacted. Just reacted. You can't make us into the products of *your* history. You are products of *our* history.

"And then there are your religions. We had no intentions in that vein. Not in any way, no matter how it eventually turned out. We were never gods come to guide the monkeys to enlightenment. We were just people from a changing environment, come here to borrow a little something to save ourselves. And after we'd taken all we needed, we went home. We left you to fend for yourselves."

"You are rather on your high horse, there, aren't you, Tom, my love?"

He blinked at me. "In what way?"

"Well, I'm thinking that maybe you have it a little backwards. Sure, you came here and wised us up a little bit. But the tiny little part that you took from us, something we never even missed – it changed you *fundamentally*. Forever. Everyone on your planet knows about us. You have to wait in line to come here. Not too many people here even believe in you, even when the evidence is right before their eyes.

"You, as a representative of your people, lord it over me, as representative of my people; you go on and on about our crossbred monkey ignorance, how in awe we were of your superiority. How we were so awed in fact, that we deemed you gods. You snicker at our naiveté. But I say you have it backwards.

"Sure, we were awed. But you had to be pretty awed, too. We have a few crumbling pyramids to remember you by, an eternal search for a missing link that's never going to be found. But what do you have? You have an evolutionary detour that never would have happened without us. An evolutionary detour that you consciously decided to take, because of us, here, walking around on this planet. You decided that our way, dumb as we were, was a better way. How much more did we shape your destiny than you shaped ours? We are not you, Tom. *You are us.*"

Tom smiled gloriously. "Indeed, we are, my love, and that's why I'd always wanted to come here. Ever since I was a little boy.

"Once we request the trip, we're warned about all the bad things that exist here, the wars, the poverty, the disease, the depravity." He grinned evilly at me. "We're taught how to recognize the cons that people run on the just-off-the-bus-from-Kansas types; we're instructed not to be too trusting. We're taught all about man's inhumanity to man.

"But all these things – war, inequality, crime, depravity," he smiled again – Tom liked that word, *depravity*. "All the sins and evils of this world are just the offshoots of mankind's epic struggle to conquer it. Something that we never had to do on Sirius. We never even really had to conquer our own one enemy. We got you to do that for us.

"Thomas Hobbes famously observed that in a world without government, there is *continual fear, and danger of violent death; and the life of man is solitary, poor, nasty, brutish, and short.*"

"Really? That's what that expression is about? About a lack of *government?* I always thought it was about cavemen."

Again that look of surprised curiosity, so familiar, now having so much additional meaning. Of course, Tom was curious. He was from *another fucking planet.*

253

"Government or no, this estimation of mankind's lot has been pretty accurate, right up until modern times. Life has been tough here for pretty much all of your history."

"I imagine it's still pretty tough in the Third World," I opined.

Again Tom dismissed the Third World with a curt wave of his hand. "They'll catch up." He could not possibly be less concerned with the plight of the Third World. Even if they did have donkey shows.

"I've made this point before," he was saying. "Mankind has done a wonderful job in the conquering of this planet. Sure, there are all the bad things, all of the myriad inequalities and evils that are the inevitable, natural outgrowths of every struggle. A hard life is never fair. People become despots. They become bitter, angry. Cruel.

"But some people are able to see the good things, whatever their hardships, and what they create is also a side-effect of that struggle. The diversity, the emotion, the pathos, the art, the beauties that mankind has created! I am indeed awestruck by it all."

I'd already heard enough of Tom's appreciation for mankind and all our triumphs. At least for the moment. Now I wanted to hear more about *how he fucking got here.* "What was that place in Mexico called? Malpimini?"

"Mapimi. *The Zone of Silence.* It's where we arrive for this side of the world."

I lowered my voice. "Is that where the spaceships land?"

Tom laughed then, actually more of a gravelly giggle. "I told you on Christmas Eve – there aren't any spaceships anymore, Liz. You don't use the *Nina*, the *Pinta*, and the *Santa Maria* anymore, if you want to go to Spain, do you?"

"Then how?"

"They don't grow spaceships on Sirius anymore, Liz. That's literally ancient history. But here, you don't need an aircraft carrier to take you overseas nowadays, do you? You just have to be next in line to go. Have your papers in order, so to speak."

"So you have your own little one-man spaceship? A flyer? I want to see it!"

"Forget about spaceships, Liz. It's an energy thing. Think more of . . . think more of a transporter, like from *Star Trek*. That's not entirely accurate, but it's close enough. You get the general idea. You saw it all pretty much, when you shared my dream."

"But you were naked. They were never naked."

"It *was* 1966." He grinned, paused. "It's a long trip from Sirius. *Imagine no possessions/I wonder if you can . . .*"

I frowned at him. "I don't care what you say. You *are* a hippie. I can imagine no possessions. I just can't imagine no shoes. In the desert. If you just dropped out of the sky, naked, in Mexico, how did you get here? To California?"

"There's an old shaman that lives nearby to the place where we, for lack of a better word, *land*. Martin. You saw him in our dream. He receives an energy pulse message as to when we'll be arriving. He's our first contact. He has clothes and money and papers and everything waiting for us. He smuggles us out of Mexico, sends us wherever we want to go. Sometimes we have another person waiting for us where we're headed, like I did. Mostly not, though. Morry and I, people from our extended family, if you will, go back a long way. Centuries, actually. Once we get where we're going, we send a little money back to Martin, for the next person, and a little for himself."

I was nonplussed at this. The simplicity. The difficulty. "What's in it for him?"

Now Tom was nonplussed. "It beats working. Third World and all. And he gets to know the truth. I sent him enough money for him to put his granddaughter through college in Mexico City. She wants to be a doctor."

"You don't make money like that from a bookstore. Even if it is in the family for centuries."

"Let's just say that some of our relatives made some good investments over the long years. Some *exceptional* investments."

Tom arose to fetch his cigarettes out of his coat pocket, and I added *independently wealthy* to the list of his good qualities.

Then a new thought struck me.

What had he said earlier? *I haven't really been here that long. There's a whole world yet to see.* So all of this, I thought, his current situation – he had to think of it as just temporary. This town, the bookstore, *us*. You don't see much of the world from a little backwater Southern California town. And you don't go to cockfights and donkey shows and fist fights *extempore*, you don't have too many adventures in Las Vegas, if you're dragging an almost middle-aged woman around with you. I couldn't compete with the world's depravity.

I realized in that moment that Tom was going to leave. *Maybe not today. Maybe not tomorrow, but soon and for the rest of my life*. He didn't travel across the galaxy to spend his life with someone like me. There was just too much world left for him to see.

The inescapable inevitability of it seized my heart and squeezed, and tears welled up in my eyes before I could gather my self-control enough to stop them. I blinked and made them fall, then viciously wiped them away with my sleeve, like a little boy embarrassed by his inability to be in command of his own emotions.

Tom sat back down on the couch, lit a cigarette and handed it to me, then lit one for himself. Another one of the endearing things he did when we were alone. He blew out a cloud of smoke, and looked at me, smiled, tilted his head, considered me.

I looked back at him, took a long drag on my cigarette, feeling the mentholated poison fill my lungs. It was enjoyable, this addiction, no matter how dangerous it was. It was not as dangerous as my addiction to him, however, it would now appear. I would not miss smoking. I'd given it up before.

But I would miss him.

We sat there smoking, looking at each other, as silent as we'd been for the first few moments when we'd first met. I took it all in again, just as I had on that first night: the tousled black hair, with just a couple grays, the fine, stubbled jawline, the enormous blue eyes, that killer smile. My mind supplied the memory of everything I knew about him that I hadn't known that first night: the way he smelled and tasted, the lean, smooth body, the things he knew how to do with those lovely large hands, that incredible mouth. His intelligence, his sense of humor, his *oddness*. I knew that I would miss him every waking minute, and I would miss him in my dreams, too.

When the silence threatened to stretch out for too long, I broke it, saying emotionlessly, "So what do you want to see, what do you plan to do next?"

"I want to do everything." He lifted his arms to encompass the whole world, and his glorious smile of anticipation knifed me to the soul. "I want to go back to Mexico, to Oaxaca, do *tlitliltzin* with the Zapotecs. I want to drink absinthe and contemplate Artemis in Greece. I want to celebrate Shivratri in India and get *as high as a Georgia pine* with them. I want to eat and drink and be merry. I want to see the Eiffel Tower by moonlight. I want to see Mt. Fuji and ride the bullet train. I want to take the Channel Tunnel to Calais and back to England. I want to dance naked around a fire at Stonehenge on the summer solstice. I want to climb to the top of Cheops' pyramid and have a picnic."

I wanted to sob then. But I didn't. My tears were held in check, because I thought, *What a bastard you are, Tom Bastion!* I took another drag on my cigarette and tilted my head at him, mimicking his idiosyncrasy, thinking, *Read my mind now, you son of a bitch. You tell me how much you love the triumphs of mankind, the art and machinery and beauty, when you are actually just a manipulative, using, heart-breaking bastard. Yes, sirree, Tom Bastion, you put the* man *in* manipulation, *do you not? You just waltz in here, with all your quirky, endearing, devastatingly attractiveness, take want you want, enjoy what you came to enjoy, ruin a girl for any other man that she might ever meet, any other man that might not be so cute, might not be so good, but who might be from* this *planet, who might not need to see and experience a whole world full of vices, might not feel compelled to try every sin this ol' place has to offer, might not need to screw every woman he meets, black, white, red, yellow, blonde, brunette, redhead. Yeah, you just waltz in here and ruin me, without a second thought, then move on to your next adventure. You rotten, careless, alien son of a bitch.*

Tom looked at me suddenly and his eyes widened. "Oh, shit, I almost forgot!" He leapt up from the couch and retrieved his coat, sticking his hands in all its various pockets until he at last extracted an envelope. He threw his coat onto the couch with a flourish, and said, "And I want this to be our first stop."

He handed the envelope to me. Inside were two airline tickets to La Paz, Bolivia, and a brightly colored brochure detailing travel to Puma Punku. I looked at him, speechless.

"Do you have a *pasaporte*, Liz Allen? You're gonna need one!"

"*You want me to go with you?*" I asked him incredulously. He wanted to drag me all the way to Bolivia and back before letting me know that he'd soon be moving on? "*Are you crazy?*"

And then a series of expressions played across Tom's face, ones that I'd never seen before. The first one was *gobsmacked: adjective, chiefly British, informal – utterly astounded; astonished.* I imagined that Tom would have borne a similar expression had I refused him that first New Year's Eve.

Next he blinked rapidly, furrowed his brow, pursed his lips together. This expression needed no lyrical British term: this expression was stunned, shocked, *wounded* disbelief.

"You don't want to go with me?" he whispered in bewildered amazement. Sadness suddenly veiled his blue eyes, so completely that I felt the stinging tears rush to my own eyes again.

I blinked them back savagely. I didn't care if he was suddenly sad because his latest Earthling plaything was turning him down. *I was sad.* I tried to keep the agony out of my voice. "Why do you want me to go with you?"

"*Why do I want you to go with me?*" he repeated my words back to me, tilted his head. But it wasn't cute this time. It was tragic. Insanely, I thought of the famous line from Macbeth: *it is a tale told by an idiot, full of sound and fury, signifying nothing.*

But fuck him, I thought. He'd just broken my heart.

"Yeah," I said. "Why the fuck do you want me to go to Bolivia with you?"

"Why the fuck *wouldn't* I want you to go to Bolivia with me?" Tom asked, with just a shade of something that might have been anger, another emotion I'd never experienced from him. Then it faded. "I want you to go to Bolivia with me because I love you, Liz. I don't want to go anywhere without you." He blinked again and the tragic, whipped pup look of sadness and disbelief was gone, replaced by a look of resigned depression. "If you don't want to see the world with me, I might as well go back to fucking Sirius."

I realized all at once how wrong I was. I flung myself out of the chair and into his arms and squeezed him as hard as I could. "Oh, my God, I'll go to Bolivia with you, Tom," I whispered.

He squeezed me back, then looked at me, unsure – another new expression. Still hurt. I'd put that pain there in his eyes, by doubting him. He'd never given me any reason before to believe that he'd ever leave me, and he still hadn't now. I'd simply imagined the whole thing.

My guilt at hurting him nearly undid me.

I hugged him again and said, "Anywhere you want to go, Tom. To the ends of the fucking earth. Only please, please, stop looking at me like that." I started to cry.

He looked at me again, still confused, but no longer sad. It was that same curious expression that I'd fallen in love with. It made me laugh and cry at the same time. "Am I missing something?" he said.

"No," I said, wiping the tears away, again embarrassed at them like a schoolboy. "I'm just crazy."

"It's a prerequisite for living here. Seriously, Liz, you've got to tell me what's wrong. I've never seen you cry before. What is it? What have you got against Bolivia?"

I laughed, even though I wasn't quite sure if I was done crying or not. "It's just that . . . just now, when you talked about all the places you haven't seen yet . . . all the adventures you want to have . . . I was just thinking . . . eating, drinking, carousing . . . *women* . . ."

His mouth dropped open, his eyebrows went up. "Oh, fuck, Liz, I've had more than my share of women. I –"

"Thank you, Captain Obvious." I gestured at him, indicating the whole flawless package, the smile, the eyes, the *prowess*. "You could be termed what we call a *ladies' man*, Tom, my love. And a man, even one as fine as you, does not get to be a *ladies' man* without having known *a lot* of ladies. And I'd like to thank them all, all of them, whoever they were, each and every myriad one, for making you the man you are today."

It was not that I was jealous when I thought of all those women. Jealousy is an emotion for *right now*, a current event, like breathing. I couldn't be jealous of what Tom had done before, especially since it had produced such fine results, which were all to my benefit. It was not like he'd ever mentioned a single one of them.

Besides, if I considered it, I'd been just as wicked, just as sinful as Tom had undeniably been. And I didn't even have the excuse that I'd been tasting the exotic forbidden fruit of another planet. Mine was just homegrown sin: sweet as Kool-Aid and just as common.

I said, "But I'm not talking about the ones *before*, Tom. I'm talking about the *next* ones. The Mexican ones and the Indian ones and the Japanese ones and the English ones and the Egyptian ones and all the other ones that might catch your eye in all these exotic locales that you haven't visited yet, on all these debauched adventures that you want to undertake! Why do you want to take me with you when all that awaits you?"

I thought I might just dissolve into an adolescent crying jag. I felt so stupid and helpless. He hugged me again and I couldn't stop myself from sobbing.

"I guess I still have a little more 'splaining' to do." His silly Ricky Ricardo imitation made me laugh a little again, despite the tears.

Tom held both my hands. "What I was going to say was, I've had more than my share of women, both here and on Sirius. Here, well, it's . . . it's . . ."

"As easy for you as falling off a log?"

He shrugged, attempted to look embarrassed, failed. He released my hands. "I guess you could put it that way. And I would like to thank every one of them, too. But it's not a cliché when I say that none of it *meant* anything. It was a lot of fun, don't get me wrong, a lot of fun, and . . ."

"Practice?"

He rolled his eyes at that one. "If you must put it that way. Okay, yeah, it was a lot of fun, and it was practice. But on Sirius, things are completely, utterly different than they are here. All the cultures here developed in such a way, once again, based on the struggle to survive. Historically, women have needed their men to stick around, here, to help provide for the next generation. And how do you women get your men to stick around?"

I shook my head. I was not getting it. "I don't know. Sex?"

Now Tom shook his head. "No, not sex. Earth women do not get their men to stick around through sex. Could we leave sex out of it for one second?"

"If you want to start leaving out sex, then you're just going to have to go back to the bookstore," I said, still sniffling a little.

259

Tom smiled, relieved that I wasn't crying anymore, that my mood had lightened enough to make jokes. I was also relieved, even though I still had no idea what his point could possibly be.

He began again. "It's just like I told you guys on Christmas Eve. On Sirius, there's equality between the genders. Everyone is provided for in such a way that our women don't have to depend on their men to care for them while they're raising the children. The children are more or less raised communally. You know who your mother and father are, don't get me wrong, but the children live separately. And the men and women, we live more solitarily than men and women do here. When a woman feels that she would like to mate –"

"Mating? You call it *mating?*"

That deliciously filthy Bloodhound Gang song ran through my head, quite unbidden: *We call this the act of mating. But there are several other very important differences between human beings and animals that you should know about.* I tried not to think of what a monstrously wondrous animal Tom could be. I wished he'd get to the point. *I'd appreciate your input.*

"Okay," he was saying. "When a woman feels like she *is in the mood*, shall we say, she has all the men in the world to choose from."

"I bet you got chosen a lot."

Again he rolled his eyes. "My point is, there are no cultural trappings associated with the thing, like there are here. There's no economic imperative that compels a man to stick around with one woman and provide for her and their children. The woman is provided for, regardless; the community cares for the child. Like I told you guys, there's no need for monogamy. There isn't even a need for cohabitation.

"There's not a lot of deep longing and desire for a lifetime companion between the genders. A sexual encounter on Sirius is looked upon about the same way you might think of a visit to a Baskin-Robbins, here. No more preparation, no more anticipation. It's fun and all that, but it's not *Casablanca.*"

"How nice for the men," I said. *You and me baby ain't nothing but mammals . . .*

"Bitch, please. This arrangement has worked forever, and it's just as beneficial for both genders. No one gets saddled with someone they can't stand because of a fleeting indiscretion. We don't even have a fucking expression for *a fleeting indiscretion*. The genetic diversity that occurs when one woman has children with different fathers is actually good for the species. We're a very healthy, robust people."

"And beautiful too, if you're any indication."

"My mother knew I would be, even before she decided to conceive me," he said, for once not only acknowledging the fact that he was attractive, but acknowledging the fact that *he knew it*. He knew it, I knew it, Maxine knew it; his mom knew it.

"There's no shame about sex on Sirius," he continued. "No unwanted, unloved children. No domestic violence. No jealousy. Sex is just not a big thing there, Liz. Just something that you do sometimes, usually with whoever you want to do it with. Sometimes babies result; most times, they don't. Making a baby is almost entirely up to the woman, but if a man decides that he really wants to be a dad, he can usually find someone who wants to be a mom without any trouble.

"There's no unrequited yearning for your soul mate on Sirius. Well, at least not much. Like I told you guys, there are a few monogamous couples. Eydis was monogamous, even if Basheer was not.

"But some people do stay together monogamously for a week or a month or a year or forever. But they're rare. Like righties. In fact, it's even referred to as a *right-handed partnership*." He gave me a one-eye-closed squint, like he was trying to gauge how I would take what he was going to say next, before he said it. He sighed. "I even tried that once myself."

Even though he'd told me that he'd been married before (on another planet), he'd never, not even once, mentioned it again, and I felt a monkey shiver of jealousy run down my spine. Apparently, he wanted to talk about it now, so I steeled myself to hear things that I might not particularly want to hear.

"What happened?" I asked, trying not to grit my teeth.

He smiled a trifle ruefully, another new expression. Tom's lack of regret about life was another thing that was attractive about him. "Ah, she got tired of me. Before I got tired of her."

I imagined that this was the Sirian way of explaining a one-sided love affair, one of those unrequited yearnings for your soul mate that he'd just said never occurred. Tom had been monogamous, but she hadn't been.

"Any kids?"

"No," he said with what sounded like relief. "It didn't last long enough for her to even consider that."

Tom seemed embarrassed by this relationship, and I reasoned that, based on what I'd heard about the culture there, it would be *quite* the embarrassment. Being in a right-handed partnership where the other person decided not to be right-handed anymore? Wow. And apparently there weren't a lot of people around who would understand, who would commiserate with you, who would slap you on the back and say, *I feel ya, brother.*

"So you felt all those uncharacteristic feelings?" I asked. "Love and hatred and hurt and jealousy?"

"We have all those feelings, Liz. Didn't Eydis encompass a history-changing capacity for revenge? And that was an outgrowth of her love for Basheer. But generally, Sirians just don't behave that way. I'm telling you, there just isn't a lot of love and hate and hurt and jealousy tangled up with sex there."

"Is that why you came here, then? To get away from this bad experience? To forget the memories?"

I was just thinking how tragically romantic all of *that* was, my beautiful, heartbroken spaceman traveling across a million billion miles or parsecs or whatever unit space is measured in, coming here to try to forget the no longer right-handed woman who had rejected him. *How cold she must have been,* I thought, *and how incredibly stupid.* How could any woman, on any planet, ever reject *him*?

He'd come here to dissipate and drown his sorrow in Earth-style excess. I was just thinking, how *Leaving Las Vegas*, when Tom started to laugh at me. It was not a gravelly giggle this time. This was a full-blown guffaw. Ha, ha, ho, ho, hee, hee.

"Oh. No. Liz! Oh, *hell, no*, you've got me all wrong! One does not flee across the galaxy because of such a thing! One does not travel to the finest hospital in Switzerland for such a little hurt; to seek treatment for a stubbed . . . ego!"

I was surprised at how much he incited the urge to defend myself when he laughed at me. "I got the impression that you really loved her."

"Oh, yeah, I really loved her." Tom stopped laughing, sighed. "I really did. As much as I could at the time, I guess. Which was not really very much. I cannot impress upon you how much of a big deal it was not. Just like anything else connected with sex on Sirius, rejection of one's suggestion of a right-handed partnership is no big deal. There are just too many other women available. Que sera, sera, as Max says. Next!

"You have to understand that I'd wanted to come here since I was a little kid, Liz. My coming here had nothing whatsoever to do with her."

He looked at the floor for a moment, obviously reliving his failed marriage, love affair, right-handed relationship. Whatever they called it.

I allowed him a moment for this reflection, but when it seemed that it would continue to drag on, I said, "So, if you don't mind my asking, what is the point to your little story?"

Tom looked up and squinted at me again. "Indeed. Here is the point to my little story. When I arrived here, I considered myself to be in the catbird seat. An entire world full of wine, women and song, here at my very feet, here for the very asking." He grinned deviously at me, and it again warmed my heart to hear him acknowledge his own attractiveness. "But you must understand that I wasn't trying to assuage a broken heart, wasn't on the rebound, wasn't looking for love. When I first came here, my capacity for love was not what it has become. Regardless, I wasn't even thinking about love. I was here to have fun, experience all the diversity of this place.

"And I cut quite the swath between Mapimi and your little town, if I say so myself. How does that song go? *I licked the silver spoon, drank from the golden cup, and smoked the finest green/I stroked the baddest dimes, at least a couple of times before I broke they heart.*"

I was amazed at how fucking surreal my life had become in a very short time: an alien was quoting Everlast to me.

"But what's the other line?" Tom was saying. "*You know where it ends, yo, it usually depends on where you start.* I might've continued on the same path, had it not been for Morry. Something that he said to me on the way to Mapimi from Vegas. And I would've been happy enough, on the wine, women and song path, with my underdeveloped capacity for love. But not as happy as I am now."

Tom impulsively grabbed both my hands again and kissed me full on the mouth, a long, slow, sensuous kiss. Somewhere in the middle of it, I realized that he was showing off. But I went right on kissing him. I liked it when he showed off.

Finally Tom stopped kissing me, and said, "No, I never would've been as gloriously, as wonderfully, as completely happy as I am right now, had I not listened to Morry."

"Does this have something to do with something that comes from Bolivia?" I asked.

Tom laughed, but I could tell that he was being serious now, that he had something important that he wanted to tell me, so I'd best stop fucking around. I said softly, "What did Morry say to you?"

SEVENTY-NINE

Tom and Morry stood in front of the *Wynn*, waiting for the valet to bring their car around. It was a 1971 Chevy Impala convertible, just like the one from *Fear and Loathing in Las Vegas* (except it was white instead of red). Morry had purchased it especially for this trip. The big Chevy was a concrete symbol of Thompson's story to him, a symbol of the pathos of his old age, his decision to leave this place where he'd known so much joy. There was nothing for him here anymore.

"We had all the momentum; we were riding the crest of a high and beautiful wave. . . . So now, less than five years later, you can go up on a steep hill in Las Vegas and look West, and with the right kind of eyes you can almost see the high-water mark — that place where the wave finally broke and rolled back."

Morry's entire sojourn on this planet had been just one high water mark after another. But when his wife died, the tide had rolled back for him, also. It was time to go home.

But he and his young friend had indeed gone out with a bang. Goodbye, Morry. Welcome, Tom.

An exceptionally beautiful woman, tall and curvy, approached Tom. She had long black hair and deep brown eyes, surrounded by exquisite false eyelashes. She wore crimson lipstick the color of the outer reaches of Hell, and leaned in and whispered something into his ear, bit his earlobe. Then she slowly slid a piece of paper into the back pocket of his jeans, and winked at him. "Call me," she said, and then sashayed into the hotel.

Morry grinned around a very expensive cigar. *"I hate to see her go, but I love to watch her leave."* He nodded after the girl. "I would have to say that they're the greatest jewel that this place has to offer."

"Women?" Tom rubbed the side of his face, considered. "I would have to agree with you there, my friend."

Morry tilted his head. "I don't think you understand what I'm saying, Tom. Not women in general. We have women on Sirius, do we not? And are they not lovely?"

A blonde walked by and winked at him. "Lovely, yes." Tom turned to watch the blonde enter the hotel. "But nothing like this."

"You have a whole world of women to choose from on Sirius, yet you wanted to come here."

"I came here for more than just the women, Morry."

"Yet, I'm telling you that the women, the women *here*, are the key."

EIGHTY

Tom said to me, "Morry came here when he was young, a lot younger than me. It was easier then; not so long a waiting list. Anyway, he climbed right on the wine, women, and song train, too, from the moment he arrived. I guess *that* was easier, then, too. Not so many *laws*." He wiggled his eyebrows at me. "Morry had never had any right-handed partnerships on Sirius, had never even come close. Morry had never even entertained the thought of love, while still on Sirius, like I had.

"Once arrived, Morry laid waste to the entire block like an alien craft from *War of the Worlds*, metaphorically speaking, did Morry, from Day One. *Coke Ennyday* was Morry, and quite the *ladies' man*, as you so euphemistically put it. But right in the middle of his conquest of the planet, so to speak, Morry was arrested in his bedpost notching and nose dusting by something, someone who came as quite a shock to him."

EIGHTY-ONE

Morry maneuvered the big Chevy effortlessly across the flawless blacktop. It was a long trip to Mapimi, almost twelve hundred miles, and only half of it – to Henderson, then to Phoenix, then to Tuscon, then to the border – only half of it would be on these perfect US roads. After that, it would be dirt and sand and rock. But Morry knew that the heavy, ancient, dragon of a Chevy was more than up for it. That's why he'd bought it. They didn't make 'em like this anymore.

They would travel at night. Morry enjoyed piloting the convertible beast across the cool blacktop in the dark, smelling the dry, dessicated, desert scent of the sage. The driving was not nearly as much fun during the day, when the sun liked to broil the very skin off of you. Instead, they would sleep during the day in hotels, in air-conditioned bliss, at least until they reached the border.

They were not in any kind of hurry. But still, it was time to go home.

Morry would miss cars, would miss driving. *No other man-made device since the shields and lances of the ancient knights fulfills a man's ego like an automobile*, someone famous had said. And that was the God's honest truth, Morry thought. Especially when you'd been here as long as he'd been, and had seen how far they'd advanced over the years. Even this Chevy was a dinosaur compared to what they were turning out nowadays. New cars were safer and smarter than this dumb brute. But it was perfect for the trip to Mapimi, where the roads were not always paved. And it carried that certain symbolism for him in its early 1970's massiveness.

Morry looked over at Tom. Tom hadn't taken to the driving experience too much yet, hadn't seemed overly impressed with it. He'd been too busy eating and drinking and smoking and copulating. But Morry had a 911 Carerra Porsche parked in storage, already signed over to Tom. He smiled. "I bet you'll tell me what that Porsche brung tomorrow, huh?"

Tom smiled back. "Oh, I don't know. I don't think I'll sell it. Maybe I'll just leave it in the garage for awhile."

"It might come in handy someday, if you need to impress a young lady." Morry looked over at him again. "Although you don't have much trouble in that arena, do you?"

Tom looked innocently at him. "That Porsche couldn't do anything but help."

"You don't need any help, Tom, my son! You're a natural." Tom rolled his eyes, leaned in close to the dashboard so he could light a cigarette. "Yet somehow, I get the impression that the whole thing is losing its thrill for you already," Morry added.

"You have got to be kidding."

Morry shrugged. "Maybe. But I think they all come too easily to you, pun entirely intended. What you need is a challenge."

Tom grinned in surprise. "What did you have in mind, my friend?"

"I think you're *looking for love in all the wrong places*, as the song says."

Tom's surprised grin widened. "Who says I'm looking for love?"

Morry also grinned. "It's a lot more likely here than on Sirius, is it not?"

Tom shrugged, thinking, *You have no idea.* He repeated, "Who says I'm looking for love?"

"If you're not, then you're wasting your time here." Morry gestured at the cigarettes on the dashboard, and Tom handed them to him. He pushed in the Impala's lighter and waited in silence until it popped back out. Then he lit his cigarette and said, "Tom, my son, allow me to tell you a little story."

"By all means, enlighten me, my friend."

Morry took a long drag on his cigarette, then sighed. "Her name was Maybelline Francis O'Flannery Doyle. I remember the day she walked into the store, as if it were yesterday. I'll never forget the way she looked that very first time I saw her.

"There was this other girl, already in the store that day. She called herself Sybil. She was beautiful, with black hair and black eyes, like your little friend from the casino. Ah, what a piece of work was Sybil! Nowadays, she would be considered tame, but for those days, she was wicked through and through, a free spirit at a time when the term free spirit had nothing but slatternly connotations. My Sybil was always gleefully up for anything.

"She'd just slipped a folded piece of wax paper full of Bolivian marching powder into my vest pocket, and I was leaning over the counter and whispering into her ear, telling her in detail about the manner in which I'd thank her later for this largesse.

"The bell on the door tinkled, and Sybil flinched and turned around. She was a product of the times, despite her sensual languor, despite what she liked to do behind closed doors, and it wouldn't do for anyone to witness a man who was not her husband whispering in her ear. She clasped her hand to her throat in shame for a moment, nodded at me, then slunk out of the store without even making eye contact with the woman who'd walked in.

267

"I despised Sybil at that moment, Tom. She wasn't a tramp out of necessity; she wasn't a sad fallen woman. She owned a big house on the hill, left to her by a doting father who'd died without ever catching wind of his daughter's poorly disguised proclivities. Sybil would want for nothing, ever. Yet still she blanched at the anticipated judgment of some stranger walking in off the street. The whole thing was sad; that such a burden was placed on women; that Sybil was so willing to pick it up and bear it.

"But when I looked up at the stranger who'd walked in off the street, I thought no more about Sybil. She was a vision. Her hair was a deep, rich brown, her skin translucent, like the alabaster from King Tut's tomb. Her eyes were a clear, cool gray. She was tall and willowy and graceful. She was an angel."

Morry paused, smoked his cigarette, then grinned a little at his companion. "Now before you think that I was unmanned by love at first sight, that I wanted to fall down upon my knees and simply worship this vision of Earthly virtue, that I had somehow forgotten that a woman is at her most beautiful when she has surrendered to abandon, her head thrown back in ecstasy, calling out *your* name – allow me to disabuse you of all that.

"C.S. Lewis said, *We use a most unfortunate idiom when we say, of a lustful man prowling the streets, that he 'wants a woman.' Strictly speaking, a woman is just what he does not want. He wants a pleasure for which a woman happens to be the necessary piece of apparatus.*

'Now Eros makes a man really want, not a woman, but one particular woman. In some mysterious but quite indisputable fashion the lover desires the Beloved herself, not the pleasure she can give. No lover in the world ever sought the embraces of the woman he loved as the result of a calculation, however unconscious, that they would be more pleasurable than those of any other woman.' Morry looked over at Tom and smiled. "Maybelline Francis O'Flannery Doyle was that one particular woman for me. She was incandescent. All other women became as pictures to me, no matter how beautiful: they were become only simple, one dimensional paintings on canvas, once I came to know my Belle. "As you've already gleaned so well, Tom, any woman, *all women* can give you pleasure. But as Lewis said, when you find that one, she is the only one that you'll want.

"I've found that the poets want to make love into something sterile, something worshipful, as if Lust hides his roguish face and flees in shame when pure and transcendental Love makes his appearance. But I say that this isn't the case at all. Lust doesn't leave. *Why would anyone want Lust to leave?* No, when Love enters the scene, Lust doesn't leave. He just changes his focus. Instead of a world full of beautiful women, he now sees only the one. No pleasure is as sublime as that which you share with her, my boy. No happiness as complete to you as when you make *her* happy, when you make *her* smile. My challenge to you is simple. Find that one woman."

"You're going to have to be a little more specific than that, Morry," Tom said. "This is a big planet. What does this woman look like? Where does she live? What does she do? Where do I begin to look for her?"

"This is not a logical quest, Tom," Morry said with a smile. "Let your heart speak to you. Your poor, underdeveloped Sirian heart; allow it to see these Earth women. They want you to love them."

"That is not news, my friend."

"That's not what I meant, and you know it. They want you to love them, but more importantly, perhaps *most importantly*, they want to love you back, in the most glorious way imaginable. With their hearts and their minds and their souls. When they only offer to love you with their bodies – that's just a way to pass the time. For them as well as you. It's transitory, like the seasons.

"But that other kind of love . . . Let your heart see, Tom. Then you'll know the right one, the minute you behold her. There'll be no confusion, no doubt. When you see her with your heart, you'll just know."

EIGHTY-TWO

Tom said to me, "Morry and Maybelline were married for fifty-three years."

"Wow," I replied. "Any children?"

Tom frowned, and there was that sadness again, so unfamiliar on his face. "Yeah. They had a little girl that died in infancy. And a son. He died in the war."

"Which war?"

Tom looked at me in surprise, but again it wasn't cute this time. "Does it matter which war?" He looked away. "I don't know which war. To Morry, it was just *The War*."

Tom lit a cigarette, offered me one. I shook my head. He blew out a cloud of smoke and continued. "Anyway, despite these tragedies, as I say, they were married for fifty-three years. When we were on our way to Mapimi, Morry said that not once in all those years had he even considered another woman. He called her *my belle*, like in the Beatles' song.

"Morry told me that this was a wonderful place, Liz. So many wonderful things, machines and art and literature and every imaginable distraction, every imaginable wickedness. None of which we have on Sirius. I'd already heard about all that. That's why I wanted to come here."

Tom sounded just like Morry when he said, "*But the very best thing, my son, the very best thing that they have here, that we don't nearly have often enough there, the very best thing, is when you find a good woman, a woman to love that loves you. There is nothing in the universe to beat that.*

"And Morry was right." He tilted his head solemnly at me, said softly, "So you don't have to worry about me being interested in any other women, Liz. I see no other women on this planet, not anymore. Only you."

I was speechless at his sincerity. My mother always said that I didn't know how to take a compliment. I struggled for something to say, some way to communicate to him that I felt exactly the same way. Then a thought struck me. "Do you remember the first time we met?"

He smiled. "I do. Like it was yesterday."

"You said, *someone like you*, do you remember that?"

Tom squinted at me. "Maybe it was a little longer ago than just yesterday. You're going to have to be a little bit more specific, Liz."

I cast my mind back to that night, trying to remember exactly what he'd said, the context of those three words that had so stuck in my mind. I snapped my fingers. "You said that Maxine told you that I wasn't married. Then you asked me, 'Why is it that *someone like you* isn't married?'"

He looked at me blankly. "And?"

"Oh, my God, you can be so frustrating, sometimes!" I exclaimed and kissed him on his nose. "What did you mean by *someone like you*? I've always wondered what you meant by that!"

"Sometimes you can be so dense," he said, and kissed me on *my* nose. "But I'm not frustrated. After all I've told you, you still don't get it. I came here looking for a good time. That's why we all come here, basically. Why else does anyone abandon their home, their culture, and go native?"

"Some people go native seeking enlightenment."

"You don't think I'm already enlightened?" he asked in surprise.

"*You're odd*, Tom. You're so odd that I'm willing to believe that you're from another planet. Enlightened? Perhaps. But most definitely odd." When he didn't say anything, I prompted him. "You were going to explain what you meant when you said *someone like you*." I loved it about him that he wasn't a babbler, but sometimes a person just had to *drag* what they wanted to hear out of him.

"You'll laugh at me," he said, and offered me a little fake pout.

"Maybe. But I gots to know. It's been bugging me forever, Tom."

"Okay. Like I said, I came here for a good time. And I had *quite* a good time, right up until that long drive from Vegas, across the dark desert with Morry. Morry told me that a good time was all right, but that this planet had one more thing to offer.

"And that thing was love – *true love*. The possibility of living one's long life out on this glorious rock with someone who's your soul mate. The possibility of sharing your life, *yourself*, with the one perfect individual that loves you just as much as you love her. The possibility of finding the other half that makes you whole." Tom smiled at the poetry of his own words. "That's what Earth women use to keep their men around, Liz. *Love*. Not sex. Sex is . . . sex is *ubiquitous*." Tom fluttered his hands to indicate *everywhere*. "It's easily achieved. That's why there are so many people in the world. But love is something else entirely.

"Morry challenged me to look for love, instead of just looking for a good time. He challenged me to go out and find it. And he made it sound so awesome, that I decided that he must be right. So I started looking. Once I decided that I wanted more than just a good time, I became a fucking monk in the looking."

You didn't want to break any more hearts than were necessary, I thought.

"After I dropped Morry off in Mapimi," Tom was saying, "I began my quest for love. My trip back here to your little town was much quicker, much more sedate than my first trip up from Mexico had been. I looked on the way back, but I didn't have any luck, not even a flash in the pan. Until I met Maxine.

"Ah, Maxine! She would've been perfect, if she wasn't just a child. That is her inescapable, irrevocable flaw. Maxine still has a great deal more of her own living to do. She needs to finish her own ride on the wine and song train. Basically, I'm just way too old for Maxine, in so many ways. Way too old to wait around for her to finish up with her ride. So I settled for Maxine being my best friend."

"You told her what you were looking for, didn't you?" I asked.

Tom squinted at me. "After a fashion. I didn't tell her any romanticized concepts about true love. She would've laughed at me. But she knew I was lonely." He puffed on his cigarette and suddenly grinned. "The stories I could tell you about Maxine! She's the best wingman ever. I had to talk to women, didn't I? To find out if they were right for me? This love at first sight thing that Morry had mentioned just wasn't happening. I figured that maybe he was being a little dramatic, a little poetic about that.

"These women I met, they all seemed nice enough; they all seemed like they had potential. But it never took more than a single conversation to figure out that whoever I was talking to was not indeed the one I was looking for. But I didn't want to hurt anybody's feelings, Liz. I didn't want to seem all interested in some woman, and then ten minutes later, not be interested in her at all. *I'm sorry, Miss, but I'm from another planet, and my friend and mentor told me that when we meet the right woman, we fucking know it. Know it for certain. And I'm sorry, but it ain't you.* I couldn't behave that way – it isn't very nice. It wasn't them, you see, it was me."

I wondered if Tom was purposely using that old chestnut to be funny, or if he was not familiar with the cliché.

"So, depending upon which scenario would scare off the prospect best, Maxine has played my sister, my daughter, and my psycho younger ex-girlfriend. Once I figured out that I was not on the right path, again, I'd just text Max. She'd burst in, make a scene, and the poor woman would consider herself lucky that she got away from me when she did."

"I sensed a long time ago that you and Maxine were better friends than might immediately be apparent," I said.

"Indeed. We are like the very best kind of big brother and kid sister. She has a little bit of a crush on me, but completely accepts the impossibility of it, without any resentment. I have a little bit of a crush on her, but I know better, and resentment never even enters the picture.

"I've helped her out, too. I've been her overly protective police officer father twice. And her psycho older ex-boyfriend three times. Anytime we wanted to get rid of someone, wanted to make sure that they never called again, we just did one of our little acts. One would-be Romeo even took a swing at me. But then Maxie just threw herself into my arms and said, 'Oh, Tom, I've been so wrong about you! Can you ever forgive me? Please take me back!' Discovering how much of a flake she apparently was took all of the fight out of that one, and he just slunk off." Tom blinked innocently at me. "It was really a lot of fun."

I'd often marveled at Maxine's ability to so completely get rid of a boyfriend once she was done with him. I'd wondered why they never called and begged for a second chance, like tedious Fred had done. Now I knew that she'd had help in dissuading them.

"You guys are mean," I stated flatly.

Tom took my hand and tugged it, so I would look at him. "It's not like I slept with any of them, Liz. It's not like I led them down the garden path. It never got anywhere near anything like that. Nothing ever got past the first date, if you will. I just didn't want to hurt anyone's feelings.

"And Max, God love her, she was usually just *done* with hers. You know how she is. But she didn't want to hurt anybody's feelings any more than was necessary, either. It's so much easier when a person can think it's not them but you."

Another thought struck me. "Does Maxine know that you're from . . . from . . . ." I still couldn't say it.

"I just told her, didn't I?" Tom grinned gloriously. "I can't help it if she doesn't believe me." He sobered a little. "No. It's not something that you go around broadcasting to everyone. Even your best friends. I told my story because I knew she wasn't going to believe me. I can't believe that you believe me."

I dismissed my sudden conversion with a wave of my hand. I couldn't believe that I believed him either, couldn't verbalize why I did. But I did. It all just suddenly seemed so logical, so plausible, so possible. I said, "Did Morry's wife know?"

"Yes. You tell your wife." Tom paused, went back to talking about Maxine. "She believed that I was just a lonely old guy looking for a nice girlfriend my own age. And she felt for me, in my loneliness. You now how much empathy Max has — she always sincerely wished me well on my dates, crossed her fingers for me." Tom held up his hand, fingers crossed. "But she was also always right there to help me ditch them when things didn't work out." Another thought struck him and he smiled. "But Maxine never tried to fix me up before you. She just came to my rescue when I needed to be bailed out."

"She doesn't know anyone your age," I told him. "Except Karen."

Tom made a face and said, "Yikes." Then he continued. "One day, Maxine calls me and tells me to meet her at the bar. I told her that I hated that bar, that I was always getting pawed at that bar."

"What a priest you'd become!" I said in surprise, after what he'd told me about the *swath* he'd cut. *Father What-a-Waste,* I thought, and smiled.

"Indeed. A fucking monk." Tom shrugged. "Like I say, I was really impressed with Morry's story. The happiness that he'd communicated to me – *I wanted that*. Nothing else would suffice, anymore. I was now always looking for that spark to happen, like he'd told me it would. So picking up women when there was nothing but a physical attraction had lost its appeal."

"Because it was so easy?" I said with a grin.

Tom rolled his eyes, ignored the question. "So, one day, Maxine called and said she wanted me to meet her at the bar. I tried to weasel my way out of it, but she insisted, telling me that it was her birthday, and that she knew a single girl my age that she wanted me to meet."

"I'd promised to buy her a drink on her birthday. But I was just about to leave, when she told me she had someone she wanted *me* to meet. She made me stay until you showed up."

"So it almost didn't happen?"

I nodded. "We owe it all to Max. Maybe we should take her to Puma Punku with us."

"Maybe next time. Next time for sure." He paused, then said, "I knew you were the one when she pointed you out to me from across the bar. From the first moment I saw you. Just like Morry had promised."

"Oh, Tom, you're such a romantic!" I said. He *was* a romantic in ways that few men from this planet could ever be. He believed implicitly in *true love*. "How ridiculous you are!"

"I told you that you'd laugh at me."

"I'm not laughing at you," I countered. "But you're just silly! I didn't know you were the one until we went out onto the patio! You couldn't have known before me!"

"But I did, Liz," he insisted. "I saw you with my heart, and I just knew. There was a spark – it was just like Morry had told me it would be. That's why I asked why *someone like you* wasn't married. I couldn't believe that I'd found *just* what I'd been looking for."

Tom was telling me, in his adorably open and sincere way, that he'd fallen in love with me at first sight. Who could resist believing such a rare and wonderful declaration? I had to confess to myself that I'd felt it, too, the minute I'd seen him and that killer smile. I'd just been too jaded to admit that such a thing existed. But I did remember practically skipping home from the bar that night. It *had been* love at first sight, for both of us. How fucking ridiculous was that?

But if I could believe that the man of my dreams, the perfect man, the man I'd follow to the ends of the earth, was from another planet, I guess I could believe in love at first sight, too.

"Oh, Tom, I love you so much!" I said, and pushed him over onto his back on the couch. "You are quite possibly insane."

He smiled up at me, took my face in both hands. "It's a prerequisite for living here."

****

Also by LM Foster

A Passing Resemblance
Contrariwise – A Tale of Twins
Corvino
Crypsis
Duck Feet
Peter's Sisters

Two Green Keys
Two Green Keys
Adapted for the Screen

One Wilde Ride Trilogy:
Part One: It Might Have Been
Part Two: An Exceptional Boy
Part Three: What Should Never Be

Stars and Guitars:
Talk To a Movie Star
Where The Guitars Play

Tom and Wiley:
This Carnival of Strange
Wiley Royce
Generally Recognized as Safe
Wiley Royce Versus The Martians

www.ingramcontent.com/pod-product-compliance
Lightning Source LLC
Chambersburg PA
CBHW061552170626
46811CB00001B/177